TIMES
of the
SUPERMEN

TOPE APOOLA

RC 878137
Bateleur
RESOURCES LIMITED

Published in Nigeria by Bateleur Resources Limited.
www.bateleuresources.com

Cover design by Ojishez Media, Maryland, Lagos.

This book is fictional, and all the characters, though there are occasional mention of known names. The author's illustrations of certain popular events are meant also as fiction or alternative history and do not in any way lay claim to verity. However, the elements of the fact page and of a few scientific matters discussed in the book may be factual.

The second paragraph of the fact page is from a non-fiction by Stan Mc Daniel, "The case for the face" and it is used with the publisher's permission. The image on the same page is from NASA's official website, available for public use. The asterisked quotation in page 97 is from Ralph Waldo Emerson.

The cover design is a dramatized picture of a young man staring at the sky. Rights to the design are also reserved.

ISBN 978-978-908-547-7

First Edition.

Dedication

To Daddy, Mr. M.I Apoola on his retirement from
the state civil service.

I hate mankind, for I think myself one of the best of them, and I know how bad I am.
-Joseph Baretti (1719-1789)

FACT

NASA Image

In 1976, Vikings 1 spacecraft spotted something that looked like a human face on the cynodia region of the planet Mars. The world became hysterical and many books purporting that a population once occupied the planet of Mars followed. NASA debunked the claims, explaining that what was spotted was only a natural landform. They supported their claims with many geological theories

But some people were not satisfied...

In 1992, Prof. Stan Mc Daniel of Sonoma State University in California organized a special committee of scientists, which made a strong case for the possibility that the anomalies on Mars might not be natural.

BOOK ONE

1

May 15, 2287 8:00 pm Lagos, Nigeria.

"I SPEAK OF THE times of the supermen, for in here shall we find the courage to proceed."
Those were the words that preceded this musing. I had kept it in my heart all through the years, praying that I find a people to listen. Now my prayers were answered with abounding generosity for the world assembled today, beseeching my own account of our history. I would open my chronicle with that line.
As I walked through the promenade in the Marina side of Eko Atlantic city, my heart played with those words, but a bitter sting clung unto that sweetness as I wondered if our story would ever be told. I realized how quickly I must write, this morning when the government of Nigeria joined the world in declaring war on the faceless enemy, the legion that loomed over us, coloring our sky with dark mistiness.
 Save for the rap song that played from a café lining the walkway, it would have been rightly said that the world became silent today. I tried to spot *Eko protector*, the massive missile shooter that was rumored to be capable of covering the whole of the Gulf of Guinea, the highest that was permissible by international laws. Where the shooter is had always been a little military secret but now, in our very eyes, it was to be launched for the first time in forty years of its existence. I tried to hover my gaze through the towers of the financial district, three miles north from where I was but my eyes rested on a family that was trying

to make it through the crowd. They seemed to be the only ones running. The father held her daughter tightly and the older son carried a younger one and held on to his mum as they hurried through the slowly moving crowd. The daughter was made to cover her ears.

"Commander-in-chief ordered an offensive against the UFO this morning," an army spokesperson announced through Marina Central Information System.

The usual bustling of that part of the town came to a hoot as we awaited the scariest act of war. Running was an impossible venture, as it would lead to deadly stampedes at the bottlenecks of the street. The people were discerning enough to recognize that.

Lagos Metropolitan bureau reported that an average of ten thousand people walks the promenade each day, mostly to catch a view of the scenic financial city from that unique perspective. On this Tuesday morning there were several thousands more. A renowned sociology tutor attributed that dramatic change in statistics to the need of families and friends to reunite once more at least, and enjoy whatever is left of their lives before the inevitable comes.

Just about when experts were theorizing reasons why enemies of the world order did not want to come to the countries of the southern hemisphere, we had seen a thing in the sky, fearful and engrossing. Statesmen had warned that the world summit would attract undue attention to the city and their fear was made real when the ship-like object appeared in Lagos sky, shading a quarter of the lagoon. The aggressors did the same before taking over Frankfurt and London. Now, it is almost sure that we would be consumed in the fire that swept a portion of the world but we are resolved to fight.

"Three, two, one..." A voice sounded from the top of the towers, and missiles flew from the coast. As we expected, the arsenals were not effective. All eyes looked to see if the ship would move at least, in response to the huge fire. No one anticipated that our missiles would be directed back to us.

"Please be calm, and try to maintain safe positions," the military announced. People scrambled as the missiles headed back to the earth. There was no place of refuge. I saw the beautiful family again, holding on to one another. They'd moved near.

"Could this have happened in your own time?" one of them asked.

"I don't know." I kept a straight face, embarrassed that they recognized me in spite of my disguise. I tried to be civil nevertheless and smiled back. Somehow, I hoped my smile would mitigate their assessment of the situation. Two thousand feet above ground level, the missile changed course and fell into the waters, causing the resultant tidal wave to pour the street a great volume. Nobody was hurt but we knew a war had started.

WHEN I HEARD the announcement this morning, I wondered if I had convinced our leaders to shoot at the Unidentified Flying Object that stood arrogantly over our heads for more than two days now. I must have, for the Presidents of Nigeria sighed and asked me to write our history shortly after today's meeting.

I had prayed the companion of my friend, the man from South Africa with whom I share this uncommon story, and I hope he joins me as I attempt this romance with the quill. A gentle man he is, and far more discerning than I. Together, we had lived longer than was human in a place so far. The color of our skin, the words of our tongue and our thoughts - we had become a new set of people ever known, we had become Martians. Now, we are back to the world we once knew, many decades after we took off for space exploration in Oron, a little fishing town in Nigeria. Our return had fallen to a time when the hearts of the meek failed, and when the peoples of the world seek only to live pleasurably, abandoning every known propositions of virtue. A few years before, the leader of the world had said in his famous speech, "we are alone."

He had, to the admiration of even the staunchest relic.

"It is time we took our destiny as men into our own hands for we have found no voice in the wilderness of space, even to the farthest ends of space."

A new turn of humanism they called it. The people of the world we have come to, live by this mediation that no one watches over them. They have seen evil triumph, heard lewdly sounds in the middle of the most saintly choruses. Now, life for them is to be lived and pleasure, enjoyed. Justice is for the strong alone and the only thing that matters is how well their needs are met.

As I speak this into the quill, the newly invented writing machine reputed as having powers to pick the writer's brain, I behold the world beyond. Lagos is in fretful silence for the world waits in apprehension. Once more, the day had come when every good proposition would be put to test. But for my friend to whom I owe the courage to speak of what we found in our wilderness of knowledge, I would have taken their condition for weakness, the good people of this new world. How they came to this day, we still wonder, the fruit of their negligence, which color the sky so.

In the middle of all these, I choose to keep my mind gathered by this reminisce, for by morrow, we will set forth to take our place.

A LONG JOURNEY from the first home where it all began, eons before this perilous time, a shining light fell across the universe, faster than the fastest of all the things that are known to us. Like a whip of fire, stretching to the ends where the earth was made. We viewed the ancient past, as it was, through the new technology of retrospective imaging.

As I looked, my face was covered with the bright light that blinded my eyes to the series of events that followed.

This morning, at the shadowy rooms of the gurus, we had come to solve the greatest puzzle; what we are, and what becomes of everything that exists, when we pass into the endless space of times gone. To think everything ends with us, some have said, is arrogance. No choice is easy as we brain storm, not as colligates, nor aristocrats but men, just tenants of this old rock called earth. Every man or woman, we have agreed as one of our terms of reference, is entitled to contribute in matters directly affecting their chances to life. And to talk of chance, the tiniest organisms have only a single digit percentage.

There, in the ultimate ground zero of human intellect, standing by the professor from South Africa, I have heard the silent whispers of yesteryears coming loud through the speakers of the magnificent hall. We were indeed in the laboratory of life, standing upon one of the greatest accomplishments of man. The most important cipher of history lay there; the hallowed chamber many men caught up with the atrophy of sentiments loved to call the pit of sin. Ironically, there laid a pointer to what had been sinful and what hadn't, of all the actions of our forbearers. There the conscience of the leaders of men are tortured, even those of the untouchable patriarchs; those who inspired us willfully, who later turned around to cast aspersions on same thing they'd imbibed in us.

From the huge screen, we had seen the baby earth, the blue wonder as it rolled in the endless space. A hope to the morose universe. If we were aliens from other planets we would have surrounded it with fairy myths, even speak of it as paradise. Indeed it is one from afar and as we zoom to view from the·heights of the hills, our judgment remained unchanged.

Many million years ago, when our history as men were yet not started, the quietness of the skies and the stillness of the waters gave this home the look of a beautiful wilderness, rumbling though with vagueness as the mountains slide and the skies, with thunder. Now, we stand on our feet, different peoples from different nations, in one voice and with uncommon sense of brotherhood, thinking, how could we save it? Our hope for the existence of extra-terrestrial life is gone, and books of such fantasies sell no more.

How shall I in the middle of this chaos, when the world's sanity and conscience and good judgment is withered? How do I speak to the finest minds, the true success of evolution whose prowess is no match for any man's my time? May I, in the manner of those we call humble say that I feel privileged and overwhelmed to see our great story, hoping to be told, as it unfolds, the great time captured in the movies of my time, and books and dreams of many men? May I, with my chest out, narrate my story with a little cynicism, exude confidence as though I have the heart of steel? Trying to give answers is arrogance that need be forgiven. Speaking with great confidence is folly that need be derided. Mine is a story of many ages, a tale as seen by one man, ending with just one assertion that there are answers; answers to why we are here, why good men sometimes live in indignity, never getting the chance to live out the lessons of poverty. Answers to why we see a hand in our lives, why we keep bumping into those faces that stay in our hearts.

I speak of the times of the supermen, for in here shall we find the courage to proceed; the glorious times when the people of the world understood the essence of everything. Of the times of the sub-humans, when there was no knowledge of what was good, or manners or traditions. The times when the chief purpose of life was to survive and when each day looked like another. At the end of it all, we shall learn that there is some truth in many orthodox propositions. Our hearts shall be gladdened for goodness is supreme among the forces that is.

2

January 1, 2003, Lagos, Nigeria.

THEY CALLED IT the Third World, and so it seemed. Across the streets were buildings having peeled paints and no drainage at all, standing beside tall ones, having wide courtyards and fountains. Just a stone's throw away from a random market place, there was a scenic private hospital which overlooked the ocean at the southern end. The hospital seems ideal for the beginning of this story.

Mrs. Oladele who used to work as a Matron at the time of my birth had told me fifteen years later when we met at a shopping mall in Lagos about a lady who shared the same floor with mum. The poor lady would hallucinate and laugh to herself every time, the laughter of sorrow. One day, Mrs. Oladele said, in the morning of my birth, that psychotic woman leaned on the railings and watched the Gulf of Guinea. The breeze from the waters must have dried her tears, but she never hallucinated or soliloquised again.

Many people had such moments in that hospital. For some, it came too late, for others, it was a new discovery. Mrs. Oladele looked longingly as she recollected. She said

"There are only short moments in our lives when we have the gift of silence and the world waits for us to take stock."

For mum, the experience was muddled. She looked through the window to see if Daddy's car was parked in the garage. Her joy was almost marred by anger, for she had planned him to be there. She curled her hands around me, as if to protect me against the wind. Her breasts were swollen and bare; her face lighted with the white diode lights of the street. She jolted when a rocket sped into the skies, spreading fire. It was her private ritual to gaze at the clock in the first minute of every New Year. She raised her head to find a wall clock. Right besides her bed was father, tapping his fingers and whistling a favourite song. His arrival had escaped her notice.

"I went to say a prayer," he said.

"It must have been a very long prayer." Mum strolled to present to him their son, looking at his face the way she used to when she was yet unsure of their relationship.

"Your involvement with the editorial has taken a dangerous twist,' she said, 'I know you are just coming from the meeting."

"It's my job," father said, like he used to, every time they had the argument.

"But you used to have a better job," mum snapped.

Father creased a smile to his face, and tried to replicate the enthusiasm he'd shown thirty minutes before, at the National Institute for Special Studies.

"We're coming up with something grand at the institute; we're inviting Chekhov over to take residence."

"Oh, you trust a man who cannot sustain the trust of his closest allies?"

"He was sabotaged."

Mum ambled through the corridors, to the other wing of the hospital, followed behind by the family friend matron and father. At the end of the long passageway was another balcony.

"You should stop this wild goose chase of fantasy, please, you are now a father."

Her voice must have been sullen. Things had turned far less ceremonious than she expected and father, even father who was once obsessed about the coming of his first child wasn't keen on carrying me in his hands anymore. His first child had arrived few months earlier- the NISS journal. That journal! He realized what he was doing in no time, and he tried to have me, but mum was no fan of such hollowness. She declined, and gave him that look again, as though she wasn't sure of his sanity. It was at that moment that the matron stepped forward to unlock the door before them.

"Science is not fantasy," dad mumbled as the door was let opened. Even a little aspersion on his love had dampened his mood. The three would celebrate nevertheless.

"To the new man."

Mrs. Oladele tossed imaginary something to the air, she must be nervous, herself.

Together, they watched the street adjourning, sprawling to the horizon, lighted only by the lights of the hospital. Fireworks lit the skies as Lagos celebrated the birth of 2003.

I WAS BORN in the first day of the New Year in a country where people live for the day and relinquish tomorrow to the unknown. In a city reputed to be one of the largest in the world and a place where everyday wit keeps people going, where many who tried to live tomorrow became stuck. A place where people innately believe in being nice and those who are not are faced with perpetual shame and self inflicted persecution. My eyes were opened to a country where every old man was king and every young man listened, a world of laughter and drama that foreigners would gladly drop their money to watch. Every time I looked at the map I felt it is the center of the world. Life was said to have begun here but I do not wholly trust such stories, possibly aimed at improving our outlook to the world and carving for us some relevance from our distant past.

I cannot aptly tell what to make from this place but I can say it is to the 'first' world a reminder of the past and to us a challenge to the future. Many nations had been faced with this challenge of nascence in the past and ours was that time.

In the developed world, the century was the time to be proactive and to worry about bridges several miles away. For us, we got to the bridge before we crossed because there were too many bridges anyway and to worry about each was to live a life of persistent fatigue. Ours was a life and a place full of comic and unbelievable stories that made us laugh under the scorching sun. A leader once said he would choose this place if he was to be reincarnated. It is a place where you fight fiercely in the morning to pat your adversaries' back in the evening. It was a place where salient issues are trivialized, sometimes given unduly overwhelming attention just to sound and look responsible. It was a place where the lowly asked no questions, even making excuses for those placed on high. It was a lovely place; a funny place. Only the thick-skinned took such thing as evolution seriously here. Among those non-conformists were father, who developed interest in the study of the Human genome system.

At the Nigerian Society for Special Studies, in a lowly ceremony begging for guests, the NISS principal had labeled this new quest, in the words of the first man on the moon, one small step for a man and one giant leap for mankind. Humanity was at the door that leads to infinite possibilities, the keys already in her hands. Like it was in the dreams of the founder of English Eugenic movement, a goathe had mentioned that the mere man is to be surpassed and that the time would come when he shall be unto the future man like ape is to human beings.

It was amazing, the path our new science chose to toe. Two thousand and three when the world was concerned with marvelous things and my own people with things which had stopped to bother the developed nations many decades earlier; it is unconceivable why the new story of humanity chose to start from here. When it chose Africa as a launch pad it must have settled for a really slow start, as the world took no cognizance of the quiet shake in history. Uncle Bode's dream had proven to be more than just a dream- He apparently had in his brains, sensitive neurons that was complicated enough to develop images of the distant past. His dreams were found to be coherent with the latest findings of science, making the group of scholars who cared to give it a benefit of doubt, to ask questions.

What if we could do more than we had ever thought? Where do we come from? Who were those who lived in the desolate planets several million years ago?

In two thousand and three, a small group of lonely scientists thought they were near the answer to the simplest of all the questions. They had no idea how many following generations would not even bother to ask.

IN THE YEAR I was born, father would drive eighty kilometres to meet with fellow historians and scientists in a motel. Five years later, when I was old enough to be left solely to his care, he would carry me on his shoulders and afford me a good view of the only white man amongst them; Mister Chekhov, the Russian naturalist who never used the microphone. I had grown to hear Mister Chekhov talk and to see him gesture before a calm audience, quietly and charmingly preaching what he believed. I think I remember the time he spoke to a larger audience in what seemed like a festival. Then, he had said

"Our lord, Jesus Christ gave us a tiny clue to this mystery but we have been too lazy, over the years, to take on the simple challenge; if ye have faith as little as the mustard seed, ye shall say to the mountains to shift and it will."

Chekhov was one of the emerging group of intellectuals who believed there was more to the human, a little divergent from core modern-day biologists because of his stance that our abilities have always been but we have not the will to harness it; the power to conquer our world from the hands of those who colonized it very long time ago, and to restore it. There and then he had met father in a manner he would describe in his next book, *The Probable History of Life*. All he had ever imagined he had seen a man from thousand miles confirm. There was more to our existence than we had ever known.

The next time he spoke, I was twelve, childishly and quietly devoting myself to the study of this new phenomenon. Father had tried to provide with the right environment suitable for kids my age, but he had never kept his journals far enough. What I had was a childhood devoid of the toys and juvenile atrocities but of questions, sometimes obsessive. Mister Chekhov's second coming looked a lot unlike the first. He had put on more weight or so it seemed to my increasing sense of perception. He had, along with his weight and newfound carriage added to himself a noticeable confidence and the reason to all these he seemed to have mentioned in his slow-paced lecture.

"The answers are coming right to us," he said, titling his head to the corner he trusted best for applause.

It looked more like the answers were abandoning him for the answer seldom come in the middle of jamborees. It has been said, the answer lies in the quiet, hardly finding a place in a blustering heart. He would learn that the sung heroes and those whose names the world might never know will, in the end, in their own eyes, account to same. That it is sweet to break new grounds, yet lonely and those who covet great glory must have their own share of persecution.

Looking back to that hot afternoon in Abuja when Chekhov declared the moment is now, we see how funny we must have been to them who had prescience. The time was near and the signs, unpleasant. Of all the mysteries of our time, we marvel most at this; why evil spoke for good and why the tunnel seemed darkest at the end at which there was light. Like it was in the beginning when we were first formed, so it was at the start of this age.

In the world gifted men see in their dreams, where great men conquered, there was a war, not of swords but words, in the chambers of ethereal beings; some advocating for us, others speaking ill of even our best actions. And how does this hallowed gathering manifest- a conference of men disenchanted from their own minds, falling for distractions, which accompanies every achievement.

Chekhov's spirit at the first meetings compared very little to the latter. Now, he had come with a little more rounded belly and a mistress with whom nothing seemed to work when they were first acquainted. In a more fitting coat that contrasted with the oversized ones he was branded with, colored lights from the ceilings narrowly falling on his face. We happen to have been there to celebrate what we will not achieve in generations for the world is to slip into another period of complacency, leaving a wide gap in the timeline of this great quest. In the space of this time I shall fill my own story and explain how a mortal is graced with two lives, how quickly time passed somewhere around the Sun, at a home surprisingly accommodating and an atmosphere nourishing our skin with the best elements, keeping our cells young and alive.

At the beginning this story was more than impossible but our ends doesn't always justify the way we had lived our lives. The finish line sometimes give no fair measure, thus, we wonder how a people consciously denying a subject evolve to be the masters of same. How a man with no regard for life could have life in abundance. The man who was kept afloat for generations was born the hot humid evening when the sky was clear for the stars to be seen.

I had read the journal of Human Genomic and father's commentaries that I found in a relinquished library shelf, *Theories on the nature of animal species*. The opening of the first volume appeared to be excessively apologetic about its 'unscientificness', a terrible term the university used in deploring it when it was forcefully published. The apologies indeed went well with me, or so with my meager shrewdness or desire for something new.

While I flipped through the second page, I felt I was baptized into a new belief, rescued from nihilism. With the funny effect of the humid atmosphere, I felt like I was drenched in the pool of disbelief, to introspect for a short while, and realize what manner of mind I had been carrying. In another moment, just like a new believer dipped into a river by a clergy then raised, I felt the sweats dripping through my body were dried. Like a new man was born. Bizarrely, I came to realize the full import of what had been for the last one hour. I had been reading in the porch with power out and a sad local bred dog wailing at the backyards. Mum and dad with his younger brother Uncle Bode had gone to offer their support to a couple who lost their kid to plane crash in the week. Although I never knew how the bereaved two looked like, I leant they lived across the street, tried vainly to get the description Uncle Bode gave and almost received a knock in the head for that. The little I could gather was memory of a fat little boy my age, always greeting. I never returned any of those how-do-you-dos or smiles, not until I had wondered or apportioned a proper ration to his reasons in my mind, but only few times did I do that early enough. Most of the time, I just didn't greet back.

Seated on a stretch chair with a piece of forbidden journal unburied from a cabined file I had always been curious about, I felt nothing unlike grandpa and I did roll up some papers to feel entirely like him. Straight faced and constantly lighting up my rolled papers like I was smoking some high class Cuban cigar, I could not but wonder why humans like myself could have been cold towards a little boy, now late, who had been nothing but friendly. Yes, I called him little though we were of same age. That was what the stretch chair and the 'nicotenless' cigar of mine did to me.

Some day in February, Two thousand and fifteen, shortly after the crazy harmattan, I was born to the world of tomorrow and a piece from the shelves made it so.

"There shall come a time,' echoed my mind, 'a time when the mere man shall be unto the new men, embarrassment."

When Uncle Bode arrived it was already very dark and I was responsible enough to light only one candle in the house. Power lines had been removed in course of the ongoing road extension and modernization projects underway in Lagos.

Uncle yelled, scaring me as he hit his toes against a rock.

"Get a lantern, you maggot!"

He meant no insult; he was the sweetest Uncle, the one to supply me with the best parts of this story. Meet Uncle Bode, the most eligible bachelor in town. Hip and gregarious, broad chested, standing at one hundred and seventy-four centimeters when anxious and a couple more when elated. His rugged composure was my first idea of manhood not until I would see him break down when he found his bevy of roses, the one whose gossip always formed a subject for our conversation and a spice for our friendship was indeed not immune to the charms of a crazy young lawyer in his thirties, who lived uptown. But for that one moment of his loneliness no one could tell he was no more than any other, except for his resolve to put up a thick and constant façade. If he was ever my symbol of macho strength, I surely had learnt one of my first lessons that we are all weak after all and our strength lies in the thoughts we entertain in our hearts.

As I tried to help him with his pained toes, father and mum entered, looking pale as expected yet energized probably because of the news report coming through the transistor radio that father was holding in his hands. Their favored candidate for Nigerian presidency had been declared winner of the February election. With their attention glued to the radio, I was provided with the chance to sneak the forbidden journals I was already getting fond of to the dusty shelves.

Meet father, a man of moderate description, slightly mustached and always wearing a pair of thick-lens glasses. He had taken everyone with surprise two years earlier when he abandoned his promising career at a multinational to pick up a job in the suburb as editor of a ghostly science magazine. He was also pursuing a doctorate in genetics. Everything I was, I got from him- the love for music, insatiable quest for answers...good enough he knew and he never resolved into aggression whenever he tried to get me to go to the church to worship, like almost every sane person in this part of the world used to, after all he was compliant in making me a critical person- he came home with big books, 'unbiased' literatures that I always devoured with the same avidness as the music CDs which usually hung between the pages of the newspapers he used to bring from work.

Father would probably make a bad politician in that, he never tried to sweet-talk me into embracing his faith, and rather he gave me a simple, honest reason why I should go to the church, one Sunday morning.

"If you keep missing church services, you will drift further and start seeing every church thing as stupid."

Perhaps, his approach was calculative and alas it was effective. I had drifted beyond all theology and reasoning and the only thing he could appeal to was my inner self- the true man who longs the fellowship of a God, in spite of all the seeming hate and inconsistencies of religion.

I was convinced that a man is nothing without the divine, as I had found myself that we do not have total power or control over everything concerning us, yet I wondered what exactly the truth was. That was where I usually seemed like an easy game to many. Asking questions, they always seemed to liken with weakness, soft heartedness and most erroneously, a will to change. It was never as simple. The more questions we ask, the farther we drift, then we should consider stopping the cogitation but that seemed like a very bad idea, as it negates the very essence of our existence, for death is typically represented by the seizure of the brain faculty which enables thinking. Our power to decipher what is right or wrong or to choose what we'd do seem to be the one sure thing that we have, and as it was said by René Descartes, we could only be sure of our existence because we think. I thought it was indeed sacrilegious for anyone to suggest that I should swallow all dogmas without consulting this gift of the creator to me- a rambling mind and a heart in love with all that is good, filled with abhorrence of many things that rob of essential happiness, even the least worthy.

I knew this mind would mellow, that I would grow to cherish symbolism over ideas. I thought that people do not always have enough love to share when they age but I know of a woman who defiled this theory of diminishing capacity for passion-mum, a fierce member of the small political organization that was looking forward to a union with the ruling party. Brief in stature and sporty, her dark brown skin was completely recessive to her white Angola mother's.

I had a sister, Dami, four years younger than I, but more adapted to the things that were. There was also a more little Junior whose dream was to be fierce and brave like movie heroes. We never got to do many things together for he thought me unadventurous and sedentary.

IN THE STREET we lived, there was a high-rise building of twenty flats, sharply contrasting our cozy bungalow which stood timidly and almost awkwardly to the left.

Life in the neighborhood was all together bright. We spent our weekend afternoons in the yard, fooling around with Mister Shrewd, our fat old dog, and turning the radio's volume so high that the sound would reach us.

Our little world was not lacking in any of those things; gossip and rivalry. It was in fact those spices that served to give that place and that time its own kind of flavor.

The little playground of the street served as our stadium for major tournaments and the smaller spaces for the 'friendlies' and trainings. Every other ground up to a cubic meter was a potential field where we played anything from balloons to the tennis balls. In one of our major tournaments I had secured an injury in the left eye, slightly changing focus of the retina permanently. I had also secured a lifelong phobia for active participation in football, thus finding more time to read and to daydream, a rather uncomplimentary attribute in my own eyes.

In that noisy street, there was a pretty one I enjoyed watching from our lowly abode, always staring soberly from the fourth floor in the holiday mornings. Then, I used to think maybe an angel was missing in heaven, hoping to be rescued.

Silence pervaded the atmosphere sometimes while everyone felt like playing other times. I think it was the effect of the weather and the tricks of the breeze that always made it so.

Saturdays in the neighborhood was a curse to the lazy folks, a day everyone seemed to be conservative about, when people always felt obliged to get busy. At evening times, kids would gather to argue or try out something new. Sometimes, we'd figure out the best matches and make for them a mock joint wedding ceremony. I do not understand why the couples always complied, there was no romance; don't hope for one. No real winning or dinning, just an envy of adult life. The joys of Christmas too were exceeding, the carols, the lights, the new clothes and the gifts, all ending in one blue Sunday evening when we remember the long school projects we were meant to complete in the festive weeks.

ONE MONDAY MORNING, I was chauffeured all over the town in search for good schools. I was rejected for my little stature in all of those places, accused of been indisposed to spending time behind the desk. In truth, I really did not know what to make from those desks.

It was two thousand and six and I was barely three, thrown into an unintended race of emerging as one of the youngest scholars in my area.

Four school years after receiving series of promotion letters I had no idea of, I was bundled into the vehicle for a better place; school of the emerging elite, sited uphill in a more sane part of the city. I had come into the hands of two girls, always giggling at the sight of me, like I was a clown. Now I had come to understand it was the signature my former school had on me that amused them, maybe the accent or the thick iron lines on my uniform. For a few days the persecution continued and I managed my anger well until the day I felt I could confide in one of our teachers.

The young man had come to teach the Christian Religions Knowledge for the first time. His first impression was great, as he talked more like he was preaching than teaching. I felt it was time to let loose. Trusting the little grammar I could speak, however poor, I rose on my feet. I felt a terrible heat, like the pupil on the next row was frying some bean cake.

"Oga...' I started, my voice hardly sounding like mine, 'is it good to be doing *ekee* to a fellow human being?" I wondered if I was anyway understandable. I thought I could hear some murmurings then I thundered more assuredly.

"B-e-c-a-u-s-e there are two girls in this class, always mocking, and if I should lay my hands on them!"
Thus I got myself emancipated.

THE PRIMARY SCHOOL was one maximum-security prison, paraded by stern-looking Ghanaian warders or teachers. There were very tall ones, slim like their flogging sticks and there were very short ones, everyone providing in their own unique ways, something for us to remember when we contemplated trouble. And trouble we always made. Fun ideas were scanty. Each time on the way to school my heart would beat so fast I'd start to worry for my health.
To worsen our already terrorized lives, father insisted the most dreaded "Uncle" take us on mathematics and geography. Thus, we lived, Dami and I and even mister shrewd who always sat far behind, missing our company, in perpetual stress till the day of my major school crime.
A drama series in the television was going violent, maybe. The boys decided to act it out for fun. I was the 'bad man' and a little more reserved friend, the actor. We ran through the school street and even defied people's privacy in their homes. More pupils joined in the madness and as it got bigger and messier, we ended up breaking a whole set of church furniture. One imp whose eyes caught mine as I quaked on a chapel desk came reporting us during a math class, accompanied by an elder clergy. Our bald headed math tutor prostrated before the clergyman and apologized on our behalf. We knew that moment that the worst had come.
We were flogged like animals.

The last days in the primary school were sweet but everything was like a horror movie trying to end up happily. The farewell songs joined with the colorful costumes of those of us participating in the valedictory play gave us new sensation, a whole new experience to savor. I enjoyed every beat of it, though my joy was tainted with a sharp, discomforting feeling of seclusion. The squad that was accused of breaking down the cathedral was barred from joining in those activities. Also, pupils who had their names appearing more than twice in the black book were to participate only by moving the wooden benches to the open venue of that ceremony. I belonged to both categories.

More painful was it that I loved the class songs to be rendered on our last day as beginners, the peculiar guitar note of the Zulu farewell song, the scenic stage and the glamour. Fighting back the tears, I savored some sweetness from the thought that I was being over-punished. I needed to feel persecuted to enjoy the piteous melody, the kind that feels like reminding oneself that God is watching.

3

THE MEDIA loved to advertise the President-elect as a lover of sciences and progressive technocrat. That was why his election was welcomed among scholars in the Institute for Special Studies. True to his words, he had invited many veterans to his house, few days after the declaration.

At his solitary country mansion that day were two German College Principals from the German Institute for Integrated Futuristic Research, Mister Chekhov from Russia and nine Nigerian Professors.

Chekhov was at that moment, on trial for secretly injecting prison inmates with a lethal mixture in Samara. There were reasons for the President-elect to be careful in his dealings with him. Should he defy the special travel permit granted Chekhov by Russian authorities, the President-in waiting would become a suspect of high crime, a possible impediment to his emerging profile in the international scene.

Although the meeting was scheduled to acquaint incoming government with ambitious and ambiguous findings which the past governments had ignored for too long, the media speculated a more dramatic thing was about to happen. It was about population control, some said. Some, a neo-Eugenics project.

The air became unsettled because the final reports of the Millennium Development Goals seemed to be enough frustration for any government to thread the paths the frustrated would. The President-elect had said in response to the Public lecture of an aggressive speaker in

January that he would run an aggressive government, hungry for growth and dominance. Now it was a thing of speculation if he would go as far as doing evil to achieve what he called 'good' for his country. But the truth as we were to find was that he toyed with none of those ideas. He was to be a learner and catalyst of the change to come.

In his outstretched gardens, he played host to the gentleman eager to sell their theories, in a Sunday afternoon with the pressmen hanging on, some covering the meetings secretly with high powered miniature cameras and microphones.

Chekhov was said to have mentioned in his presentation how medicine and pharmacy and agriculture stand the chance of being revolutionized, taking Nigeria to a new threshold as an emerging light from Africa. Another researcher argued the new field of science would pass into the hands of the least intended, should authorities continue to disown it. His suggestion seemed to have fallen on deaf ears for the incoming President waved his hands dismissively, showing an early sign that he fancied no undue pressure.

While some accused him of treating respected academic authorities with contempt, others claimed he was speaking with perverted geniuses who lacked the will to put the days of dramatic history behind them. We watched it all on the television; the elites and the middle class in their offices and hangouts and the peasants in their workshops and little kiosks. We all watched out for the gestures and manners of our President. For a very few, they watched out to see if the rumors were true.

I WAS TWELVE, glided out of my rebellion when Chekhov gave the most important speech of his career. He was at that time writing his *Probable history of life*. He was breathy that night yet he mesmerized the audience, not with his gestures this time but the content of his words. He closed his laptop and had the screens shut as he spoke.

"We have seen in this time of boundless knowledge that eons before the first of the stories we have ever heard began, several mighty asteroids flew around space, breaking into pieces and hitting the planets. Our home was to become desolate and formless and void for many thousand years. A thick dust was to cover the atmosphere, blocking the rays of the sun from shining forth."

He raised his head and a smile of conquest came to his cheek.

"When the dust was cleared, and the waters separated and the huge beasts were buried, our earth sprang forth to a new day and everything flourished again."

He faced Dad.

"Perhaps Mister Oladejo, it could be true that there used to be a fully civilized population in the Milky Way before this time."

He turned on the computer one more time and I thought he showed them a thing on the large screen.

"We have found a tiny clue to this emerging hypothesis that there existed a deliberate design somewhere on the face of Mars. If this is found to be true then we would have a reason to suspect that a legion of superior creatures once lived on Mars."

He barely comported himself as he clicked the computer, and he bellowed

"This formation was found on the surface of a rock in one undisclosed location in England."

A frenzied noise followed. He had projected a picture that showed striking semblance with the one earlier shown from a rock on Mars.

"These symbols appear to have been carefully crafted by same super-intelligent population many million years ago. Should there be a semantic relationship between them, I'd purport that these ancient beings once visited the earth."

He paused to catch his breath.

"Could it be that these strange creatures were the ones described in the words of the famous young man of Frankfurt who suffers from schizophrenia?'

Chekhov drew his glasses out of the case and read from the journal in his hands.

"Men once had great abilities and their cells used to embody genomes of infinite complexity, bequeathing them with the power of seamless vision. Their lovely voice, their clear conscience, beautiful body and eyes and mind were to live side by side with evil. Those were the days of ignorance, when wickedness ruled. The days when men were harmed with great abilities, yet cowed by the whims of impish beings that lived before them, the tribe to whom a race of celestial beings had instilled false passions. In the times unspoken of and the lost ages, our fathers gathered in a great quest to conquer their world from the hands of those corrupted, uncouth and malicious race.

Lined on a long row, from the mouth of the valley to the mountaintops, men hummed the

tunes of war but the truth was heartbreaking. Majority of the army of men had been bought over and the great match was made a charade, to satisfy those whose delight was to speak for the time with the quill. But there came a time when men who understood love and justice and freedom took their place by force.

Since then, the world had seen relative peace and prosperity. There were times when it was crude and dark, that blood flowed more than wine and boastful words of threat took the place of good music. Through the thick and thin we come to a great day, sleeping and slipping away, forgetting that the little piece of evil left behind would hardly die."

Chekhov removed his glasses and wiped his sweaty face. He threw the papers down.

"But we find a major inconsistency in this. If we take the words of this young man with a pinch of salt, then we would assume that these unknown people arrived in the earth at the same time with the Homo erectus or the Neanderthals. We may want to suspect that the early modern human is being referred to. This is never true. The formation on this rock is found to precede the advent of *Homo sapiens* yet it evinces modern craft, so modern we cannot hold the homos of those times responsible."

A man from the audience raised his hand and hastily remarked.

"The dating must have been wrong, sir."

He was made to introduce himself before going further; he was a science journalist from one of the dailies.

"How sure are we that there were no *Homo sapiens* in those times?' He said, 'I guess we have only found a clue as to what happened at a point in history that made the modern human to replace the older species completely. There must have been a war of the worlds."

Chekhov replied sharply from behind, "No. The mystery design as found in the planet Mars is older than every known living thing, and it is unclear how a people so sophisticated could have lived at those times. If you will agree with me that both designs from the two planets were from a common origin, then we might as well say that these people were extraterrestrial and that they visited our planet about thirty thousand years ago."

He strolled through the rows of the audience to smile at them and prepare them for his bombshell.

"The preponderant position is that the findings of science and the claims of this young man are mutually exclusive. The man must have made a subtle reference to the missing link between *Homo sapiens* and their older neighbors with whom they co-lived about thirty thousand years ago, not this mysterious otherworld race. There must have been a great war between the homos and this must have accounted for the sudden disappearance of the older species, the brutish creatures, around this time."

He shut the computer finally and gathered his papers.

"As for the rock, we are working to uncover the mystery symbol that we know to have formed once in a prebiological time. Perhaps we might be diving beyond the waters of science."

THE DAY that followed, I sat before the television and watched every bit. Chekhov's thinness glared at me. He must be working twice the time he was being paid for.

"The answers are coming right to us," he said again.

I was there the first time he said it and now it had become his slogan. Chekhov promised us that the age-long question of who we are and why we are here would be answered in no time. He was a quick-witted man who feigned progress each time there was a meeting. He needed to be on his toes because of the manner of people he was leading-severe people who waste no time. In spite of his efforts, his authority dwindled in my mind and I thought he hadn't really achieved much than to confuse us further.

Everything seemed meaningless. I was relapsing into my life of unbelief yet I loved to massage my psyche with his grounded words, especially when he told us we were more than who we thought we were.

Not very many believed a new history was starting, even the journalists, with their zeal in covering the proceedings. We did watch it on the television as Chekhov met with the newly elected President, those of us idle enough to do. He was careful to leave out his rather mystical hypothesis to pursue the more genial one that we could annihilate sorrow in the name of science.

Chekhov introduced the concept to the skeptical middle-aged politician who looked uncomfortably to the fishpond twenty meters away like he was losing interest

"The Human Genome Project was formally begun in the year 1990 by the United States Department of Energy and the National Institute of Health with a projection that it would be completed in a decade. However, the project was completed in 2003 before the targeted period, because of the rapid technological advances which enhanced swift completion. Then, the President of America had remarked with pride, "Today we are studying the language in which God created us." The goal of the project was to identify all the 20,000 to 25,000 genes in human DNA and to determine the sequences of the 3 billion chemical base pairs of which it is made. We will soon be able to determine the function of each gene in the body. We will live, knowing what risk our health will face in the future and if we stand chances of transferring diseases to our children. Once we know what risk we face, we will decipher what diet or lifestyle we should adopt to prevent those risks from coming to bare. We will develop an enhanced and almost perfect judicial system. We will develop a superb agricultural system that will put an end to malnutrition and hunger permanently. Also, biochemical information will be adapted to pools of data bases, enabling future references that may be needed on occasions where distinctive 'unnatural' chemistry is discovered and explained."

That moment, a young gentleman came in through the garden gates, stealing their attention. He was the thirty-two year old doctoral student of the Harvard College of Sciences, rumored to be on the new president's ministerial list. He had been invited for the talk and he was flown in to meet with party leaders for an informal interview which was necessary in deciding if he would be nominated as a Presidential Special Adviser.

For a moment, all eyes fell on him and all lenses. It was in that frenzy that a journalist with a permit to record only the sound was caught with a button video camera. The rest of the proceedings of the meeting we would not know but for the President-elect's press officer who tried to narrate how useful the meeting proved to be.

If legislated, he said, parents or guardians of kids having family history of classified crime would be mandated to present their children or wards for special therapies. A medicine could be administered; the so called 'Cheknosin' which was formulated by Chekhov in 2010 and outlawed in his own country the subsequent year, after it was reported to contain mutagens capable of causing inappropriate levels of mutation in the cell. The press officer argued all possible mutations was ninety-nine percent safe, and that the government of Nigeria mustn't follow the conventions of other countries in adopting new technologies.

"We are fast emerging as one of the world's most populous countries and we bear not only the advantages but also its attendant problems," he said, 'It is high time we started discussing pro-active measures, to ensure a livable environment and to keep responsible citizenry in the face of this social challenge."

He never mentioned that the young man from Harvard suggested further enquiries into the true nature of Chekhov's mixture.

THOUGH I WAS born three years after, it was never difficult for me to imagine how it must have felt, witnessing the end of a millennium and the beginning of another. Uncle Bode did mention it several times, as it was his own time of true loving. He told several stories that I quickly identified with, and sometimes I would feel intimately close to those stories as though I was the firsthand witness. Perhaps Uncle was responsible for my occasional psychosomatic false memories. Sometimes, the memory would be so intense and so clear. I used to have some problem understanding that I was not part of the millennium party and the prayers. I must have mistaken one of those year-ends, in 2005 or so as the beginning of our new one thousand years.

Uncle Bode was always generous with the story of the new millennium fever, how it was like, flying between two great ends of time. There was anxiety in the air as the world data banks were said to be at risk. He said the first morning of the new year was just like every other morning that he knew. No celestial festivities, he sure wasn't expecting one because he was then, twenty-six but he said so to arrive at his point that time flies without itself being aware of it.

"A new beginning is best started today and sometimes we might just start what will spin like carousel, never ending, sometimes when such carousel spins, we lose the vision of head and the tail and what we see is a perfect cycle."

That, I was told, was how many heroes of history were made.

"We are idols for the future for everything we do today with love, however blemished shall be improved in the eyes of tomorrow. Knowing that those little things we do matters greatly for tomorrow, we could go on, floating within our best, knowing that it will someday amount to something. We needn't bother about when, for it is like the water. Though sucked from the earth, it comes back condensed."

I was afraid for the look in my eyes as he spoke those words; those sermons. His life had been nothing like his principles and there was a look I could not help giving whenever I was skeptical, baring my dirty mind. He was the type in love with life, deeply more with bachelorhood. He was the one who made me understand that people do preach to their own selves by their words because they hope they would be better off if admonishment comes from their own mouths. It was not being phony; he was too lovely to be. Not hypocrisy, he was far from it, just a margin between who he really was and what he wanted to be.

He had grown up as a man having to live with the stigma of psychoses. His dreams, his anecdotes and wise words were youthful luxuries, seductive only to willing children and fat yummy cream-licking kids. I was a fan until unwitting realities crept in, draining my appetite for his fairy tales. Life in the street was a fast one and those who walk along the lines of written words always find themselves out of the lane. I wanted to be in the lane, to be contended with the boring meditation of my time and to live with the world more than I live with myself. I grew up to become a rebel against knowledge itself, and proverbs and sermons, hating every smart quote. The shorter it was the more odious it got. I was saved from my rebellion in the most unusual place and the most unusual manner. The texts of science were forged to spell spontaneous, yet it made me to suspect that there was some truth in those old witty lines I loved to say out loud alone, like a crazed lad.

AS KIDS, we contend with our fears and grow up to overcome them. In the neighborhood, there were children who feared Santa. Those cowards always spoiled the whole fun for the big boys who were usually able to figure that it was only a harmless man from 'Rome'. There were kids who feared to see people with excessive facial deformity. We grew up to reason it was all normal and learned to live by those sights that used to confront us everywhere and every time. Yet we grow up not accepting our own selves.

It was interesting, our willingness to hide from our own selves, to answer to other names and to deny who we obviously were. In the more lively moments of school days we always had occasions when everybody came out to announce they were not what people thought they were, occasions when the obviously arrogant ones pleaded not guilty of arrogance, when the promiscuous denounced what fascinated them. Drunks also used such avenues to renew the faith they had in themselves, they loved to remind everyone how well they could restrain themselves.

It becomes even more familiar when a boy tries to talk to a girl he wants. It was always the same old game, changing only with the venue. All the time, at the libraries, it was always a boy fidgeting with some book he would never read only to end up saying 'hello'. In the church, it was always a boy not listening well when the preacher calls out the bible passages. And why do I mention?

A junior boy trying to be witty in the school library had thrown me into a round of sleepless hours the previous night and I woke up to a rainy morning with heavy eyes. By his insensitive comments, understandably made to run a smooth conversation with the school's cutest, I was told that any sophomore in the Senior Secondary School without any career idea in mind was heading nowhere. I was angry, maybe not entirely at his comment but his decision to sit between the miss and me. That hazy morning, I went to the class with a resolve to fall in love with one school subject, hence decide on a career. The magic would not come, the famed sparkle in the eyes. At the close of the day, the school's senior Geography teacher announced the formation of the Space club. Interested pupils were to gather in the Geography laboratory after school hours. I knew immediately it was time to get down with something. I would shun my routine for the after-schools.

After several futile efforts to go with a friend, I stepped into the said venue to be confronted with an empty, cold room. I paused for a moment to think. Perhaps, I was mistaking with the time and venue. I sighed and yawned until a voice came from the far end. Robinson Crusoe would have sounded more cheerful.

"Please take your seat; the teacher will join us in a moment."

I could not see clearly who spoke because a strong beam of light fell across the room, right in front of him. I stood and wondered how I could possibly cope in a two-man club and it dawned on me that space trips were lonesome ventures all the way. Apollo never went with a crowd, nor did any of the men who had been there. In my desperation I chose to rationalize the situation. I took the front seat, wondering what kind of sadist I was stuck with. I felt like I was in a space ship already, traveling with a moribund geek.

In the next moment, I stood close to the huge map of Nigeria, which hung next to the writing board. My eyes went to Bakasssi, the little region that I learnt, used to be part of Nigeria. Right before the map, I went dreamy, remembering how pale the day had been. I had started my day with my leg stuck into a bucket of water an overzealous pupil fetched as early as four, that cold morning. I had also missed breakfast by a hairsbreadth at a time I just went broke. The rain had beaten me, running errand for a teacher who didn't even like me. Now, I was in a large room waiting for a teacher who would not come.

As I stood drenched in self-pity, I received another instruction from the same corner.

"Take your seat now, the teacher is here."

I decided that moment I was not about to be part of a losing team but the teacher was already at the door. It was too late to walk away as it would be rude to do so at that moment.

Bothering himself with a casual apology, the teacher ordered the boy at the back to move nearer and he rolled up his sleeves.

"Welcome to the space club."

He browsed through the passel in his hands busily. Just before we said the opening prayer, I had seen what made me glad I hadn't given up on the new club. The girl at the library was at the door, leaning on a taller girl friend. My day started off so bad, but that never robbed it of a happy ending.

IN THE EVENING, I lay on the sitting room chair, hanging my head back, worrying about my first impression.

I was no different from the guy I despised; who always bothered the library girl with unnecessary details, I thought, and my pick up lines were too generic.

I hid my face in the cushion and yawned, instinctively moistening and giving me the warmth that I needed. A voice came from the television as I breathed into the foam.

"And now the new president of the Federal Republic of Nigeria delivers his speech."

I leaped to the television and waited for my eyes to clear. How I had almost forgotten to watch the presidential banquet I don't know.

The President, a slim young man looking a lot more handsome than I expected, walked slowly to the podium. He filed behind a long procession and when he arrived at the podium he was greeted with a moderate ovation. Noon papers said he spent a great deal of time deciding on whether to leave controversies for another day or to spell out every detail of his widely publicized social policy. A close campaign manager had advised the Banquet night was a good avenue. They had developed cold feet in the morning inauguration and they weren't ready to repeat the same in their victory night. The night of many colored lights.

"Today we shall expound on a few factors; our population, our space and of a clique of aristocrats who knowingly or not, speak eloquently and inadvertently against this noble proposition- that the world is ill and a reward awaits those who make attempt at reviving it. Here I am using the 'space' word, a favorite vocabulary from one of history's object of opprobrium, the man who craved more breathing space for his countrymen, using the most inhumane tactics."

The President picked the papers which lay on the podium; he was so overwhelmed that he could not read from it. It was better to speak from his heart and damn his aides.

"Someway, somehow, evil had given wicked men foresight for a reason too clumsy for good people to understand. Even before the first whisper of a saving word for us, evil had echoed its own sounds, giving our yet to be struck chords a bad reputation."

He looked into the audience, many people sat on the edge of their chairs, stunned that the rumors were true.

"Long before we would ever venture into tackling this great societal problem decisively, our noble approach had been given a bad name by the real sinners- those who knows what is right and do what is wrong or those whose vision were so blurred that they found themselves committing greater atrocities to humanity which they seek to preserve. Sure it is more convenient to oppose this art and to adopt inaction. And we throw this debate open to you, hoping to speak to the minds of the proponents of inaction, a stance which is no less humane than the theories of the so called liberalists but this is the thought of a man not stating what is ultimately right but what is essential. This is what a man whose house is on fire would do if he were besides the fire fighters' machine and lived in a country where it is an offense for a non-staff to pull the fire fighter's noose."

Now the place had become really tensed. He could feel it in the air.

"Every passing seconds, evil multiplies, every minute too, good people increases but the net result will always be evil because one is multiplying geometrically while the other only adds up sluggishly. We need not be psychic to know there will come a time when people who hold virtue in high regard shall be outnumbered, that a time will come when the virtues of today shall become shame and the shame of today, a thing of pride. It is an act of unforgivable complacency or mere suicide for the aristocrats of a nation to think what comes around will not go around, presuming the walls built around them would be shield enough when the time of uprising of the misused comes. We have seen several cases where those who presume to be beneficiaries of a system turns out to be the victim of the same system they created. We have seen greater evil consume lesser ones from which it was rooted, this is why I think no one could afford to stay at the other side of the road in matters like this, even bad people themselves."

He paused, worried that there was no applause.

"Understandably, those fathers of faith who teach us against such population control practices like abortion have sharpened our conscience the same way they have done to stir our emotions against clearly unacceptable vices like murder and theft. To underestimate their contribution to our society is to do a great disservice to our hope for a safe, livable world. We owe them in return not only our respect and gratitude but also a good debate in matters where the same conscience of ours that they have graciously buoyed seems to be unshaken."

He raised his head and looked straight at the audience.

"Anytime I muse over these conditions of dilemma, my mind would be drawn to the sentiment, to which it is eternally tethered- that it is a sin to deny nature what it is her honor to decide. As much as we use the 'nature' word, I doubt if we had truly paused to discern what it really means; what are the determinants for what is natural and what is not. Have we ever looked into history with suspicion, that probably we had been rushing down our gullets a flurry of secular laws that might not be perfectly fitted for our modern and ever evolving age?"

He could tell he was picking up a little, for a few big men in the front rows nodded and changed positions on their seats, a good sign that his tutors had thought him to watch out for.

"If there is a culture that celebrates bravery and goes overboard about it, have we ever suspected it is the hands of leaders who want to encourage young men to enlist in their armies at work? If there are costumes that bare a good flesh of the ladies, if there is a tradition that makes them dance and twist their buttocks, have we ever given it a thought that probably the authors of those traditions were inspired originally by lewdly motives? If there are traditions that preserve them from all forms of exposure, do we suspect the integrity of the male is being selfishly protected? What then is natural?"

He grew fierce and raised his voice. His politeness increasingly gave way for his real person to show and his real intent came out of the cover, shining to those who were familiar with the games politicians play.

"Several centuries ago when capital projects were labor intensive and when there were no leverages it would be insensitive of anyone to encourage such things as choice.

In the times when large number of people were needed to fight wars, to build bridges and walls and tall castles and palaces I understand it would be highly unpatriotic of anyone to argue against any system of rules that encourages quick multiplication of people, even if their coming to the world would lead to becoming slaves to the more fortunate ones. Every time when we see the sweet smiling face of a little one and learn it is a child that could have been aborted, a chill goes through our spines and we find it difficult to imagine the world without that particular lovely human. Every time we hear the story of a child once presented for abortion becoming important in life, we draw nearer to a conclusion. Every time we watch the advert where a fetal blood begs not to be flushed out of the mother's uterus, we feel strange about the whole idea of making choice for our own selves. If these are viable arguments, then no man should speak for choice no more. If these always hold true, everyone who has terminated the process of conception even minutes after the fertilization of the mother's egg should know that they have sinned greatly. But these whole rouse would have been easily laid to rest if only there are no kids who wish they were not born to their parents or to where they were born or in the time they were born. If only it is true that the uterine blood, even in its formative stage could speak, if it has a mind and a purpose. If only it is true that good people are not shut away from coming to the world the same way we have come, to have a chance to breath in the same air that we do, to enjoy the same things that we enjoy, eat well and see how they could improve the world and their own lives. What obtains in reality is not as simple. It is a bogus entanglement of what is morally right and what is socially responsible; what is good for our senses and what is good for the world at large. Perhaps we may never come to terms with the ultimate truth or realize fully, the significance of individual preferences on the larger society. Perhaps a single rule may not apply to everyone from different backgrounds and this is where it gets a little complicated."

He waited to catch some oxygen. His mouth was getting dried up and the potency of his words, faded.

"For a nation that wants to empower its population, build a generation of people who are surrounded by innate abilities to unlock their potentials for their own good and the good of their country, this becomes necessary- to multiply what is desirable and decimate what is not. This could be achieved through strategic means, reward-motivated control and far-reaching propaganda, but also with total regard for the fundamental human rights."

A timid and then intense round of applause interrupted him. Presidential aides had come to save the face of their boss at last. For that, he was truly grateful.

"Also..." he wanted to continue but he could not help laughing at them overdoers, especially those who for the purpose of wanting to be noticed, struggled to be the last to finish applauding.

"This is a purely circumspect system yielding not to poetry but the prose of life. It is like the terse and seemingly tactless orders which captains reel out when their ship is about to capsize."

He turned around to face the part of the audience he'd been backing hitherto. When he moved, he did with grace, and restrained self-admiration. He hoped his antagonists would at least have a single good thing to say about him.

"Yet again, it sounds mean for the captains of our ship to throw people off this boat to reduce the weight being carried and the risk of getting drowned,' he said. 'The captain should have ferried with a safe level of mass from the beginning, dispelling frivolities, allowing only swimmers and people who could fight off pirates in the high sea. It is criminal to invite more than he could cater for, into the ship. It is heartless for him to think he would bring more people on board, hoping it would be merrier when they get to the harbor, or to think he would have more fighters when pirates show face. He is no better than the captain who watches the weight of his ship from the start, who gives others the chance to board another ship and arrive at their own destination safely. This proposition would have been rightly dubbed thoughtless if there were no passengers who regret boarding the ship when the wind comes storming."

The President lowered his voice and reduced his pace.

"My thoughts concerning the choice of the woman, the captain of her own ship and the state who owns the ship to decide who is ferried over the sea is surely guided by the precept of freedom and this is paradoxical, for everyone who steps on that ship becomes as free as those who were in before him or her. He is gifted by providence, the right to roam freely and even to perpetrate evil, giving the law enforcers more job to do and becoming a threat to every person with good intent on that same cruise. She is at birth bestowed with the right to coexist with altruistic persons and to throw her off the ship becomes a heavier moral issue than stopping her from boarding it in the first place. The good lord had blessed humanity with science and the wisdom to join the seemingly unrelated components of life into one piece. We have been commissioned to christen other creatures and by my own understanding, to make laws that are not opposed to the fundamentals of God but which guarantee happiness for most people and possibly everyone who lives. The law of the state is supposed to be the landlord, holding brief for the ultimate landlord whose presence cannot be fathomed by all minds. I do not know of any landlord who does not care about the population of his estate and who cares less what kind of people comes in."

He packed his jotters with an air of accomplishment.

"In exercising some of the propositions above, I recognize there might be serious loopholes which stands to jeopardize individual freedom upon which this sets of believes are based. Some may rightly consider it as dehumanizing for the state to apportion limits to the population of a people. There are genetically disadvantaged people who clearly lack resources to maximize the little potentials of their offspring through education and who love to keep large families. Such people of course are entitled to their own unalienable right to pursue happiness, which in this case, they acquire by having a sizeable family. What is in doubt is if this right really belongs to them because a second person is involved. A new man who is given too little to start with is born. It is this new man who suffers and not the father whose pleasure lasts for the period of babysitting. It makes perfect sense to assume that a right that involves a second party belongs to the state. This is why I think it is not totally out of place to suggest that the state could have a say in apportioning limits to family sizes. Also, there exists serious issues that may want to arise from this doctrine because the capacity of men to do evil, as said by a world leader friend, is still very much high but it will be totally naïve and inept to discard a topic only because it has been explored by heartless men once in the past as there is hardly a thing immune to the caprices of selfish men."

The President moved as though he had finished his speech, but he was a deceiver.

"For the sake of preserving every basis for human existence, it is important for good people to stand up to their God-given duty; first to step to the fore and second, to create a society where evil, though remaining inevitable, is greatly minimized and most importantly, made to stay in ignominy where it belongs. But this is never simple as care need be taken that evil should not be met with an equally disgraceful culture of prejudice or stereotype. The brilliant idea of evil to preemptively discredit this noble proposition could be quashed by doing what ought to be done rightly, without taking away the rights of anyone, even those who are not aware of their own rights. Science has provided headway and we need the will to engineer our common destiny on our quest to make our world a lovely place, not to produce a perfect generation but to minimize the tendencies of each child born to become tools in the hands of selfish individuals. A system needs be created where no child comes to the world except they are planned for, where it becomes criminal to deny them proper education. A suiting environment needs be created where their minds would be buoyed with bright and progressive doctrines. They will grow up to become strong and peace loving. They will grow up to understand the essence of brotherhood and love. They become free and will hold no fellow man captive because their mind is freed from the shackles of hatred."

He tapped his finger, a habit his tutor hated him for.

"In conclusion, we believe our number was meant by the good lord to be a blessing and we will work to harness the good it provides. We will work with the legislature to start a thorough thought and fair campaign of social responsibility; reward motivated family size control, better and compulsory education for children below the age of eighteen. Also, individuals with history of classified crime are to cooperate with relevant authorities in this concerted effort of raising a generation of our dream in Nigeria."

As he left the podium exchanging pleasantries with new arrivals, a lawyer friend whispered to his ears with a snicker. We heard series of things about his private chat with the President but popular conjecture was that he jokingly called him a Nazi.

 The President's speech on the proposed policy was set to let loose a fierce legal process, the kind that would incline the ship of his government at a dangerous angle, preparing it for sinking like the Titanic. Even before the new legislature resumed for a new session, there were debates on television shows and the pages of newspapers. Organizations were pitched against one another, sects against themselves. In those times, one newspaper editor stood out when she said

"We are all related one way or the other to the so called classified criminals."

Others argued there had been great fuse over just one item out of the many good ones proposed.

Rejecting knowledge was to become a crime and the nation was to find her perfect sanity.

AFTER A FEW months the proposed social policy had almost become an object of ridicule, attracting rude sarcasm and jeers even among the handlers because of the new government's inaction. In a budding daily it was remarked

"The people suffer when the President of a country is stuck with old literatures and shy about the realities of freedom and justice."

The Institute for Special Studies became more and more a social liability than a symbol of foresightedness. Everyone was caught in the frenzy of debates; of accusations and counteraccusations so much a daily suggested it was a deliberate ploy to divert attention away from the government's non-performance in the Microeconomics. While the arguments raged on, a clergy warned a permanent polarity was about to be created.

And a permanent one it did create. Along party lines and cultures, there were different opinions; schools of thought that believed it was a divine intention for the wheat to exist among the chaff. There were people who believed deciding one's descendants was a sin unto nature itself. Some said that evil was non-inherent, that it was a product of circumstances, even becoming necessary when those in authority does not govern responsibly. And who could have thought that our redemption would come from that conflict? We had lived years under a vague system; preaching a common good, yet blind that it could not see the route to that good. We had been punished and subjected to the rule of those who had no prescience for tomorrow, condemned to answer to the calls of those who could not protect us; those who slept and snored when our common gates were besieged with infamy. And thus came the time when the foremen were torn apart, not for the sake of money or fame. Thence, we asked, "for how long shall we be here?"

From the floor of the legislature where men and women fainted, voicing their deepest beliefs to the courts of law where order was barely maintained, there came tension to the land, dividing the leaders of thought, and making us realize that we could become an embarrassment to the world of tomorrow if we continue to lag. I saw the panicked faces of our leaders. Suddenly, a dark cloud came upon their minds and they stooped to think, everyman taking a shelter betwist the two-everyone to the dictates of their conscience. Times had gone by; the times of weak patriotism when we were fed with those lexicons that never made us want to believe.

THE NEWLY issued police warning proved incapable of withering the morale of them protesters. I was home on a school day like many other kids whose parents anticipated rowdiness and I watched every detail on the television. Dad was off to the work, mum to her friend's for a mock interview in preparation for the real one coming up in a fortnight. Uncle Bode left for the airport early that morning. He was returning to his family in New York after a month in Nigeria.

That morning, I watched a live show that would be replayed countless times in many TV networks in the country. A governor and his own deputy were publicly picking on each other over the proposed federal social policy. A big church was at the verge of splitting over the morality of controlled and discriminatory birth. News flashes kept buzzing as protesters gathered at the city square. It was supposed to be a day of rage and disquiet, but for the heavy presence of the anti-riot policemen who shot into the air and drifted the people farther from the square with bullet proof shields.

By twilight, it was publicly announced that a conference of community representatives was to be convened. If legislated, representatives from each ward would come together in a weeklong effort to arrive at a decision.

AND TO THINK that my school, the High school would be left out in the whole frenzy is to be condescending. We raised during the weekly debates, many questions that would have made the principal fear for his grip on the school if he was aware. For those who cared, our classes were split too, a huge majority of the girls being conservative. We had seen potholes on the road to our school, heard about preventable security situations, heard of the comforting technology of the developed world. For us, nothing could be worse and it wouldn't be unsafe to ask for change. We might have gotten it all wrong or we might have gone a little overboard. For us, the conflict was about the wheat getting rid of the chaff; and for the opponent, it was about the biblical injunction that the two should co-exist.

They argued it was a divine intention to keep it so and we posited it was not our own grand plan as humans. We might keep the weeds off our gardens, knowing surely that it would spring back, but for every moment spent without them, we would be thankful. The ladies objected and asked how we came about our own definition of 'weed'. If we knew weeds could be of benefit to plants at certain times in their lives and if it would be fair for us to decide what ought to be nature's honor to do. We replied 'weeds' are unproductive, antagonistic to development and that it represents every negative agent on the garden. The meager benefit the weed tends to give at certain stages in the life of the plant is dwarfed by the adversity it brings. We also said that humans have always been guilty of manipulation and if we decide to speak for nature, it would not be the first time that we would be doing so.

The debate would not end until we had decided to invite two senior students from a nearby federal college to stand as moderator of a grand debate we were going to hold. The finals would commence shortly after Friday evening assemblies so as to enable day students to participate.

As the class proceeded with the preparations, the news grew bigger, the rumors wilder and wider. Even staffs were not spared in the surprising euphoria that ensued. Every day, each idealist drifted more apart. Every day, we added some truth to our belief. There were dissenting opinions among the boys as there were among the girls but we agreed wordlessly to assume Friday was not only a battle of ideas but also of the sexes.

And the Friday afternoon showed an early sign we were about to do something as big as the weekend parties. Invited judges arrived two hours earlier in their school's bus for a motive that paled my enthusiasm a little.

Pupils arrived in droves and gathered before the locked school auditorium. The Principal had just introduced a policy of keeping all keys to the school's properties in his office, three weeks before, when we were accused of partying too hard in the hall. Slowly, the evening took its form and just as I noticed a rush from surrounding gardens, the student chaplain opened the door and headed for the microphone box.

I smelled good perfumes and saw many happy faces. Our ladies looked more beautiful with their hairs down and their faces lit with the white halogen bulb which hung from the ceiling. I could see my library girl from the dais where I was seated as the timekeeper. She smiled like some Egyptian princess, as though she was the prize for the evening. I'd chosen the angle I was to reward myself with the view and I spent some time wondering why God would want to break a boy's heart so.

Each time I rang the bell, it was always two seconds late. I had given two seconds of each minute to feed my eyes with the beauty of the hall at night and of the twinkling eyes of my colleagues, each sheltering unique vanities.

Guys sat haphazardly and laughed their heads off for the witty jokes of our Judges and the girls, cautious of their fabled femininity, sat with great poise. Both of the groups sat facing each other, leaving me with an irresistible imagination that their eyes were engaged and their minds were not in conflict as we, the organizers intended. For me, I managed to put on my fighting garments and it wasn't difficult to, as our opponents pushed us to the defensive, almost to the verge of retreat.

"The world has learnt to be suspicious of even the best rhetoric," said the little devil. Her gracious carriage, slim body and daunting gestures kept my eyes off the audience for a moment.

"The veil of civility is not enough and will not blindfold us into repeating the sins that was committed in Germany about a hundred years ago."

I tried to stick to my guns and remain on my guard. Her soft mien grew fierce and her voice, shaky yet she smiled convincingly – the kind that shame opponents and make them wonder why they choose to oppose.

"When a man chooses to assign a destiny to an unborn child, or to establish a virtual caste system within a civilized population, we cannot but suspect he has some sinister motives, more evil than the evil he pretends to fight."

Now it was like she wasn't doing the debate but engaging in name-calling. I could see someone whisper to our own speaker, who nodded with a knowing smile. To our delight, she continued the trend, building for her team, points that we would crash with only one phrase. She did notice the smile on the faces of those who knew the rules, for she was smart, but the wariness on her face also suggested she was at a lost. Her voice shook more as she continued.

"Not knowing how to come about what we want is just as bad as not knowing what we want. Any leader with neo-Eugenics tendency in this twenty-first century is no better than Hitler himself. He is an apostle of hate and its legacies."

She clenched her fist, a rather awkward gesture for the word that followed.

"Hitler knew what he wanted. He wanted a nation free from criminals and homosexuals and feeble-minded. He wanted a great Germany but did not know how to come about achieving that without emerging as a criminal against humanity which he supposedly seek to preserve"

With that, she ended her argument, strolling to take her seat in the right corner of the stage. She was greeted with huge applause all along; with a

loud noise and many personal comments entangled in between. Comments like
'You rock, girl', or 'Go to hell' or 'damn you'.
It didn't matter what they said for all was in the tone of cheers; making us fear for our own speaker. We wondered if he would fare better with the audience.
'Jelly lily' was what we called him, for his soft demeanor and teeny-weeny voice. He spent more time with the girls, hated football, and as if his sins were not enough, he was also an avid reader of Fashion, food and house shore magazines. We loathed him for every comment he used to make, we were too young to understand how not to be chauvinistic. We derided him for his excessive groom. He looked to us more like a gay but we respected him for one thing- his eloquence. In this I dissent but most of us cared less about politics or history. Our passion was soccer, rap music and a little mathematics as it was important for any boy who wanted to spend his leisure at the school café to know how to play his way around calculus.
Jelly Lily walked to the podium cautiously and with a teeny but firm voice that stole people's attention, he started.
"Thank you Miss Debater for mentioning most of the points I forgot to include in my presentation."
He pocketed his hands.
"Firstly, I would like to say that I consider it as blackmail for you to mention a name surely capable of arousing negative emotions and disapproval among the compassionate and modern people that are seated here."
His face was lightened with an insolent smile as he looked to the eyes of the opposite speaker for admission of guilt.

"There is no comparison and no analogy. What we are about to have is a social policy simply concerned with our future place in the global village. We seek to join the world of tomorrow with a little more speed and spirit and passion but also with just one sacrifice. We seek to give to this nation and the world just the gift of good offspring with minimum tendency to constitute hindrance to our noble vision. We do not promote hate, not even for those brothers and sisters whose deliverance came from the confines of the prison walls. We do not build concentration centers or train men for a secret service. All we do is to preach the message of change to our people; to trust them for a social revolution and rely on the strength of their will in this hardly acclaimed but godly mission."

He was greeted with a resounding applause, coming yet from a minority. As the deliberate and excessive applause subsided, the judge gave a brief comment and introduced the supporting speaker for a last word.

"I don't have much to join with what my co-speaker said," she said to a mocking and intimidating male audience and she continued angrily,

"I will like to ask what the opposing speaker insinuates by saying that we need to refine our genes to be fit for his ill-inspired vision, and his utopian world of tomorrow. Do you suggest that we are truly what the racists called us; some human in urgent need for improvement?"

Triumphantly, the girls chanted, and she raised her voice because she was not done.

"Let them tell if the haters were indeed right when they called us names."

About ten minutes later, the winner was announced. They won and we managed to come about a lewd story that had to do with the judge, the coaster bus, the curtain and the girls. We were Nigerian. A Nigerian my time never loses.

AND THE RULERS hardly bow out of tough situations. The President's popularity soared by the day among people who shared similar ideology and diminished among people who felt differently. It didn't really matter what each of the parties said, for there was strong bias. Now, the new president was unto those who believed, a persecuted revolutionist and they were consoled by such thoughts that if he should be impeached in the process, he would be taken for a 'martyr'... a more dreaded being, like ghost is unto the living. His learned antagonist, fully acquainted with the lessons of history, cautiously desisted from taking extreme positions. He was to emerge as the worse maverick the country would have as a leader, constantly chasing fantasies.

On his hundredth day anniversary as President, he hosted a grand night ceremony that a session of the media would deride as a "modern day fascist rally." To the very last day, he showed optimism that his seemingly dead proposals were alive. Indeed it was alive and would not be easily put to sleep as it was like a seed, germinating in the minds of many. The new team also was alive with youthful vigor. Chekhov was seated that night, in the rally, laced on the right side with his model mistress.

4

HIS' WAS THE perfect story of a prophet without honor in his home. The honor that he enjoyed in a foreign land, unlike the one in the saying, did not come easily too. It was the one of inconvenience, highly volatile, and maybe merited.

After several failed attempts at securing the doctorate in a Russian University, Chekhov had ended up establishing a private laboratory where he encouraged himself more about the authenticity of the findings that his mentor always felt ashamed or afraid to discuss. He had relocated to Abuja at the instance of the Institute for Special Studies, after several correspondences. He couldn't have been so recognized but for the compelling resemblance his work bore with those of a few local researchers.

His story as a controversial scientist had started in his days at the Timeline laboratory in Moscow where in 2000 he worked as a keeper. He was said to have stolen highly confidential materials from the place, but failing to understand the use. He worked hard to find his truth for he was convinced that a great answer lay in the cryptogram, which some men had just smuggled to Moscow at that time. A thing of global heritage had suddenly become an enigma. Many old hands came around and worked round the clock in the Timeline lab but their activities were shrouded in darkness. Even some invited researchers knew very little of their mission. Chekhov nevertheless knew that the famous ancient ciphers were being decoded. He was too clever not to know. He knew also that some people were out to gain private advantage in what was supposed to be for the public and even all living persons. Chekhov, though a graduate student, had disguised as a peasant to take the job of a keeper in that place. He knew the plotters would be less careful around him, being an uneducated person they would think he is. Even before taking the job, he knew what to expect. He could see what the municipal government had failed to see. A gifted schemer he was, and only very few things he'd done in his life had come by chance. He had been nursing the ambition of uncovering the wisdom behind the famed prebiological inscription of England since then but with little success.

When he was derided in the Nigerian media as having lost touch with reality, he must have felt just at home with himself because he was never in touch with reality and he knew it. He always believed that there existed a race of flying men or women with a voice like rushing waters and eyes emanating light rays. He had come across many things, mostly mystical, to arrive at that. The rudiments of his findings shared only little semblance to modern Genetics and most of his propositions were ill explained. He always hoped for vindication, that a university would call for the DNA he had secretly obtained from Timeline, examine it and discover the bizarre nuclear base sequences he thought that he saw. He never envisaged a step as simple as that would take so long; that nobody was in haste to be convinced about his sanity.

After series of disappointments, he had ended up assisting a college governor who was also a Biology instructor, a job he would give up quickly. His last resort was an old private laboratory in the heart of Volgograd, Russia. He bought the lab with the last heritage of his endangered bloodline, leading those who called him mad to think they were right. With proceeds from forensic examination services, he managed to raise a huge sum with which he hoped to establish his science in America but he was to be met with huge resistance. Several publications later, he found a home in Nigeria, devoting most of his time to organizing a world network of those he called the new age geneticists. He would never tell, but in his mind he might have believed he was coming to an easy place; that he would be accorded immense respect and that his colleagues at the institute would grovel at his huge but unattested profile. Again he was to be met with a rude shock and quickly too.

Three officials of the institute, all wearing big identity cards with NISS boldly written had received Chekhov at the airport in Abuja when he arrived in 2008.

The tallest among them who stood to the left moved forward to receive him, stretching his hands with a grin. In the foreigner's view, his big smile and lively continence seemed to be in contrast with the long, overdone tribal marks on his face. Chekhov was happy to find his first word at that moment. He had read about Nigeria from various Internet sources and he knew the man whose hands he was shaking was a Yoruba. In a very friendly tone he greeted.

"Happy to see you mister, you must be Yoruba."

The three laughed, impressed at that, yet a little surprised at his terrible accent. He had been speaking English for only one year.

As they moved towards the lounge, the eyes of his hosts glued to him. His funny coat and his unbelievably long nose only made them want to laugh and roll on the floor but they would have to think about getting another job to do so. Chekhov felt the tribal mark on the face of the dangling tall man among them was excessive too. He had read about it and seen pictures of the typical Yoruba man on the Internet but he hoped it was all exaggeration and at worst, an old practice. He feared he would lose his manners and laugh too. Each laughed at another, not making it clear what really amused them and trusting cultural differences for a cover.

Chekhov sited the high-rise NISS building under construction for the first time the Monday after; the second floor of the older building, a hundred meters away, was to be his office. The institute occupied the first four floors.

He sighed audibly when he was as ushered into the office. His expectation was nothing close. Like his Yoruba friend whom he later understood was to deputize for him, he knew the thought in his mind was written all over him. The tall NISS staff confirmed what he knew.

"You must have heard a lot about Africa but it is not all factual, one thing we do have in Nigeria is taste."

He looked away, pretending not to hear. Seeing someone boast about a developing country was a huge turn off for him.

Walking across the long passage at his new office, he noticed a mini gallery of the timeline of human development, something that brought a genuine simile to his face for the first time since his plane touched down. He crashed into his seat, a big chair of about ten- inch fluff, heaving a sigh of relief with noticeable feeling of satisfaction. With that, the tall man having facial marks said, "Welcome again," leaving him alone in the large highway view office room.

He began to nurse that old thought again, that apathy which kept him from answering to the Institute's call for so long. Be it real or delusional, he thought he was the next big thing to happen to the world and now he was full of regret that his learned empire was to be founded in Africa, a place he never really liked.

A week to his arrival in Abuja when he broke the news to his only daughter, a precocious eight-year old that his trendy mistress refused to accept as her own, she told him what they both never expected, what he recognized as the lowest point of his life.

"Now I think your doctor was right about the psychosis," she said with a film of tear slipping through the cornea of her sad eyes.

Probably he was truly a freak; the last man standing had joined voices with those who felt he needed help. He knew that moment an end had finally come to his battle, his denial. For him, when a battle ends in retreat it only gives an avenue to remunerate and take another look at life in a little more docile light. He took another look from a meek angle, and suddenly felt an air of peace about his journey to sub-Saharan Africa. He always moved on. Always found excuses to stay away from suicide.

That same day, he talked to Rosemary about his journey, suggestive of her company.

Rosemary was the one with whom he had shared the greatest times of his life, painting the streets of Piano red when the going was good. She was a tall blonde with fabulous eyes and skin, tattooed at the shoulders with Chekhov's initials. Their story had changed with a modeling contract they both signed the previous year, when the contractor suggested Chekhov was not good enough. Whenever he felt that he sucked, the scene would play back in his head,

"I hope you'd understand when I say your style is not complimentary with Rosemary's." The agent had said politely. He buzzed in and out of the room, emerging in another T-shirt. His guilelessness seemed to have irritated the agent who now told him to his face that he wasn't a good fit. He looked up, not believing his ears. Rosemary gave that peculiar look of hers, her lips embedded and her cheek muscles fidgeting in an effort to hide her dimples. He stormed out of the office but kept his eyes on the mirrors. He hoped to see Rosemary follow him or show solidarity at least but the least happened to be too much. That evening, he received a stern lecture on how to be gentlemanly. Two nights after, he lost his life's chance of marrying a hottie.

Years after, he found in his arms an unsuccessful club entertainer, a year on, with a baby girl and another two months, a weeping wife and mother begging for forgiveness, explaining what it meant to her to be fulfilled at the clubs.

Ever after, Chekhov had fathered the little child, his broken heart shuttling between his estranged wife's and his project. It occurred to him several times that he was chasing the genetic theories to keep himself monogamous, till his wife would consider herself fulfilled enough to come back to their marriage. He would find the worst was yet to come. His wife would rather sue for divorce and register another marriage with a local DJ than return to his judgmental life.

One day, in a city pub, he covered his face between two bottles of beer, wondering if his days would ever be bright again and like an angel touched his shoulders, he raised his head to see

Rosemary, looking every inch like she used to. Then, he slipped back to his old life, a life tinted with a lovely baby Rosemary would never accept. Two failed marriages and several sizzling romances later, the two came together in one last effort to start a home but the baby girl would remain a factor, not until Chekhov decided to grant her wish to stay with her grannies. He knew he was being selfish and he feared he would never forgive himself. The little one was 'kind' enough to offer to live elsewhere. She never really wanted it but her father was aging hopelessly in a loveless life, muddling everyday through the common misconception that he was a freak or a mad man. A change in their lives, she believed, would save him – any change at all.

He realized how wrong he was in no time but he came across a love far greater to him than the charm of a lady or the plainness of a child. When there was a chance for him to lead a 'normal' life, he fell in love with his new findings, shifting appointments, and missing job interviews. His entire life was to change forever, one night in the laboratory when he had a dream. A dream too vivid to be just a dream.

IT WAS TIME for the hearts of men to be opened to a great new thing. He had colonized the earth over the years with grandeur of an author, yet he is only a tool in the hands of the ultimate author. He is the tiller of the earth and doctor of her herbs but there is no success he achieves that is not granted and nothing he knows that is not revealed. Around this time, a random people found wisdom in the comfort of their bed, visited with visions in the quietness of the night.

Famished and lying ingloriously on a large laboratory desk, Chekhov saw in his dream, the world of sparsely dressed men with caramel skin, their hair frail, covering a large portion of their bulged faces.

He was there amongst the crowd of primitive people, chanting in a tongue unknown. His hands were raised amongst the crowd and his eyes, shut. When he opened his eyes, he realized he had forgotten why he screamed, or why he was there. Tapping the man standing next to him amongst the sea of heads, he asked what was going on, to the man's surprise. The man seemed to speak in Akkadian, a lost language of the ancient peoples of Mesopotamia, but the dreamer understood him.

"Crazy man,' he said, 'you have been here all day, echoing every word that comes from the crowd yet you ask what is happening?"

He paused and joined the crowd in chanting *dapānu*, then looked back and vouchsafed to reply.

"We are here to take our land!"

While Chekhov was trying to absorb the terse information provided him, he saw the beautifully setting sun at the ocean's horizon, silhouetting a young lady whom the crowd cheered almost riotously. Her gaits were bold as she strolled to the crowd. Suddenly, the cheering stopped. An anonymous bowman struck. She fell to the shores, her face swollen and her eyes closing. Many rushed to help with the stick that was stuck to her chest, more to catch a glimpse of her final moment.

"Promise you will find me," she said to the man who held her up as they both sobbed.

In a manner that saddened Chekhov even when he found it was only a dream, the strange man replied, "I promise."

EVERY DAY, a great child is born. Every day, a happy story is started but each new wine is fated to age in an old barrel. Each happy story met with distraction, even greater amusement than it is intended. Thus the world remains the same and its story unchanged. Sometimes, he is obsessed with passion, and the world is turned, to the right or left, for evil or good. Sometimes a hand is seen, stirring the ships of men, leading them to a shore unknown.

And when Chekhov turned his computers on, he agreed a bigger mission awaits him. Seeing Goggle return a website where he came across a picture; the same face he had just seen in his dream, he looked through the sliding windows. Another day was breaking and a cold breeze that sent a shiver down his spine blew through, almost violently. It was drizzling and the radio was playing an old Tu Pac rap song. He had fallen asleep after a long day at work, unusually at his laboratory. As he sleepwalked to check his fax for a new message, he shook his body to the beat of the old hit reminiscent of his college days. His true mood would surface with the message.

"You can as well stay in that laboratory for the rest of the week," his little girl said.

He smiled agreeably, knowing that he was a freak, a bad father and that his every life was falling apart. Somehow he believed everything would fall into place when his ship comes in; his dismembered family, his sanity, his finances. He had entered a huge debt with his ambitious human genome-sequencing project tailored towards finding the missing link between the modern man and the earliest of the early men, the aliens who he believed, once visited the earth in the Ice age. He had worked on DNA samples that he secretly got from the Timeline gallery, tried to reach out to a few respected figures in the universities to announce his findings. To his surprise, they always showed little enthusiasm like they knew something, like there was some secrecy or conspiracy.

When he took another look at the picture showing on his computer, he stood still to think. He was afraid there was more sense to his fantasies and experiments, sense he was not prepared for. He was called mad and he was happy to be, with his career and not mysticism.

Hurriedly and with a fast pulse through his arteries, he made for the printing machine and copied the pages. In the head was written in bold upper case, *National Institute for Special Studies, Nigeria.*

He browsed through the seventeen electronic pages to find who it was, the man whose face appeared down the first page. His name was Olabode Oladejo. He was a consultant for the institute but that was just a title apparently given to make him feel special. He was in truth a volunteer who shared a few stories with the institute in course of their research a decade and a half earlier. He had received a huge sum in exchange for his privacy and he followed the institute where needed, to share his story first hand. He learnt from those pages that the young man gave fifteen years earlier, a non-scientific account bearing striking resemblance to the account of the institute.

Chekhov ran his fingers through the small fonts, tried to strain his eyes to read. He had gotten his glasses broken the previous night to release some stress. In the middle of a long third paragraph was written

The confusion as regards the origin of the Homo sapiens, which is the modern human, has deepened because of a recent research which nullifies the proposition that we evolved from a common ancestor with the Neanderthals. The true origin of our first fathers remains a subject of contention.

Chekhov's eyes opened more widely and with great excitement he browsed through the pages on the computer, clicking on hyperlinks to further reading. His feelings were mixed, as he was at the same time happy and afraid and confused. He knew the nervous similes with which the trio at the college greeted his findings were meaningful and suspicious. He knew there was something a group of the highest clique among the elitist scientists knew that he didn't. Without hesitation, he penned down the contact of the NISS, starting eight months of electronic mailing and correspondence between him and the institute, especially the young man whose face he saw in his dream, Mister Olabode Oladejo who was also my Uncle. All these he had narrated in the prologue of his book, *The Probable History of Life.*

5

I BECAME de facto leader of the space club but always felt a clog in the wheels of my excitement each time a new pupil indicated their interest to join. I always felt they were coming for the library girl's sake and that paranoid thought alone turned me a tyrant in my own right, giving me for once, an insight to how the minds of some debauched leaders work. Every day, the library girl grew more beautiful, more aware of that fact and I, more jealous and more desirous of the leadership I had received reluctantly.

Like injuries, my dwindled rectitude was restored and I remembered once again, the spirit with which we were supposed to carry on, as youngsters who wanted change. Our meetings got more interesting and the mischievous yawns and sighs gave way to real discourses.

One day, the teacher spoke about the legislature's refusal to append to the payment of Nigeria's quota in the African space center. If the July deadline elapses, according to him, Nigeria would not participate in the epoch making event of the coming four years which would see African men going to space on an African mission.

"Space exploration is on its way to becoming a normal business, and very soon it will no longer be an exclusive reserve of the elitist nations," he said then, arousing our own interest in the daily national news. He spoke about India, how they made it to the moon nine years before and how a couple more of the erstwhile undeveloped countries tried to follow suite. We also learnt NASA was launching the first manned mission to Mars in the coming months, and that a small village was to be erected on the red planet's surface on subsequent visits. The old, long forgotten race of making it to an extraterrestrial body was on again, this time among the less successful countries which happened to have yet one more thing in common- massive resistance from home.

At the space club, we shared details of international planning of allied sub-Saharan African countries and the teacher gave us fresh updates. Every week came with new turns and degeneracy. There were too many questions in the air, the question of morality; if it was responsible to sink so much money into a single project when the country harbored so many poor people. A senator referred to the project as one that has no other benefit than to massage our battered sense of worth. He declared such motive as immoral to the dismay of a colleague who cautioned an agreement to which the country was appended should not be ridiculed. To him, there will always be poor people and since the country's prosperity of the past few years could not stop poor people from being poor, it should also not stop the country from pursuing some of its ambitious projects.

With a smile pleading for leniency among those he knew would be mad at his comment, he said

"We have been blessed superbly in recent years and I think it is time we stopped playing the second fiddle. It is time we stopped being coy about a few contemporary issues. It is time we loosen ourselves from the apron string of our uncomplimentary past."

When he said it, he knew he was giving his valedictory remarks and that his career as a politician was winding. Strangely, he enjoyed saying so. He thrived on controversies.

The easier and the commonsensical path which majority followed won easily, path of the working class. There is no sense in chasing pride when the stomach aches for hunger. Active space activities were to be suspended, giving room for more independence, more gut and ambition, preparing the world for a story.

At the space club, we felt disappointed as we would not be going on a sponsored trip to South Africa to witness the take off no more.

Our teacher came with another parcel, right before our finals, announcing federal scholarship to members interested in becoming astronauts. He served us a thin volume, an elegantly printed prospectus that we read interestedly. Whoever gets sponsored was to go for a year course in the United States after a two-year preparatory course. The package was nice, the remuneration rewarding. I felt I was heading somewhere for the first time, but in the weirdest way. A look at the streets from tall towers always made me cringe yet considered a life of heights. I was comforted by what I knew. I knew my country very well – that I might conclude my career not having to step my feet on a spacecraft. I realized later that I mustn't, and there were so many people whose life dream was to be in space anyway.

I would learn it was a whole life of its own, with rivalry and competition and frustration; the new space technology institute where I would spend a great part of this story. Of course there was a little bit of skepticism from home and I won by arguing the Nigerian factor, coupled with the fact that no one would want to put a whole history to my trust, a spacecraft of many million dollars.

That way, I was in for the preparatory course at Abuja. Just as my mates were preparing for college or battling with entry exams, I was auspiciously chosen for the latest career in our world.

SUDDENLY I REALIZED what I was advocating. I had signed up to a life of extreme hard work, chosen to spend two years with humorless kids. From the very first day, I had gotten started to the very life I imagined; geniuses from different corners of the country staying awake into the night, sorting different textbooks, assuring their mums on the phones that they would butcher others in the class works. I had suffered to be here... the school crimes and undone home works, the revelries unsanctioned...I had survived all, and when I perceived the smell of the oak tree before the Admin block, the rain dripping through, I knew I was in for the toughest part. Yes I knew the smell of trouble.... everyone except me had come with the wicked ambition of being the best. I had come wondering how much fun it would be, floating in the space laboratory. I came hoping an instructor would announce a new planet has been found with better people living in it. I thought the curriculum was too boring and undemanding.
Monasteries seemed better as there was no need to be reminded that one is being paid for in other's expense. There was one humor and slang in the dormitory ... the boys loved to call one another the government's property, an idea I never really liked. Also, they loved to calculate how much is being wasted on each kid who failed to show up in a class.

In the dormitory were spacious rooms of five beds, each with distinct views. Next to my bed was a little geek, Dotun, never doing much of the things normal people do. He hated to admit, but he was battling with Leukemia and seasonal depression. Since our first day together I had noticed his obsession with clairvoyance and eastern literatures. He was hoping secretly for a miracle in the place he trusted best.

There was also a twin, both living each day to see their dreams of becoming Africa's best astronauts come true. With time I would see they were already deluded by their dreams. There was a South African with whom I shared the longest part of this story, a fifteen-year-old math wizard whose parents migrated to the country to start a business two years earlier. I had developed the habit of seeing the city through his eyes. In my opinion, the city of Abuja was perfect but I was also very familiar with people's funny judgments. The South-African had been to many big cities in Europe and a few in Asia and I always asked for comparison. The highest remark he ever gave was 'okay' and I felt like I would hit him each time he did. It was difficult to, but I had to admit that I belonged to a world far at the back. I resorted into annoying him with a proposition I never explained satisfactorily- that Nigeria is the giant of Africa. Every time he asked how, I would answer tersely, massaging my psyche with his roused temper, "Because it is the fastest."

On our first meetings I never thought that I could stand him for half an hour. Though he was rarely at fault, I thought he was having an aura of ethnocentrism, a self-absorbed sense of national identity, leaving me with a feeling sandwiched between envy and irritation. I wished I could honestly trust in a first generation leader of my country like he did trust in his Nelson Mandela. I wish I could feel comfortable with the face of a dead or living statesman hung around my neck. I tried it once but the feeling was not genuine. When the South African asked some questions about the smiling man at my chest, his conquest was complete. I knew too little about my supposed icon and when I spoke, we both knew it was from somewhere not the heart.

I agreed his' was an exceptional heritage. I had just gotten over the dance movie; *Sarafina*, brooding over the proposition that a nation begat with afflictions have more recipe for love and passion. I wished we had such story binding us; such persecution reminding us that the things that make us differ from one another is unimportant, considering the things that we share together. Maybe I was being funny, or selfish for I would rather be part of this easy generation when people hold dearest their simple and humble lives, yet, I loved us to have a thing so thick we could hold, that our minds would go to when our flag waves.

I wanted to love and have reasons to do, not because my South African colleague claimed to be a patriot; I never really liked him or his own expression of patriotism. I wanted to love for it gives some sense to everything we perceive. Gradually, the will to be a good astronaut set in; to take the colored skin to space just for glory. To walk into those places we were hardly found. As I read more about our history I learnt we did have a great story too. As I read the lines on the face of my roommate, I came to understand there was already a need to be chauvinistic about my country. Again, I acquired a fresh momentum and energy, promising myself to remove the sneer on my friend's nose with a blow, for a start. I hated the way he used to sniff every time I discussed the streets of Abuja and the markets of Lagos.

Meet my South African friend, the one to become a professor of astral physics and only witness to this impossible tale, Shederach; A skinny big haired lad with grimaced face and goggle eyes. At first sight, he looked slightly awkward with his oversized plain shirt and rounded specs. When he speaks the first impression becomes unimportant and what comes to the mind is image of a young genius with a clear vision of what he wants. When he spoke, whoever heard believed he chose to be colorless and old fashioned. I felt so too and was charmed by his smartness, yet loathed him for almost everything he said. That was how complex everything was, but all our differences and complexities would vanish that frightful moment when we discovered we were lost to float in the space forever. Then, we both found what every human mind was destined to become- flat, gentle and serene. We both found that in the absence of everything that we crave for to suit our body, we are as lovely as the angels.

At the preparatory school there were loads of things to compete for. From the grades to fame, even unbelievable things like the rumors and attention. We did crave for crazier things than standing before the beautiful blue lights lining the magnificent assembly hall of the school at nights to get noticed when gorgeous young people frolic the stairs. Our conversations and even the thought of our mind seemed to be shaped by what surrounded us- the colorful, scented flowers of the gardens. While some pursued their dreams with dignity, some lost their faces, receiving their blessings on bended kneels. For Shederach, he fell on the thin line of the ideal. Always did. He knew too well the good measure of everything and how to achieve without trading his dignity. But for his fat lips with which he uttered careless words and his haughty eyes, he would have passed for a really cool dude. However, classmates considered him sociable enough to listen to complaints of the twenty-three class members, nerdy enough to traffic their weekly projects around the school.

IT WAS A DEFINING moment for my country, a time of truth and a time of birth when the mother labored to conceive. The coy tiny cracks on our mud houses had stretched widely, ready to give way and give us the chance of a new beginning. We watched as it all unfolded in the fourteen-inch television hung up at the left corner of our room, as a group of people vowed to put an end to the government of the day for its reluctance to repent. Another group of persons took it upon themselves to educate people about the proposed social policies. Everyone with a fresh awakening. For some, it was a game for the day, and others, a subject for the future.

One evening, after the weekly Thursday chapel, Dotun and I ran to the dormitories to catch the 2020 Olympic opening ceremony. We needed to rush as Shederach and the twin would want to watch the Science Daily, an educational program sponsored by Shederach's parents on a local channel. While searching for a channel to watch we noticed that there was 'breaking news'. The Nigerian Television Authority showed the President talking and hitting the table like he used to, also, mister Chekhov smiling uneasily at journalists in front of Independent Corrupt Practices Commission office. Nevertheless, we ended up in a sport channel.

The ceremony had just begun and a reddish gas rolled in the air, gradually taking the shape of a bird; symbol of the year's Olympic. The media reported earlier that a new technology was to be showcased at the games. Hypnotized by the view, we jumped round the room, yelling and singing the praise of the west.

"*Oyinbo ti loo.*"

We hastened to the corridors and knocked at other people's doors, starting a round of crazed revelry. The hallway, a little wider than the average and flooded with white florescent lights used to be our madhouse in the very few evening times the boys try to be fun. As we tried to be decorous and watch the Iraqi hip-hop artiste's opening song, 'Bird in the sky', I noticed the twin had arrived and went to try getting them to join us in the little Olympic party of ours. It appeared they were no less bubbly.

"Your president is in trouble," the friendlier between them said, stocking his cheeks with chicken pies. His brother smiled awkwardly, his eyes implausibly glued to the television. On the screen was written, 'Chekhov linked to an experimentation that goes awry. Two found dead.'

IN THE MORNING after, I yawned quite loudly to wake my roommates up. The television had been on, all night. The President's press conference of the previous night was being replayed. He dissociated himself from the mess and pledged to instruct the government's attorney to take the case up.

"In this turning point of our nation we should not be so complacent to rule out the possibility of sabotage or blackmail. The man at the center of it all, Mister Chekhov will of course be treated as innocent until proven guilty. He has come not of his own accord but on a special invitation to join hands with the National Institute for Special Studies in their wholesome task. We must also put it at the back of our minds that he is here through a special agreement between the government of his country and ours."

When asked if he was aware that Mister Chekhov was under investigations for the same accusation in his home country, the President chuckled and muttered to the microphone,"There was no time in my career as a politician that I was not under investigation. Even when you give to the destitute, you will be investigated."

He seemed to realize fast enough how watery he sounded. He left at that moment apparently to escape tougher questions he was anticipating from the press. A local news channel reported that he was being advised by the government attorney to meet with some lawyers, including his own personal solicitor before giving further press conferences. A junior press officer mounted the dais, castigating people for making mountains from a molehill.

"The president's humane disposition to this case should not be taken for granted,' he said, 'although the President seems to have waded into this case, it remains a private case and should be treated as such."

An evening newspaper reported that Chekhov tried to divert from his earlier stance that the President knows about the experimentation. He gave every reason on earth to why he mentioned the President when he first appeared at the Independent Corrupt Practices Commission's office in the morning. No opponent seemed to believe him about the President's unawareness. There were too many contradictions upon which the opposition worked. A legal cloud was hovering over the executive.

The day after, a middle-aged plump, dark skinned woman gaily dressed in *iro* and *buba* was aired on the television. The cops escorted her. I learnt that she was a wife to one of the killed inmates. She had been arrested for struggling for the corpse of her husband which she claimed, needs be cremated before dawn in respect of her husband's wish at his deathbed. Her strife only helped arouse suspicion that she was trying to cover up a thing. Firstly, there was no deathbed.

The next of kin to the second victim and his only family, a close-to-thirty year old call girl from the suburbs was also reported to have absconded over the night. Though two men on a legal death row were killed, the case grew in fame, topping the list of issues of the week in the newsstands.

In the day that followed came the ice that broke the camel's back. Autopsy result showed the two were indeed administered with poison which was later identified as the so-called Cheknosin. Before the end of working hours, Chekhov was charged to court in what would be a landmark case.

Even from the preliminaries, the case had started getting messy, as a group of lawyers believed that government needn't be the plaintiff. The legal process was to start with an argument concerning representation. No one and not even families of the victims seemed to be well disposed to the idea of joining issues with anyone. The group of concerned lawyers suggested they might have been blackmailed into keeping quiet or they might have been threatened. Their suggestion appeared to have merit because the next of kin to one of the victims had absconded in the heat of the moment. Also, the second victim's wife showed no interest, even when medical examinations showed that her husband was murdered.

The government attorney argued that families must have been keeping mum because of the social stigma of being related to someone on the death row. He announced that hearing was to commence shortly at the high court having jurisdiction over the case. He said in a rather too familiar tone, "The case has been taken before the court of law and as a custodian of the judicial process, I want to enjoin everyone to abstain from making further comments about it."

Whether public commentators complied with his 'directive' we could only presume but the columnists surely were not impressed or hypnotized. A self-acclaimed biased contributor to an evening newspaper wrote in plain terms what was widely whispered. The President is in the know of how Chekhov smuggled his mixture to the maximum-security prison. According to that writer, the President threw caution to the dogs to pursue his objectives. He is guilty of abusing his powers as the chief executive, for granting Chekhov an expedited access to the prisons. Many other questions were raised in the column. Why there was not a single relative of the victims willing to appear in the court at least. Why the warders on duty in that night were swiftly dismissed without given a fair trial. Why the government was both the plaintiff and defendant in the same case.

The court of law dismissed the group of concerned citizens' case for the group's lack of standing to file the suit. There were no firsthand complainants; hence the police was advised to forward a case. The judge said he would not bow to pressures from those who were bent on making it look like it was more than a regular criminal case.

"These are men under a capital sentence for goodness' sake,'

he said wearily in the middle of an interview. 'If the executive wants them dead they would have done that simply because the highest court in the land has ordered their killing anyway."

The judge also tried educating the masses, he couldn't help it, but there were too many funny stories making the rounds.

"This is a case of medical ethics,' he supplied 'Mister Chekhov is a suspect in the case involving unauthorized use of a yet to be validated pharmaceutical substance on two adults without their consent. If convicted, he shall be guilty of homicide and he shall be referred to his country for final action."

He took the pain to explain the condition with which Chekhov had come to the country.

"We can say it is wrong for the executive to have appended to such arrangement but that doesn't mean we can annul the agreement at will."

Hearing was to resume the following month in what the public believed was a charade, unworthy of mention. The government was both the claimant and the defendant. Leader of the 'concerned citizens' seemed to be giving up the fight when he remarked in one of the newspapers that nothing was to be expected as a big judicial manipulation was being committed. Indeed nothing was expected because everyone believed the executive would stop at nothing to safe its own head. Gradually the case became dry, enjoying only a tiny attention in the media.

The first round of examinations was approaching in the preparatory school and we kept vigils, spending less time to amuse ourselves with those contemporary issues we used to find interesting. Whoever slacks in the exams, it was announced, would have his or her scholarship dropped. Also, whoever shows distinctive abilities would have the scholarship extended to the main program we were hoping to run abroad. The greatest drama of the Chekhov case took place around this period, allowing us only a scanty time to update ourselves with the news. Chekhov had finally thrown in the towel, telling the court that the President was indeed aware of his plans to test his mixture on the convicts.

That evening, a press statement duly signed by the President was issued.

"Mister Chekhov has always been our friend, always contributed positively to our dear country' he said, 'Chekhov did earn our trust but we have learnt to place our trust even more carefully. I ought to have inquired more about his mission to the prisons before making recommendations and I humbly apologize for this great blunder."

While some fell for his thinly acclaimed response, a lot raised more discomforting questions. The president, they said, lied and abused his office more by trying to overturn the judiciary. The heat would be intense for the next few weeks. His pet project brought to disrepute.

On our way to the dormitories one exam morning we learnt of his decision to resign. Chekhov was extradited with a recommendation of life imprisonment.

A BUSY MONDAY it was, especially in the government official districts of Abuja. The president had resigned under the most unusual circumstance and in the most unusual manner.

Though his letter was tendered on a Friday, it was agreed among a few Senators, Representatives and other officials at hand to receive it that it should be kept as confidential over the weekend. However their top secret made it to the headlines they could only wonder as most of the 'suspects' were enemies of the press avowed. More disturbing were the comments credited to them in the tabloids. They were said to have mocked the President for being cowardly, developing a cold feet and doing it so obviously. Also, they'd supposedly remarked that they would draft a bill mandating aspiring public office holders to have their brains tested as one of the requirements for the offices. There were lots of opinions but all seemed to have come to an agreement that the manner with which the President left the office was irresponsible.

In the busy thoroughfare that led to the National Assembly, a thick human traffic transected the crossroad. Many parked their vehicles to walk down the government district to the executive wing. We had come to witness the passage of the bill establishing our own preparatory school of space science into law. Now we had become pretty sure that it would be postponed for the umpteenth time. Nevertheless we were happy to be around on a day of drama. We looked forward to watching the proceedings from the gallery. Before the gates leading to the domed structure with a scenic rock behind were men of the State Security Service, busy mounting some security gadgets. Also to the right and left of the gate were policemen patrolling with Rottweiler. As we approached, one of them pointed the gun at us apparently disgusted at the audacity the driver evinced in bypassing the traffic right in front of them.

"*Yaya kasua*," the driver greeted, making efforts to hide the fact that he was jittery. He had spent the last few minutes bragging about his frequent visits to the place.

"*E pele*," replied the policeman.

"We are changing the government today."

There was excitement on his face.

"The constitution is clear about it,' I interrupted, earning for myself a very scornful look and I managed to finish. 'The Vice takes over."

One more policeman joined us, trying to be a little more assertive than his colleague.

"Are you on visit or just checking around? As you can see, today is a very special day."

Shederach tendered the letters in his hands and they browsed through, with a funny expression of contempt on their faces.

"I doubt you would be able to do what you have come for," he said and beckoned to the officers who were forming a fresh barricade to let us in.

Few meters ahead was the famed doomed structure of the National Assembly. As I stared, my mind was occupied with a thorough assessment of the architecture. It looked imposing from the western streets, but looking from the front, I felt it could be bigger and more awe-inspiring. I was admonished for caring too much about the trivial and I took a second look at the building. There was something Nigerian about the place, the background rock maybe, or the color of the atmosphere. What human ingenuity had omitted, nature had graciously provided.

As our vehicle zoomed, we saw the legislative buses preparing to pick men in flowing *agbada* to an obviously short distance. The new President was to be sworn in by noon, just five minutes away.

No one was having a ready insight to his politics but he was generally agreed to be a centrist and liberalist who would pursue even the most radical agenda subtly. Over the months, the new President, as the vice, had been conspicuously silent about the issue of the moment- transformation of the nation's human capital. When he spoke at the handing over, he left no one in doubt that his predecessor's legacies would remain. From the reception hallway that leads to the outermost offices, we watched as he made his first speech.

"We must not create an impression that we have come to a promise land we cannot till."

Many of us heard his voice for the first time. All we knew about him before then was that he was the yes man with dyed golden hairs who always laughed awkwardly to the jokes of his boss, always nodding to affirm the President's overstatements.

Most of them uniformed receptionists nodded affirmably as the new President spoke on the national television. They seemed impressed at his guts.

"Even the meekest man knows what to do with power," the chubby, short man at the lobby said mind-numbingly. He was underdressed; seemed to have taken a long holiday off salons. Our driver whispered the man was an assistant to one of the representatives and that he wielded great powers in the assembly. He will not stop making us sick with his know-all attitude and his incredible rumors, the short chubby man. Maybe it was a delusion but it seemed like his eyes were fixed on me as he talked, forcing me to nod compliantly even as I wondered how a man of his kind managed to get to that hallowed place. For a moment, my gaze fell on his waist too, measuring the distance between the waistline and where he his belt was. Though he managed to make some chivalrous gestures in his conversation with the receptionists who stood watching the TV, I could sense he was a political jobber, those whose stories were urban legend especially at those times. His fingers were permanently on his face, pressing the many pimples. Perhaps, I thought, he should make use of one of the pointed rings on his fingers to burst those pimples. He sniffed like he was catching cold and cleared his thick moustache with the back of his hand

"*Were ni baba*," he boomed as he picked the handkerchief from his pocket to wipe his oily face. He meant the President when he said *baba*. He seemed relaxed, even more than our principal who arrived few minutes behind us. Shortly, and just before a staff came to usher our principal into the VIP, the man was cautioned politely to take his seat. We were not meant to know what was whispered to his ears but he was lighthearted enough to echo the simple instruction given him. Suddenly, there came a moderate level of silence, providing us with the opportunity to hear the erstwhile Vice President now the new President more clearly.

"Having scaled through the frightening web of economic crisis, we are today, at a seemingly more comfortable juncture. We are faced with two or more options. Whether to adopt the conservative stance, which I honestly believe, is safer or to dare take measures which I fear might be followed with varying degrees of consequences. It is tempting to take the easy way out but anyone who detests mediocrity will understand that inaction is no choice."

Our bully friend, obviously uncomfortable with the sentence of serenity recently slammed on him, muttered from the smooth upholstery in which he was almost completely subsided

"I said so; he will never depart from the ways of his boss."

I had shushed him before I realized how rude I was.

"Our population now stands very close to two hundred million' said the president from the television

'Our population growth rate is projected to rise over the coming years because of our overwhelmingly young population. This I believe is a major challenge to us as a people; whether we would make this factor of ours a blessing or otherwise. If we could make every child born within our borders or born to a parent who shares in this vision to be a resource or liability, If we could give to the world the gift of good and productive people."

"Nonsense!" the male receptionist closest to the television quaked. Another receptionist, tactically making apologies for his colleague remarked

"The man said it himself that the policy is prone to bring consequences."

We tried to catch up with what was said that earned the president audible jeers. We were angry to have missed out and we protested indistinctly.

Three hours later, when we had become conditioned to the place, we were called upon almost in whisper. A uniformed female receptionist who was standing by the door gestured
"You may follow that gentleman in gray suite, please".
Our eyes were heavy and when we stood up, our trousers became tucked in our buttocks. We stretched our muscles widely, savoring our newfound sense of freedom. It took no time to feel at home, no time to assume old habits especially after the comfort of a sound sleep. The principal had admonished us to be as courtly as possible at the National Assembly complex and there we were, yawning loudly and uttering vulgar words. We were mischievous teenagers, deliberately defying the ambience of that palatial lobby. Nothing seemed to be immune to our mischief.

Thirty minutes later, when the house committee was fully convened, we rose to our feet in greeting. The chairman of the session did mention in his long memorandum what helped us dump the idea of sleeping with our eyes opened (something we had become accustomed to, a necessary practice in the killing schedule of the institute).
"Space science as we all know is a tasking one, requiring the absolute attention and devotion of technocrats involved," the chairman said fumbling with a brochure. "We expect you sir to guarantee that the three hundred and seventy gentle men and ladies in your institute are the best we could have ever had out of the thousands of potential technocrats that we have, scattered all over"
"A hundred and fifteen, sir,' the principal stuttered, 'many states did not comply on time."

It did us well to see him tremble.

"Very well, sir,' the rep cut in. His politeness was that of convenience and the manner with which he held the brochure in his hands showed that he meant not to be interrupted.

"I have gone through the files carefully, in fact taking two whole nights to digest it," he said, removing his goggles which he moistened with his breath.

"For every student, the government is to spend approximately half a million dollars." He paused to rub the lens with a face towel before he continued. He seemed to be proud of the fact that he was versed in the figures.

"We have seen occasions where young men whom this great country tried to educate decide to forget their benefactor time and again." He paused again, trying not to be negative as a decision had already been reached.

"I wish to inform you sir that the House has included in the Acts an additional curriculum among which is citizenship education. You may want to go through to see if there is any objection you want to make before it is being passed."

The principal nodded

"I have always considered it a good input."

"The house committee will like you to seize this opportunity to tap from your wealth of experience concerning the space mission. May I ask that you wait behind for a closed session?"

We were asked out of the room and led to the exit where our bus was waiting.

In the evening, the principal and his wife joined us for the dinner, surprising us pleasantly. He must have been heartened by the good news. The House was to set up a commission to draft the road map through which Africa's space mission would be realized.

Many years later when the party of expectations was over, I looked back to that October night. Our dreams had lived with us for so long. Like it is for most dreams, it was a lot less complicated than what reality brought. Like it is for most great stories, it began with a shy wishful word.

The principal and his wife sat barely at the edge of the long table specially prepared at his bidding. Though we felt discomforted at his sudden humility, most of us were encouraged and challenged.

"Someday,' he said, 'very soon, some of you boys and girls would be controlling Africa's space stations many hundred thousand miles above the earth, becoming our heroes and heroines."

His eyes came to be dreamy as he spoke, sparkling with the light of the florescence bulbs. As it lingered in the rows, it seemed not to have any expression of doubt. Principal seemed to trust us more than a few of us trusted ourselves.

From the back row where I was seated, I saw the face, glowing with hope. My mind drifted far away, and I wondered how one could get to love the unlovable, especially some kind of job. I contemplated taking a sip from the orange drink served, though it was only proper to wait for a toast. I was determined not to be inspired. I thought I knew my country too well. I was probably defending my psyche because I was clearly not a candidate, not a real part of that dream. My phobia for heights was far-reaching.

When it was toast time I did mine with an empty glass. We toasted to a great dream that night. It was 2020.

THOSE TIMES, our mothers' breasts were blessed and caused to bring forth seeds through which great feats were achieved. The wind of change blown across the oceans reached our shores, starting a glorious age for everyone. Our eyes were opened to a few more details, a happy chapter from that old book slowly accomplished. We did feast on glorious words, becoming numinous, our feet threading on a spotless floor, tempting us with the thirst for greater things.

It started the moment it was conceived that a creed needed be written to our minds, when it was agreed that some wicked men could be turned around. It began when it was understood that the world was ill and a reward await those who made attempts.

The Yorubas say the child we refuse to build shall sell the house we build in his stead. They were better off when they realized that the mines were not greater than their minds. A wise man once said that the power that resides in them is new in nature, and none but they know what that is which they can do nor do they know until they have tried*. When our emancipation came, we almost became like the lords of the ancient times both in thoughts and crafts.

Truly our story was not as enchanting as many would tell. There were no cherubs in the skies or emerald in the horizons. Some indeed called the difference meager, people whose nature was hopelessly cynical. For those who tell the cup is half full, it was a splendid time as everything the world did in one accord flourished. My own account is a little complicated. I had grown to the world where the tales of genocide and open wickedness sounded like fiction or story from the very distant past. We had seen too little of straight wars to appraise the sharp difference that the new era brought to us. Many brave and passionate people had tried in the past. There had been times when the leaders of the world seek even greater things than we had seen; yet failed.

When the new men in whom the wisdom of the past was imbibed came, they understood that they were living to accomplish the happenings of those eons, in the world unfathomed, in the first home to which they would return.

Sometimes and someplace where our earth hung above and the shining eyes of the lords of the ancient times behold lustfully our place, there was a great rebellion, starting the long story of evil and of good, of love and of hate. Though they found there was no greater pleasure than the ones provided, they wished for a change to choose for themselves their own path, leading to no where certain even in their own eyes.

The rebellious lords knew less how great the kind father's wrath would be. Like a meteor, they fled to this home they covet, flying for ages till they got here. The place they had always dreamt of entering with great glory, now they have with shame. For them there was no other place to go but here, as our youthful earth had come back to life, surviving tons of million other planets. And when the people of the world saw the drama in their sky, the sight of which made the meek hearted faint, they fled to the caves.

The flesh eaters and hunters stayed in the caves for many days till they withered and when their fears subsided they hovered within the hills rejoicing, not knowing their world had become a home also to wiser beings. Everything that belonged to them was left to corruption. Slowly, they lost their merit and forgot the sweet song with which they communed with the lords of the ancient times, in the good old days when everything was beautiful.

It came back to a select few in their dreams. They were tutored with morals from the past for men were to be like gods, as wise and lovely as they were originally intended to be. Maybe it is true that the future is of no use without the past. Maybe it was time for us to know our history, our true fathers. In a subtle manner with which it is known, wisdom came to a few, a select few from different places, and creed and faith through dreams.

We dream in the nights, of the life we would have loved to have, the lovely gift we crave, doing things we might not be able to do in the 'real life', sadly of the awful things that we fear. But what could be more real than the world where everything is decided, the puzzling world where the shy words of meek men were like the roar of lions, where the cry of the anguished is so loud. Perhaps it is a process of reverse learning as it occurred more vividly and more frequently to those who shun the things with no immediate consequence to their private lives, those who tried to deny what was coming to them. Their dreams were likely a way to unwind the bizarre perception coming to them, a way to negotiate with the giver of inspiration. Little wonders so that such man as Uncle Bode shared in the burden of our unfolding history.

He told me of his dreams, a world and a contiguous story line which used to come to him in his sleep. At first, it was funny and he shared the experience willingly. He started feeling weird about it and I saw uneasiness in his eyes. He was obviously ashamed that he needed help. Before things started getting a bit sour, I had always loved to listen to his never ending tale; the 'urban tale of the full moon night'. When the going was not only good but also hilarious, he used to speak of the gothic imageries that always confronted him in his sleep; chinless and short stout men with slanted fore head and frail hair, dragging their thick feet awkwardly over the icy earth. As ugly as he deemed his constant friends of the other world, he seemed to like them. Their humble demeanor, he said, strangely contrasted with their viciousness in times when foods were to be shared. Though he ate and made fires with them in the cold caves, none seemed to be willing to involve him in their senseless melee, none dared look into his eyes, yet he was the centerpiece of their attention.

He was unto them like a god and they groveled to give him his own share of the meat even when their own were underfed. In the world of his dreams, he was a leader with no idea of the vastness of his territory. One night, Uncle Bode dreamt that he was ferried to the ends of the seas where a transaction was to be made with fairer people who lived in the other side of the world. There he discovered the world of his dream was not as crude as he thought. There lived a people of his own kind in that world and there lived a maid whom he loved.

ABOUT thirty thousand years ago, somewhere around the Mediterranean coast, there lived a boorish race. That time, our home was cold as a cave made of glaciers. The treeless plains of Europe were covered with rivers of ice.

Neanderthals lived dispersed in the caves, the cliffs, also beneath huge stones, each of them minding their own businesses. Though their life was free from vices typical of the modern world, they were alien to the virtues of brotherhood as they barely muttered a speech. Each mind was largely left to hover alone through the vast and vague realities of the time. There came a time when only a few rodents and deer and horses roamed the wilds, making these early men to become more rustic and violent scavengers.

Those times, there lived a pretty young man in the land of these chinless men; a man belonging to our own race. He had grown among the Neanderthals from infancy, since the time he was abandoned during one of the series of wars between the two races of the world, the real human, our own fathers and mothers, and the race of brutish homos who existed before them. He had grown to love the chinless men, more than his own people and he had become like a prince to them and conqueror of his own people.

When the baby prince was seventeen, he had designed a grand plan of abducting the 'modern' and better looking people who lived hundred miles away to mate them with the race upon which he was lord. His real intention was not as simple. He hoped to mix the races and become the ruler of the world. Barely two years from the time when this idea was first conceived, the Neanderthal race had built many knifes from stones and stored many pebbles for the silent war of the worlds soon to commence.

Many thousand years after, when the echoes of this unfamiliar past reached us, we were stunned to know that a race like this lived in the same time as our own fathers. More bewildering is it that the chinless men were exterminated at a time in this long lost history. The first among the remains of the early men whose story appeared in the dreams of men my time was found in a valley near the city of Düsseldorf, Germany in 1856. Many other skulls and jawbones of men who belong to this lost history were recovered from a cave in Iraq, a mountain in Israel, a peninsula in Ukraine and in Uzbekistan. Slowly, we came in contact with our own history but He who holds the sway of history made it so. We were like a grown up son pestering the father for his history. The father waits for the right time for knowledge is like a crown in the head of the strong and a knife in the hands of the weak.

6

HIS EYES were swollen. The room was dark. He could not remember a thing except that he'd been flown to Moscow that morning.

"You should speak the truth, Mister Chekhov, because no one is willing to save you."

"No one?" He raised his head and a drop of blood mixed with sweat splattered on the white paper on which he was expected to write a word at least. He wasn't able to think clearly and so he asked about what sincerely concerned him.

"No one is saving me?"

His interrogator emerged from the dark.

"You are between two sworn enemies whose only agreement is on secrecy."

"Enemies?" Chekhov panted as he shook his head, the poignancy of his forgetfulness was as much as the physical pain he was having. The interrogator, suspecting that the suspect had lost memory, stopped passing electric current through the metal interrogation chair.

"Okay, Chekhov, I will help you remember your sins. Firstly, you took a job in the Timeline, lying to be a second grade school leaver when indeed you were a graduate student. Secondly, you stole from the lab, selling a priced technology to a people who would at best use it for their private gains."

"They believed in me."

He looked up as though he had said something grave and his interrogator's compassion melted down into rage.

"You almost destroyed the works of the world's best geneticists, almost started an apocalypse single-handedly."

"But I did the same in Samara and no one budged."

"You were arrested for man slaughter."

"Yes, but no one mentioned treason."

"What happened in Samara...that was before the government and the researchers agreed to be mute until a decision is made."

"I see.' Chekhov tried to be stoic, 'now that I know what was not meant for me to know, what do you intend to do?"

The interrogator was silent.

"I bet you do not want me to suffer the penalty of my misdoing because I know what you do not know, what is good for both the good and the bad people of the world that a greater evil is waiting to be born, that will conquer all nations."

A moment of silence followed.

"How do you know?"

"The prisoners of Samara started to speak ignoble things as soon as I administered the mixtures on them. The malevolence that I saw on their faces was beyond compare.' He reduced the pitch of his voice, 'Cheknosin did not kill them. I did."

The state security officer stuttered as he struggled to remain on his feet. Apparently he'd heard of such before. He'd listened to the few invited people who came from all over the world to debate in that chamber.

"A man is not corrupted by what enters him."

"But an evil lies within him that could be made passive only by obedience. You should take heed to my warning. Disobedience makes a sin to be sinful."

The man standing in the dark hollered. He had conceivably been told what he hated to hear, what he suspected was true.

"How can I trust a mad man?"

Chekhov ignored him. It pained his heart that he was called mad.

"Authors of the cryptogram seek vindication in our corruption. They will rejoice when we decipher their message and yield to their counsel."

"IT IS ALL for his pleasure."

Those words blew past his ears gently as he trotted along the street in April rain. The breeze had carried the waters in different directions within a very short moment, creating those familiar syllables, "all-for-his-plea-sure."

He gazed at the amputee sitting in an isolated park, close to the prison gates, soaked and shivering. He shut his eyes and pursed his lips in an exaggerated emotion- a new habit of his' that was meant to assure himself of his humaneness. He felt warmth in his eyes and wondered if he had shed the tears for a stranger. It was difficult to tell, for the rain was all over his face, signifying the vague feelings he had caught from the prisons.

The past few days had been pleasurable, though poignantly. Every current that was passed through his body, every bone that was broken affirmed his resolve, and his pains were finally numbed when he started to reason that the actuality of cruelty could also be construed as the realness of kindness.

His gait had changed on account of his contemplation. He had barely spoken for three days now, three days after he was finally coerced into divulging the secret of how to decode the mysterious designs. He wondered if he had, by that 'cowardly' action, began an era of gloom. Too much evil from one man, he thought. While he was beating himself up, he remembered what his senior colleague at the college used to say; *everything that happens is for the pleasure of God.* He wondered if what was about to happen was for his pleasure too. As he moved to join the waiting car at the road close, he remembered one evening in the early 1980s, when religion was scarce in Moscow, in the time when he was still a passionate Presbyterian.

The room was moderately lighted; the ambience of the place was calm. Quite a few adults had come to learn about God, or about their own selves, how to live well and better their lives. A lean man wearing goggles indicated he'd like to ask a question. His look reminded Chekhov of the perceptible intellectual dads, one whose demeanour typified and characterized the weekly Tuesday evening assembly of the children of God.

"A recent report claims that a place has been discovered in one planet where an opulent mansion stands,' he said, could this be heaven?"

The teacher smiled politely, for he dared not be insolent in his objection.

"If it is decipherable to human devices, then it is not divine."

With that laconic reply, the question was assumed to have been answered, and the curiosity of that man, satisfied.

He knew it sounds modest and even devout to conclude that if it is decipherable to human devices then it is not divine. Though it sounded like the perfect answer that should be expected of someone who had come to teach the bible and not astronomy, Chekhov realised at that time, even with his pre-teenage sense that a sharply contrasting notion may be observed in occasions when the same question is being thrown at theists; if they think heaven is a physical place, having a physical location.

"It must,' many would say. Such would be the answer of the same people who would, at first instance, readily assume that the things of God cannot be visible to the human eye. Through that simple exercise of his mind, that quick imaginary poll, he'd seen the actual nature of the minds of many people, that they have the capacity to reason, yet make pronouncements too many times without intellectualizing, that even where they are right, they do not know why, and whatever virtue they posses could easily be eroded when confronted with empty logics.

He reasoned that as human beings, it is hopefully rational to assume by default an initial position that what is incomprehensible to human mind is within the realm of human cogitation, implausible. Through this truism he mounted the dais from where the real contentions of most controversies became vivid to him.

It had once being said that the God characters are incomprehensible to human mind; the ominipresent and ominiscient attributes, all righteous, and all powerful. The possibility of an entity having such attributes, it is argued, is remote but against this proposition, one of the greatest scientists of the 20th century had said an entity of similar character is necessary in explaining the universe's harmony and the apparent conscious and careful design of the cosmos. Even within terrestrial realm, certain things happen to be poorly understood; the nature of the electric current, and the mathematics of infinity, among others.

Beyond the euphoria of knowledge, or the grandeur of being the discoverer of one of the most rudimentary laws of matter, Albert Einstein once came to the conclusion that the universe couldn't have been without the existence of an entity known to theists as God, or gods and to him as one whose existence is conceivable only in the order of the universe, who does not necessarily bother about human affairs. This great scientist was apparently acquainted with the teaching of the 17th century fellow Jew, Benedict de Spinozoa on the nature of that entity. He, she or it is the determinant in everything that happens in every bit of existence. Hence everything that exist comes from this entity, both wickedness and kindness, evil and good, thus the essence of creation is solely for His pleasure, not to be taken serious, and meaningless.

Chekhov, through his resolve to weigh all propositions with common sense, he saw that pure pleasure was not enough explanation as to why he existed, why he had to suffer torture for if it is so, then it could also be said that justice is unnecessary, that goodness is nothing more than a wilful choice, and that evil is permissible among the cycle of existential possibilities. The speed of the earth in its revolution around the sun, the violence with which stars explode at its death, the sheer opulence and the awful images of the galaxies all does not resemble the product of pleasure. The purpose for existence, is to his humble mind, beyond mere pleasure, and if it is, he thought, even pleasure itself as it is known is for a further purpose and is not self-determined.

Many answers surfaced as he brainstormed while he was in that prison cell, among which was the one he heard from his parish vicar in the good old church days, that people were primarily created to worship and praise God ceaselessly. While it seemed plausible that the creator desire to be served by those He had brought into being, Chekhov concluded it remained unsatisfactory to reduce the purpose for existence to what he called a simplistic desire. The reason for human existence surely includes serving the creator, he must agree but their purpose may not be singular. There seem to be something more, he said to himself, that is expected of every person.

If everything is based on what he termed the 'pleasure principle' alone, then it could be deduced that the ills of the world is equally pleasurable unto Him, for nothing that was made for the purpose of pleasure will the maker gladly keep when it loses its purpose. He wondered as he tried to shut his ears against the noisy insect in the cell, the night before.

Why then are we here?

Too many times, the religious folks had tried to demonstrate the presence of the righteous God by showing the beauty of nature; natural plains, the gardens and waterfalls. The land is lush, and the flowers are beautiful. Nature rejoices and everything is perfect. God is indeed with us. On a closer look, Chekhov realised, what really goes on in those forests isn't as idyll as it always seemed. Any observer, on moving a little closer, would hear the agonizing noise of preys and ruthless groans of predators; they would see that even waters harbour the crocodiles, that some animals practise incense. Indeed, the righteousness of the creator, he could not exemplify by jungles where supremacy of the stronger is incontestable. Chekhov remembered the tsunami of the previous years and concluded that nature had too many times added to people's suffering.

He was absent minded because of the thing that had weighed on his heart since he was advised to keep mum over the new human genome project inspired by the ageless design, because of the threats of those who took custody of him when he returned to Russia after being deported from Nigeria. The dons had arranged for his bail, and magnanimously offered him a teaching job in the city college to keep him busy. Idleness, they reasoned, was the mother of mischief.

On his first day on the job, he presented himself before the faculty board as was the practice of the place. He was to introduce himself and talk about the piece that he published in 1999 which had caught their attention. The board chair, wanting to amuse himself by Chekhov's propositions, had suggested the meeting.

"Forgive my frailness, my voice, friends,' Chekhov said, 'how could I show more charm after I have been dealt with so brutally." He looked away to avoid whatever pity or solidarity the congress wanted to offer with their eyes. After all, he thought, they were all guilty for the torture he was made to go through.

"I am commissioned to discuss an issue that I raised twenty-five years ago, which had stood the test of time,' he said, 'a most interesting phenomenon which I had ascribed, with the chair's blessing, to the realities of our world. Although my version for the interpretation of these things had been grossly discounted over the years in the community of researchers, mostly because of their disdain for superstition or my perceived disrespect for their subject of study. For their fear, I pledge that I do not wish to explain science with religion or classic philosophy but to expound on the seeming reality between the tiniest of all known substances and the largest of all things. Through these things, we arrive easily at a conclusion that the universe itself is on the match to a certain goal, that everything is for a reason and there is hardly randomness in the course of our history."

He switched on the neon light at the end of the room's breadth.

"Speaking of the origin of life, I cannot but mention the findings of the great English man who fathomed sometimes in the 17th century, the nature of light. And why do I start with light? It is for the reason of our friends, who in 1997 demonstrated that matter could be created from light. People have always suspected ever since Einstein arrived at his famous equation, that mass could equally be produced by light. It may not be utterly idiotic to assume that a special light existed before a certain primordial matter through which everything was made. It is not the existence of this special light that bothers me, but the behaviour of that light, knowing that it could explain, if deciphered, our purpose in this place."

Chekhov moved to the end of the room, making his new colleagues to turn their heads. He loved it when he made heads turn. The beating had not cured his delusion of grandeur.

"If you will permit me to use the visible light, the one to which we are accustomed as analogy in attempting this explanation to the nature of the first light, I would refer us back to the findings of Newton, who showed how the white light gave birth to different colours of light on passing through the glass prism."

He pointed at the bulb right above him.

"Newton referred to his discovery as wonderful, and it is indeed, seeing that many colours emerged from white light which epitomizes purity in our crudest consciousness. It is for this reason that I have raised a concern, that evil could be quanta of goodness."

Chekhov cleared his throat and returned to his seat, saving his colleagues from having cramps on their necks.

"But the light that was intended for us might not be that which we behold, as nature is not divine and does not exemplify perfection."

The board murmured. Most of them were aware that Chekhov was a confused man, a know-it-all who couldn't even clinch a doctorate for himself in his own alma mater.

"And those who do not deny substantive evidence know that even this light couldn't have produced the first matter accidentally. A force must have given birth to nature, hence allowing the laws therein."

Chekhov tried to keep his voice down but he found he had little control over that.

"And I wonder why we have consistently mistaken nature as the mother of all mothers, for it is finite, a created thing. Taking a cue from Newton, we deduce that purity preceded impurity, and unity before division. Probably there was unity of will before creation, before the existence of this glass prism which made other wills possible.

The board chair smiled. Chekhov was really entertaining him.

"What is this glass prism that denies our consciousness of this unity of will, this special light that preceded even the big bang?"

Chekhov saw that members of the board were beginning to lose interest at the point he wanted to make the climax.

"The dark matter is my suspect,' he said, 'a mysterious occurrence in the universe whose composition is unknown to all people. It is this unseen matter that exerts a gravitational lensing on the distant waves, it is the divergent will that occurs in the vacuum, providing not only the force of gravity to us but also acting as an obstruction to this unity of will, the pre-existing law, providing the alternative law that we have come to know as the laws of nature. And there was a man who showed the understanding of these things, a man who lived in the times of the Romans, yet knew the science that is yet unknown to us, *if ye have faith as little as the mustard seed*, he said, *ye shall conquer nature.*"

Chekhov finally looked into the eyes of those who occupied the front seats.

"Please do not think of this as magic, because it is not. The phenomenon of the dark matter which I have proposed could be understood in the instance of what a dark environment mixed with boredom could do to a child who seats alone, close to a plate of porridge which he is commanded not to take. It is what the right weather could do to healthy adult male and female, mutually attracted to each other, who becomes safely trapped in an isolated building or what the lack of physical movement or any form of excitement could do to a man who had just lost his job."

Throughout the conference room, there was muted discontent in the air. Even a Friday evening ought not to be wasted so.

"Mister Chekhov,' the board chair, feeling guilty for the way his little symposium had turned, called the new staffer's attention, 'I hope you are acquainted with the latest news of the dark matter, that it is indeed useful to the harmony of the cosmos."

"So is evil,' Chekhov snapped, 'you know very well that there is nothing without an anti, nothing created without one, I mean. There are matters which reflects the radiations that we know, and there are ones which choose not to, becoming even completely transparent, possibly affecting our minds and judgements."

Chekhov saw that a man in the middle of the table was preparing to walk away but he would not allow that to happen, so he quickly made his conclusion.

"Everything was made perfect,' he said, 'but there was a reaction to the action that brought about the big bang. Einstein's question is answered, Spinozoa's dilemma resolved if we presume that the reason why the creator had allowed this seeming antagonism by the work of his creation is what seem to me like an act of trust or the act of love, to see how many will overcome that force of gravity before it will be finally destroyed, returning life to the unity of will."

WHEN I read Chekhov's book, I remembered why he had become so disillusioned that he could no longer differentiate physics from biology or mysticism from science. He would return, that Friday evening to no family. His daughter had been taken by the provincial government and there was no life for him elsewhere.

7

IT PASSED, the days of the National Institute of Space Science. In the morning of our graduation, I forsook the early send forth revelries for the news. A cable channel had promised to broadcast the German president's speech on the recent discoveries at Frankfurt University the previous night. Perhaps my fellows slept late, diving through the obscurity of our discipline with wishful words. It was our last night together, our last chance to receive enough words of encouragement from one another. We recognized we were about to face the world of little understanding, to be sneered at for the subject of our study. Almost everyone of us went from one room to another, from one optimistic person to another just to gather enough words of encouragement to last a lifetime for those of us who were too arrogant to admit that they their coming to the institute was a mistake, to last few years for those who wished to take the next 'bold step'.

News from the German institute had been confirmed over the night. More than a hundred paleontologists and historians had recognized there was a major semblance between the dreams of a few men around the globe, Uncle Bode inclusive, and the real findings of highly reputable scientists. Now, the world was in the threshold of a new understanding and each of these fateful days, we came closer to the mystery of where we came from and how everything works in the bulky cycle of predestination and free will. Each of these fateful days, the strong voices of the past came back to us subtly, in the dreams of humble men in different places and at different times. The milestone to this notable age had begun in the eve of the new millennium when a lad suffering from schizophrenia put into writing the series of dreams he had that night in a hospital bed in Germany. About twenty-one years later, the Frankfurt University press had published hundreds of similar individual accounts, spread all over the world within the space of two decades. Also, they had proven ostensibly that there once existed a world, some thousand years old, almost as refined as ours. Now, Uncle Bode's two hundred pages account of his dreams had become a little better than a subject of ridicule and amusement.

In the eve of our graduation, I saw in the television, eminent persons discuss what was at stake just as the world awaited the pronouncement of the German Chancellor. He was to say a word the next morning when he was billed to address a seminar at the Frankfurt University. It was a live show, hosted by a great reporter from New York with persons like the chief researcher of the American institute and the discoverer of the latest and most agreeable piece of prehistoric bones, speaking. They expressed a very skeptical concern; how bad the reputation of paleontology would be affected as a science, and anthropology, even the field of genetics should the whole new development be found to be false or to be some grand fraud.

Just as the world's history unfolded in our eyes so did mine as I wore the space institute's academy regalia, adorned with the emblem of the Presidency itself. It seemed to me like a ploy to play down our fears and boost our tattered morale. At the solemn farewell party to which we had no choice but to attend, the Principal stole from the German president's words, a speech I wouldn't have missed even for my own graduation ceremony if I had the chance.

"Now we live in the time of unrestrained knowledge but also with the challenge to see that an end does not come to every good culture we inherit."

The principal's speech was greeted with a spirited applause in a manner reminiscent of how it used to be like when we still believed that we would be pioneers of the coming change forged with great ambitions.

Somehow I noticed his optimism had waned, that he now spoke like the pot-bellied leaders we were so used to. Even though he was a professor, he must have learnt the ways of the world afresh. One cannot stop learning with the politicians and one of those lessons better learnt early is that passion alone does not work the magic. Our Principal must have learnt that change ferries not only those who wants it but also people who do not. We could see the signs that the promises of the institute were dwindling. There could be no clearer sign as the Principal preached job creation for the first time. We wondered how we were supposed to create jobs from the knowledge we had just acquired- a totally fresh know-how that made sense only to the elite of the elites.

That morning, as the Master of Ceremony took the microphone from the Principal to engage us with the institute's anthem, I took one long last look at the oak tree before the admin block. Waters of the early morning rain dripped through the leaves of the big tree very much like it did the first day I created an impression from it. It was a reminder of my fears about the overly serious institute. Now it had become a lot easier for me to stare as I have come to understand that only a few things should be held in awe and the space institute in Abuja was not exactly one of them.

"We make others stare at the sky for there we are. We fly so high," says the song. Our synchronized voices were joined with a soft key, and we sang quaintly like a lonely congregation in a gentle Sunday morning.

That evening, I barely concentrated as I gathered my things, waiting for a ride from home. The German chancellor's speech played again and again in the radio. Journalists hammered every bit of it. While some called it a case of scientific recklessness, some chose friendlier words, citing it as a comical endeavor, needful in our fast and boisterous world. Indeed if those who called the dog a bad name always have it killed, the new knowledge would have disappeared. Weird as it may be, a powerful executive had given credence to a very radical thinking that the past indeed came to a few of us in our dreams, that there was a world, vague but real, another world where everything first came to be.

I OFFLOADED my last items from the car just before the news at nine, right on time to see our graduation ceremony in the news. A congratulatory message from the presidency was played after a short flash at the day's event, tempting me to flirt with hope. Whatever would happen to the promise, I was determined not to give it a place in my heart, as I would like to keep it unbroken. To choose another career might be the answer. I was determined to try out a more conventional career for the part of the world I was born. The path I chose to thread was a lot more conventional but my reasons quite unconventional. Though I worried for a lot of things, I would learn not only alcohols help people forget their worries. Though my nerves were strained in anticipation, wondering, whither my ship come, I would be given a break from above. The kind of break that makes us wonder how on earth we clocked thirty, what we've been doing with our time.

At night, I hid myself in the thick blanket, savoring the freshness of the smell. I guess it had been washed and dried in the day's scorching sun. I was thankful for the breeze that blew through. Temperature high for the day was thirty-six. I guess a good man among us must have prayed God to bring the cold wind. As I lay on the bed, I stirred up in my mind the beautiful scenery that capped my day. I had seen a sleek duchess in purple, while offloading. Too perfect to be real. I could hardly tell if it was one of the brief flashes of dreams that crept halfway into my short sleep. Indeed I could not tell if it was real for I was entranced both with the suddenness of the sight and the strong wind which blew as I packed my things from the car.

Before I could sleep well it was already five in the morning, just an hour from when daddy's morning grating voice usually called. Several times, that same voice from the adjacent bedroom had ruined my nightly moment of glorious musing.

"Rise up and go help me tell Omotayo that I might not be able to make it to his party in the evening."

For whatever reason, he never treated the boys with morning courtesies. He yawned knowingly and loudly too. When I got to his room, I met a sly smile on his cheek.

"I wouldn't be available for the party. I am talking to the national teevee tonight."

Mum hissed playfully at his jokey boastfulness. She lay next to him in the large bed positioned close to the window.

"Why not pick Dami and Junior from the boarding house because you are having an interview with NTA?"

She stretched her muscles and yawned. She was obviously excited at my return, maybe also anxious about the said interview.

"I learnt Uncle Bode's face was on the teevee all day," I said, my blood racing with excitement.

"What are they going to ask you in the interview? When were you contacted? Where is the interview going to take place?"

I was asking too many questions at once.

"Hope Bode thinks you could tell everything to the teevee," mum asked.

"Of course yes,' daddy snorted, 'he has changed a lot since the last time he left, maybe those guys in New York are paying him well."

At that moment, I remembered that the nameless girl I saw while packing my things the previous night actually showed up from the backyard porch of the Omotayos. Luckily I was provided with a chance to check out if I had been having delusions. Moving to the door, I turned around.

"So I should go now and tell them you aren't coming?"

I saw the look in Mum's eyes; she was too smart not to know the reason for my sudden sense of duty.

"Tell him I am very sorry," Daddy said as I hurried to fetch my sandals.

The Omotayos lived in the second floor of the building that casts its shadow on ours every afternoon. It was a four bedroom flat with a striking layout plastered with a snow-white paint. From the top, our own single flat looked a little lopsided. Curiously I worried for the aesthetic effect of that tiny blunder. I tried to trace the tiny pass that led to the street football field with my eyes, forgetting to knock at the door.

"Long time," a young lady said from inside the house in a cold, suspicious voice that got me wondering if I had not been mistaken as having a sinister intent. She must have been watching for a moment.

"A message for dad," I said, consumed with a needless sense of shame. She flung the door open and disappeared into the rooms, her slippers slapping her feet lazily. The last time we saw she was all over the streets with an oversized top and a cheap pair of sunglasses. I was a little surprised now to see she had mustered enough courage to treat anyone with contempt but not even her newfound gait would do me the trick of seeing her in a new light. Perhaps the new company she kept would. The girl whose face I tried to remember for the better part of the night came in through the main door. She was apparently making her hair for the coming party. She looked overly casual and not as stunning as she was the previous night. She hollered 'Glossy' in a strange accent as she walked briskly to the rooms. She had forgotten something by the name 'Glossy'.

When my old times home girl appeared making excuses for her daddy, I replied he could take his time, earning for myself another suspicious look. The world seemed to be content with the fact that this new girl was amazing. She seemed decided.

She'd stand aloof. She must have had a brush with a few dudes in the neighborhood. I thought I could see their faces in hers. When she whispered a word to her friend, I thought my ears were tilted like the antenna. Her pleasant accent coupled with her reluctance to speak too many words combined to leave me with an impression. Though a little grimace dotted her chubby cheek, I could tell it was not her fault, it must be the handwork of a few mischief-makers in our street. A fiction was gathering in my mind and I had so much comfort believing it. When I said 'mischief-makers' I meant some people, I had my suspects, those who cannot keep their cool 'in the face' of a new hot girl.

With a faked haughty mien, I watched the mute little television two arms length away. Uncle Bode's face was in the news again. I felt the urge to boast about it but no word formed in my mind that was not marred with innuendo. Giving up an attempt to make a new friend, I paid more attention to the news showing in a cable channel. The Americas had included their voice to the growing uproar but with an ominous restraint.

Few minutes later, mister Omotayo appeared in flower pajamas, joggling a bottle of syrup. He looked fleshy and tall and knew exactly how to carry such frame. With his creamy skin and flat belly, he could pass for a young man but the mass of flesh at the back of his neck betrayed the number of years he had spent putting things together at his successful conglomerate. His well-trimmed bears and wavy thick hair reflected his modish personality. Most conservative folks and a few more jealous people hated him, that he presumed the contrary upset them more. The previous year's party had almost gotten him into jail. A sophomore at the state university and beauty queen had been killed in the pool during the wild party. Then, haters thought his end was nigh but when he stormed the courtrooms with evidences of the presence of lifesavers and security cameras, they could not be more heartbroken. He was a lascivious widower, a fervent lover of life. Walking down the stairs that led to his cozy living room, he waved and I greeted.

"Daddy said he would not be able to make it to your party and he is sorry."

"Okay." He smiled. He knew about the interview.

I cannot tell if I hated him or liked him but he was a lot nicer than anyone would expect.

"But you will come to my party won't you?" He looked intently at me.

"Yes sir," I replied, sure not to show my eagerness.

IN THIS PART of the world it was acceptable and totally glamorous to come late to parties. The most affluent came latest most of the times and when they do, they wave to the cheering crowd, politely making excuses for their lateness. Mister Omotayo's party was an exception. There was no need coming late as it was a party for both the old and the young, more like a feast to celebrate a simple life which had eluded the affluent in that area for a time. It never came without some drama too. The previous year, it was a college student and beauty queen exposing a great part of her fair skin to the disdain of older ladies who wished the party was strictly an old people's affair. Before the next morning, she had gotten her clear velvet skin exposed more than she meant to. Though our area was sobered by that occurrence, people easily forgot cheerless news especially when their senses wanted its due.

Half a mile away from the compound where the Omotayos lived, a steady pop song echoed. There were four huge lamps standing at the corners of the stretch of lawns, emitting white light and a stately podium with a giant cake on top. Omotayo was billed to make his speech from there like he did the previous year when he preached all virtues but fidelity. It was seven in the evening and the sunlight was still shining. The lush garden behind the high-rise group of flats had been styled as the venue. There was a tiny aisle in the middle, impressively covered by arches of balloon. As I walked through, I was met with a vision that turned me a stalker for the rest of the evening.

"Good day," she said hurriedly, squeezing through the tiny aisle. The smile on her friend's face was borne out of a momentary joy and it was never to last.

"She is my cousin," the little hostess enthused, 'Fisayo'

Chivalrously I leaned in and she moved back a little. The smile on her face was both beautiful and contrite.

"She speaks only French and German," her friend supplied, mocking her condition. That evening, when a blessed old folk song played, she flew into my sight again, this time in a black gown. I had seen that sight before, that same face, she, resting on the backyard railings.

Thence came my calling. I tried to hide it from my self my main reason. I would learn French and become an interpreter or translator in a software company.

A fortnight later, I started getting my nose into the books. The manner in which countries filed to state their position on the new science was interesting and I was inspired more to learn a few foreign languages. There was no other comforting thought than to believe one day, my sudden new love, French would get me to one of those chambers where countries proudly lend their voices, a rather obscure ambition. I was right but not exactly for language and science would get me to a far loftier place to be humbled with great revelation.

THOUGH THE GOVERNMENT of the day started on a weak footing, it quickly became more assertive and less shy about its creed.

"We may never know when is the right time to start joining the world in the voyage of high-tech endeavors," said the President at a lecture.

"While we stooped patiently and humbly to care for the peasants, those who by lack of opportunity or cheer providence find themselves in a discomforting position, we must not forget to pursue great ambitions in trust for everyone."

Speaking with burning passion characteristic of his predecessor, he remarked

"We will indeed become great when we thread in the path of greatness!"

Now the crowd of young fellows became ecstatic, making noise and waving the little flags in their hands. There were twenty thousand of them in that dome.

His body was damp with sweat though the air was well conditioned. There was a pile of good will cards at his feet. Leaning on a tiny stand, a piece of thick glass with the seal of the presidency, he chuckled.

"No more shall we sit down and moan in a less than glorious atmosphere of self-pity."

His voice was dampened with a long round of applause. He looked at their faces like they were his ministers. He was not a rock star with the older populace and the daily papers loved to publish a caricature of him carrying the plaque 'Under eighteen can vote'.

"Someday, one of you would be here,' he rubbed his hands on the stand he was resting on. He had been speaking for two hours.

'Very soon this nation shall become a home to the homeless black peoples of the world and to those who has a home but feels not at home."

He had also appeared on the television few days after commissioning technocrats whom he sent on a classified mission a year and a half earlier. There he said

"The time is now when money and material possessions shall be the least of all measures for success. Today we create a nation where those who serve it with their heart and might, directly or indirectly shall be considered as truly successful."

We believed not his easy rhetoric though a great revolution stared us in the face. Firstly, it was an upturn in the schools and then, the construction of sixty domes that many were inspired to fund. Sixty castles of peace covering an area of a hundred and fifty thousand feet each, a fortress for men and women to lift their minds from the shackles of impossibilities. We knew not change was among us though a new optimism captured our fellowship of doctors and engineers and researchers and inventors. The time had come when providence would take us to a glorious age. The skylines of our cities were changing and fast too, a new generation of people who understood freedom, emerging.

Though the world around wears a new look and the fortune of those who worked hard is turned around for the best, my own story was not stirring yet. I was stuck in a lifeless pursuit of a career in French language, a quest rooted in a wobbling amorous desire. Shortly before starting another round of schooling, I had seen on television, the President talking about the space program to which he was committed. Afri 24 was to take off by the first day of October 2024, barely a year away.

Afri 24, the mission of nine interested African states including three French-speaking countries was formed five years earlier when a few regional leaders decided to reconcile the erstwhile third world nations with the dreams of the *new promise*, the phrase by which the leaders of the world called our time. Twenty-four people from nine assenting nations, twenty-four astronauts and engineers were to fix a few satellites in space, a rather little fit in the eyes of the 'first world'.

My old school was a consequence of the memorandum and it was commissioned solely to provide in their words, able young men and women to convey the lingering black pride to space. Only two people were to qualify in a single country yet a hundred and more were made to try. No one really cared what happens to the remaining one hundred and eighteen who passed the tests. No one really told us the whole truth.

The first glimmer of hope that a couple of years in my blessed prime of life were not wasted flashed when I received a mail from the Institute. That moment, in a Sunday- after- joy melancholy, I tore the dazzling envelope bearing my name in fine prints. I was then, at the peak of despair, almost certain for some vague reasons that a restitution was underway. French as a language had been more painstaking than I ever thought. I always believed it was merely an extension of the English tongue but there were too many intricacies than I thought was necessary. My friend said I was being ethnocentric and insensitive to the need of the French to communicate distinctively. Anyway, I managed to utter a few words, mostly flirty phrases to prepare for my little dates with Fisayo. I was impatient and yet hesitant as I tore the brown envelope sealed with the space school's stamp. I was devoured by a strong sense of anticipation for the thought of reading a trifling mail seemed unbearable. What I needed was a clear turn around, a huge quake to wake me from my slumber. As my eyes hovered through the letter, I searched for some words as though I had an idea, words indicative of a good fortune. I saw 'thanks' and my heart sank for they rarely thank people at the opening of the kind of letter I desired. For once, I tried to pretend I had come to terms with the worst and it worked, for my heart pounded less.

"Invitation to participate in mission training," the heading read. I was thankful till a thankless thought crept in. I wondered how many people were invited. I was afraid for the worth of the invitation. "Everybody," said my inner mind. I hated that part of my mind that always said what I disliked, the part of my mind that cared less how I felt. Alas it was right. Though it sounded terse most of the times, it was to be trusted. Everybody and even people who never attended the space school had been invited.

AGAIN AND without credit to what we might have learnt, we were subjected to a round of solemn training under the tutelage of the new crop of scientists who loved the president and followed him. There was a sparkle in their eyes, a fire of passion that burned more than the wailing test rockets that sped into the heavens from the wilderness a mile away. My South African friend, Shederach, happened to have come to his paradise because he craved no better life than this- to be trapped in a sober life of lofty quests. There were many kinds of people in our camp but more people were like him, more with a story like his' as their love was lost for many things but virtuous glory.

In the evenings, Shederach would stare from a miles distance, the huge rocket waiting to be launched and he would lay his back on the sandy ground. I was there with him once, one tired evening as he babbled his opinion about anything that flashed his mind. That evening, we stood in awe of the grand site of the setting sun, halved by the little flat top mountains as it cast the rocket's shadow to the dam, few meters away. Perhaps those who sat to watch with us thought of it as the object of their dream. They loved to be inside one of those shuttlecrafts and they did in a fanatic way, almost with a touch of insanity. For me, the feeling of fear towered above the quest for glory or the search for adventure or money so clearly I could not deny. Also, that feeling of fear did not stay as fear but changed to a more assertive thing-cynicism.

Neither the dark cavity of the near vacuum inside which we felt bizarre nor the strangely harsh light from the 'celestial chambers' changed my mood or view. I was sure another six weeks was to be wasted but the loyal inner mind of mine was wrong that once.

Two fortnights after we had acquired a substantial flight experience, a circular was passed requesting us to come for a proficiency test. That evening, a list was published, a list with my name atop. I was to be part of Afri 24 for a reason I wasn't quite aware of. My Shedrach was at hand to tell me why. I had a little background in French language and half of the crewmembers were to come from French speaking states. Shederach's name was next to mine on the final list.

At the firelight rally of that night, we stood atop a makeshift dais, eighteen of us, with big fluffy ribbons daggling on our necks, cursing the DJ, cheering and dancing whenever he played our favorite. The current from the river was heavy. Our clothes became wet and clung.

The playing music was interrupted sporadically with sudden bursts of surprise here and there for those whose parents surfaced. When I spotted my own folks, I screamed too, but infelicitously. How I looked that moment I don't want to know. Just as the crowd started wondering, a new hit song rented the air, throwing them into a boisterous round of dancing, saving my face. That moment, Shederach withdrew himself to his chalet, a snug house with a single parlor and bedroom, a kitchen and bathroom.

There were two hundred of such houses lining the tranquil bay. I guess the foreign instructor on space psychology must have been keeping an eye on us to see how well we adapted to loneliness and boredom. I was certain there were some cameras in those needless conduits at the walls. I was at my best, each of those four weeks already spent; handling not only my loneliness but also despair in the best way I thought was normal. Though I seemed carefree about everything at the surface, I was no less desirous of being a part of the mission than those who worshipped the sight of the take off in the twilight but to let it show was to be at the risk of feeling disappointed when I really didn't mean to.

For a moment, I was lost in thought and the loudness of the crazy new music seemed reduced in my ears. Now everything seemed like it was meant to be, like I had seen just that sight before; young people and a few bareheaded men dancing with good cheer round a burning fire in a beach-like wilderness, spilling beer to the ground. My body level of dopamine was changing, I guessed.

"Hey buddy!" Dami yelled

I wondered how she had come to pick up a totally different personality but she had become a lot sophisticated and I was quite comfortable with that. I turned round to see where she was calling from as I could only hear the voice.

"Hello big brother," she said with a knowing smile. She was a career imp, always up to something. Her dress sense and carriage and make-ups, no one could tell. She had grown taller by four inches or so, since the last time she was home for the holidays. Now she was about 5'8, adding just a few pounds to her weight. She had become well adjusted too, a miracle we never expected. She was seventeen, four years younger than I, and well ahead of her time.

Junior came hugging too. He seemed resolute about being short in height. His dour countenance was in line with the hip-hop culture, I never failed to remember. Mum was at the back, unwilling to embrace. Somehow I thought she was afraid everything looked too much like a long farewell. She had been wrestling with her new public office and I doubt if it had been fun. Having branded herself with a new look, a white dye on the left side of her hairs, she looked ready to carry on with her political career but her recent fears and anxiety made the signature look seem more like old age. I could tell she was having a running fight with dad over my involvement in the space mission.

Dad slapped Junior in the ass playfully but so hard that it hurt. He was like his brother, Uncle Bode whom you never can tell when he was playing or not.

"It is safe dear,' he said, his eyes were brightened and he looked a decade younger in his short pant.

'I have seen your commander, read about all I need to know and trust me, you are safer than we are."

Mum chuckled, visibly relieved by the exaggeration.

"Come see my lodging house," I waved, anxiously reading Mummy's countenance. "Each person has one to himself but the ladies prefer to stay together in there," I pointed to the multistory house some meters away.

"Yea the Captain told me there are four of them; Ghanaians and Nigerians," dad supplied, apparently to convince me that he knew everything including the safety measures.

As we approached my suite, a mate reported

"All astronauts are to converge in the newsroom in an hour's time for a press conference."

I thanked him and flung the door open. There in the parlor were Dami and Fisayo, laughing.

"Surprise," they yelled
That moment, the evening sky shimmered greatly and beautifully with fireworks. Shederach had withdrawn to go and prepare the fireworks and it came as a pretty surprise to me. I had seen many instances yet I had not fully absorbed the fact that workaholics like him are too smart not to know when to celebrate. As the multihued light and the thunderous noise enveloped the camp, Dami and Fisayo screamed, locked in a playful embrace of pleasant fear. How they got to meet I wasn't sure. A couple of friends from the streets was there too and one old mate with whom I shared my high school laboratory desk. They laughed; the look on my face must have been funny.

THE YORUBAS say that the word of the wise comes out from the mouth of the fool loudly. They are not only better for the sake of their precision or good sense but also for knowing when to act or when to delay the thoughts of their minds. And there is a wisdom that mocks it all; watchfulness and slackness and bravery and weakness. There is a wisdom that looms behind, bidding to captain our ship.

Though we planned to sail the vast universe to pen our name in a closing page of history, we were met with a larger charge and though the old chapters of history closes, our names were written in the front page, bold and clear. We were a people shackled by the past, and now we were to be the light of a new time.

In the eve of the launching of Afri 24, two more researchers from different Universities joined, and four veteran flight captains from Nigerian air force. They seemed calmer than the rest of us and they were clearly aloof. Together, we practiced necessary routines in the simulator.

By the dusk, a battalion of soldiers had surrounded the little Table Mountains that fenced our camp in readiness for the President's visit. Also, a row of flags was erected and it flied brilliantly in the windy bay. The mood had become tenser than was necessary. My stomach was unsettled that night, more because my personal camera having a lens adapted for space shots was lost. I had tried to use it four nights before, when my folks came around visiting. My pocket French dictionary was lost too. I spoke far less French than the selecting board believed but I was determined to do a real crash preparation, and cover up that minor hiccup forever. Little dishonesty it appeared has its own ways of becoming big embarrassment. But above all the conspiracy of probity to embarrass, I found a way to survive.

The calling bell rang by 4am. It was the morning of Nigeria's sixty-fourth independence anniversary. The president had touched down at Calabar airport just about a hundred kilometers away from the campsite. He was in company of a few other regional leaders. Just as the bell rang, a gentle knock came at my door and I opened, to receive my new uniform, crispy and smelling nice.

"Good morning. Would you bring me a picture of the earth by night?" the waiter quipped.

"Of course yes," I chuckled. My breath was becoming labored. I switched on the little radio at my bedside, ready to go to the bathtub. I was thankful for the soul jazz it played me through the night.

Forty-five minutes later, the bell rang again. The President had arrived and everyone was to be seated before he does. I looked at my phone. I had missed a few calls.

When I opened the door that led to the windy court outside, I noticed the radio was playing the same police band song that was playing outside.

"Good morning ladies and gentlemen," came a dutiful female voice. "As we all know, today marks the independence anniversary. We enjoin everyone to be seated and stay quiet as the President addresses the nation."

The ushers led me to where the green robed astronauts were seated. I was the last to be walked through the rows and as I took my seat, I felt the commander's piercing eyes on me. I had become bolder over the night, maybe because of the blissful songs of the old Jazz masters that calmed my nerves. I believed I did not deserve to be looked at with contempt any more.

While the President gave his speech, I went for the zs, waking up at intervals to behold the spacecraft, seated about forty meters above the earth. With its own height, it towered close to three hundred. It was not quite an improvement over what the world once had, except for its smaller weight. We had the chance to carry more payloads and perform more tasks in space but surely, we were still tethered to our culture of selective modesty.

I anticipated the speechmaking would take few minutes but it had turned hours. My mind was shuttled through series of dreams in the windy open, under the President's husky voice. The scenic sun of the early morning climbed over the mountains, shining down right at our faces. There were lots of mists in the air and the dawn's dim light formed thick rays. It was a beautiful site to behold. Just as I was waking up from the hazy dreams, I heard the closing words,

"Be it little, be it late, generations after us will say that we were neither weary nor disenchanted in the face of challenges."

Someone from the last row tried to get us applauding but no one bulged. Together, our eyes devoured him.

"When they become fully integrated into the world of tomorrow, they shall remember that once, there lived a people who did great things."

A loud ovation started from the same timid young man and the guests took it on, to the middle rows and the left, then the right. We stood to herald the moment the President left the dais.

Just as we started taking turns to shake hands with the President and other regional leaders present, the spacecraft wailed and a bright green light showed from the metal tower atop the main office block, a hundred meters from the launching site.

Filing past a crowd of over three hundred officials, we moved slowly to the waiting ship. I never remembered to smile. Shederach went for the seats before everyone else. His confidence and smoothness was a recipe for my own composure. In some way, he felt slighted by my newfound confidence. He was surely more comfortable with me fidgeting and he got me back into my former state of mind effortlessly.

"The stage of initial propulsion is usually the most risky," he said and the lady from Ghana gave him a long look, a rather subtle way to beg him to shut up.

"Ladies and gentlemen, I am Oguntoyinbo Oladare," called a voice through the radios. "It's such a long difficult name, I know," he chuckled.

I could sense nervousness in his voice, even through his efforts to make us laugh.

"You can call me Gtheebo,' came the voice 'and I would follow you through the trip from here, in the control room of Nigeria Space Institute."

In the middle deck we sat, eighteen of us tied to our seats, waiting for the fabled thrust to push us into the skies. Others were at the upper room apparently running their hands over tens and tens of switches.

"And now, Afri 24 is set to go," Gtheebo said.

And the last hatch closed. I busied myself with a little literature I found by the seat. It was a leaflet containing information about the safety measures put in place and how to handle various cases of emergency. There were too many dos and don'ts. I tried to learn them by heart. Though I had passed several hours in different simulators, being in the real thing posed a different challenge. Fear was inevitable, yet it was cowardly to exhibit it. I was stuck among the best and the brave and it took no time before I started thinking that I deserved it. One of our teachers had thought us to always respect our inner man, that there was a power in us that we might not recognize. I believed him.

We saw the waving crowd from the nine-inch screen hanging at the right corner of our room. Everyone smiled and wore the cold faceplate hanging next to our seats. It was necessary to smile at this minute, more than it is to the beauty queens. We were supposed to be heroes and in the days of the simulators, we were told to smile like heroes, not like people who had been seduced with great remunerations and insurance packages. No doubt we had intentions of socializing at least during break times in our lengthy schedule but we all felt compelled to keep our mouths shut at least for the moment. My mouth couldn't stop drying up as I waited. I was having a strange reaction, something never covered in the six-hour medical course that we took the previous day. My pulse raced faster as I looked into the screen.

About a dozen men in suits ran towards the President, almost getting themselves shot. Apparently there was a little argument. I was relieved because Gtheebo sounded optimistic enough for me to know all was well. The president's closing remarks started replaying in the radio. That time, the rigorous, almost violent reaction producing water, heat and light proceeded.

Our ship shook and a thick cloud of flame surrounded it. The engines wailed louder as it consumed fuels coming from the giant system of metals to which our ship was clung. About five thousand liters were consumed in a second. Two years ago, a local inventor proposed an updated means of propulsion but it was too much to chew at once especially for a maiden voyage.

Struggling to hear the earthly words of the President in the unearthly moment, my mind was engaged for the first time in several minutes. We had waited for some time, having no much to do but to wish ourselves good luck. For a moment, I thought about a number of possibilities. If backing out in the very last minute would make a big difference, if the mission would be cancelled due to some technical problems. Gtheebo seemed to have heard my mind.

"Five, four," he counted.

Afri 24was lifted off its base, hesitating for a second, and then she sped aggressively into the skies. Though it took only a short moment and giving us no time to observe any subtle thing, I could see a red clot form on Shederach's fore head. He looked like a dead man. I looked to the windows as we moved past the towers. After the initial velocity, Afri 24 started to move at more than four thousand miles per hour, pouring the earth a great load of burning gas. It looked more like we were blowing up.

Having propelled us half way into the earth's atmosphere, the two Solid Rock Boosters flanking our ship fell off into the Bight of Biafra perfectly and on time. Now we were moving almost twice as was expected. There was something strange about the velocity that the captain hoped to change. There had been a serious conflict in our mathematics. We could see from the computers as he tried to dispel some energy off the rocket and we could see the meters flashing some warnings. Something was wrong and the captain was getting nervous; a very ominous sign for a pilot of many years standing. He was crazy to have tried to stop the thrust prematurely, as we would fall back to the earth the same way the Solid Rock boosters just did. He was surely loosing his mind. In the midst of the panicking, a voice came from the radio. We thought we had lost them.

"Too much!"

Whoever it was, I guess he was screaming. The ground control room was getting unsettled and noisy.

"Alright, we will make it," said someone else.

Shortly, the radio was tuned off. The captains had shunted it to the upper cabin, leaving us to speculate. From the computers, we saw our ship approach the orbit. We had gotten to space a lot faster than we intended, moving at a speed far greater than was necessary to keep us under the influence of the earth's forces. Twenty minutes after takeoff, we had gone pass the orbits, still very much with our propellers which failed to let go. Bewildered, and scrubbing for breath, Shederach exclaimed

"The tank is fueling itself!"

There was a reaction no one understood that kept us going without the chance to bend, not even giving us the prospect of heading to where we could maneuver our way around. If there was a calculation we could do that will take us back home, we were provided with no time to work it out.

We were also at the wrong trajectory, heading for a place unknown in the sea of vacuum. In the middle of those things, something was happening to us more bizarre than the mystery energy that carried us ten times the speed of any craft ever built by man. We felt and evinced no signs of panicking or regret as we progressed. We had attained a new nature, so calm and so at home. Except for the violent thrust that kept us fastened to our seats there was no other sign anything was wrong. From the screens, Shedrach watched in somewhat patronizing admiration as our ship raced into the unknown. The nineteen year old from Ghana was busy with her iPod. No one was afraid as we were all deluded by some powers that seemed nearer and nearer as we moved deeper into the Milky Way.

A voice came from the ground office twelve minutes after Gtheebo's last words. The president himself had taken on the radio.

"Gentlemen and ladies, thank you for your service, courage and bravery." His voice was laden with guilt and it was more hurtful for him that he would have to express his feelings in a hurry. All communications would be cut off in a few seconds until a few diplomatic contacts are made and fresh connections are established. All he could remember to say was to give his thanks. His voice sounded final and pale, like the great generals of old must have felt in the valley of defeat. The radio slipped off as he panted.

"We will keep you in sight and ensure the best happens. Our love and our resolve know no distance." We could feel the monetary implication of keeping the faith in his voice. There was a lot to be apprehensive about. It was quite unclear if a government would trade the future of millions with the chances of just a few, as there was no major agenda for space technology in the budgets, yet we trusted him. He seemed more like a person who would wear the burden to the end. Such was his sense of morality and values. He perceived us not as servants of the country or the continent but his'. He was the embodiment of change and the way things had turned, change had been dealt a great blow, the book of history smeared with an inglorious clause. Should we be lost, the world shall inherit a lie that there exist such things as limitations.

WE SEEMED not as fearful as we ought to because our ship was wrapped in peace, with no adventurous particles or asteroids. We all felt certain by a new instinct, and a new heart that a planet was on our path where we would live happily thereafter.

Twenty minutes after we took off from the base at Oron in Nigeria, the external tank forsook our ship, falling quietly in space. It might have made quite a large fire but there was no background against which it could be seen. How the fuels had regenerated we wouldn't know in a hurry but the radars said we had travelled ten thousand miles. By then the sun had risen upon our ship and fallen five times. We looked, kept quiet, stopped thinking and we slept. Thus we rode in space for days, eating and drinking, using the toilet and doing all sort of things that made little of the thrust by which we advanced.

Every time the sun turned its face away, we would look through the windows to see the earth. She looked beautiful and calm as the light of the sun shined on her.

Two weeks afterward, there was yet no feedback, not even a scratch in the radio until the morning of the twentieth day when we heard a clear female voice.

"Please reply if you can hear me, this is the National Aeronautic Space Administration agency of the United States."

Vouchsafing to move closer to the phones, the commander of Afri 24 replied

"Yes we do."

His response was followed with an uproar in the agency but the lady's voice climbed.

"An entreaty came from the Nigerian embassy a week ago requesting us to link up with you,' she said, 'and I am happy to inform you that we now work together. First we need to know what happened that took you off target."

Our captain, angered by her comment, answered tersely

"Nothing happened."

That moment, Shedrach looked at the televised images coming from the cameras attached to the exterior, in the arms of the Remote Manipulator. No one had bothered to look before then, for we were all engrossed in grimly peace.

"It is the hand of God," said our captain to the NASA agents. Shedrach panted dreamily from the utilities

"I guess it is."

We all moved to where Shedrach was standing to see what it was that dropped his jaw. A bright spot of light like a comet was hanging to our ship. The captain rushed to where the hundreds of operation buttons were, looking for the fault as a muddled voice from NASA tried to call our attention.

With his eyes blinking for surprise, the commander said quietly

"Something is pushing this ship at the rear,' he moved briskly to the doors. 'I have to check it out."

"Attention, Afri 24," came a robust and assertive voice from the radios. We tried to ignore the call and follow the captain to the hatch. There were four astronauts at the flight deck, trying to take charge, yet lost in the series of events that was taking place.

"Attention!"

The caller repeated. He was getting anxious. NASA seemed tensed just as we, but fear was no possibility in the half conscious mind we were carrying. We had come under the influence of a nameless power.

"NASA has been able to locate your position in the cosmos," the caller informed, his voice filled with guileless glee.

"We know exactly where we are," captain moved to the microphones and tried to destroy the communication system. He was insane and so we were. Someone argued in the background that we might have lost our sanity due to the extreme trauma of having traveled three hundred and ninety thousand miles per hour. The NASA agent gave his information anyway and he rushed in doing so as it was clear to them, our hostility was abnormal and could lead us into cutting the cables.

"We have been able to locate you. You are totally on the plain that might get you landed on the surface of Mars."

From his voice, he felt weird saying it as there were no such propeller in the world capable of achieving that fit. Again NASA called, this time with outmost certainty.

"You should reduce your velocity and change your orientation to prepare for a maneuver. Please follow the following instructions carefully."

Now we became a little apprehensive as we were at the risk of crashing on the face of the red planet. If we do, we might be faced with the strangest situation ever known in the history of the exploration of space. I realized it was best for me to think of it as nightmare for the thought that we might crash in unscheduled location froze my brain. It was a moment not to be remembered.

We were getting closer to the Martian atmosphere but we waited for the right time to act, that we might pass by. That moment, Shedrach's eyes became wet and the muscles of his face strained, forming lumps all over. I could feel a strain on the muscles of my face too and I was certain it looked like Shedrach's. From his watered eyeballs I could see our ship flying at a tangent to the planet. Whatever made us brave, it did to preserve our hearts that we might live.

There were flashes of moments when we realized that we were two hundred and thirty million miles away from home. For once the humane part of us showed up but not for long.

"Eighty-two hours from now you should make the following provisions and you will be on course of return. We wish you luck." The ground agent spelled many figures painstakingly and repeatedly. Our computers were failing but we could see through the windows, the red planet as it got bigger by the hour. Though we loathed the voice from NASA, a part of us was resolved to follow their instructions and head back home. We could only remember faintly, how things looked like where we came from. We knew we needed help but our sense of how much was greatly diminished. We had become allured to where the massless thing at the engine of our ship was leading us.

At the eighty-second hour, we moved to put all measures in place to return to the place we barely remembered as home. We were moving close to the Martian orbit through the southern hemisphere. Slow it seemed but the radars still read that we were travelling at our unearthly speed. Though we intended to maneuver, the force that pushed our ship from behind was too great to be overpowered.

Two hours before the given time, we reached the Mars' orbit, and our ship slowed down without manipulation. Softly, we were removed from the orbit and we fell like a ball of fire through the thick clouds of the planet. Our screens got blurred with a misty brown substance as we descended. Few minutes later, we bounced over the surface, rolling through great distances.

I clung unto a metal for support but nothing was enough to keep us from floating violently. The guy from Angola hit his head against the hatch and Shedrach floated uncontrollably to the ends of the cabin. He must be dead. I grabbed him midway as he swam back. The bleached pupil of his eyes confirmed my fear. I forsook him and tried to get the giant helmet that I remembered was attached to the back of my seat. Flashes of light came shining through the windows; we must be falling into a deep cave. My hands trembled so vigorously I could not get the helmet. Determined not to give up, I held the pole that ran through the middle deck with the last bit of energy I had but my hands slipped. The voice of my mind grew weak, fading into whispers of prayers.

8

LIKE THE REST of us, I slept inside the ship. When I regained consciousness, I delayed the opening of my eyes, wishing that I did to see it was all a dream.

I woke up to see that everything was real. Nothing had moved that couldn't have been moved by a person. I heard the faint chanting of a brother, the voice was shaky and it seemed incongruent. I stood up to look, he pressed his face against the window, weeping and singing a church song. A yellow light was cast on a half of his head, on his miserable eyes.

I had no idea how long we had been there. The quietness of the place was both saddening and eerie.

"Shedrach!"

I looked around, ready to fall down in grief. My voice hardly traveled beyond the tip of my nose. Our space ship had landed without any mishap, only for a few fire-shielding belly tiles that we lost. It must have flown off as our ship scratched its body over the rocks some meters apart as we bounced on descent. The ship's side door that led to the cargo bay was opened and so was the one which ultimately led to the exterior. I walked through the hollow walkway arduously, ignoring a crewmember who lay on the way snoring. As I moved to the door, a lonesome voice approached. I was relieved to know that someone was talking (in the inside of me, I was also introspecting and examining my own sanity). As I emerged from the door to step my feet on the rocky surface, the captain stood up from the rock he was sitting upon and gave a pregnant smile. He had been discussing with the lady from Ghana. Only the two of them were yet awake.

"I am trying to link up with the ground offices," he said calmly.

His body was firmly fitted with the newly designed model of the Life Support System. The lady from Ghana looked keenly at me. Apparently she was wondering what sort of humans she was stuck with. Shedrach had given me a bad image for his elitist and insensitive comments.

"I am Nana," she said tersely and retired to the laboratory. Her skin was very dark and her eyes appeared reddened probably for the acute fear with which we entered the desolate and dusty wilderness. Obviously she was sworn to speak only to the captain and not even the dreadfulness of the moment would drop her guard. The captain must have been telling her stories that played down the condition in which we had found ourselves. Also, he must have exaggerated our chances of being rescued.

I checked the Nigerian time; I'd slept for almost a day. Next to the Central African Time was the Integrated Martian Time. I stood to observe the sky. It changed colors but mostly it was pinkish, quite cloudier than the earth's. Sometimes whilst the cloud shifted, the Phobos and the Deimos adorned the sky, perfecting its awesome appearance. We had landed in a low land, about three hundred feet from the level of the surface we suspect as volcanic. That was something to worry about but I was preoccupied with looking out for a satellite. I wasn't sure how spotting one would help but it was a lot more helpful to hope for something, however silly.

As I stared, I felt a hand on my shoulders. I was hit hard as I turned around. The guy with the big round hair among us had given me a blow. Spoiling for a fight, I leaned back and watched him grow weak. No emotion is not to be expected in our situation.

"Where are we?"

"Mars," I retorted, still angry at his painful blow. He must have spent the whole energy left in him to make an impact in the forceless atmosphere. He broke down in tears but not well enough to earn my embrace.

"Come on," the captain called in his baritone voice. He was every bit a captain and he knew it. With the six packs of muscles at his chest, his height and his strong build, he looked like a hero and now he felt like one. I really was apprehensive about his confidence; somehow I thought I could see through him, that he was hiding his hopelessness and wanted to enjoy his last moments pretending to be brave.

"We have one another."

He walked up to the gentleman and gave him the hug he so much craved.

"Something really brought us here,' he said quietly, 'everything that has happened so far shows someone is following us."

He rose briskly and smartly, his own words had given him life.

"Ladies and gentlemen, I have a thing I think I should share with you."

We gathered to hear him, our faces brightened with a new hope.

"Last night, while everyone was asleep, I lay outside here," he pointed to the stoneless plain five square meters behind us.

"I think I heard a voice from the top of this valley."

We snorted, at least all of us except Nana who had come to have faith in everything the captain said. He grew angry as we muttered different comments.

"The voice I heard was so far, yet so near," he said, scanning through our lines to take a brief count of those with the look of contempt on their face. The little gravity of the wilderness, the freezing temperature, the non-existent atmospheric pressure, the lethal oxides and the knowledge that he would starve to death should we be there for another three months (even if we survived other impediments) had done nothing to his ego. We grew defensive and more determined to ruin whatever he was suggesting.

"There is no life in Mars," someone said and we laughed. And a tyrant was born. The captain drew out his gun and pointed it at us.

"I won't have any of those from you fools".

He seemed lost, almost broke down in tears but something in him spurred him to carry on with his faked show of strength.

"All I want you to do is to listen,' he fought back the tears, 'someone out there is trying to talk to us, we must listen and we must ask for help."

He pointed the gun down.

"Sorry guys."

I never mistook his apology for repentance as he was still holding on to his gun. We had been forced to see a merit in his proposition. In the evening, while we dined with canned beans and bread with some wine, I thought about the possibility of hearing voices in that wilderness but the more I did, the more it seemed to lack merit. My fears were rekindled that some of us were losing our sanity for the sake of the fearful sight that confronted us two nights before. We might have been captained by a mentally derailed who would not let us have access to the communication systems. As I stocked my mouth with the wheat bread, I flirted with the idea of holding the captain hostage to gain access to the radios and be able to see if there was a satellite anywhere we could link up with. The captain was no longer capable of taking responsibilities for us anymore. He needed help and so did we but to leave our destinies in the hands of a man whose sanity was in question was to commit suicide. I watched him eat, looking for the last thing to justify the plot that was gathering in my mind. He was a leader, looked like one and talked like one. It felt more relaxing to be led by him than to be followed by a multitude. Maybe I was being indolent but there was a thing about him that pleaded for a benefit of doubt.

We did not realize until the second day how blessed we were to have landed in the large ditch. Whatever brought us there, we were being shielded from the freezing cold climate for the elements of the sand surrounding us gave so much heat it felt like home. The shades of the day had been unstable and the colors of the sky ever changing. Shedrach explained it was the dust from the ground and the little moisture above that combined to give different shades of pink and red. I was happy for him to know his mind was still gathered. Mine was intact but changed with the colors of the sky.

Sometimes my mind would be clouded with fear, other times with joy. There was a joy for we felt like humans of a new age, still under the watchful eyes of a father. Inside the brightly lit cabin, under the ravaging skies of the wilderness, many million miles from home, we feasted. In the middle of the endless desert we celebrated the unknown. Our story shall be told to many generations.

AND IN THE night it all came back to me. The captain was right. There was a whisper in the empty planet, a voice from the past, eons before. As I looked into the night sky, tracing with a telescope, a satellite that moved across the horizon, I was mesmerized by the sight of the part of the sky whose formation seemed like humans.

"Men once lived here," I thought. I was half asleep and I perceived pictures from the past; thin in the atmosphere, whispers from the lost years.

And it came upon my mind. Somewhere here, when the red planet was yet pleasant to life, sometimes whilst the news of the blue planet was fresh, there came a multitude of grey fellows, strong and more beautiful than the races of men. They had come to feast and to have a look at the earth, with their excellent telescopes.

The people, dressed in immaculate robes with dazzling ornaments, filled the place and they were like snow in the winter as there were millions of them. Atop the hills, a hundred feet above to the levels where clear waters flowed, a legion sang. There was a striking interlude in the choral song, made with an instrument yet to be known to us, happy so much that it became sad, a sound not to be heard again in this part of the cosmos for many thousand years. Then came the morning, when the earth appeared from above. Her glory surpassed the Phobo's and the Deimos' and the Moon's and Venuses'. They loved it and to love was good. But there was a feeling in the dark that made free will perceptible. They had come far away from the light of the Father, out in the world new to them. In the night, their robes were like white lanterns, illumining the place. They took turn to have a look at the mystery that stood a hundred million miles away. The planet on which it was said, a new race of intelligent homos shall live. Rumors were in good supply that the new planet was prettier, and that great treasures lay within the crust, but they must not go to the unknown. A leader of the congregation explained that the new people must find their truth even without clear testimonies.

Now, a member of the tribe, having stared for too long, raised his head and the light his eyes turned orange.

"*Anbassu,*' he screamed, "if only I could get there, I'd ask no more favors."

He tried to finish with the map he was making from the image of the telescope. His mind had become corrupted by constant covetousness and now he had found the courage to speak. Leaders who sat close to him were bemused for he spoke strangely. In the world known to them, grace abounds and bright radiance used to come from each of the millions. And there was a single color and a single mood. Now they had seen one of them who was a leader shine forth an irreverent light. They gathered around for a thing had happened that had never occurred before.

Happy to see himself surrounded by hundreds, he raised his voice higher and reasoned the way he had never done before in his entire existence.

"A great new thing beckons at our timeless history that a creature like us is to live away from the light of the Father."

His light got dimmed as he spoke till darkness came upon him.

"Those new men will behold the unknown and see corruption."

He moved away from the camp because he felt shame.

"I had beheld the unknown for too long."

"But father knows the unknown and He commanded that we stay away from it," one of the nobles said.

The former, consumed by the curses of his disobedience, climbed a hundred feet to the top of the mountain that was forming a volcano. His feet were meshed in the flood of fire that sprung forth. Now the whole assembly stood to watch him from the ground level. As they reasoned along with him who stood up high crying, their garments lost its glow until there was darkness amongst them.

They stayed away from their home for many years, forming an army to fight the armies of the Father. These were the times of the lords of the ancient times.

I WOKE UP the third morning to be greeted with a pleasant surprise. Nana and the Captain stood a few meters away from the ship, eating and talking. I looked closely. They weren't putting on the Life Support Systems and it took me some time to realize that they were breathing in the breathless Mars.

Captain yawned with a knowing smile.

"We are pretty lucky to be here, six hundred feet below the surface level."

He looked up at the frail Sun like the retina of his eyes could not take the light. He dipped his hands into the ground and heaped a mound of sand.

"There is something in the sand that reacts with a gas in the atmosphere to produce more oxygen as it turns over, and there is a boiling river beneath the ground, a lake of boiling spring over there."

I looked at the laboratory as though it was the place being pointed at. Something was cooking.

"Whoever brought us here did to make us live," said Nana as she ran her fingers over the Captain's head. They had become content with the fact that they might never be found and with the smile on their faces, seemed to have given up trying the radio for signals.

"We have to do something or we die," Shedrach said from behind. He had been acting strangely for the past days. All of us had changed quite much from whom we really were, each of us dealing with our unique challenges. If abnormality was to be measured by the variance we exhibited with our original characters then none of us would be considered as normal.

Shedrach's own case was a peculiar sadness for me. I had come to know him as a haughty boy who claimed to know everything. Now that he had become so withdrawn, so unwilling to speak, I feared it was the ultimate omen that we might be heading for the worst.

"Hey." Shedrach raised his voice, picking up a piece of rod that fell off the laboratory compartment. He was getting aggravated and the Flight captain did not fail to notice.

"Calm down, dude," the captain replied gently. Perhaps he was civil because of the presence of a woman in his new life. He chuckled and cleared his throat. That moment I remembered the impression I once had of him. He was a brilliant officer and there was wisdom in his head.

"Whoever brought us here did to make us know something," he said. There was a look in his eyes that showed he was ashamed of himself for sleeping with Nana. He hadn't done enough to be a leader he was supposed to be and fortunately he was good man enough to understand.

"I am convinced there is something important God wants us to know," the Captain explained with an awkward posture, arousing my pity. I was more comfortable with him being detached.

"Two thousand two hundred and eighty seven," Shedrach whispered as though he was letting out a secret.

"Someone said something to my ears last night and I thought it was you,' he pointed his chin at me. 'The world will come for us in the year two thousand, two hundred and eighty seven."

He sounded crazy, seemed to have lost his wit to the weird myth of ours. We laughed and that moment, he realized Captain and Nana weren't putting on the Life Support System. The look on his face made us laugh more.

"2287," I hissed, remembering to take off my LSS.

Captain laughed even more. The iris of his eyes showed heavy wrinkles. It must have being long since he last laughed. He would not stop until he farted. He paused and excused himself.

"Shedrach," he called as he emerged from the cabins with a little diary in his hands. A tiny smile was still dancing over his cheek but he tried to feign seriousness.

"You obviously heard or read it somewhere that Mars would be five times closer to the earth in 2287."

Shedrach fell on his knees and stared on, like he would cry. He had changed a lot since we got there but he seemed to have retained his habit of being dramatic.

"You are right, Captain,' said he, pensively, 'I think someone is trying to talk to us and we must listen."

"Yes I think so." Nana joined. We were silent for a moment.

Each day after, we gathered to share our stories with one another. More than any other thing we had become convinced that there were answers to it all, and the world is not a meaningless cycle of random events.

We joked, we laughed, feasted and danced. We did all manner of things that contravened even our own expectations. We discovered new things that helped us survive. We quarreled and forged a common law by which we lived. Though our battery went flat, we invented new means of lightening. We made walls with the sand to be able to respire and to warm up the place. Beneath the surface was a good tilled soil and waters almost completely free from infection. With time we adapted, becoming fairer and bigger. Our eyes became smaller and nose tinier. Our immunity to diseases became perfect with time. We made music and tried to keep up with the calendar.

There was a time we got a signal we could not sustain through the radios. Captain said it was the American robot that was fooling around at the old Opportunity landing site, a place on the same planet with ours that we do not know. There was a time we formed a policy that we would cultivate more and make more things than we give birth. Nana was the first to conceive. By the time we had celebrated three Christmases our numbers had risen to fifty. It was a necessary blessing because everything boomed there though it looked like a cursed wilderness.

We learnt from one another that the stories that culminated to ours started subtly in many places around the world. One day I told mine. My Uncle's. He was one of those recognized by the Institute of Special Studies as having in his brains, cells capable of receiving transmissions from distant past. It was a new science. Slowly it came to us that there was a time and there will come a time. The times of the supermen.

BOOK TWO

9

May 15, 2287 11:15pm

TUCKING the window blind, I saw a battalion match across the road. Several incongruent voices sounded from the street below and the one above. I tried to listen. The martial orders chanted were neither in French nor English. Cries of the commandants faded into the after-rain tranquility. I felt the compulsion to see what was happening in the upper street and looking through the telescope, I saw hundreds lined on the road bridge connecting Eko Atlantic with Victoria Island, standing guard, pointing their arsenals to the sky. A fleet of armored vessels dotted the seascape. A few surveillance planes hung about four hundred feet above ground level.

I went back to my little desk, bustling with life, seeming to my supercilious mind like an altar. I had written quite a volume of our history, but I must add that in the world where nothing is known about virtue and rulers alone are served even when no service is returned, in the world where homicide and genocide was but a sport for princely kids, there was found an atom of something new.

This old Cimmerian world had slipped into oblivion without a record, only a trace in the age of carbon dating and rigorous excavations. Forever it would have been a waste if there were no single new thing found among them. Scholars called it sudden, biologists my time, mutation, but we have learnt that only few things happen by chance. Out of this little, almost non-existent chance came an atom of good judgment and fairness.

For the sake of a feeling transcending vanities, a man chose to end barbarity, leading the earliest population Darwin called many funny names into another era; the age of men whom cynics loved to call advanced animals. As time passed we have seen their undoing is imitation, stereotype, hypocrisy and countless more. They are lovely for their sense of shame; shame to stand up for their private evils and voice out the very thoughts of their minds.

There was also a time when they raise their bars to the skies and stoop 'humbly' to the grass when the sun is sunken to feast with insects. In their quest for public approval they had been faithless to themselves, sadly more, to the father whom they mostly claim to serve.

The man, my time had normal, predictable patterns. There were times when he feels the urge to do a thing. There were times when he has the adrenaline surge. Sometimes he goes out of the ordinary to be good. Oftentimes he had done great things, raising his towers to the skies, giving the pale evenings the colors of delight, improving the love he'd got with music. In him was the great drive to be good. Within him was the reality of love. Amongst those people came the promise of the glorious time of the supermen. A great man among them once said,

"Let it be known that there was a time when good people lived in the face of the earth."

Indeed they are great people, not for their actions for it was mostly meant to impress, not for their homilies for it was tradition, nor words, for it was hardly eloquent without lies. They are great because of their humility. No mortal my time told the whole truth.

They are great for recognizing the temptation of freewill, taking only a little space of all the spaces freely given. For keeping the world livable for you to be born, sheathing the sword when darkness slipped the nuclear into their midst, looking up to the father whose face they never see; living their life with naïve complacence or with complete trust of the divine, trying to be happy, disregarding the cloud of questions hanging over him.

They lived in the shadows of the new men that will come, some, so well that their names flourished over hundred more years.

Perhaps the sweetest of all he had accomplished; recognizing that he is meant for a higher pedestal, that he is to strive to be the man he was meant to be.

Even the feebleminded gave credence to this. They had ended up though as lesser species by the quality of their minds and in the annals of nations. They had no further understanding than the need for them to transcend mediocrity. In their dreams was a great revolution. First it started without them realizing it for they lived in the mirage of bliss, spreading fire to the skies to buoy their joy.

At a time we least expected, the world was awakened to a new promise but through a tortuous journey. A few in the past worked for a closely knitted dream, yet dark, preaching selective breeding and a people to dominate the world; the ideal place where there is no frustrating divergence but harmony and as an actress would put it; the world where the men are real men and the women are cherished.

This aspiration, though around for a lengthy time, gained wide acclaim amongst some patriots my time. Their rules were the pass to life. And those who fell short were exterminated. The time of the new men was near and the world was pregnant for another form of evolution, so long delayed.

At this time, the world was tired of the mere men. Then came Eugenics, the doctrine by which many men fell into the black book of history. In those times when there was strong desire for a race of human to dominate another, governments and people felt the need like never before to let go of any hindrance to their dream for an ideal world. Interestingly, a session of these ideologists believed it was the evolutionary responsibility of supermen' to crush mere men.

Darwin's theory was having an important consequence he couldn't have imagined in his lifetime.

He had postulated the theory of evolution earlier in 1856. According to him, environmental and a few intrinsic factors leads to variation, which he said, cause the good variants to predominate and evolve into a higher animal. Sudden changes occur in hereditary materials and new variant arise with the advantaged species getting selected by nature. The consequence of the budding theory of natural selection was immense as it brought to life or fortified several arrogant practices of imperialism, racism and sexism.

Although Darwin had postulated that weaker species would die out naturally, a set of powerful people thought a task of such magnitude should not be left to chance. Thus the world was plunged into a time of opprobrium, when fellow men were paraded nude. In the middle of these came a whisper of hope that we could be good. While the guns raged and the doors were shut, the cold floor vibrating for the fury of men, a little one wrote. Though she lived underground, in tiny rooms with only the grace of a faint light, her mind was not trapped betwixt the thick walls nor her wit within the cursed time.

"Despite all these I still believe in the goodness of men."

10

May, 27 1999

WHEN they were home, she discovered she had not prepared her mind about who she really wanted to be and before she could make a resolution, she had already carved a career form arrogance. She had sent away children who came pestering her to gist them about America. She had also turned down neighbors who wanted to treat her to a feast purposed for showing that life in the street had improved.

When it was night, it appeared sleep and not only neighbors would snub her. She stayed awake in her old room and childhood memories came flashing through her mind. Each object that she saw helped to enhance her memory, like it would, a recovering amnesia patient. An old pleasure painting that stained a once covered part of the wall reminded her of her old passion. She saw them as sacred for the messages of the paintings amazed even her. She discovered that she had been who she was even from childhood. Reminiscing about Tunji was not pleasure but she couldn't stop regretting every little thing that she did the last time they met. She had come after eight years to see none of her loads of sin would move an inch.

She remembered the letter Tunji wrote, narrating how his father abandoned him in the rehab. Each time she remembered she was right in the street where it all happened, her heart would pound.

She had been a precocious child but no one had any idea. People did look at her with pity and she had looked them back with pity too. Contrary to everyone's belief, she was positive and calculative. She had planned to make her first inroad to the field of her choice before she clocked twenty-one and she was right on the time. She had a number of things to be thankful for but a persistent sadness clung unto her heart. Something was wrong with her, same thing that made her struggle with a strong feeling of self-disapproval. She had cried several nights for no apparent reason but it was a little more disturbing for her that she would cry in the night that ought to be her happiest. The phone rang as tears gathered in her eyes and a very familiar voice said

"Gotta meet at 31A, Kings' avenue, 4pm tomorrow."

CLAD in a sky-blue gown with a pair of sunshade glasses, she searched the said venue, her eyes radiating with suspense and her face with uncertainty. She looked more beautiful under the gentle evening sun. She walked an aisle, pounding the floor with her heeled shoe, enjoying the imagination that the paparazzi were squabbling on both sides. An old best friend appeared from one of the high-rises at the road side.

"Surprise indeed."

Her smiles were never lasting for more than a few seconds. She followed her friend up the stairs to a room full of party people. A surprise anniversary party was being organized for her. She selected her toes down the stairs and got lost in the crowd. More guests arrived, Tunji, Uncle Bode and Obi. And the Disc Jockey took over. She was a bad dancer after all but she made up for that. Every eye that met hers was rewarded with a genuine smile and a shallow bow.

Uncle Bode and his friends stood close, observing her every move, hoping to find more reasons to hate her, more things to motivate them to be willing to do a great harm without the aid of some drug. Their silence suggested there was none. Only envy could make them want to, but they hated to imagine there was envy in their blood.

"Cute, isn't she?"

Tunji looked away and swallowed the saliva, not knowing exactly what to say.

"Cameleons hardly count as cute for me.' He looked sideways to be sure no one was eavesdropping. 'She is a chameleon, always looking for attention and the saddest part, no one is noticing."

"Is that her?" Obi asked. He'd been by himself all the while, missing the drugs. He was the fattest and the shortest among them and he talked only when necessary.

They stared as the one they'd come for blew the lights of the candles.

Uncle left his friends and went ahead to take a snapshot.

"Hey, who... a photojournalist?"

Her gaze was hardly on whom she was challenging. She was too absorbed in her own elegance to get into catfights.

"A fan who wants your picture in his room," Uncle said after a moment of silence.

She giggled and stole a gaze of him. He seemed quite comfortable with himself, sounded apposite with his smooth talk.

"Private cameras are not allowed," she said quietly like she was ashamed to. "There are exceptions for friends of course."

"Then I am one. Lets do this."

She posed for a few shots.

"Happy birthday," Uncle said as he vanished into the party. His voice managed to climb over the music.

"I am Bode Oladejo."

UNCLE Bode was glad someone understood him. It's been a while since he last had the chance. Dr. Akinola was a friend not only to his father but also him. He was a grey haired granddad, now lived with his wife whom he once abandoned. He had come to understand forgiveness and a few other things as well because he was himself a recipient of forgiveness he hardly deserved. He had pledged to spend the rest of his life making up to his family. When Uncle Bode finished with his own story, the doctor grabbed his shoulder and snorted

"You can start a new life, my boy."

He never said it like it was easy and Uncle was impressed at that. Uncle wanted to trust him with a secret but he was not particularly brought up to trust anyone easily. He had been to churches on invitation of his girlfriends, those he fancied, he had been threatened with altar calls severally without bulging but he was experiencing his miracle now with the doctor. That moment, without much hesitation he decided to heed to some of the advices and go for help. He was resolved to stop taking marijuana. Smiling unconsciously for the sweet thought of his heart, the great new idea that seemed to bring his mind peace, he tried to speak but gave the doctor a chance to finish. His throat was rough and he spoke without clearing it. A terrible and a hardly audible voice came. He tried to speak but had a rethink.

"Guess you wanted to say something?"

'Yes... No sir'.

"You should trust me son."

The doctor loved to call him son, partly because of his own urbane lifestyle. Uncle Bode enjoyed being called a son too. The only person who ever did was his girlfriend's pastor who ended up parting them.

"I am afraid it is personal," Uncle Bode demurred, remembering to mitigate his objection with a bow.

"That even after the war, your mum and sister refused to show up?"

Uncle Bode nodded, taking the easy way out.

"I can remember vividly, how some separatists burst into our compound during the war," he started. His face was expressionless.

"Daddy fled with my brother and I, leaving mum and our baby sister. He couldn't save them in that instant, tried to, but he couldn't. Perhaps mum never understood."

The doctor sighed, sorry that he had nothing important to say.

"I pray you guys return to be the perfect family I once knew."

He was too perceptive to believe Uncle Bode's story was that simple.

He heard a rousing noise and he looked through the window to see where it was coming from. His favorite staff walked past the door, singing an old Baptist hymn. She must have had a great Sunday.

"Good morning, *oga,*' she yelled 'you must be wondering what is good about the morning?"

Her voice was louder than was necessary and her face was lighted with a mischievous smile. They had worked together for twenty years, and they were the only remaining first generation staff of that hospital.

Dr. Akinola was not in the mood but they never conversed in morose tones.

"Guess you what?' the fat nurse came to the door. Her big tummy pointed downwards and her bum, it was like it was stuffed with a pillow, 'Sola Aderomoke is at the reception and she come in after she is through with some camera-carrying pests."

Akinola hissed playfully, feigning ignorance

"Who is Sola Aderomoke?"

"The world broadcaster of the year, the one who was interviewed on the TV last night."

Her eyes brightened with excitement. The doctor loved her ways because she always reminded him of a simple life he once fancied. He thought she was funny too.

"So do we roll out the drums now?"

"Better do, doc."

She took a file from the desk and ambled away.

Uncle Bode excused himself and he met Sola Aderomoke at the entrance.

"Morning, Mr. Oladejo."

"O Mister," he echoed, his head bereft of words. He'd prefer to be addressed as Buddy.

"You walked out on me last night."

She said, holding his belt for support as she adjusted her heeled shoe.

The nurse came and delivered the doctor's message to Uncle. He was to accompany the doctor to the handing over ceremony set for the next day. The first civilian president of Nigeria in fifteen years was to be inaugurated on the twenty-ninth day of May.

"I am reporting there too,' Sola said, 'would you like to join my crew, see how we make the news?" the way she gestured and giggled, he wondered what she really was, introverted or receptive.

11

HE LEFT the clinic for a near phone boot. An idea had crept into his mind. He wanted a job. Many who heard him inquire on phone to speak with Sir Gbajumo thought he was name-dropping and those who weren't humored by that condemned him for whiling away the early hours of a working day. He knew he was been mocked and he tapped his fingers, making music to keep himself focused.

"Hello Bode," said a voice at last. "Do we have another deal?"

"No Sir I just want to talk to you."

"Alright fire on."

He cleared his throat and began

"Sir, I think it's high time I took a more conventional job."

A moment of silence ensued, Sir Gbajumo was hesitating.

"Can we see?"

"Absolutely."

He dropped the phone, wondering if the onlookers' impression of him had changed. He headed for the road trying to ignore escorting eyes and hurriedly took a cab to his place from where he picked his dusty file.

When he got home that day, he tried to take a rest but the thoughts of his mind denied him sleep. His discussions with Gbajumo had been futile. He remembered how the man crushed every suggestion he made, how he had once been promised a good job. He had been asked to wait for six more months. His sadness made him sleep.

"TOMORROW is the D-day," said the radio. Uncle jumped out of bed with a sudden fever and watched his pocket calendar lazily. It was 28th May, 1999. He carried through the day with pains in his head and it was more like he was being anxious for the evening.

Abuja noon flight was pegged at 2pm. He flied with Dr. Akinola and lodged in a downtown hotel with him. Sola Aderomoke, Engr. Ogungbemiro and a technician with the SBCTV Nigerian office took rooms at Chelsea Hotel but they all met at Nicon Hilton. Beautiful evening scenery crawled in, just as a fuji band set the stage. The five lay faced up beside the learners' swimming pool, each appreciating what they cared for. It was a night to remember; Soloists sang beside the pools, Painters displayed their colorful works, swimmers had a felid day, elected politicians celebrated their victory and young lovers made fresh vows. Uncle Bode looked at the face of the moon for half an hour but his mind was not as serene.

He broke the blissful silence. It was obvious he had been thinking all the while.

"Can we start a game?"

Everyone nodded and listened. They looked at him attentively, more than he thought he deserved.

"We will match and dance by the pool edges and anyone who does not stop with the music would be thrown into the water."

Ogungbemiro clapped his hands; Akinola smiled and Sola pulled her hair together. Uncle Bode begged the fuji singers to provide music and the game began.

"Whoever cannot swim should signify by raising his or her filthy hands," he screamed.

I will make you fishers of men, sang the fuji band. Their music was pop mixed with Yoruba Islamic flavor. In the manner with which they were known, they praise-sang eminent persons present, in the middle of the choruses, ensnaring those who were cycling the pool to dance more. Many people joined the madness until the row became tight. They threw one another into the shallow pool till it was crowded. Amidst the pleasant chaos Uncle searched for his own fish. She was in the water, looking lost as the crowd grew more and more tumultuous. He bended over.
"Help you up?"
She declined, shrugging, and Uncle laughed, this time at how she looked in the pool. Drips of water ran over his face and hairy chest as he struggled to pull her out. He coughed and spat. He must join the rows back.
"I will make you fishers of men if you follow me," the song went on.

DEMOCRACY was back in Nigeria after fifteen years. Sola Aderomoke was happy she would be able to present her country in the light deemed as good by the developed world, in the upcoming documentary. She'd promised herself to make at least some good reports about Black Africa to measure up with the stories of violence and poverty and diseases. She'd also prayed that her foreign managers query her for doing just that because she was resolved to lecture them about the ills of prejudice. She was a little naïve and full of many positive youthful ideologies.
She mounted the SBCTV gadgets with the technician's help and Uncle Bode, and two local camera men she hired a day before. She covered

the people more, showed many faces and she spoke brilliantly on how their lives might be affected by the change coming to them. She joined the crowd in singing *Ose baba* just as the new president moved to the dias to take his oath. Her voice was cracked for stress but she didn't mind. Again and again she reported Reverend Jesse Jackson's comments. Uncle Bode joined her when almost everyone was gone. She decided to grant him an interview to use up the half minute she was having left.

"What do you expect from the new government?"

"Job and most importantly, sports development."

"Your priority, sports?"

She stopped the interview abruptly and continued with the packing. She was really stressed out.

"See what they mean by job ethics," Uncle Bode said as she unplugged the microphones for the last time in Eagle square. He was getting on her nerves.

"I was wrong,' said Sola Aderomoke wearily. She looked ten years older when she did. She was to stay behind for updates and further broadcast for another one hour.

"I guess you are...' Sola began as she sat on the bench, 'I think you are..."

"Oladejo?" Uncle Bode cut in, his eyelid raised.

"Yes you are. But I am not sure if you..." Her countenance was dour, 'you chaperoned someone to my party didn't you?"

"O, guess I do that for a living?" He laughed and she joined, but her question seemed like it remained.

"I am about leaving my present job for a better one at Sir Gbajumo's metallurgical firm." Uncle Bode supplied

"And what are you doing presently?"

A difficult silence ensued but she helped him out
"Don't wanna be called a minimum wage local cameraman?"
She laughed, unsure of the cost of her joke. She leaned back and brushed her sticky hair away from her face. Her shirt moved up a little as she stretched her body. There was a little scar at the belly.
"I grew up in Owolabi's castle of joy,' she said. She seemed determined to talk about her life against her own instinct. 'We call the place Kiddies Den."
Again she grew uncomfortable with what she was doing. She beheld the small television set hanging above her shoulder, slightly hiding her face. SBCTV was showing. The gathering tears she was hiding dropped and she was consumed by shame.
'I think I am the worst friend on earth. I reported my best friend to the police and caused him to linger in the jail for eight years. He must be old and haggard now. Do you think my friend will forgive me?"
When she spoke Uncle thought she sounded ingenuous and sweet. He nodded and tried to get rid of the patronizing smile on his face.
"He will. I am so sure he will."
He had learnt from the doctor how to listen. Sola smiled back, impressed but also amused at his efforts to feign empathy. She understood every unspoken word. She had been with many people and she had come to understand the game of attraction perfectly.
"I hope so," she said.
He looked into her eyes, only heaven knows what was more beautiful; her cries or smiles.
"You love him, don't you?"
She looked away and mustered strength, "I am traveling to the east tomorrow, I will miss you."

12

OBI of Ezukala splilled two drops of gin to the earth and said
"You are welcome to the land of a thousand heritages."
He also introduced Emeka Uwakwe, his special aide to the SBCTV crew. Emeka was to orientate them. He took caution to enumerate the intricate rules of the village and to lead them to the house Obi offered, a neat little bungalow shivering at the corner of a compound almost the size of a stadium.

One of the rules of the land was against unrelated, unmarried men and women living together. Emeka decided to give the only female among them, Sola Aderomoke, a room in his own house.

Before his compound that afternoon were two identical, young light complexioned ladies in colorful blouses and skirts. Their long hair was plated in big rows, falling down on the concave arch at their broad, dimpled backs. One tapped her feet against the earth and the other danced to the rhythms that came from afar. They both went to welcome their father.

"Sorry girls,' said Emeka loudly, 'you may go and watch the wrestling but not until you have met the world's broadcaster of the year."

"Haba! I am only SBCTV world broadcaster of the year and not the world's."

"XPZ and the world are all the same,' he replied, 'meet my bevies, my twins, they will pioneer the school of Arts that is coming to Umu Akwu."

Nneka and Chichi lowered their heads in greeting, to the embarrassment of their father, who now took his leave. They did not know they were three years older and their father cared for those little details.

"Will you be coming with us?' Chichi asked, 'you are going to see our handsome and powerful men."

Nneka didn't get on with the new guest like her sister. She was characterless.

Sola agreed to go see the wrestling. It was a God-sent offer to keep her busy, as there was no electric power that afternoon. A shadow of sober quietness was looming over the sleeping village.

At Ogbonaya square, Sola Aderomoke found herself dropping decorum and shouting to cheer favored wrestlers. She tried hard to make herself believe that she was having fun and in the end, she came to enjoy it, at least the view of the hefty muscled men sweating and swearing in *Igbo* to kill their opponents. It was unclear what it was that really annoyed them; the fact that they were challenged to a fight at all or the fact that they hated their opponents so much. More amusing was it that in spite of their rage, they still could wink and even smile at girls who waved and cheered.

By the time the wrestling competition was over Sola had known many names. Chichi pointed at persons she knew, ascribing different idiosyncrasies to each, crumbling the complexities of the world into a few terse statements. She had also talked about her aunt; Nkechi who she said, left the village for her farmstead two miles away after she learnt that she was having a terminal disease. Nkechi lived in the outskirts of Ezukala alone with herself and her two-month old unborn child. The twins were the secret benefactor to her for the village was awash with rumors that her rashes were contagious. Sola Aderomoke became interested as a story was coming to her on a plate of gold. She could not wait to see the said lady because there was an intuition in her mind that one more person was only getting killed by ignorance. She was also going to have a firsthand story for her documentary. She asked to visit Nkechi that evening.

They met Nkechi toying with a dirty doll and singing the ancient song of the ravaged persons of old times. Her hair was unusually long and curly, her lips dry and cracked. Her limbs had become like a shepherds' staff. Everything about her told a story of a diminishing beauty. There was sorrow in her eyes and hopelessness. Even a visit would not cheer her. She fetched a seat for the visitors and muttered

"The spirits love to send you to me whenever I am thinking of suicide."

She spoke quite unlike the way she looked or would have looked; spoke like she belonged to an ancient generation. She was having a peculiar disorder- probably a type alien to psychiatry.

The twin sisters stirred at each other and sighed.

"Don't you dare do that,' Chichi burst out, her voice was firm but low, almost at same level with the sounds made by the gallivanting rats from the rooms. Tears ran over her rounded cheek

"I won't even bury you if you dare give up."

Nneka held her sister. She couldn't believe that she just said 'bury'. Her sister understood her wordless apology. They both looked at their aunt, the one who taught them all the folk songs they knew, standing with impaired posture before them. It was difficult to believe their once charming aunt could be dealt cruel fate so badly.

"Its okay,' said Sola Aderomoke, 'you two can leave, I will bring my crew and we will pass the night here."

"Don't be silly girl,' Chichi hollered, 'no one must know that we were here in the first place."

"Obi and papa would be very upset with you." Nneka broke her silence. There were tears in her eyes but a fresh one rolled down as she spoke.

"But the poor lady needs someone." Sola said.

"And we've not given her some?"

"O, Chichi, can you ever give enough?' her voice climbed, 'I wanna stay and speak with her, trust me, I will call my friends and they will join me in a jiffy."

Chichi like Nneka, shrugged. They'd always hated to go to fast cities because of the fear of adventure and now someone was bringing it right to their doorsteps. They would play the game for a change. They left, committing a blunder; they never introduced their new friend who was to stay behind.

When they were gone Nkechi stared at Sola wordlessly for a couple of minutes. The usual wind of the dusk at raining seasons was starting to blow and it was getting dark fast because the sky was cloudy.

"Who are you and what do you want from me?"

"One question by each," Sola took a breadth. A slight feeling of embarrassment mingled with the sense of guilt she was having in her mind. She was expecting to meet a wasted and gentle fellow, now she had met a sardonic and confident sick lady.

"What do you want from me, dumb?' Nkechi moved a little too close, 'Heartless! Wicked!! What else do you want, to take her pictures halfway around the world?"

"I want to help," Sola Aderomoke shouted back as her fingers ran over the buttons of her cellular phone. She knew Nkechi was losing her sanity but never expected her to show aggression.

"You want to help me? Nkechi hissed, 'Help indeed."

Sola Aderomoke was upset but never intended a word to slip from her mouth.

"I can see what Chichi and Nneka meant when they said I could not pass the night here," she said to a crew mate on phone, quietly. They had arrived at an unpaved tiny road that led to the farmstead and a local was bringing them to Nkechi's part of the farm.

Nkechi broke the bottle containing one of her concoctions and aimed it at her. Sola dodged the missile, stooped and grabbed Nkechi's tiny legs. She took the bottle away from her. Nkechi fell back to the floor, stupidly pretending to have been killed, until she slept off. She was once of good repute but her sense of integrity had diminished with her fortune.

Right next to her head, Sola sat on a little stool, so little her buttocks could hardly rest. She had seen worse situations. She smiled as a beam of light flashed from about a meter away, in the bush. It was already getting dark.

"Show time," she said as Ogungbemiro tried to park his Land Rover. The crew mounted some cameras secretly, hoping to capture a useful scene of Nkechi's lonesome and dejected life.

In the morning, Sola stood at the terrace, thinking where next to go. She was reneging on her determination again like she always did. She had now come to feel like her seniors at SBTV used to, now believed it was unnatural to cover Africa without covering the gloomy scenes. There was a person in her she loved to get rid of that she couldn't. In her very eyes she was picking up the traits common to her seniors that she used to detest.

When she decided to leave, she rose and walked towards the car, tapping Ogungbemiro who was dozing off at the door. Nkechi walked up to her. She was looking somber

"What happened last night?" She asked tiredly. She hadn't really eaten in days and her energy was never to be expended on weeping. Sola hugged her, holding her breadth for the smell that oozed from Nkechi's body and mouth. She looked at Ogungbemiro, hoping that he would not wake up yet.

"I am afraid I won't come back to normal like this next time I black out."

Nkechi beamed a sad smile. Her teeth were beautifully arranged though it had become smudged. She moved nearer, oblivious of her pungent odor.

"Per adventure I lose my senses, tell the baby I planned life to be a lot better."

Tears rolled down her bony cheek, watering the scum of the previous cries.

"Tell the baby that I love it." She smiled but tears did not stop from coming forth. She mustered strength in five minutes and told her story.

Her parents separated during the civil war when she was three. Her father fled with her four year-old brother, Olabode and another older one to be seen no more. Since then, her mother had become unenthusiastic about the family life she dreamt about all her young days to have. At nine Nkechi had become accustomed to watching sex movies with older neighbors. By the time she was fifteen she had been gang raped severally. That was the life she knew, till when she joined a dancing troop in town and started thinking differently. Six months earlier she had discovered a small lump at her back that developed into lesions and rashes. She had been knocked down with persistent fever, finding it hard to keep up with her dance group who had started becoming wary of her company. Unyielding to all pleas, she had left home for the family farmstead to live alone and enjoy the feeling of self-pity. Somewhere in her heart she hoped that the eyes of who stares from above would behold her with compassion. She needed to come out of the crowd to make herself more visible to that mysterious eye. She needed more austerity to win His pity.

Disgusted Sola asked if she still saw the men, the culprits and she answered some. She asked if she had made any attempt to sue them and almost made the sobbing lady to laugh. She yelled suddenly after a quietness of frustration, "I bet you aren't tested!"

Nkechi nodded and Sola smiled but was careful not to raise any hope.

"We shall go to the lab one of these days."

One of those days hardly came. She hardly kept her words, never really practiced the altruism that she preached. She was busier than she could have ever envisaged. Time rolled by, and then came July and August and December.

"SILENT night, holy night, all is bright...."

She tried remembering the lyrics. She'd not been singing carols for ages but a magic brought her to the mood in that year. She looked through the windows. Someone was playing Saxophone at the living room. She stood still to enjoy the music and the sight of the huge silhouette, dancing on a feet to herald the end of an Africanized *Silent Night*. Then, Emeka came and held her by the neck, jolting her.

"Where have you been?"

She stood speechless for a moment and stuttered

"You need to understand, Nkechi is not mad, she only needs help."

Emeka had no idea what she was saying. Sola was mistaking, he hadn't ask about her visit to Nkechi, didn't know about it. Even if he knew he would have given his support anyway. In truth Sola was a bit engrossed in the smooth rhythm that played inside the house and the fragrance, a smell she had come to attribute with fine successful young men. It's been long since she last spoke to an urbane person.

Members of Emeka's household clapped their hands as the saxophonist bowed. There were eight of them and three more in the dimly lighted sitting room. Sola clapped a little more. She wondered why no one bothered telling her about the little family carol. Her hands kept jamming even when everyone else had finished applauding. A light complexioned woman with an aura of affluence and slightly hunched back walked up to her.

"Is she the world broadcaster of the year?"

"She is', gestured Emeka 'can't you see she's as beautiful as my twins.... and Sola, my wife, she arrived in Nigeria with my boy few moments ago."

She had learnt to leave jollity to extroverts but her smiles told she was pleased to meet the woman of the house, at least a little.

The saxophonist was not done. The music *Have yourself a merry little Christmas* played, thrilling and tender. Emeka clasped his arms proudly and droned.

Sola smiled coldly, that which betrayed her lack of concern. In her mind, she tried to reconcile many facts. It was difficult to understand why they allowed Nkechi to waste away in a lonely place. Again and for the first time in two months her mind went to Nkechi, the young lady who she believed must have lost the sense of Christmas and forgotten the essence of it in the first place. A loud applause brought her back to consciousness and she saw the saxophonist come nigh.

SHE WOKE UP to a rather sordid reality for her dream gave a feel of heaven and it was like entering a hot desert from the cold tundra. Her mind was filled with a pointless joy.

She was supposed to go on a date with the saxophonist at seven in the evening but it was already forty minutes late. Just as she was beating herself up for failing to keep yet another promise, she heard someone knock at the door amidst the noisy storm. It was December yet it was storming. Nneka and Chichi stood by the door, shivering and panting with anxiety. Nkechi was in pains and they had no idea how to help. Probably she was dying. Sola Aderomoke took the lantern and followed them. They had barely conversed.

Their breadth and the slapping sound of their slippers alone were to be heard though the sky was warming up for a torrential rain. They could hear Nkechi's agonizing cry from a mile away. Her voice echoed in the wilderness, forming a rhythm with the wailing thunder. Flashes of lightening provided intermittent light and by it they trekked down to the place Nkechi lived.

Nkechi was in coma and a baby's head was already protruding from her. She rested her back against the wooden pole at the porch of the farmhouse with an unpaved floor stained all over with goats' urine. A lantern hung to the pole, just above her head.

Her voice had started to recede when the ladies arrived. She had been having false contractions for the past four hours.

"Golves!' Sola hollered as she threw her bag to the dirty floor. 'I think we need gloves to do this."

Nneka replied with a confused smile but she would burst into tears.

"Yes we need gloves but we went for the result today and it was negative."

"I said it," Sola hollered and that moment, she felt like a nervous silence ensued, something that never really happened but which she perceived as a result of her constant misapprehension caused perhaps by feelings of guilt. She was a little disappointed in her own self that Nneka had to go for the result after three weeks of procrastination from her. She knew what it was to be good but never learned how, never on time. Her face was a little sweaty like it normally used to whenever she felt uncomfortable inside her own skin. Her voice was strong, yet shaky

"Now girl, push."

Nkechi made another thrust and the baby came forth.

Sola, Chichi and Nneka stared with disbelief; a sad nightmare had suddenly ended. They needed no one to proclaim their new gospel. Everyone in Ezukala would see for themselves.

Obi of Ezukala honored the SBCTV troop with a farewell party on the eve of Christmas, the day they were scheduled to leave the village but the rave ended on a sad note. News of Nkechi's death spread over the village square when the party was almost over. She was killed by complications of delivery.

13

FIVE hours to Christmas day, he decided to hang out at Oniru beach alone. There was a vacuum in his life that he did not want to deny. He leaned against the hip of sand freshly built by a group of merry makers and sang *In the bleak mid winter* with them.

"Christmas is a day of reflections when Christians should examine their deeds and turn back to Christ."

He had lost count of the number of times he had listened to such.

"I have decided to stay indoors tomorrow and weigh my relationship with God but trust me, I have no plans of passing a minute indoors on Boxing Day."

He laughed, couldn't have if not of the remote peace that made him perceive any word with a tint of sincerity or simplicity as amusing. He heard his own voice as he laughed and noticed another had joined his'.

"How dare you abandon us?" Obi thundered.

Uncle Bode was taken aback but he mustered courage. He had experienced peace and to be discomforted with anything less would spark a fury in him.

"You know we can't be together forever, Obi," he replied defiantly and he seemed proud of himself that he did.

"Yes of course,' Tunji caught in, 'I knew we will start another life someday but not like this, not this time."

"Sorry guys,' said Uncle Bode calmly, 'I understand Sola wronged you but I also think that your approach is not a very good one."

Tunji moved closer to him, flaunting a knife
"Tell me that you prefer that brat to us."
Uncle Bode smiled contritely, looked down and chuckled
"I choose the brat."
An eerie silence followed
"You're doomed."
"You won't attack your guy, will you?"
Uncle Bode gave a seemingly threatening grin that earned him a hard blow. He fell to the ground and the two fled.

A MOMENT later, he heard a faint voice.
"Come on, he's moving."
 A thick veil was covering his head that he couldn't see. He wanted to rise but a hand pulled him back. A strange voice advised him to relax and a familiar one mocked him.
"Maybe he is missing a Christmas party."
"I have got a broken neck," said Uncle Bode tiredly. He remembered clearly how his two friends attacked him. He knew he must have fainted, wasn't sure if it was still Christmas day or the eve. Though it felt like a dream, he knew one of those voices he heard was Sola's. She had called him on the phone an hour before and he had answered half consciously.
He decided to quit complaining, and sat up.
"I know who it is."
Sola uttered no word but she removed the veil from his head.
"We gonna spend the Christmas here?"
Uncle laughed for no apparent reason but he stopped on spotting an observer.
"My friend,' Sola gestured, 'she brought me here when I was looking for you."

The stranger's eyes scanned through him briskly and rested on his groin. It was an unkind look from a protective friend, meant to convey without mistakes the message of hostility. The way Uncle laughed was stupid, showed that he was clueless on what to do next, maybe even embarrassed to get what he never really asked for. It was clear from that moment she thought Uncle an impostor.

Uncle thanked the friend like he would, an old enemy and before he could inquire about the baby that caught his attention Sola had nervously stated that she would like to talk about it later.

When the bells were no longer jingling Uncle Bode sat to reminisce on how he uttered those words at the tranquil beach, things he wouldn't have said even if he was hypnotized. He shouldn't have been so consumed as to talk about the deepest things of him. Probably the veil was not only covering his head that moment but also his cerebrum. Sola seemed to understand his bizarre story. She was a news girl and she had made documentaries on far more complicated family issues in America. Though she was only twenty-one she had surrounded herself with huge profile.

"That you're asking to be forgiven is strange even to you. Unexplained feelings could be divine." she had said convincingly. Uncle believed those words. He was going to beg his father for forgiveness, something he had lacked courage to do for two years.

After making a couple of attempts by the phone he dialed the number that brought him some poignant memories. A part of him still believed he should be the one to be begged but he was determined not to go back on his resolve.

"I will be home," he said.

All he heard was a very weak voice from a seemingly indifferent receiver.

"Please do."

His fingers trembled on the phone box as he dialed Dr. Akinola's number.

"What's up with Dad?"

Akinola explained that his father was suffering from acute depression and told him to come over for an advice on what to do. He realized at once how close he was to losing him and a pint of regret came to his heart. He never knew how much he cared until then.

Uncle tossed his car key and matched to his 504 and Akinola followed behind with his Land cruiser.

The new millennium fever was thick in the air and the romance of anarchy and festivity begat rowdiness. Uncle Bode's sobriety melted away to the buzzing air easily as he tried to get around the rowdy highway. He loved life and chaos. He enjoyed the noises of the little fireworks that was being thrown around and curses rained by passers-by. Though he was on a serious and symbolic mission, more important because he had attached a superstitious deadline to it in his mind- he still found time to cheer street urchins who ran across the roads celebrating and even dashed some of them five naira for throwing the bangers astutely. His happiness gave way to apprehension as he drove into painfully familiar streets.

His heart skipped a beat as he spotted the large signboard that read Olaiya Street and when he got to number nine he felt it would stop with the car's engine. He looked through the rear mirror. Akinola was locking up his car behind them. The smile on the man's face was helpful to his psyche though he knew it was a plastic one. He looked to the right and saw his father with open arms. Things had turned far easier than he expected.

IT WAS seven in the evening, just five hours to a new millennium. Crowds that besieged the roads grew riotous and fowl sellers transacted business almost in the middle of the streets. As though the chaos wasn't enough, one more trader started to play some local gospel music to join with the fuji that was coming from a barber's shop. Uncle Bode moved his head to the music and tried to sing along even as the gospel came intertwining. He had become livelier than he had been in years. A huge weight had just fallen off his shoulder and it was ironical that Sola was just about bestowing hers on him.

"The baby," Sola screamed. 'It is eight days old today and we've not even chosen a name for it."

She sighed,

"So much for parenthood."

"You promised to tell me about the baby, didn't you?"

Uncle's voice was meshed in suspicion.

"Yes but we've got to get out of this first."

She looked sideways and scowled.

The way she played down the question angered him a little, especially the manner with which she waved her hands.

Uncle Bode whined and panted. He was not done yet working on his temperament. He had spent too many years with unmannered friends.

"Okay," and smacked as though she was remembering a thing. How she had come to care so much about Uncle she did not know and she wasn't ready to let a stranger get between them.

"The woman asked me to keep him."

"Before she died?"

"Yes."

"O, I see she really meant her child to live a good life, knowing that you have the means," Uncle remarked. His selfishness was evolving as meanness.

"Please don't say that, the baby needs us."

"Us?' Uncle tried not to laugh. 'I hope you know the family."

"Yes, I do."

The mention of Nkechi reminded him of his lost sister. His Ibo mother had named her Nkechi.

Uncle sighed to relieve his heart of guilt. He took her hands and looked at her face. Worry and guilt was written all over.

"We will have a party for him," he said.

"Not about the party," Sola tried to say but a loud burst that sounded from the rear got her gasping for breath. The car's tire had ruptured.

Uncle rushed to go and see what was wrong and he saw two joker cards bearing Tunji and Obi's names, on floor just by the car. Some people had visited them with terror, bursting the tires and draining the oils. What Uncle saw he kept close to his chest.

"It is nine-forty and vulcanizers are miles away.' Sola lamented. 'Where we gonna be by twelve?"

Uncle Bode took the two joker cards in his pouch, cleverly covering the names writing on them in what looked like blood.

"Pick Ace, we go to the club house, pick Heart, and we go to the church."

He shoved the cards and placed them on the car's hot bonnet and she picked Heart.

"Got to get the baby," she hurried away and boarded a cab.

"Think about the name."

That bustling night, the clock's hands moved desperately towards the vertical. Uncle Bode imagined himself pulling it back but when it dawned on him that he couldn't, he decided to create interest in the worship song that sounded from a distance.

After waiting for nearly two hours Uncle Bode saw Sola come nigh. He had kept his eyes on the taxis with anticipation, many times mistaking ladies who alighted from them for his girlfriend. Now she had emerged from the dark streets, looking nowhere near the perfect picture in his head. For a moment Uncle Bode worried about his luck- for he never got what he expected. He was expecting his girl to emerge with a black strapless, backless micro gown, beaming a seductive smile. He wanted to take her home after saying a few wishful words at the church gate. When Sola arrived she looked famished, barely talked. She whispered with the strength left in her

"The baby," she panted.

She couldn't find the baby. Uncle Bode broadened his chest for her to rest her head but she hit him even harder than Tunji or Obi had done.

"You took the baby," she screamed, her voice deeply toned in an American accent. She had been forcing herself to speak easy all along. Uncle felt strange. He focused his attention inadvertently on how the veins of her neck stretched when she mentioned the 'police'. He'd been threatened with the police several times in his life. He had experienced a difficult history and everything that reminded him of it he hated more.

THE STREET WENT sleeping in the dawn, no obstruction to its almost perfect silence. Uncle Bode and Sola watched the mechanic a kind worshipper and passer-by referred to them as he fixed the car. Their dispute was far from over.

After one hour, the mechanic shook his head and declared it would take him hours to finish.

Uncle stopped a moving car and begged for a lift. He headed for his former place of abode where Tunji and Obi lived, ready for a fight.

When he got there with his infantile rage, Obi spoke incoherently; he must have taken the drug.

"You aren't seeing anything yet man, think about it; the innocent son of nobody flushed down our dirty toilet or some thousands for you.....The TV star, a kid trafficker, don't you get it? Don't want to make some money?"

Hemp was all over his nose. Uncle took time to think and then gave his consent. One of the two hefty men by this side held his elbow and shook hands with him.

"Sorry we met this way."

HiThe story of his cruelty was legendary to them and they felt inferior, as it was their dream to be as dreaded as he once was.

"Strong man," the second fidgeted his hands over Uncle Bode's chest.

"Don T said you were great..., care for a drink?"

Uncle laughed and grabbed the bottle Obi offered. He was to pay for every bottle.

Tunji studied him as he gushed the drink

"When last did you take a dope?"

"Long," he yawned.

"She changed it all?"

He sipped the whiskey and coughed like it was his first time.

"She changed it all."

He stretched forth his hands for some but Tunji ignored him. He read out his plans instead. Uncle listened to see where he could implicate them, he planned a counter action in his mind but he consciously refrained from creating any room for suspicion. Shortly his eyes began to close and he slept away.

Late in the night a bar attendant tapped him by the shoulder and told him they were closing for the day. He staggered but he woke up fully when he saw the clock that was hung against his face. He could see the day was gone but he could not bring himself to believe that it was 1am in the morning of another day. He returned home and sleepwalked to his bed but the note lying on the terrazzo floor attracted him. It was in Sola's writing. He took it and read.

A stranger called this evening and told me about your plans. How could you?

His sadness made him sleep and he remembered the poignant experience of his childhood. He was eleven then, and a fresh man in the secondary school. On his way home, one unlucky day, he had seen two rogues boggle a neighbor's house and he had shouted at them. The men fled but some people bounced on him claiming that he was the thief. No one cared to listen to him, not his subservient father. He was forced to apologize for what he hadn't done. Though it seemed trivial, the pain was to haunt him for a long time.

HE WAS ABOUT driving across the junction when he decided to suspend his work and head for the police station. It was the first Monday of the year. Christmas was gone and reality had taken the place of sweet dreams. It felt like the world was cross with him; students who agonized over their lateness to school, workers who lamented their lost house keys. He drove with less care and almost recklessly to police division D Tejumade close.

People waited to see the most important officer there, the lady Inspector having red hair. He was selfishly saddened that the world would not spare him the ordeal of queuing for the sake of his situation: he was relapsing, becoming unstable like he once was.

A lady in police uniform showed up after the people had waited for thirty minutes, and she apologized. She appeared too made up and the loudness of her voice, she seemed not to care. She pointed at Uncle and told officers at the reception to let him, not minding the people ahead on the queue. Uncle entered the small office room, his hands tucked in his pocket, his eyes lingering on the written vision statements of the Police force. He sat down as the Inspector entered. Kemi crashed into the noisy leather upholstery facing her desk. She clearly meant to be informal.

"Shut the door and give me two minutes," she ordered a junior officer who wanted to tell her that Uncle was the last on the queue. She looked straight and talked freely with an irritable mien. Uncle realized she was the one he once heard about when she removed the cap, revealing her dyed hair. She combed the short hair repeatedly as she sat on the long upholstery of her office as though she was expecting a compliment from the stranger who stared. Uncle Bode did not give one, but not because he felt it was improper. He wasn't done yet with the lessons of how to be a lady's man. He did not thank her for making him jump the queue either.

One more thing that was hilarious about the lady; she seldom pretended, not out of virtue but of the notion that there was nothing too bad as to be ashamed about. She was an achiever and no amount of scandal would eclipse that. She was proud of her Range -rover, a gift from her eccentric former fiancé whose life story inspired her to pick up a very bizarre investigative job. When Uncle Bode presented his case, Kemi told him to come to pick her up by 5pm for her to see things by herself. She ordered the arrest of the suspects too.

Uncle Bode went to pick her by five forty -five, the African time of five O'clock. They started off as good friends, and maybe old lovers. For Uncle Bode it was just another fling and for Kemi, a chance to fathom what really happened that made her fiancé of two years slip away. She was a cop, a great one and she was discerning enough to notice there was something common to her ex and Uncle Bode, something that first endeared her to the German. When Uncle Bode entered the station he had worn a look that made his eyes dim as though it was beamed with an headlight. Also, he had stood motionless for a split second to give a peculiar audible sound the same way the German used to. Though it seemed trivial, that strange mannerism of her betrothed had landed him in the psychiatric hospital where he penned down bizarre things that came to be the subject of her investigation. She was having an ample chance now to get to learn firsthand what it was that was claiming the sanity of hundreds in different parts of the globe. It would be easy for her to learn for she loved the company of those who pleasurably mystify her. Also she was discovering a thing about herself too- something that had always depressed her and made her to wonder why she was always attracted only to freaks.

"MY HUMBLE abode," Uncle Bode sighed on getting to his fenceless compound, hurriedly kicking away a few disfiguring stones in front of his house. There was a skinny cock he hated that kept coming to his door. He picked the last stone by the door and threw it at that annoying fowl with stunted growth. He would kill it the next time it comes around because it seemed hell-bent on defacing his place every time a new catch comes by. He was hoping for a smooth night but it appeared the world was averse to it.

A police jeep was parking and two policemen were waiting impatiently inside. One of the police officers carried the lost and found baby to him and announced that Tunji and Obi had been arrested.

THREE letters awaited him in the office, one a query, the second, a recommendation to Lagos Business school and the third, a letter of provisional appointment as Manager of AAF Guest house, a division of the Aluminum recycling firm. His best friend in the Alpha Aluminums Firm Charles had waited vainly on Monday to see him pick the dazzling white envelope lying on his table. He was late to work because he went to bail Tunji and Obi out of detention. He was proud of what he did and he could not wait to tell Charles about it. He was at that time getting obsessed with a bestselling book that preached forgiveness and it was quite natural that he would want to forgive. He knew how Charles would react, he knew his

Belgian friend very well and he loved it when people said he had a good heart. To his outmost surprise, Charles was not interested in his story however hard he tried to embellish it. What mattered was the white envelope.

Charles gestured his clueless friend to pick the envelope and read the letter. Uncle smiled as he uncovered the mail and asked if Oga was around, Charles nodded and he matched to the chairman's office with a somewhat infantile chant of joy. No one dared interrupt his jubilation. It was a little surreal for him to have been appointed as he was unknown among the circles of acclaimed performers. Again he remembered his private philosophy and conjectured that sometimes, good things just happen and when it does, it happens fast, quickly before nature gains back her reason.

"I guess you are Oladejo?" The chairman asked to be sure. His glasses were failing him. He was the perfect figure of the big man stereotype, with his robust neck and unexcited stares. He never forgot to add a potbelly too and the way he breathed, the world would have to wait. The world was with no choice but to condone and even love his slowness because his every move was money. When he spoke, his voice was ordinary and genial, suggesting that he meant not to be intimidating.

"My son has been bothering me about it for two months now,' he pointed to the middle-aged man leaning on his rotary upholstery 'he said you have the foresight, the will to turn AAF around."

The smiling chap looked familiar, Uncle Bode had conversed with him before, sometimes in October when he came complaining to his dad about the services of the AAF Guest House in which he was lodged. It was a boring evening during the hours most workers traditionally kept straight faces. He had just arrived from the airport then, harmed with two new certificates, determined to work only where the true worth of his expertise would be appreciated. He had got talking with Uncle Bode while waiting for the board meeting to end. That time, he was having a running fight with his dad who thought he should come back to head his conglomerate. There and then, he had discussed his vision with Uncle Bode who seemed to understand and he had fallen for him. He had been a little egoistical, used to wonder if anyone in that group of companies could indeed match him but when he spoke with Uncle his assumption had lied flat on its face.

"Your reputation has preceded you,' the multi millionaire boss of AAF said, 'everyone here knows you as the guy who finds a solution no matter what."

Uncle smiled, astounded by the chairman's insincerity.

"I will justify the confidence reposed in me."

He smiled at the chairman's son.

"Thanks Mr.Abdulkarim."

"O, he is Alhaji too," a courtly laughter followed.

Mallam Abdulkarim. His brown eyes and thin hair never did much to tell his story- the story that had him attend Harvard Business School and make friends with many top flyers. He was lean because of his frequent fasting perhaps. With his peculiar posture, askew but not awkward and his more-than-average height, he seemed to provide a good alternative to people's imagination of how he should look like. He always defied people's stereotype but his alternatives were not bad either. His father was fat, huge and good-looking but he grew up himself to be lean and moderate, not too cute. He used to see disappointment in the eyes of faithful servants each time he returned for a holiday. For Uncle Bode, he had found a muse, one who sees the world from the prism of a struggling man and not from the prism of a millionaire. Uncle Bode found himself worshipping him- the young millionaire was good at making the most unlikely person idolize him. Mallam Abdulkarim understood too well the darkest secrets of power- churning out self-debasing words, yet asserting his superiority subtly. His arrogance was complete and indecipherable because of the mask of humility, that which made him win the heart of many, even as he crashes their defensives. His influence on Uncle Bode would last for a lifetime as he gave Uncle the fortitude to accept his own self and to worry less about his own 'abnormality'. I guess he was the one who told Uncle Bode this, "Being a freak is nothing to worry about because we are all freaks in unique ways but what is worrisome is when one does not accept himself as a raw piece to be worked upon to produce a better man."

I came to realize years later that most of the words he told first came from the lips of this gentleman.

Uncle Bode learnt hundreds of Hausa vocabularies and before anyone knew it, he had become the chairman's favorite, conversing in an accent the family found adorable. He ate dinners with the Abdulkarims in their mansion and slept in their guestroom when it was too late to go to his own house, prayed together with them at their private mosque on two occasions. The urge to become a successful career man in him grew again. It would make a funny graph if plotted against time.

He met Zainab, Musa's only sister and Pearl and Maryam, his half sisters. They looked very much like Arabians. He was never tired of saying how beautiful they were, especially when they were putting on their pretty, expensive fedoras and gold, not until Pearl called him a sycophant to his face- an early sign that he was becoming a member of the family and due to be strip of all special courtesies.

Pearl was fourteen and the youngest; her father's adored. Everyone thought she had changed her real name two years before, out of her own thirteen-year-old mind but in truth, her pedophile twenty–one year-old boyfriend had christened her 'Pearl'. Pearl had mailed Dolce and Gabbana several times, supposedly requesting for shipment. On her tenth birthday she had 'charmed' her dad to buy her a set of costly jewelries and clothing and she had become noticed at 'The Vogue' magazine, turned down many times for faking parental permits but known for her persistence and her emerging style. One lonely evening she had whispered 'Mrs Pearl Bode–Oladejo' to herself and looked into his eyes through the mirrors dreamily, a rather curious thing because of their relationship and the years between them. Uncle Bode would never be her type but he was the most visible, having a body closest to the firm, clean ones she saw only in the magazines. Her sisters were no more girls than she, perhaps. She was the sole music star of her school, still learning the guitar and taking an afternoon course to train her voice. She would hit a record deal in few months if she could live up to the hype. There was a peculiar air around her already and she was beginning to look like the diva she wanted to be. Her school uniform soon began to irritate her, her soft blue shirt and long black skirt. She was quick to invent her own style and almost got away with it but in that one week of rebellion she had warmed herself into the hearts of the little boys who knew without mistakes that she was not cut out for any of them. There was a thick 'Uncle' with a white 504 who comes for her, Thursdays and Fridays after school. Those times, she would run into his arms and seize a cup of ice cream and muffin from him-her constant present. Though she seemed a lot clever, she was apparently harboring in her mind many wild thoughts, one of which made her think Uncle Bode really stares at her little pair of butts. For her fans at school she was the most glamorous, the first to live out the dreams they caught from the movies. Had any classmate found the courage to suspect she was not infallible, she would have found true friendship and easily outgrow her weirdness, maybe.

UNCLE BODE AND KEMI watched little Bamidele fumble with the cake before him, their eyes studded with pity and admiration. They had both agreed to have a party for the baby in Uncle Bode's house. Kemi danced all day, in her little top and pant, drunk and sassy. The room was lit with a dim blue light for the party, made darker for the number of people inside. A lot of them had come on Kemi's invitation and there was one who never kept his hands off her waist, even when the music dictated otherwise. The cutting of cake was Uncle Bode's idea. He hoped to stop the trend he was noticing.
The lady she hardly fancied seemed to have become attractive to him all of a sudden. He was

stupid to have downplayed the evening. Now he was catching his own fever right in the middle of the party, his hungry eyes stationed on the crowded middle of the room where tens of couples were dirty dancing. A moment earlier he wouldn't mind seeing her dance with some daring dude but now he'd noticed her big, fair thigh and a flat tummy streaming down to a perfect hip. It's been long since he last worshipped a woman's body.

He gushed the juice on the shelf he was resting his weight upon and belched. His eyes were fixed on the trespasser's wandering hands and the twisting waist. He had better watch than be tormented by his mischievous mind.

"Hey guy," he called, eight inches away, stretching his ankles to feel taller, wishing his muscles to be noticed. He intended to move closer before talking but the strange enemy seemed too fast, and his face was rested on her head already, smelling the big glossy hair.

"Would you mind?" he blew a threatening smile.

"Thank you," his eyes followed the kid as Kemi's sullen voice cut through the loud music.

"Will you be a better dancer?"

He nodded for no word was important but the speechless and sensual interaction he was hoping for. A Yoruba Hip pop song that Kemi loved was playing but she barely moved.

"Quite a music for a child's first birthday," he supplied after three minutes of no speaking. Kemi turned around resignedly and shook her buttocks against Uncle Bode's groin- a gesture he failed to interpret correctly. He grabbed the waist.

"You should dance, boy."

Her voice was both stoic and firm. He tried grabbing once again; he must have been looking at the couples next to them. The third time he did, he saw a glare on her face. Few months ago he was a 'hero' and now, a laughingstock. He retired to his bedroom, straight to the corner where a pint of marijuana was wrapped in a paper. It was the only pint that survived his self-imposed repentance. He had only remembered the previous day that he was still having the powder somewhere between the books. That night, he missed his former life; never remembered the bitter part of it that made him try to change in the first place. He took the powder and he thought that he smelled a thing that reassured him of a huge conquest. He sniffed it voraciously, more than he ever did and he remembered immediately why he wanted a new life. He would go mad- the visions were coming to him again.

IT HAD BEEN six years now that he first dreamed of a world bleak and fearsome and desolate. There was a hill to the left of where he seemed to recognize as home. This time his eyes scanned through the whistling mighty hill about fifty miles away and dropped on his own feet. He had suddenly remembered something about the feet of everyone he saw in his previous dreams though he barely recalled a thing about his other life. He was anxious about his image for a faint knowledge of how he was supposed to look pervaded his clouded mind.

In that dream, he rushed down to a tiny stream he remembered was somewhere near his home and bent forward to look at his face in it. He feared that he looked ugly, like the human race he seemed to have lived his whole life with. He was impatient that he dusted the soil over the stream, causing ripples. He waited for the ripples to clear and looked at his face in the water. He was nothing like all other people he had known all his life- his face was a little oblong and his dentition was perfect. He thought he was handsome and started reconciling many events as he remembered them. Everyone treated him nice because he was the finest- he was a god. He had fallen from the sky and his destiny was to rule the country where a boorish race of funny-looking people lived. He could not understand; he knelt besides the stream feeling frustrated. He was lost and there was a picture in his heart he could not place. The more he tried the more impossible it proved. He raised his head to try again. The hill ahead of him was familiar; he had spent all his life staring at it. He remembered there used to be a tiny fire under the hills at night. He had probably been there before. Now, he could recollect he had a family. He could remember a stone knife and the hideous practices perpetuated beneath the hill in the mornings. He must have slept for so long that he forgot his own life. He tried to smile- his frustration was melting away but he sighted a strange fearsome beast- a tiger with saber tooth and he struggled out of the vision.

KEMI and Dr. Akinola watched him closely.
"He is convulsing again," Kemi whined but the doctor waved her to be quiet. They kept observing Uncle Bode who was lying uneasily on the bed.
"Nasty boy," Kemi chuckled like she admired the fact that he took cocaine. Her efforts were to mitigate Uncle Bode's offense and to convince herself that his condition was trivial but she appeared confused and deeply worried. The beat of her heart was faster but she tried to remain

calm and waters hovered her eyes as she smiled. Things had turned for Uncle Bode almost the same way it did for her former fiancé and she felt a fear that reminded her of the last September when the German, the man she loved, spoke of bizarre things in his sick bed, chained and clothed in the hospital's uniform. Her intuition was eerily right; there was a semblance in the conditions of these two young men who lived in separate continents. She would be the first in the world to uncover the mystery and her face would appear in the papers. She thought briefly, how much naira that could translate to but quickly scolded her own mind for daring to. It was unspeakable to contemplate feasting on other people's misfortune.

Uncle Bode shuddered as though he would storm out of the bed and out of the building. Kemi stared helplessly and Akinola scratched his scalp.

"I think we need a psychiatrist, he is hallucinating."

"Where...what?" Kemi was becoming afraid of the obvious. Her lips were dry and the little piece of beauty on her face melted with her courage.

"Never mind, I will take him to my friend, Olanusi."

Dr. Akinola was torn between downplaying her fears and saying something vindictive to Uncle who he noticed had become conscious.

Uncle choked. Saliva had passed into his larynx.

"I am sorry,' he said with an honest sense of guilt 'I will try harder this time."

"You've got to,' said Akinola firmly. His anger had vanished.

"Next time I see you drugged I'll report you to the police and you'd better believe its not just a threat."

He vacated to his car and Kemi joined him
without uttering a word. Uncle Bode followed
behind with an exaggerated show of remorse. The
snow bed sheath followed him to the door and he
threw it back, taking a time to pick his breath
freshener. Their destination, University Teaching
Hospital annex, Iluimo was 45 miles away.

14

A LARGE yellow sun was sinking into the horizon and its image was reflected on the still waters- the little lake adorning the endless piece of land he once called his'. There had been such moments in the past and there will always be, moments when a man looks at the heavens because the thought of his heart has become unearthly. In such moments the patterns of the clouds of the sky would seem unhappy. Such moments always came in the twilight of an eventless day or a sad one. It depressed his soul further, leaving him with just one reason to live- to finish his long essay, which he hoped would slip into the hands of a great one someday.

He had lived a long life, most of it within high walls and he had come to that part of the town to have crosswinds blow over his pale skin and enjoy youthful memories. His eyes had seen more than a lifetime would permit.

When he heard a teeny noise in the quiet place his weak heart came alive. His sight was blurred as it had been fixed on the evening sun for ten minutes. He looked to the direction of the noise and allowed his sight to normalize. He did not only look, he smiled, for the first happy sight in six weeks had finally come to him. A pigeon was born and that alone made him smile. He had lived alone for too long that a little thing from nature gladdened his heart. He stared with inexplicable interest, as the little pigeon broke loose from its shell. He had become drawn to such things and he had grown to be fascinated by everything in its beginning. His life as a celebrity had ended the day he was told that the growth on his throat was malignant. Since then, he had come back to his old opinions, when he was still pursuing his doctorate in Oxford as a temperate young man.

He was an exceptional psychiatrist; the best among his peers. He traveled two hours every other day in the nineteen-forties to a little place near London to treat a wealthy man who was sick with mild psychoses. There, many great people came around visiting his patient. The old aristocrats who came loved him and some loved him too much that they opened up to him on everything under the sun. He was a humble, slavish genius and there was no need hiding anything from him. It was in fact pleasurable to bare their dirty linens to his young face.

Fifty years after a fabulous career he had returned to his hometown, Iluimo where he continued to wrestle with journalists and young doctors in need of inspiration. His wife who was also a psychiatrist was hardly around. She needed to represent him wherever he was invited to speak because he was sick and old. None of his children or grandchildren ever returned to Nigeria. Once again, he was alone most of the times, like he used to when he wandered in the mansion of the wealthy British, snubbing ladies from different continents who wink at him.

Though he responded well to treatment, he had become too pessimistic about his survival. He was ninety-two years old after all. The day he was told that his chemotherapy was successful, he went out alone to the hilly side of his village to have a feel once more of what it was like to be strong and healthy.

The day was drawing to a close and fellow sightseers were packing their things already, preparing to catch the boats that plied the heart of the fishing town, forty miles from Lagos. He reached for the camera on the muddy earth and cleaned it with the arms of his shirt. He had taken a few snapshots with it- silhouette of a father teaching his daughter how to use the telescope and of a fisherman sailing home after a disappointing fishing day. He had also taken the town's picture, the meek little town that prided itself with producing the world's most distinguished psychiatrist. He needed a little contact with the world to finish his essay. He wanted to fill his mind with the thought of everyday men and speak to them the way they would feel bothered. He had lived too long in an esoteric conferment where words are not cheap and are not to be used cheaply. Now he labored to be understood by the world of another generation for the clearest of his words were like ciphers to the most discerning. He was not going senile, only that he once lived with those who shaped the world, whose assumptions became the basis for conventions.

His eyes were sunken with age and several lines extended from the sockets. It used to be a beautiful pair of eyes that brighten up at every new fortune. There was a time in the middle of those years when his eyes would shrink even at the sight of what seem to be good. His long hairs looked healthy though he didn't intend it to, he had lived his life taking only what enriched his body positively, not by choice but necessity for someone who lived with the smartest. His broad face was with a gravely calmness as he was amused by nothing but preachers who swear to be honest.

Olanusi was the kind of legend people always thought was long dead, the kind who heard fables about themselves in market places. Most of his mates at Iluimo high school were either dead or too absolved in societal issues to socialize. The few unsuccessful ones were too egoistical to come see him and relish old memories over a bottle of beer the way he had always dreamed of. If they still exist he would never know but it was sure they would know about him, as he was the shining light of their little town. He still had contacts with Dr. Akinola though, the little boy of the nineteen-forties that he mentored.

Akinola had chosen to take Uncle to the old psychiatrist to make it look like they were only meeting a great man for social reasons. He envisaged Uncle would consider it demeaning if he suggests him to see a psychiatrist.

When Akinola arrived at his old mentor's house with Kemi and Uncle Bode, he looked around the array of awards hanging in the passage that led to the main sitting room. He had been told Olanusi would be back from the hillside in few minutes and he waited patiently, bragging to Kemi and Uncle Bode about his relationship with the old man.

Olanusi spoke from the door, beckoning his visitors to join him in his private study. He needed to prepare another paper for his wife who was going to represent him at a conference in Johannesburg.

"*Ot'ojo meta sir.*"

His speech though impaired, still carried a little authority and he was courteous as ever. Akinola worried if he'd still recognize him and when he grabbed the old man's cold hands he tried introducing himself.

"How is madam?' Olanusi inquired concernedly, he apparently remembered that Akinola's marriage suffered a major crisis. 'And my boy, the one who climbs the tree to eat, uh, Tokunbo?"

"O' Akinola was dazed at Olanusi's sharp memory; perhaps that was why he was a genius, 'Tokunbo is on tour to Europe with his family, he sings."

"Great,' Olanusi remarked as he offered his hands to the other two visitors, Uncle Bode and Kemi.

"We thank God for everything,' he chuckled, 'here I am after fifty years of service to just one man."

Akinola wanted to say that was an exaggeration but remembered how true it could be.

Olanusi had finally found someone to pin down with his talkativeness. He hurried to the bar where he fetched bottles of wine.

"In those fifty years I saw what I'd better not seen,' he took a breath. Sadly, his fever was returning. 'There seem to be no heroes anywhere but men who just want to court our admiration by some means."

Akinola took the cup of wine he offered.

"Tell me doctor, rumor has it that your patient kept the largest multiracial help center in the world."

Olanusi turned his face down; he was old yet he was shy.

"It was ranked the largest for a particular year but it is a shame that his noble efforts were marred by his own demons."

Akinola looked at him the same way he used to in old times when he came to his room in the village to plague him with questions about Oxford.

"The first time I caught my lord in room with one of those young ladies, he knelt down and begged me not to tell anyone. The second time, he explained he was going to take another wife, the third, he wept and said he was losing control over himself."

Akinola stared bewildered.

"When I see that look in the eyes of anyone I tell that, I become even more bemused,' Olanusi beamed a smile of despair, 'why do people ascribe infallibility to others while they wallow in their own sins? It is all illusion when we make others the object of our worship."

He ordered his maid to get him a sweater, he was feeling cold and his body temperature was rising.

"Perhaps it is necessary to suppress our desires with religion and morality. Where the two is absent or where the ego is no longer worthy of defense we abate to the levels of animals as I have found in the case of my lord."

The visitors looked genuinely affected by the revelation.

"What is the world turning into?"

"Nothing, gentlemen. The world was never better, so it would be unfair to lament it is turning. Like I was saying, I found my lord had excess libido, accountable from provisions of his genes. Shall he be guilty of the dictates of his genes?"

"Not exactly sir,' Akinola demurred, 'everyone is obliged to deny their senses to make themselves better people."

"So did my lord,' Olanusi responded, 'studying his medical history, I learnt that he was pedophilic. Setting up a help center, for him was a way to stand up to his own stress, but in the end he could not stop being himself."

He paused briefly to observe his visitors.

"Somewhere along the line, I gave him my own professional advice that he could go on living his life without guilt. His mania is cured alone by his sins."

Akinola sat back and heaved a sigh.

"Yet I am astounded by the number of people who agrees a sin could remain as private,' Olanusi continued, 'our little sins derive its true satisfaction in expanding, the same way our genes sought to outlive us."

He stood up to take his medications.

"My lord wished to be a good man but in the end he built the biggest brothel in the world where many great men freely surrendered to their senses. I watched him as he graduated to a greater evil, becoming even blasphemous to his God."

Akinola, like Uncle Bode chuckled and a look of surprise was on Kemi's face.

"Almost everyone have the potentiality of becoming wicked; the kid who enjoys sadistic movies, teachers who spank their pupils unnecessarily in the name of discipline, clerics whose best topic is apocalypse."

His breath became labored and Akinola tried to make him stop. He was obstinate. He hoped all those months of his sickness to preach to the world and sadly, only three people were listening now. He had tried in the past but every time he did, he saw the eyes of the little men. All they had ever wanted from him was motivation for personal success and where motivation failed, some money. No one was willing to listen to his satire, as he was himself the greatest among the elites. To criticize the systems of the world was to stand the risk of sounding phony. Everyone had forgotten the truth that he owed his success and his whole life to a clique of people whose veneration of him was most of the time, patronizing. He did not really feel a sense of self until he retired. It was then that he remembered his true love.

One morning when he was driven pass his old school at Iluimo, he was met with a familiar feeling. There was a time when he wished to turn the town around for good, and neighboring Lagos, even the country. He knew he could, as there was strength in him that he alone felt, there was an aura of strong will all over him. It was not difficult to feel that way for he was brilliant and wise and brave. When he saw the fences of the school he wondered what it was that took away his mind, making him to waste five decades in the service of a man in a strange land. Perhaps he hadn't wasted the years. He took big tasty chickens in the mornings with sublime coffee and cooled off his head under the armpit of voluptuous Bahian girls. Even in marriage he was never subject to the pressures of family life. He lived a great part of his life in a hedonistic nirvana where guilt and fear is to be conquered. Whether he truly conquered, he did not know but he felt strange when he heard the cries of children used for 'experiments' in the presence of the lord of the castle. He felt strange those times he noticed a child had suddenly stopped crying. He felt strange when he waved his servants bye as they mount the truck to be ferried to another place like old time slaves. He did not intend to be wicked, neither did any of the aristocrats who frolicked at the castle but they tried too many times to assume their sins were private.

The harrowing memory of his past came to him as he spoke to Dr. Akinola. He rubbed his eyes, muttering.

"Whoever sees wrongdoing and is entertained, whoever feels pleasure at anecdotes of bad behavior threads on a sloppy pathway to wickedness. Even nature, complaint in those offenses, does not behold such with delight."

Akinola tried to help him with the cover sheath he was spreading over his body. The poor old man must have been lonely all the while for him to jump at them with multitude of words.

"I was hoping you could bear us out on a little problem my boy is encountering."

Olanusi smiled.

"Akinola, you see that I am sick."

"Absolutely sir,' Akinola interjected, 'you should take a rest. We will come back next week."

"Next week,' echoed Olanusi, 'I am clinically well and what I feel is somaticized. I need some altruism to get pass this feeling."

He laughed at himself, "I am in Erik Erickson's last stage of life; ego integrity versus despair."

Uncle Bode sat up interestedly, neither Kemi nor Akinola knew before then that he was anxious about his own mental health. His eyes met Olanusi's as the old man let out a tired voice.

"So what is it young man?"

"I..." Uncle Bode sat up some more, almost shifting out of the chair. His composure always failed in the presence of great men, making whoever observed to wonder if he was the same person who was fond of flaunting his intellect among his peers.

'I do have these funny dreams," he said at last, awkwardly wading through his newborn humility. 'I do have a constant dream and it's so like reality. I seem to exist in two worlds."

Olanusi removed the wooly sheath covering his body and joked, "No, you belong to us."

He looked longingly at his study room; the urge to smoke was coming over him. He took a pen from the floor; he'd lost it two days before, when he defiled his illness to write his essay with a suicidal courage.

"Does it affect you in any way, I mean your dreams, does it interfere with your daily routine or make you be who you don't want to be?"

"No sir' Uncle Bode replied.

"Do you engage in any irregular habit, sir?" Olanusi inquired, mirroring Uncle Bode's politeness.

"I am recovering,' Uncle Bode stuttered, almost unintelligibly.

"He takes cocaine" Akinola supplied.

"I see,' Olanusi hiccupped, careful not to sound censorious.

"The so-called abnormal disorders cannot be properly diagnosed in the presence of stimulants which produce similar symptoms to theirs', young man."

Uncle Bode made effort to suppress a coming yawn.

"You will do something for me,' Olanusi continued, 'abandon cocaine for three weeks and come back to me, let's see if you'd still have those dreams."

Uncle Bode looked away, dissatisfied. It feels terrible when the world's best does not understand.

"The mind has many layers of varying complexities," Olanusi began. He studied his patient's countenance as he droned. "Distant memories may affect adult minds especially if such memories find its way into the unconscious. As I have found in my recent research, the patient might develop instances of disturbing visions or perpetual dreams where there is serious conflict in the superego."

He paused for a moment; a new idea had entered his head. He ordered his attendant to get Uncle Bode a rest couch.

"Through the series of my unfinished researches I have discovered that dreams prepare us for those challenges we procrastinate. Through dreams, the neurons of our brains rejuvenate. We could get to know what our true problems are by analyzing what the lazy neurons sneak to the back of our eyes."

He took the couch from his attendant and placed it for Uncle Bode to sit. His passion for duty made him forget his pain.

"Can you narrate one of your dreams, maybe a recent one?"

"I saw a cat with long teeth, a big tiger."

Uncle Bode shuddered. The thought of his heart was repugnant in his mouth.

"Do you remember reading stories about tigers, ancient cat families?"

"Yes but that was when I was in the primary school."

'And what else did you see in your dream?'

"Nothing," he lied.

The truth would make even the broad-minded shiver.

That night, Uncle Bode read a lot about saber-toothed cats, how they lived on earth many thousand years before. He read about the happenings of those times, the prehistoric times and a cold shiver went down his spine when he discovered he had been dreaming of it.

ALPHA Aluminums Firm Nigeria had its administrative head office and main factory covering 12 acres site. Beside the road that led to the gracious seven storied plaza were stunning gardens and fountains. The gentle noise of the central air-conditioner and that of the 'almighty' central factory engine created a rare impression reminding people of how serious the world should be. There were virtually no human movements between the ninth and the fourteenth hour of each day. Uncle Bode drove sluggishly into the compound. He had not been to work for a week, though he was excused for only three days. He prepared himself for the questions his leanness asked. He looked drained and lost. He tried so much not to, but his eyes against his wish called for help. He reported to the welfare unit where he learnt that Musa Abdulkarim had finally taken the chairmanship post and later to his office where he slept.

WHEN HE SLEPT, he did not just pass into the dream. It was a little more chaotic. He felt like his every substance including his blood and mind and the tiniest strand of his hairs passed through a tiny tubule of a single infinitesimal strand of neuron in his brain. It was especially painful for him this time because his system was free from all stimulants. He fell on the floor, besides his desk as he gasped for breath. His head was aching. Gradually, as he traveled through that delusion, he felt increasingly better till a soothing feeling of cold breeze overwhelmed him.

He was in the wilderness, in a hunting spree with Neanderthal men, climbing the hill he remembered to be near his home. One of those creatures beckoned him to come nigh. The monkey man was dumb, like hundred others, but they made unintelligible noises. He rushed up the hill, seizing a little boy that looked more like humans. Uncle Bode thundered from below.

"Stop!"

His own word was in a strange tongue but he knew that he asked the monkey man to stop. He ran up the steep after him and protested. The word from his mind came as a lost tongue, like the old Mesopotamia's in his mouth. Before he could intercept the monkey man the child had been stabbed with a sharp stick. He looked as blood splashed over the hill surface.

He looked and remembered. He could have died like the boy few seasons back when there was a war between the kingdoms of brutish men and his own people. He remembered the time when a woman carried him in the middle of the war, as men lined up, forming a human fence round the village. He remembered the dust and cries of agony. He remembered as men of his own kind fought against one another even as the monkey men rounded them up, something he really never understood. He remembered how one of the monkey men abducted him. He'd lived with them in their own part of the world ever after, denied the knowledge of his own people.

As he watched the boy's lifeless body a flood of memories ran through his head and he recalled the series of events that led into the war in which his people suffered defeat.

In that strange world, there was a colony of men, a tiny hamlet of a hundred and twenty people, Nērubu. The people, barely clothed and unevenly toned were ignorant of how expansive the world was and they stayed in their dire land, for fear that they might fall into the 'ditch' if they moved further. There was a system of mighty hills, encompassing the little settlement of theirs and none of them had ever advanced the hills. They were gentle, they were pure, living each day to create things important for their own lives, making music and forming laws, learning everyday how to make better use of the soil and seeds. At the other side of the hills and beyond, there lived several groups of brute creatures that were rumored among the timid people of the valley to be the real owners of the world. A few among the people of the valley who woke up early often spotted them when the morning sun starts to climb. Though these 'modern' and timid humans seemed more intelligent, they never wondered where those creatures lived, if indeed there was a dish surrounding their world.

At the back of the hills was a large expanse of land where monkey men lived. Even in the other side of same hill, under, they tore the flesh of one another apart and ate, took one another's mate and invited the crowd to witness their sexual conquest. To meet their immediate needs, whatever was possible was done even if it meant offspring crushing the parent.

The people of the valley were no better but they knew what was evil and did it in secret. Among them were Şibtu, a seasoned fighter and owner of the largest farmhouse in the hamlet. He had seized the opportunity he had during one of those periods of famine to gain fortune and influence over all other men. He had passed that legacy in full measure to his children. He hoped to make Nērubu into a structured society but his life had turned out to be one dominated with guilt and bitterness. Şibtu was extremely formidable and feared by all, he smiled to no one all his adult life but he saved some smiles for the most favored among his mistresses, the one with the biggest breast, Ir'emum.

Ir'emum had two sons from different fathers, Dappanu and Asiru. Dappanu had grown into a bright, influential man and envy of his contemporaries. Once, he heard şibtu whom he grew to greatly admire talk about his ambitions for Nērubu. He grew up to be as ambitious as mighty Şibtu and imbibed in his mind the will to change the destiny of his people, the only people in existence who seemed to have the sense of guilt and the power of speech. He was born to Ir'emum's last lover who died in one of the streak of random conflicts Nērubu had with the imps who sneaked into the valley at night to steal produce from their barns. Being a child from a lowly father, Asiru worked hard to create a niche for himself and that propelled him into becoming a proud owner of hundreds of animals and a shelter. He always felt like he needed more, that he should organize Nērubu into a place with rules. He felt it as a personal need and he expected a personal glory in return.

Uncle Bode recalled the folklore of his dream. One day in the season when ice came falling, Şibtu invited his both children to his shelter.

"The cold is severe and I am afraid I cannot make it through the night."

He wanted Dappanu to start an empire but he called Asiru also, because of his considerable influence.

"I have a dream but there seem to be no much time to see it come true,' he said 'my life had been full of fantasies but I need you to do justice to those time I spent fantasizing, I want you to organize these stubborn people, to be lord over them because they need to listen to someone when the crazy creatures over the hills come with their rage". He held Asiru's hands ruefully 'I need you like I need him; I want you to support him".

That way he died, forgetting to teach that power corrupts, assuming that evil was a monopoly of his heart. There was a moment in the middle of those seasons of madness when Asiru ordered his own to make a mark on their right arm as symbol of solidarity. Dappanu did the same for his cohorts and the little hamlet of a hundred and twenty people became divided. It did not only divide, each of those sides employed the services of monkey men as mercenaries in conflict. The weird creatures they hated to see on the hilltops they had now invited to the valley.

Finally, Uncle Bode remembered everything that happened in that world, how the monkey men taught them not to fear, to satisfy their desires without guilt. The monkey men hid under the shelters of humans at night, making them happy. Whether their intimacy   advanced to the sexual he could not tell but he saw the eyes of men as they watched the monkey men and women worship one another in sensual bliss. The monkey men couldn't speak, yet they taught the real men about their world and about 'wisdom', that it was crazy to satisfy another when they are not yet satisfied. They taught men to determine what was good for themselves and go for it, even if all barricades to their wanted end was to be destroyed. The villagers taught the monkey men their language in return. Uncle Bode understood even in his dream that the monkey men's influence on them was evil but he was bemused by the fact that the monkey men also taught them an ancient, entrancing song. It was a song of justice; a song of redemption and it was puzzling who taught monkey men the song because they do not understand even the lyrics and they hardly spoke.

Uncle Bode recalled in his dream the most important discovery of their lives, when the monkey men illustrated a story for them on the ground. There was a time in the monkey men's folklore when their world was visited by a mighty host, huge and smooth, a race of men that flied, who seemed to have the powers of magic.

"You pride yourself as beautiful creatures but their own beauty dwarfs yours" one of those monkey men seemed to say. Seeing the real men green with envy was their delight for they were the most mischievous and the most odious creatures who ever walked on two feet.

Neither of the rival camps of Dappanu or Asiru owned up to the atrocious act that was going on in their own land; that the creatures they behold with disgust from the valleys now live among them. There was a time in Uncle Bode's dream, in this lost history, when the monkey men sneaked human daughters out of the valley to the outside world, behind the hills. Men who were not aligned with either Dappanu or Asiru rose up in conflict. At the beginning of the war they hoped for easy victory because they believed they were fighting a just cause but they found evil does not fold its arms and look when confronted. News of war traveled beyond the valleys earlier than they expected and in the morning they saw monkey men do revolting things at the mouth of the valley where they could be seen from below. The monkey men butchered a young boy, forced incense upon captured families and even beheaded one of their own and threw the head down. It was an act of war. The day promised to be a day of war but none of the great fathers of the village had the nerve to confess that monkey men lived among them and were receiving lessons on how to use sharp sticks in war.

Uncle remembered in his dream how monkey men descended on the camp of men, bringing atrocities of the morning a little nearer. He remembered as a monkey man soldier took him to the plains where he would live to adulthood. He hadn't seen creatures of his own kind since then and now that he had seen one, the boy had fallen.

He picked stones and threw it at the monkey men in protest and it was like the crude creatures felt no pain. They ran away contritely, making sounds that annoyed him more. They never intended to frustrate their master and all they wanted was some teeth for knife and flesh for meat. Uncle Bode knelt besides the boy and watched the monkey men whine. He could not believe he had lived his whole life with such creatures. He whispered to the boy's ears, grabbing his ribs desperately but the boy could not understand. His own version of speech was awful. He taught that he asked the boy where he came from but there was no answer.

As he sobbed he noticed something was moving in the bush. He jolted when he realized someone was watching. It was a woman, stern looking and evincing no fear. She was brown but fairer than anyone he had ever seen. A piece of tanned flesh was covering her privates. He had always wanted to invent such clothing but the monkey men laughed at him each time he tried (they were most of the time, nude). When he looked, he remembered how the monkey men pounced on humans during the conflict. He had dreamed all his life to repeat the sadism. A familiar feeling of cruelty rushed through his blood but he hesitated. He was wise enough to understand the woman was calm for a reason. He was human.

"You born this?" He said.

The woman nodded. There was too much sadness in the air and it was a waste to weep.

"How long have you been living with them?" she vouchsafed to ask. He was happy that she understood his dialect and he postponed his thought.

"Been living with them for too long," he replied

"How many cold seasons?"

He gave a look that warned his friendliness would be short-lived.

"We do not know numbers here."

She moved briskly to lift the boy's head. He was dead but she cuddled it and kissed the head.

"We?" she queried as she dragged the corpse to rest its head on a fallen trunk. He stared, enthralled by the strange culture of the woman for there was no memory of kindness in his head. All he had ever seen was men finding pleasure in inflicting pain on another, scavenging on corpses. The best of kindness he had seen was them riveted by one another's body and that itself was no kindness for each tried to subdue another, even to the point of death. Now he had seen a creature of his own kind and he had seen a piece of meat treated with so much affection. He knew humans were beautiful; he needed no further proof for the perfect young lady he had just seen. He knew they were of somewhat progressive nature. He was completely thrilled by the piece of clothing he saw that only existed in his imagination before then. The dark thought of his heart was overshadowed by the new desire to be like one of them, to show kindness even to a piece of meat.

15

SOLA Aderomoke's reputation as broadcaster had skyrocketed. Even the bigwigs of the teevee made crazy offers and turned nuisance at her door. She had boosted her profile with a new degree and she had read a piece from her research before world diplomats in the United Nations. Two weeks after she returned to New York, her thin but elegant frame had graced the cover page of Marie Claire. Her documentaries were getting far less attention and she appeared bigger than even her employers more and more. There were occasions when she received big proposals from big style companies, mouth-watering proposals that could see her resign her job. She knew very well that style was not one of those things she'd got, the bones of her chest were unbecoming of a lady's and there was a leather shirt she could not stop wearing. The world's eyes were blind to it all and everything she laid her eyes upon slid to her feet.

A decade earlier, she was in the remotest part of Lagos. Her father whose limb got broken in an accident would look at her in her mother's hands and think, *poor unlucky girl, she shouldn't have entered her mother's womb*. His disabilities had cost him his means of livelihood because he was a tailor, fully dependent on leg driven machines. He learnt about the wealthy phinaltropist who owned a large orphanage, Owolabi. In the week that followed, the poor man tried his luck with the philanthropist who later agreed to assist him in raising his baby girl and keep her among children his foundation was catering for. Sola Aderomoke was four then, too young to feel embarrassed by anything but she could understand she belonged to the lowly class. She had learnt to be quiet in the midst of kids from affluent families and to listen. Even at seven, she would wonder what was it that made her own father care so much for a small piece of bread while other kids lived carefree lives. She wasn't a sweet little girl, she was as cautious of life as she could be, having seen poverty and diseases face to face. One sweet memory of hers was not of Christmas but the day her only brother was born. In her own mind she allowed herself to believe that a new fortune would follow the new baby but she noticed they could hardly afford a meal in a day. The new child was twice unlucky; his poor diet suffered him his brain and growth. His intelligence quotient was not even up to twenty. A physician had disclosed later that he was not a cretin that he would improve with time and the family lived on with hope, as did many people who ever carried on.

Sola Aderomoke as a little girl would withdraw from the "ten ten" game whenever a couple of kids she perceived as privileged came around. She expected to be discriminated and hoped to be persecuted. Since the time she heard from the pulpit that the persecuted were blessed, she felt a comforting feeling that God was on her side. Most of the times she found the little persecutions she sensed from time to time was illusory, making her to doubt if she had any reason to be blessed. Every time she was treated with kindness she would fear that the blessing she desperately needed was being diverted to who was blessed already. The 'privileged' ones who tried to be her friend was more like "Jesus' children" than her. When they smiled, they smiled well. They used to cuddle her and talk about her long hair and exceptionally white eyes, but for Sola, she swore too much and she always pretended not to understand when a male friend from the neighborhood explored her body.

Sola Aderomoke was a child bred in penury and she behaved like one, but in looks, she never looked like one of her family's. The nerves of her face were calm and the hair on her head was healthy and shiny. The way she looked at people, she seemed to expect no miracles from no one; she looked like she was anxiously waiting to grow up and become like one of the women her mother worked for. When her father told her about the kiddies' den, he felt a little weird about it and he feared for the kind of glare that would permeate her face, not that he cared but for the reason that Sola 's Mona lisa's smile was both frustrating and piercing.

When Sola learned about the kiddies' den she felt excited and she laughed like was expected of a little girl. It was her last bout with ego and she gave in to the fact she could never use the kind of sunglasses and butterfly-hair-bind that her two friends use. Her new romance with reality brought her peace and she learned to be the humble and lowly little girl she was always afraid to be.

In the 'Kiddies den' her new life was easier than she anticipated. There were thirty boys and girls and one of them was like her. She made her first best friend and she fell in love with the place fast, calling it 'home' after living there for only a fortnight.

Mr. John was the tutor. He taught English, Mathematics and a bit of Geography. His English was more like pidgin, his arithmetic horrible, it would have been better if he hadn't taught the innocent kids at all. He would enter the class at his own time and say '1983 elections, no cheating' and the kids would reply 'no foul play'.

Behind the 'Kiddies den' was a large coffee plantation covering six acres land. None of the kids could have possibly imagined that there was a field of such magnificence behind their hostels. Mr. John told them the little they needed to know and gave them portions. They handpicked ripe cherries from the trees, then soaked it in water and left it to ferment. When the cherries were fermented and its pod extracted they washed and spread it out in the sun. It was during the harvesting period that Mr. John told the kids that Nigeria was burning. The kids gathered around him then, and listened to his rumor. It took Sola years to understand that what actually happened was a coup attempt. It was also in the harvesting period that Sola met Tunji Owolabi.

Tunji was three years older, gregarious and popular among the fifteen girls of the 'den'. With the way he talked to them and the love he showed them, it was difficult to imagine that there existed a more special room in his heart for yet another person. He recognized there was one with a peculiar face whose laughter was always short-lived. His wit was good for his age and he made everyone laugh but he worried for the enigmatic little one who only chuckled. One afternoon when Sola seated beside a coffee tree he walked into the shade where she was, and babbled

"I feel we aren't doing you guys any favor here."

Sola smiled, her face brewing with innocence and strength.

"I feel you are doing us a great favor."

Her words were pregnant and the more he wondered, the more he loved her. And they became best friends.

While others worked at the coffee plantation she would study at the Owolabis' family library. It was the defining moment of her life because she read the weirdest books from the strangest authors, listened to the most ethereal songs inspired by the most solemn parts of ancient history. It was not the best way to grow, she knew. She knew what ought to be as she watched her self grow. A great destiny was awaiting her, and she felt it from the breeze that blew through the lonely windows, but the powers that beckoned were not of light but of gloom and desperation. She'd seen a man once introduced as Mr Gbajumo peek at her with an older man who seemed a lot more cautious and who spoke in hushed tones.

On the eve of her seventeenth birthday, the day that she read *The shift of powers* as translated by an alumnus, she felt like she would faint and she fell into the hands of Mr. Gbajumo who was snooping to know why she was always alone. It seemed so like accident, yet so like fate as she fell into the hands of whom would tell her that all she ever suspected was valid, that the road to success isn't necessarily glorious. The new girl of the spotlight was born the day she first spoke to Gbajumo one on one. When Gbajumo spoke, she concentrated on his moustache as it moved up and down and wondered what it was that made her thought that the man was peculiar. He was not the comfort that she wanted, in fact he was a new page of mystery, almost as mystifying as the book that took her stamina away.

Gbajumo ran the Lagos branch of an hedonist society which started two years before as a parody to organized religion. 'The believers' as they are called, gathered every Friday nights and Sunday mornings. On Sundays, they would tell and listen to different testimonies mocking faith and making travesty of any hymn that came to their minds. They had good laughs, even words came around that a couple indeed joined the society because they loved to laugh. Friday nights used to be a short version of Sunday activities but now it had become a party of some sorts. Those nights, there were dim blue light, soft jazz, coffee and quiet giggles here and there. A good fraction of 'The believers' wanted more but there were few dissidents who only wanted to laugh. It is being rumored that the branch in New York did more than talk or party on Friday nights. There were only a few members and there was a need to fly in more emigrants to participate in the sensual revelries. Gbajumo was the first Nigerian initiate of 'The believers', approached by the World Chancellor when he stopped by a night comedy club during a business trip to Lagos. Gbajumo was a failed career comedian at that time but he did made the visiting old man laugh, at least with what he said about the rosaries and the crucifix.

"Spread our message to Nigeria and inherit the world," the old American said that night, his eyes blinking for the blue neon light that shined directly into it. Since then, Gbajumo's fortune had turned around for better and he had convinced dozens who were giving up on the systems of the world, dozens more of people who wanted to run away from their past and make light of what was left of their lives. Gbajumo met Owolabi through the foreigner and ever since then, he had conducted meetings of 'The believers' at the Coffee Hall, an auditorium within the "children's den" having a capacity of about six hundred.

When Sola clocked seventeen, Gbajumo told her to "Spread the word to America and inherit the world," then gave her a visa and student scholarship notification. That day, she felt a little dizzy because a lot of things happened too quickly and she slept off in the library. In the middle of the night she was awakened by a creepy sound. She hid herself in a dark corner behind the shelves. The sound came closer and Tunji finally opened the door. She gathered her books with a sigh of relief. While she was thinking about how to scare him back, she saw him inject himself with hard drugs. He was strangely unaware of her presence. That night, Sola stepped back, stooped and rested her head on a fat book. She never intended to sleep, not with the fear of being caught peeping, but she eventually opened her eyes to the next bright morning.

Gbajumo and a senior Believer came early the following morning to formally inform Owolabi about the scholarship. That was the first time Sola saw Owolabi eye to eye. He was a huge man with rough chin, the man who peeked from the library verandah together with Gbajumo about three weeks before. He sat on a low upholstery and faced Sola who stood five feet seven into the air.

"Lucky gir," he droned as he stared. Sola recognized the look on his face was not that of someone that was seeing her for the first time. Owolabi wrinkled his brow as he spotted the scar on her neck but he seemed generally satisfied with what he saw, as though it was important for her to look good.

"Young lady, I bet you must have seen actresses, dancers.. singers' he shrugged, 'you see, some of them sell their skills for peanut. They loose because they are not smart enough to assume their rightful place and become great, powerful and rich. If you work hard and obey, you will be like one of us in no time"

She did not hear him; she was busy studying his face. He looked a little different from how he did in the dailies. She had seen his face once in the newspaper with the caption 'I will transform coffee production in Nigeria'. She felt proud that she was conversing with a man of the papers but the things she was noticing terrified her. It was scary thinking those things and she even scolded herself for being so distrusting. What was undeniable was that she was unhappy in spite of the good news. She was used to difficulty and disappointment so much that she presumed her journey would bring either. Her new best friend in the kiddies' den told her not to worry but she noticed a familiar tone in her friend's voice; a tone of artificial positivism that she despised. She looked elsewhere for a chat and Tunji proved more convincing; told her it was okay to be paranoid sometimes, that she was afraid only because her life was to change forever, for better. Inside the Kiddies' Den garden, below the scorching sun that bright Monday, he declared a new day had come for her.

Sola felt she owed him a favor. She could do him a lot of good by taking the drug away from him. She remembered the Nigerian police slogan, 'Police is your friend' and reported him to them, believing he would be slapped in the wrist. She was a seventeen year old whose education never centered on the basic things.

FINALLY the Limo arrived and Gbajumo lightened up. He'd been waiting at the airport for hours to hire one. Sola opened her eyes to spot the car; white and looking bigger than she anticipated. She'd been having funny dreams about it in the past few minutes. She even dreamt that

Gbajumo said it was a surprise present for her and she saw her mother in Virgin airline hostess' uniform applauding. When she saw her mother, she remembered the woman was supposed to be in Lagos and realized it was only a dream.

"Thank you Richie."

Gbajumo's voice came quietly in the middle of the street's crunching noise as Sola stretched her muscles.

A new hit urban song that she just fell in love with played inside the car. She tried not to sing along but she moved to the music as she looked through the blinds to enjoy the view of downtown Brooklyn. It didn't take long before she felt the New York magic. She'd learned about Verrazano Narrows Bridge in school, once the longest single span suspension bridge in the world, connecting Brooklyn with Staten Island where the castle was located. Over the Narrows, Gbajumo stopped the Limo contemplatively.

"You got me jealous, girl, the master seem to have special interest in you,' he got a little chatty, 'you are to become the finest tevee presenter in two years, owner of the largest media outfit ever, in fifteen years."

He chuckled as he took a white envelope from the three-deck cabinet dividing them. Indeed there was a document detailing the road map for that plan.

"But I do not want to be a presenter" came Sola's jittery voice.

"What do you want to be?"

"A doctor"

"Oh..doctor' he raised his brow as though he was giving it a thought 'some folks are taking care of that already."

"What do you mean?" Sola's confidence was building up and she was surprised herself that she could speak in the face of so much intimidation.

"Take a look at this,' Gbajumo detached an hanging mirror to her face, 'what do you see?"

She looked away coyly, to the giant cables that supported the bridge, the Narrows wasn't narrow at all. Gbajumo looked down her skirt.

"What we see is glamour, Oprah. You will become the most influential woman of the media and those cowards will marvel when you speak good of what they've known all their sorry lives to be evil."

"Evil? Sounds scary.' Sola tried to breath 'Sir, do you want to scare me? How are you sure I will like this idea?"

"Nobody sees the glamour and the splendor of the castle and turn back. Every passion is rooted in power and power we give freely."

"Teacher says power corrupts.." she paused and realized it was a faux pas what she was about to say. Gbajumo smiled and nodded

"You may speak."

"I don't want to be evil, I don't want to be a bad girl."

She looked at Gbajumo's face for the first time since they left the airport in Lagos.

"Neither are we forcing you."

"I want to leave."

She opened the door to threaten him. It was too unfamiliar outside, too unnerving. She went back inside.

"I am sorry girl, you may have to rest and eat before you call your parents, and it's been a long day."

They were both silent for a moment, as the car sped over the bridge. Only the smooth fuzzy sound of the car and the FM alone were audible and the outside seemed like a movie as Sola looked through the tinted glass. Gbajumo broke the silence just about the time Barry White's *Practice what you preach* played.

"I see you never vouch for yourself like some people do. Trust me girl, your doubts will melt away when you live the dream."

Sola faced him and the sly smile on her face was beautiful.

"What makes you so sure that I want your kind of life?"

"You indicated in the quiz that you want to be a star, you want to be rich and famous and successful..."
Sola interrupted.
"Teacher taught us to say those things. You know, you aim at the sun so you don't fall below the moon."
"Teacher taught you to speak the truth. You would do anything to become that woman you dream to become."
He started the car.
"When I mentioned that nobody sees glamour and turn back, I see that you never refuted my claim."
He stopped talking because Sola was not paying attention.
"Look at that."
He pointed westward to the tower carrying a beam of light about three miles away, 'that is the castle where you will live and school but I am taking you to my house first, you've got to see my wife and friends, they cannot wait to meet you."
Sola looked through the rear mirror. The tower was rising above other buildings that overlooked a body of water. As the car moved into the east wing of the Island farther away from the tower, she turned her head and kept looking till a truck blocked the little view that was left at the skyline. She looked forward and asked calmly.
"Sir, why do you do what you do?"
Gbajumo sighed as he negotiated a bend in the road.
"Same reason why your fathers invented religion."
He hesitated and then continued.
"Power. We are tired of being judged, tired of making excuses for who we are or what we do. We want to take over everything so that we might be the one to write laws and enforce it. We will become the best doctors and lawyers and soldiers and politicians and ..."
"Stop!" Sola shouted, almost in tears. She was horrified because she saw Gbajumo's face was becoming red as he spoke, reddened with passion. She looked away panting, opening her mouth a little to breath and she jolted as

darkness came over. The car had passed under a huge tree.

LIFE SEEMED a lot different at the wooded side of Straten Island even though the business district wasn't too far away. There was a majestic tree at the side of the tiny road that led to the street where Gbajumo's New York home was sited. The tree's roots were damaging the road surface and the trunk was taking almost a quarter of the road at the sharp bend. It seemed like no one was paying attention to the dangers of that infringement. Over the bushes were medieval buildings that were either tall indeed or standing upon a hill.

Sola noticed a graffito on the side of the road: *I hate the police*. She was starting to find the place interesting because there was something in her that really cocured with the ambiance of that countryside, same thing that made her lampoon in a quiz essay, the fact that she had to be busy working by all means, every morning. She saw girls her age in scanty dresses lazy away in the streets and she thought that one of them looked back with a puckish smile to see if anyone was lusting after the view. There were burnt facilities adjacent to the junction where the road parted to Gbajumo's house and the rest of the community. Sola could not help asking about it.

"A couple of guys set the place on fire some years ago.' Gbajumo supplied, 'they went mad when the police tried stopping their party."

"Why try to stop their party?"

She tried to douse her tension because they were at their destination already and dozens of people were waiting to receive them.

"They made too much noise," Gbajumo replied. He smiled when he spotted a slim beautiful woman among the waiting crowd.

"It happened a long time ago and those two boys are grandfathers now. They own large corporations and they founded the movement of the believers, they are to become the first among the free men of the world in the glorious time when there will be no more laws or nations."

Sola opened the door and for a moment she felt her legs were weightless. The crowd cheered and applauded. She looked sideways and realized the cheers were for her. It was totally weird to be applauded; she had never received a card on her birthday before then. There was nothing commendable about her and the cheering did her no good. She walked up to the crowd at Gbajumo's bidding, her steps fast and filled with apology.

"Here she is,' said the woman whose eyes met Gbajumo's from the car. She introduced herself as Gbajumo's wife. 'Dear, you look every inch like you think, so free and so beautiful."

Her breath was fast. She took Sola by the hand and introduced her to the strangers towering above her meek figure.

"I love the part where you called your little teacher an opportunists, it's my favorite," said the tall one with funny dentition. Sola returned a smile and respired as she bowed, having known the reasons for their affection. Apparently, everyone was acquainted with the short essays she was asked to write in the last school term, an essay about punishment and fear. She never expected anyone to like it, as it was the private indulgent thoughts of a girl who saw too much hazes whenever she tried to see her future.

She followed Gbajumo's wife through the rows of those twenty people who wanted to speak to her. At the end of the row was a plump woman in a light blue uniform. She had the biggest smile among them. She was the one assigned to be Sola's attendant in the castle.

"Happy to meet you, ma." Sola smiled back. There was something about the woman that calmed her nerves, maybe the smooth light skin and the sweet look of a mother.

"Call me Aunty," she said as she took Sola's hands.

The buildings within the castle seemed to have been constructed a long time ago and if it was not, it must have been planned by a brilliant architect whose mission was to create a feeling of old, maybe a feeling of barbarism because there were underage half naked girls in the upper passageway, ambling to the delight of a certain old man who rested his head on a rail like he was sick. Sola looked up as the woman in blue uniform pulled her by the hand. The castle was more than eighty meters high and there was a rectangular courtyard in the middle. Passageways extended into the courtyard at the ground floor, and in the upper floors, it was simply suspended into the air above the yard and it was lined with railings. There were more girls in the castle than she could have ever imagined, young ladies from different stock and culture but they shared one thing in common; they were orphans and they were all beautiful. As Sola would learn, each of them had mastered a craft that would see them becoming the best in their chosen fields. The life of 'freedom' and pleasure for them, went beyond the quest to sooth their bodies for they were thought the principles of intemperance- that which would wash them clean from guilt that religion and culture bestowed upon them. There were young good-looking boys in the castle too.

Sola examined her own skin for a moment and wondered if she was qualified to live with those perfect creatures. Aunty Bay took her through one unending piazza, lined on the left side with rooms. They finally arrived at Sola's designated room after fifteen minutes of walk.

It was a large room with very high ceiling. It felt like another world inside because the room was shut away from the outside noise. Closest to the door was a twin bed adorned with bouquets of flowers. A plasma television was adjacent and few inches ahead, there were transparent curtains draping over the Vinyl floor. There was a bathtub at the other side, and a toilet, which was the only facility secluded with a door.

 A knock came at the door as Aunty Bay showed Sola to the room. Bay went to answer and she returned with a white pajamas and towel. After boring Sola with details of how a great interior designer from Italy flew in to design the rooms of the castle, the maid finally handed her the towel and the sleeping cloth.

"Thank you ma."

Sola had suddenly felt the urge to make her stay and talk more, she's been staring at the pajamas in the woman's hand for the past ten minutes.

"This place is nice.' she pulled the maid's hands, hoping to start another round of discussion 'Guess I will always see you around ma?"

"Oh dear!' the woman tapped Sola's round cheek, gave her the look of assurance, and faced the door.

"Save for a last minute alteration, I will be deployed to L.A next week."

"There is another castle at Los Angeles?" Sola moaned

The woman finally walked away.

"Yes dear, we stay too long in a place, they become uncomfortable."

"Why?" Sola's eyes followed her to the door. The woman rolled her eyes and left. Sola sighed as the door jammed "Wow."

She must have nauseated the woman with too many questions. As she turned around, she noticed a mirror hanging next to the wardrobe. She was looking radiant. She never expected to see a pretty face after the stress of carrying a heavy luggage through the endless passageway. The fresh smell of the towel around her neck was relaxing, and the rock music that played quietly from the room adjoining. She smiled at herself through the mirror and inspected the perfect set of teeth. She was not looking too bad at all and she would fit into the opulent castle of beautiful men and women if only she could get rid of the little scar on her neck. She resolved to start acting like a lady and she yanked her cloth as she slid the dividing curtain at her room, ready to go and bath. The moment she dipped her foot into the Roman bathtub, she noticed a small window at the top right corner of the room and shadows of two men talking. She understood whoever showered was to be spied on, and she became convinced that she was in a kingdom of perverts. She stopped the running tap and slid into the tub, at least she'd seen one in the movies. She tried to listen to the two men who must have peeped.

"Happy birthday, doctor' one of those men said.

"Guilt' the doctor sighed audibly, 'every time I try to run away from guilt I feel drawn to it the more."

His accent was Nigerian.

"Meaning you aren't trying enough," the second man said, dropping the glass in his hands to take a quick look at the castle's latest catch who was scrubbing her body with a loofa, eight feet below.

"This black one isn't bad at all,' he chuckled 'And she is seventeen."

Sola looked away, pretending to be unaware, wondering if they cared that she might be listening.

"That is the problem, buddy,' the doctor said, 'what we are doing is wrong."

"Says who?' the other's voice came a little louder, 'who tells you what is wrong or not, the magistrate who came around to our party last night or the mayor from Europe, the bishop who begged for a face mask?"

"The law," answered the doctor with a pacifying voice, he seemed intimidated by the second's temper. The second man rested his hands on his friend's shoulder.

"Wait until we become the law."

He walked away from the windows but his voice remained. "When we become the law, we decide what is right or wrong. We become real leaders who do not leave their destiny into the hands of one hypothetical omniscient being."

"No,' the doctor interjected sharply. 'You speak like devil these days, pal."

"Could we be more like him? We evade taxes, yet we punish peasants who try to imitate us, we finance the media to preach what makes us happy, we recycle children here every month, African, Asian kids."

"I can't do this no more' the doctor screamed. The testament of his friend had pierced his soul. He left the window too but his friend must have intercepted as he approached the door.

"You gonna spend the rest of your life in courtrooms if you walk away. You've sinned too much to become a saint."

Sola tried stepping out of the tub quietly and she tiptoed to the walls, paying attention to the low voices that was coming from the upper room.

"Are you gonna act so cheaply, blackmail me?" came the soft voice. There were no replies.

"I choose my former life."

Sola thought that the first man left but another voice came, jolting her.

"Go ahead and choose the life of fables and baseless hope."

"You choose a life dedicated to your own impulse and it alone," the other replied. He must be sitting now. The second man chuckled dryly.

"You speak of impulse as though I made myself. Who made me to love making decisions for my country and to love spending my holidays in the Caribbean? If impulses were to be denied then I would be denying nature itself, a greater misdemeanor by my own reckoning."

The doctor moved to the window, "when I still lived with grandma, she used to say: the world is doomed and every man who loves it."

"You listen when they tell you the world is doomed? You'd rather be in love with some hypothetical world against the one you can see?"

"But you are not an humanist either," the doctor replied

"Yes I am not and I do not pretend to be one. All the love I've got is for who I choose to give, not for my country, not God."

The doctor, shaken by the other's resolve, spoke more compliantly.

"I suppose we are being mocked. We hear speeches and get inspired but we learn every time no man truly wants brotherhood. We donate our money to men not worthy to clean our shoes."

The second man took the words from his friend's mouth.

"We are fed with lies, always. Now it is our turn to play the game. Let the thugs become the masters."

The two would never stop talking. Sola withdrew to the bed and breezed into the duvet. There was a magazine on top of the bed and a menu list indicating events of the week. She was to be called upon to meet other members of the castle in an hour. She read through the magazine; there was a poem in the fourth page, written by an inmate from the state prison. That wasted poet had pleaded guilty to charges of burglary early in that year, rapping the judge to his face- a spectacle that dominated the media for many days, triggering his notoriety. Sola saw her write-up too. She'd said almost the same thing as the prison guy and she wondered why. She must have written about pain and punishments, as her teacher instructed her to write, one moment when she realized her family had abandoned her in the kiddies' den. Someone had placed that magazine on her bed intentionally. She read intently and her appetite for eavesdropping sharpened more. She went to the other side of the room to see if the men were still talking. Like hell, they were.

"You speak of these men as evil, most of the people the world once celebrated yet you plot to carpet their legacies with greater evil," One of those men said quietly.

"Senseless?' the other reiterated and tried to laugh. A dry cough came instead. 'You see, everything is senseless; a thief takes from another thief. I am afraid it is all about survival."

"And what is the use of this survival knowing that someday everything will sedate to nothingness?"

A deep sigh of contemplation followed.

"Remember our classes at the College? Every time we are shown animations of the sperm cells rushing to the egg, I feel there is a reason for that rush." He paused for a moment and it was like he was panting.

"There is no such thing as nothingness. There are countless instances in nature where a tiny range of conditions need be met for life to be sustained."

"Sounds like luck?'

Sola was lost, not certain who was talking.

"Maybe luck, but what is the place of a man whose mind find no rest? Every time I muse over these things I become lured to the comfort of my mind, that nature itself is indifferent to what is good or bad."

The other man sighed too.

"Every time I leave the door,' he pointed northward, 'every time, I feel like a mark is being made against my name in some book." He rubbed his face and made a silly laugh, "Our doubts, my friend, might well be the greatest prove of all, that someone is coming for all persons who desecrate common sense."

"But I have found too many exceptions to every law that I have put to test and I can't help concluding there are no laws at all." Sola was sure now it was the second man that just talked.

"But we learnt there was a conscious design for everything. There seem to be someone who obeys the laws of the cosmos to put everything into place."

"Did he form the law or did he obey the law?" the second man's voice was pensive and coarse 'If the latter is the case, then I'd be more confounded, because the laws of nature itself is inconsistent and most of the time, unfair. Spare me your sermon, friend, I don't want to believe that I am right in doing what I do."

The doctor laughed quietly.

"I bet it is safe to conclude that nature itself is indifferent and inconsistent but there exist a power outside nature that corrects the wrong, which will ultimately redeem the cosmos."

The doctor swallowed the tot left in his glass.

"There is nature and there is a hand greater than nature that makes it perfect."

The room was lighted more the moment the first man talked, casting a more distorted shadow to the curtains.

"Look at this." He paused for a moment. He must be showing his friend a thing on the computer. "I have used so many permutations thinkable, to see what becomes of an entity which entails different combinations of these chemical compositions but none seem to make any sense."

"Like I said," the second man interjected

"Yes. All these components are meaningless except a conscious external force acts on it to give it a meaning. Good reasoning has made me to conclude that in the end, a law greater than the laws of nature shall abide."

THERE WAS NO spectacular view for that room. Sola looked from the windows curiously and all she saw was the tiny road that she took during the day. There was only a single streetlight by the roadside. She remembered it was fall when she saw the tree that was encroaching on the road. She was a little sleepy but she needed to stay awake till 10pm when she would be called upon for the last schedule in the day. Her stomach was unsettled because she was to be hosted by the whole community in a dinner. Suddenly, she stopped blinking and became watchful for movements within the bushes. She thought that she saw a thing run across the road. Just as she was about giving up, she saw four men run across the street into the bushes and she started hearing the whirling sounds of a helicopter. There came a bang. She closed the windows swiftly and ran to her bed. There was another burst and she lay on the hard cold floor, her heart throbbing. The gunshot came nearer and nearer, it seemed like it was unsafe to stay in that room but there was chaos in the courtyards too. Hundreds were scrabbling for safety. Suddenly, the screams of the ladies and the men came louder. She raised her head to see the door to her room was opened and she saw people's feet as they ran to the west wing of the castle.

"Come over, dear," a woman waved from the door. She was a little relieved to see it was the maid assigned to her, Aunty Bay, but the loudest of the booms that came in that instant spoiled her joy.

"Come quickly!" The maid was loosing her patience. Sola rose up to meet her, shivering and keeping her head down. The crowd ran towards the right and another group surged to the left, forming a stampede. The maid held Sola tightly at the fist and pulled her through the desperate crowd that was screaming and cursing their luck in many strange languages. The maid took her through one secret emergency stairs that was unknown to no one but the big sharks of the castle. The Police hoped to capture men who took that route but no one was falling into the trap. It was drizzling outside, and several police cars were waiting. The maid flung Sola into the car

"You are safe, dear."

She slipped into a bulletproof jacket, and fetched herself a gun.

"You have caused one hell of a panic over there," she rushed to the car having a microphone and announced, "everyone is advised to empty his or her pocket and raise their hands up. This estate is under the surveillance of the state police."

Still shivering, Sola watched a brown fume rise above the tower. The powerful halogen lights from the helicopter must be tricking her sight. She gasped and tried to be calm. Police instruction echoed, the car microphone must have been connected with the central sound system of the group of buildings. Sola's heavy eyes searched for a good way to lay her head. It was supercilious to try to sleep, she quickly realized. She tried to stay awake and enjoy the pride of witnessing a drama of such magnitude. She began to percieve the gunfire as friendly, knowing that she was in safe hands. She felt like the princess of the cops in the car and the old blues that played inside helped perfect her quaintly special moment. Her new confidence would not last. She started noticing a different tone of fire, wild and fierce and she noticed the partying cops were loosing their cool.

"The air is poisoned!" came a voice from the radios. She heard the officer's voice thin out into the surrounding noise of gunshots. The suspects were fighting back.

"Reinforcement," the lady officer who manned the cars cried to the phone, 'members of the castle are being killed with an air poison, one of our men possibly lost."

Sola came down from the car, no one was guarantying her safety any more and to run to the bushes was suicide because young men and ladies fled the dark woods, throwing up and falling to the fields with their faces down.

THE EARLY MORNING SUN climbed over surrounding forest, right down to her skin. She opened her eyes to see she had been covered with a white sheet having the state police insignia. Not many woke up to see the beauty of that morning or the beautiful mist that formed in the bushes. There were dead people all over. She saw the faces of the remaining few that was being gathered- young beautiful people who was in the process of inspiring her interest in fashion. She had a little problem seeing the fly hover the face of one with piercing on the lips. She walked up to the men who were packing the corpses to a truck.

"What happened?"

"You fainted."

She puffed, "I mean what happened to these people?"

"The bad guys killed them so they won't talk."

She moved close, attempting to touch the body.

"I saw her dance at the balcony yesterday. She seemed pretty sure of everything."

"Not anymore, girl," The cop scoffed at her childish wit.

She turned back, miffed by the officer's coldness. The woman that she met at the castle the previous night approached from the East gate.

"Surprise?" she stretched her arms and smiled. Had Sola forgotten the face, she still would have recalled for the quirky smile.

"Glad that you are safe,' Sola walked into the embrace. 'You don't look like a policewoman."

"I work with the state Counter-terrorism agency' the woman supplied.

"Those guys, we've been at their backs for many years and what you saw yesterday ought to be a major defeat for the greatest threat to the freedom we all enjoy."

Sola objected that those people also talked about freedom.

"Like almost everyone who ever tried to rule fellow men," a male security agent butted in. He looked quite friendlier than the one who was packing the corpses. Sola understood the easiness on his face. He was the boss and bosses find it easier to be cordial because they are not the ones doing the dirty jobs. His face was unshaven and his hairs unkempt but underneath that mess was a very good-natured man.

"Mister Bay,' he shook hands with Sola like old time friends, 'perhaps you've met my wife, Mrs Bay."

The maid of the previous night smiled and then remembered it was out of place to smile at that moment. She turned her body towards her husband, assuming a more professional posture

"We've gone through their fact file and we see that they have a very brilliant and all-inclusive roadmap to what they called the Ultimate Takeover."

"Takeover?' Sola hovered her gaze between the couple. 'Mister Gbajumo told me about taking over. I guess those people have serious problems with the government here."

"Not only here,' Mrs. Bay leaned in, they co-opt vulnerable people around the world; neglected war veterans, homosexuals, underpaid geniuses, unemployed ex-convict."

Sola gave a long look

"Am I vulnerable?"

"No sweetie,' Mrs. Bay palmed her soft cheeks, 'they also co-opt young men and women who have great potentials, they train them with the hope of using them for their so called ultimate takeover."

Mr. Bay lifted Sola's luggage and headed to the last waiting truck.

"Their budget for last year was $900 million, this year it is half because the state is already frustrating their finances secretly.

"I wonder why they are so resolved," Mrs. Bay looked into her husband's eye for an answer. 'Why does a group of people map out a strategy that spans through generations, why do they network the world?"

Mr. Bay dropped the bag and quipped

"Why did I abandon the med school in Quebec for a criminology course in New York?" he looked around playfully like he was sorting for an answer in the air. "Passion" he supplied. The wife sank herself into his arms. "And when you kept asking about my school during the student exchange program, I wondered why," her voice was meshed in a sober nostalgia. 'I can't even remember giving you my address then."

"Yes I left your dormitory immediately after you mentioned it to your hostess because I needed to pen it down."

They both laughed a restrained and cautious laughter.

"Remember the Prof who introduced us when your bus arrived in our campus? He was my instructor and a preacher too. He preached kindness but refused to give his recommendation when I needed it because I performed rock music against his counsel.

His wife turned around to face him as he raised his voice

"I hated everyone who preached anything."

"So what happened?" Mrs. Bay's sullen voice was barely audible.

"And I left Quebec for New York to find you."

THE BAY FAMILY lived in an isolated countryside, on a steep grade, sixty feet above the old basal route that led to the castle. It was difficult to understand how that big piece of land was an integral part of a bigger, tightly fenced estate. Visitors never knew, as it was a security secret necessary for the preservation of the agents commissioned to investigate the castle with a few more nasty urban groups. The Bay family had been living there for five years since the time they signed a security contract with the state. Before their snuggery was an extensive lawn, the site of birds' evening fiestas. One of the first things Sola noticed in the house was that it wasn't too homely, not even for the couple. Their baby stayed with the granny somewhere in the heart of the city. There were no hanging frames, no pictures or shoe racks. The couple also spoke in hushed tones even when it was certain no one was eavesdropping. They lived not too far to the enemy whom they were stupendously paid to smoke out. They did not know the true capacity of those weird guys, weren't even sure if the enemies were having their own counter investigation. Every time Mrs. Bay went to work in the castle, she attached a remote alarm machine to her skin. She was the only servant whose face never brightened up when the great men of the castle perform their deadly fetish acts on the kids; she was the only maid who never joined them. She knew her days in the castle were numbered and that was the reason for the hasty and poorly planned aggression that left none of those men arrested.

Sola jumped to her bed and slept off when she was shown to her room, waking up twice to eat, twice to make a call to her parents and one more time to take a medication Mrs. Bay promised would calm her nerves. The couples seemed apologetic about the fact that she was made to witness the ugly incidence of the previous night and they assumed that her long sleep was a mild protest. They planned to make her see a therapist before she started talking to any state agent; they were too descent to think it was proper for anyone to see what she saw without getting affected. She was indeed affected not by the sight of kids her age dying, but by the continuing twist of her life. Everything seemed too much like a movie, and she was occupied by the thought of how it would end.

She woke up around 2a.m with memories of gunshots and shatters of glass of the previous night. The door to her room was wide open and a white florescent light was reflected from the sitting room. She moved towards the light, half-asleep.

The couple were sorting files in the sitting room, both wearing glasses and sipping a cup of some hot drink. They looked tremendously tired.

"Here in the states they are called Human Renaissance, in Africa they are called the believers."

Mr. Bay paused abruptly.

"Wait a minute."

Sola stepped back because she feared she would be forced back to bed. She wrongly presumed Mr. Bay's sudden outburst was because of her.

"They exist too in the UK," Mr. Bay whined, 'we must have been fetching the sea with cups to make it dry."

"How did you know?" Mrs. Bay yawned. She was unmoved. Sola lay close to a glass door, enjoying the view of the couple in white pajamas.

"You won't believe this, in the UK the group act as a fully registered orphanage and it administered by well respected men."

He sat on the floor and took a closer look at the files. Mrs. Bay rubbed her palm against the mug.

"Darling you should take it easy, this work is overwhelming you.' She paused and shook her head, 'we don't have to suspect every institution in the world just because we are right this once."

"No, you gotta see this. Last week, there was a major exchange between the Human Renaissance and the orphanage, sited at a countryside close to London."

Mrs. Bay's undecided eyes fell on him, but there was also a mocking smile on her face, making it seem like she was oggling.

"Many innocent people work in the castle without even the slightest idea of what goes on there, everyday."

Mr. Bay ignored the objection

"Whoever it was that prepared the travel documents, that fellow has the habit of using a particular address, although it is non-existent, I have found that same address in one of the HR journals.

Mrs. Bay left her chair and draped her waist over the couch her husband was leaning against, combing his hairs with her fingers.

"I wanted to tell you this. I notice school curriculum is same for the HR and the orphanage in UK, even the kiddies den in Nigeria where this child comes from."

Mr. Bay stretched his legs but did not move his head as not to let loose from the caress of his wife.

"What do they teach?"

"Normal things,' Mrs. Bay replied 'only that they appear not condescending. They seem to teach with immense respect for their pupil's intellect."

"Do they teach citizenship?"

"Surprisingly, yes but I think they do it as satires."

Mrs. Bay scowled,

"Those guys mock everything any flag ever stood for and they teach what they called the true brotherhood of men, transcending borders or religious creeds."

Mr. Bay chewed his tongue as he tried to skip the playing song to his favorite track.

"There is no denying we need that kind of brotherhood."

"Yes," Mrs. Bay replied, pausing a bit to allow her husband change the music. The man would not stand up to do his thing for fear he might cut short the sensation.

"But they speak of God as evil; creating diversities and wars among them."

"So they wanna be God?" Mr. Bay exhaled as the song started.

"It sounds eerie when men try to take the place of God."

"You are right, and from the article I am reading, a mention is being made of Nietzsche' he removed his glasses and clasped his wife's hands around his neck. Their hectic schedule was killing them both. 'They accuse societal norms of obstructing the free manifestation of science and they borrow from Karl Max in declaring the times when uncompromising scientists would become the masters."

Mrs. Bay exhaled "I smell the same old conspiracy, men seeking to take hold of the soul of their fellow men."

"And they try to justify their wickedness with some theories, even pretending to be subverting evil,' Mr. Bay joined, 'even people who do good happen to be doing it for the wrong reasons. How easily my questions get answered when I wonder why the common end of every man is death."

"Yes, muse, the ancient teachings of rebirth could be right after all. We pass through this fire for our hearts to be purified and our energies for evil to be watered down."

Mr. Bay paused hesitantly, like he did when he first asked if Mrs. Bay would like to stay the night with him, five years before, in college days.

"It sounds fair to propose that anyone whose heart is unpurified would be denied the greatest evolution that would see men becoming supermen."

"Yes, superman,' Mrs. Bay unbuttoned her pajamas. 'And if there are evils locked up in your heart, I am taking it away."

She pulled him up the couch, mocking his grumpiness.

"HUMAN Renaissance group accused of murdering three hundred minors, charges of genocide likely."

The adrenaline pumping musical prelude to the morning Super Broadcasting Channel news woke Sola up. She greeted Mrs. Bay who was ironing a shirt from the adjacent laundry. She had forgotten to shut the door to her room the previous night when she spied on the couple. She rose to find the television.

"It is Monday, February 12, 1996, 6a.m in New York and 11am in London, this is the World News." came the voiceover. She spotted a little television in the laundry and watched. Videos of the castle were being played. It looked deserted, without a tiny vestige. From the television, it appeared quite smaller than she thought it actually was. She looked away from the screen hesitantly.

"Why hasn't anybody quizzed me?"

Mrs. Bay dropped the pressing Iron. Apparently, she wasn't expecting a question.

"There are too many things about the castle that should not be discussed with a minor."

Sola looked away to the television, irritated by the 'aspersion'.

"I am eighteen."

"Not exactly about the age,' Mrs. Bay replied, 'my husband and I have decided to make you see an expert, first. We want to be sure you gonna say the right things on air and we wanna know how safe it is to speak at all."

"Such luxury', Sola snorted, 'things work out here as though everything is right."

"What?" Mrs. Bay's attention was glued still to the shirt she was pressing. She meant to say 'pardon'.

Sola ignored her.

"Those guys doesn't seem dangerous to me at all."

She fixed her gaze on the screen as the Police Borough Chief made his statement, but she faltered.

"I hate the way Mister Gbajumo stare when he speaks of his dreams, though."

Mrs. Bay switched the Iron off and moved closer.

"Nobody seems to understand in the office whenever I try to illustrate that look on the faces of those men when they talk about their coming glorious age."

Her shoulders were a bit more relaxed, as though she was conversing with a peer.

"Did you see the capillaries of his eyes thicken?"

"Yes, I did," Sola nodded.

"Those people, their quest has taken the shape of religion, nothing seem to be immune to such transformation."

She looked away contritely; she had been warned not to bother the kid with such discussions.

A commentary played as the cameras toured the castle.

"The manner with which the faceless men and women of the castle beat the state intelligence has been described as unnatural. Speaking at a press conference at which details of the failed operation was unveiled, the state police chief alerts the nation of a possible come back of this cabal."

Sola's attention was glued to the television but she asked questions at intervals.

"How come everything looks so serious on the television?"

"Common, it is a serious thing that three hundred people died" Mrs. Bay admonished.

"Three hundred people from different parts of the world who has no family, no ambition or something to live for." Sola said sarcastically. Mrs. Bay had said those words to console her the previous day when she was weeping.

"Baby, you gotta forget what happened the day before and carry on with your life. We have applied for residency for you and with your parents' consent you will study and stay here for as long as you want."

A film of tears came to Sola's eyes; she was either touched by the woman's kindness or felt pity for those who died and missed her kind of luck. She kept mum and looked at the television, wiping the little tears left on her face with the back of her hand. She said with a sullen and very coarse voice, "The man who brought me here said I could become a newsgirl. I want to be a broadcaster."

FOUR YEARS later, she recalled the teeny voice that came from her vocal cord. Her decision had stemmed out of her own will but she wondered sometimes if she was living the dream of the one who brought her from Nigeria and told her on the Verrazano Narrows Bridge that she could become a TV presenter. Gbajumo had said then that she would become the most heard voice in fifteen years and the way things were going, it seemed the prediction would come true. She flirted with the idea that it was mystical, her rise to the top. She felt a deep connection with her past, maybe the wanted men of the castle whose identity remained unknown. She knew Gbajumo was following her career, wherever he was hiding, or wherever he lived as an impostor. She'd seen strange e-mails beseeching her support in popular issues susceptible to media manipulations, strange messages reminding her of her obligations to those who brought her from obscurity into the limelight. Either providence or human maneuverings had taken her to the top but she was at the verge of being coerced into believing the latter. She did muse over this, as she hung her head down in the green room, waiting to be called to give a speech. She'd received another message that morning, begging her to keep mum over the issues of the previous years, which they had successfully clouded.

She'd rehearsed her presentation for two hours till a person from the upper floor called her trainer's attention. She'd been thinking all the while, her make-ups were disappearing and she was beginning to wonder if she would ever be called. Just as she was about raising her head to complain, her trainer's quirky voice sounded from the stairs.

"You don't have to put your hands down, you need to gesticulate indistinctly and emphasize your phrases where necessary."

Sola took the coffee and tried again.

"The vision of Baker Edison is vibrant broadcasting..."

The wardrobe manager interrupted. She attached a more fashionable cell phone to her suite and bended over, "Oh my."

The etiquette tutor played a video featuring Gloria Steinem in a session, expecting her to learn from it.

"Jesus, why can't I be myself?"

'No, babe, you are representing not only yourself but also the majestic SBCTV, moreover you are bound to do what I say."

"Without minding if I've got any idea?"

"I know you are almost bigger than the company, girl but we call the shots here," the tutor smiled to douse the fire of her remark.

Mrs. Bay entered the green-room and called anxiously "Sola, your name is ringing and people are applauding."

She walked briskly to the doorway through which a dim blue light reflected, feeling as the bible's Jonah must have felt when he was halfway into the shark's belly. Her instinct was driving her to mention the evil of 1996. Rumors had it that she witnessed it firsthand, and that she had come to the states through the faceless antisocial institute. She was expected to open up in the conference and put an end to rounds of claims and counterclaims. She was decided. She would tell the truth about her entry into the states and about the fact that she was indeed one of those kids intended for the 'Great takeover'. Her resolve, like the many good things she had done, was not for altruistic reasons but for the will to be accorded a little more attention on the media.

"The vision of Baker Edison is vibrant broadcasting..."

The voice that came from the speakers was too fine to be hers.

'We gather here tonight to celebrate this vision, to be part of this achievement. We are resolved; we shall build upon the foundation, those steadfast legacies already laid by our founding fathers especially Baker Edison of sweet memory."

She joined her visiting colleagues at the newsroom when the Media Dinner was over. There was no proper arrangement for the press conference because the idea was conceived not long, to help a budding news-bureau and she was to moderate by herself. The first question came from a journalist from Florida.

"There are reports that you narrowly escaped in the incidence of 1996 which saw three hundred kids of the castle at Straten Island killed, what do you feel about the progress of investigations so far?"

Sola nodded as if she was expecting the question.

"Thank you Florida. Four years and eight months ago, I saw wickedness in one of its ugliest forms; I saw a brown fume rise over the majestic piece of architecture, which used to be the pride of the area. I saw children die. Years after, we are yet to uncover the true rationale for this heartless behavior of a group of people a magazine alleged in the third anniversary of the tragedy as influential. Today, we keep wondering; why has cruelty survived all moral establishments, all political engineering and all attempts by our religious leaders to bring out the best in us? We may be yet to see the worst of men's inhumanity to their fellow men but we are committed, as professionals to report every bit and to bring these issues to the round table of all people because there is a happy fact in the middle of it all; there are more good people than evil people and with the right education and right information, the good guys become potential solutions to this age long problem bordering on all human societies."

Mrs. Bay who was seated at the back smiled at her. She was proud of her then than any other time.

16

HE STARED into the gloom and allowed himself to be hypnotized by the mournful silence of his room. There was an abandoned promise that was having his mind haunted and a thin voice from the past that was coming to him as a noise.

"Promise I will find you."

Uncle Bode's transition to the dream was vague as he came from darkness into another darkness. Now, he was back to the world, thirty thousand years back where monkey men lived. He walked down a steep, muddy earth desperately to where there was a tiny fire. There was no moon and not a star; there were no noises either, except one intermittent growling of an animal whose red eyeballs alone could be seen in the dark. As he moved closer to the fire, he heard the sounds of flowing waters. There was a river at the other side of the huge mountain that had become a common feature of his dreams. He'd always seen streams in his dreams and now he'd seen a river. He took breaths and fell on his kneels. A monkey man sounded from behind. Though its tongue was senseless, he believed he was being warned not to move too close to the river. He lighted a dry stick in the fire and ordered the hunched creature to explain. The monkey man barely spoke a word but he believed it said a people from the other end of the river do traverse at night to sell stolen goods. He raised his touch and looked ahead; the river was more than a quarter mile wide, probably opening to a sea. He grabbed the rope tying a piece of wood that was laying waste at the riverbank. The monkey man warned him again, climbing a tree apparently to demonstrate the depth of the water. He asked it to come and it obeyed. They must sail together. The wood was thick and safe enough to ferry two. He held the torch in his left hand and the paddle in his right. The monkey man's cry was making it difficult for him to concentrate. Just before he cut the rope, the monkey man leaped over to the waterside, weeping and running till it disappeared into the dark. He sailed on undeterred but his anger would surface when he encountered the first piece of obstructing ice.

The world was silent, not even the wind blew pass his ears. He felt like his auditory canal was impaired. Twenty minutes away from the riverbank, he started hearing whispers from the opposite end and he stopped paddling. He was divine and no one would harm him. He moved on, faster with renewed courage. A voice ordered him to slow down. He stopped paddling and tried to see who it was. The light of his torch could not permeate the darkness. The one who spoke lighted a big stick; his brethren likewise. He shook his head, bewildered by the multitude that kept vigil at the riverside. The two men who came nigh was surprised to see a man of their own stock come from the other side of the world, he too was surprised that there were so many people who looked like him. One of the two men surged forward, violently to slap his face.

"On your kneels," he commanded.

Uncle obeyed, for the fellow who slammed him seemed ready to kill. Sadly, he was skeptical about his divinity for the first time.

"He is a traitor,' said a man within the crowd. 'He goes to the monkeys at nights to divulge our plans to them."

"No I am not," he stuttered

"Shut up!" The hefty one thundered. He loomed over the stranger, panting with anger. He was fierce and scary, almost like a beast. The muscles of his chest were big and strong and thick hairs blanketed it. A belt of leaves hung around his waist and beneath, a big dark scrotum. There were deep cuts on his legs.

"Tell me, you,' his husky voice was accompanied by the hissing sound of a dark serpent. 'Are you the monkey man's machinery?"

"No,' he replied staring down, 'I was lost in their land when I was a little boy and I grew up among them."

His speech was incoherent, like someone who hadn't been speaking all his life.

The hefty man took a closer look at him.

"Now you will tell me all that you know about the monkeys."

He rubbed the serpent on the head. It was now wrapped around his neck, stretching forward to the stranger under investigation. It seemed like it understood what was on. Uncle shuddered in his dream and his feet jerked into the soft soil of the riverside. As he tried saving himself, the serpent stretched further, with a fierce look of warning. He paused and watched his leg sink. The world was silent again, and the serpent's eyes were only an inch away from his'. Someone broke the silence and the creature glided away. The one he saw in his previous dream appeared, offering a hand, and pulling him out of the mud. She looked a lot older. Many years must have passed.

ABDULKARIM stood up from the sessile chair by the lawn tennis court and headed toward the bar. Musa stopped the game and looked.

"Not all old hands grow weak."

He made an ace. Uncle Bode yawned wearily, asking what the count was and Musa moved to the service court.

"What is it you are thinking about?"

"Nobody,' he started contemplatively, 'nobody knows that I didn't do it."

"Kemi does and so does Charles, Maryam, Zanaib and I. We all believe you."

"But she?"

"'Make her do, write, fax, do all the shit till you make nuisance of you."

"Come on Buddy, you should expect I have been doing that."

Musa returned to the borderline to serve the ball.

"Have you been to your house today?"

"No." He panted and returned the ball skillfully but Musa failed to shoot it back before it bounced twice.

"I saw a note signed Chichi at your door."

"My lost cousin's name," replied Uncle Bode trivially.

The ball flew off the court and their eyes traced it to Pearl who was just back from school. She was in her own version of her school uniform, a very short skirt and a tight shirt. She ambled, up to Uncle Bode with the ball, ignoring her big brother's wry face.

"I came first in Physics."

"Really, your classmates must be very bad in Physics.' He smiled. 'How about eating out tonight?"

Abdulkarim stepped in, interrupting.

"I want to take you round my palace," he curled his hand around Uncle Bode's shoulder, casting his weight upon him. His potbelly protruded restlessly from his vest. Uncle strolled with him to the plots adjourning, where there was a commercial fishpond. Abdulkarim leaned over the bordering railing. He had bought the pond in one of the darkest seasons of fishery but luck was always on his side.

"I can see that you are getting on with my boy, he will surely give the dividend. He only does not like to be under pressure."

Uncle Bode did not know that Abdulkarim was basically retired before then and he marveled more at his person when he did.

"Young man, there is a thing I want to ask of you that I cannot ask of my son."

He bended over, blowing forth a good smell. He'd never been so near. Uncle Bode looked at the wrinkled face. He'd always known him as a man of integrity and now, he feared he was about to be given a shocker.

"Three months ago, I received a message from the states that we will be having visitors who would like some security."

"Security?' Uncle Bode forgot his manners and interrupted, 'they can always contact the police."

"Nope, young man, it isn't as easy as it appears."

Abdulkarim picked a piece of note from his pouch; he had been folding it all day. Apparently, he had spent the whole time wondering when it was best to talk.

"Our visitors are under serious threat and they would never be comfortable in any place during their stay here. They want to be around for just a while but do not want to be tracked."

"Sir..." Uncle tried to remonstrate but Abdulkarim's mind seemed made up.

"I understand this seems suspicious to you but believe me, it's nothing bad. I am just meeting my obligations to my foreign trade partners who helped us in recording eleven-digit profit in the last financial year."

"But you are not running a security outfit sir. They might be running to the wrong person for help."

"Young boys make me laugh,' Abdulkarim puffed, 'achieving fortune as a fabulous business man goes beyond the metrics of business most of the time, man."

Uncle Bode whispered to him, as though he knew someone was eavesdropping.

"I sense blackmail. You are obviously unsure about this."

Regretfully, Abdulkarim exhaled.

"Yes. Those guys know very well how to make a felon of anyone. They would stop at nothing to have their way."

"And who are they?"

"The Human Renaissance," he supplied. The world had suddenly opened its eyes to their sins. Every day, my clients move closer to their waterloo. Their finances are being frustrated; the clearest omen that their identity is already known."

"So they want to abscond?" Uncle Bode tried to feign decorum.

"For just a moment,' he replied, 'they plan to come back stronger, they plan to bring chaos so as to be able to vilify the government's pacific policies."

"Chaos?,' Uncle Bode sighed. He was beginning to fidget. 'Sir, did you say chaos? I am appalled. I believe you are a man of peace."

"Yes, boy,' Abdulkarim felt incredibly ashamed of himself, 'there are mistakes we make that we spend the rest of our lives covering up. I have made one of such mistakes."

"But what on earth could make you speak for violence?" Uncle Bode whined. The muscles of his neck were straining and his eyeballs were reddening.

"I am sorry.' Abdulkarim looked away, hiding his tears. A goose descended on the water few meters away. He turned around to look, backing the one he was conversing with.

"Things will become worst if I take the path of honor and turn those guys over to the government. A lot of people who look up to us would be de-motivated, many people will loose their jobs, AAF would become one big tragedy."

"Where do I come in now?" Uncle Bode asked, unwilling to push him further.

"You should ask the present occupiers to leave. You accommodate those visitors in the guesthouse and tender pseudo Identities to the office of Municipal security."

Uncle Bode shook his head, "No, I can't"

"Two months and it will be over. They'd figure how to save themselves in two months."

"We could get in a lot of trouble in two months. Those municipal dogs are more watchful than you think."

"And you think anyone would suspect?"

"Yes they will when travelers stay in a place without an explanation for so long. I bet their pricks won't be hiding too. They'd go out in the streets looking for girls someday and you know how fast things get blown up."

"Come off it, boy. Those guys are too smart to be caught by Lagos security."

Uncle Bode combed an imaginary mustache in deceitful contemplation.

"And why not tell Mallam Musa about this?"

"He is not the Manager of AAF Ventures, you are."

"But he is my boss."

"My son was born with the silver spoon,' Abdulkarim sneered, 'he thinks of integrity as important, not wanting to know the details of his fathers' affluence."

Uncle Bode nodded.

"I guess you made a mistake retiring the time you did."

"I retired to save the company because those guys were overwhelming us.' He pursed his lips, 'you cannot understand."

"I still do not understand what you meant by chaos, sir."

"Not to worry' Abdulkarim patted him on the shoulders. 'Everything will soon be over and we will live to right the wrong."

Uncle Bode threw the hands down and regretted doing so immediately but he screamed.

"Don't talk to me again."

He walked out, not looking back for it was a nightmare seeing the man he adored watch him do so. He forgot to remove the glare on his face as he entered the driveway.

"I am so proud of you. You had a fight with dad."

Pearl walked up to him and locked her shoulders in his. He feared she must have overheard their discussion and he tried ensuring she hadn't.

"Yes, fight,' he stuttered. 'And do you think I was right?"

Pearl shrugged and gave a puckish smile.

"I was only happy for you that you don't have to fake smiles anymore. You are now one of us," she said, twirling around to look at the garden her brother asked her to water.

"Wow" she sighed lazily. Her brother was wicked to have assigned her such portion. Uncle Bode, not knowing the reason for her hesitation, looked on idly. He wasn't sure if his reaction to Abdukarim's plea was proper, he wondered if he would have done the same if the man hadn't retired. He tried to justify his actions in his mind. He faced down for a moment. When he looked up, he saw Pearl was just as pensive as he was. Her short legs were fat. She was bare footed and she hadn't changed into a housedress.

"I remember asking, would you like to eat out tonight?"

"Absolutely." She turned around, 'I could get back to this unfortunate garden work when I am back."

LINING the streets of the new Lagos Islet were corporate offices, small and impressive. The government proposed to reclaim more land but many organizations had already acquired the little piece available. Among the buildings at the road's edge was a restaurant. Uncle Bode struggled to secure a space in the parking lot but all seemed to have been reserved. He was about getting kicked out of another space before succor came. Someone had passed a note that he should be allowed. He stepped out of his new looking but not too elegant 504, wiggling his wrist to fix his watch. His white shirt had been stained in the armpit, and the collar seemed dislocated. He was visibly in a rush but he tried to be sweet still. He was surprised to see excitement written all over Pearl's face. She had been to many exquisite places on summer vacations, and even to the fabulous restaurant in the heart of Paris where she posed with a Hollywood goddess in a picture. A Hip hop artist was billed to perform at the restaurant, that evening. They had come at the right time. He stared at the bill posted on the wall as he locked the car, wondering if he had parked too close to the building, then he shrugged and walked to the door, assuming the posture of a very responsible brother. Pearl's own mien was conflicting, she asked for his hand, and clasped it with the confidence of a lady, smiling the smiles of accomplished women. She sniffled as she took another look at the poster. The artiste of the night was steamy in the picture, wearing dark goggles, holding nobody knows what.

"Excuse me sir,' a guy in white tuxedo approached. 'Hope you're aware that our charges are going to be a little different tonight?"

Uncle Bode nodded indifferently.

"We are sorry we didn't indicate in the ad," the waiter said, 'but we did remember to say that under eighteens are not allowed."

"She is my sister and obviously I approve of her presence here."

"No problem sir,' the waiter showed them to their seat.

They both wondered if indeed she looked younger than eighteen in the gown and with the makeup. Some assholes are just too smart as long as what is in question wouldn't do their lives any good.

Somewhere at the back of the curtain was a deejay, mixing and playing rap songs. Before they could check the menu, a female dancer had taken the floor, fetishizing a chair, and with fast instrumentals, the artiste entered the stage and started his performance.

"Whoever leaves at some point is cowardly."

The red neon light at his back dimmed progressively as the music and the dancing got more suggestive.

"You sure don't like this."

Pearl took a rectified spirit mixture from the dozens at the table. She had conceivably talked to divert attention away from the strong alcohol she was about to take. Uncle Bode sat back

"Says who?"

She took a stick of cigarette from her bag, though she knew there was no lighter. She had tried to smoke several times without success and it was starting to worry her that she might never learn how to smoke.

The song climbed to the climax, and the audience grew intoxicated. The artiste beckoned to the one whose eyes caught his', Pearl, and she hurried to the stage, smiling with excitement. She'd lived her live dreaming about the stage.

"Now you want to see some dance?" the artiste's ferocious face was covered with sweat. He twisted his hips, if there was one at all, and encouraged her to do the same. Pearl danced as though she was drugged. The music started to wind up and the disco lights from the ceilings rolled faster.

"I think this is not right," Uncle Bode said to the waiter who had now arrived with their food. The waiter smiled as he poured the wine. Uncle Bode tried fixing his attention on the foaming drink but he found himself bursting in on the dancing two.

"If you want to do this, you should give yourself some privacy."

Pearl stood terrified, her chest heaving. Uncle Bode grabbed her arms and pulled her away to the greenroom. She sat carelessly on a bench, staining her clothes with lip-glosses and crayons.

"I was drunk," she wept.

"Then you should go home now."

Uncle led her through the kitchen to the place where the car was parked. It was 8:30pm, and the fresh street was getting less busy. Another song played from the restaurant, a slow one. He couldn't hear more than the beats but he knew it was a popular song. He saw a shadow on the walls, tried to look back but decided it was nothing. He realized he was wrong to have embarrassed her.

"I am sorry, Pearl," he bent his kneels to wipe her tears.

She jolted, rose and stared down at him.

"Take me home and don't you ever talk to me again."

She tried entering the car but she tripped. Uncle Bode helped her in, needlessly grasping the belly.

"You aint so clean either, are you?" Her eyes were closing and her stretched arm was making it impossible for the door to be shut. Uncle nodded like an animal and bent over to kiss the tummy. He noticed the light from the streets had been blocked off. He raised his head to see. Abdulkarim was right besides the car, looking.

ABDULKARIM BLEW SMOKE through his nostrils. He hadn't taken the pipes since when he arrived from pilgrimage.

"No father sees what I saw tonight and remain calm, especially when a man he trusts is involved." He looked away wearily. He was a shy man and everything he had done within the last couple of days was so hard for him.

Uncle Bode sat next to Abdulkarim and kept silent as they both watched the electrician fix the bulbs at the swimming pool side.

"Her brother loves her as much as I do, we all love her. I cannot imagine how it would look like if they get to learn about your behavior."

Uncle Bode tried to utter a word but Abdulkarim did not give him the favor.

"I cannot believe this, you try to take advantage of a fifteen year old, and someone you once took as a sister? You could lose everything you've ever worked for if I press the charges. My son could show you hell!"

He looked behind his shoulders, he'd raised his voice and he didn't intend to. He moved closer, and spoke to Uncle Bode's ears.

"Hope you still remember what I told you about the ware house? You should prevail on the board to sell it. I'd buy it for 25 million."

"Twenty-five, what if they refuse?"

"Then you should lease it out at least. I'd drown if I dump my white friends."

"I see' Uncle Bode mustered courage but his voice was pale still. 'I don't understand why your friends want to keep away from the eyes of the law. I guess they must have done something very bad."

Abdulkarim grew a little more restless.

"I am no longer interested in your sanctimonious disposition, young man. I was wrong to have compared you to my boy, my son who truly cares about what is right and what's not. We have both seen you are nothing but a pervert."

"Sir,' Uncle Bode shook his head with sorrowful regret. 'I cannot hide my mistake with a more grievous one." He paused to allow the electrician give Abdulkarim the leftover of the wiring work, thought more about his decisions and gathered confidence. 'Once again I want to say that I am deeply sorry sir, but I do not feel its wise to harbor fugitives."

He walked away, his feet feeling like a rock and his eyes blurred like he was in a dream.

THAT NIGHT Uncle Bode sleepwalked to his place. Life was too harsh to be fully awakened to. He took solace in pretending to himself that he was drunk. He had almost run over the flower at the front of his flat. There was power cut and he had to use the light of his phone to see. He noticed a note was hung to his door. He struggled to read. The note was bearing his lost cousin's name. He gave up reading and he tried to find the right key for the front door.

"God punish NEPA," he roared, as the door finally got unlocked. He wandered to his bed and a neighbor spoke from the flat attached

"If God punishes NEPA, there will be no more lights and we will suffer more."

He slept and the note fell off his hand.

He was also sleeping in his dream, under a roof made of leaves.

Everyone had gone to fetch water from the stream, he remembered. His eyes were fixed on the big, black serpent, crawling above. Having failed to make its way through the roof, the snake fell to his chest but someone stoned it hard without wounding him.

"I'd kill this slimy animal someday," said the brave lady, who was carrying a jug filled with water on her head.

Uncle Bode watched the snake move away.

"Why not kill it now?"

"I dare not,' she gestured for help but remembered the gentleman was being chained to the floor. She offloaded the jug alone, pouring some water on the captive's body. 'It is master's pet, I would not kill it, but I am afraid I might run out of patience one of these days."

Uncle Bode realized at that moment he was being chained and that he was in mess. It was embarrassing for him especially because a gorgeous lady was standing right in front of him. He looked away with shame and the lady smiled.

"I am Lā kēnu "

Uncle tried introducing himself but found he had no name.

"I will call you kuzbānu"

"kuzbānu?' he mumbled

"*Anna*, because you are big and strong."

He faced her, having received the boost his ego dearly needed.

"And you are small and beautiful."

She smiled, surprising him. She must have been frowning all her life.

"And is it true you are a thief?"

He tried to remember. He had been wrongly accused several times, both in the modern life and the otherworld of his dream.

"I am not a thief."

A thick voice came calling

"Lā kēnu!"

She walked away to answer the caller.

"And why do you believe me?"

She turned back and shrugged with a smile that exposed her little teeth.

"Big and strong men don't lie."

The one who called came to her face before she could run.

"This is how you flirt with every prisoner we keep here?"

He landed her a slap that jolted the crawling animal.

"How do I know you are not one of those who sneak to the monkeys?"

The lady sobbed, "He is no monkey."

"But a thief; goes to the other end of the river to trade stolen items."

She walks away.

"Papa calls you"

The old man was near already, and the lady greeted him, touching the ground with her head. She received a second dose of beating. He was to die in few days, yet he falsified strength.

"How wrong I was to think the child of a whore would grow up to become responsible."

Lā kēnu raised her head from the floor

"You remind me of my shame everyday and it was you who made us who we are. You made us harlots to please yourself."

The old man smashed her neck with a stick, causing her to bleed.

"You do not talk to enemies and thieves!"

She stood up, covering her wounded neck with the soil.

"I am going home to my father."

"He sold you off to me' the sick old man laughed 'you belong here."

"May I ask that you release the thief that I may go with him?"

The man puffed.

"You see, those men and women you see around, you can never be like them, you can never be with a man, you will kill him and come back here someday. You are corrupted beyond redemption and you are useful for us alone."

She faced him, still pressing the soil against her neck,

"Why do you possess my life so covetously?"

"Simple. You look good and when you speak to those men and their mothers, you speak well. You are to keep them humored in my camp."

The lady tried to remain on her feet but she felt weak. There was still tears on her face and blood on her neck.

"You don't have a camp."

"Wait until you see me build one," the man replied. The color of his face changed; the prisoner saw it go red.

"When I build my camp, I will make all young men into an army and we will fight the monkeys and the human tribe that live in the north, becoming the sole owners of the land. We will take everything, from the hills to the ends of the river."

"You sound funny when you talk like this, how many times do I tell you that the world has more tribes than you know."

"Keep telling me girl, the old man's brains need be hammered. You are the wise one and you were born to do this for us."

"And freedom would be my wages? I desire to go with this man."

"Do not take the old man as one of those you charm with your sweet words. You will go someday but not with the enemy. Cursed be anyone who goes to the enemy!"

"There is no greater curse than living another man's life. I go tonight and I wish you luck with your conquest."

She turned her back on him, an act the old man despised.

"You cannot go, not with the thief."

She faced him for the last time

"You said I could do anything, watch me do it for myself."

There was a full moon that night. It seemed bigger in the sky and there was another body like the moon, smaller but whiter. The old man woke up from his sleep to keep watch over the prisoner. He never took the lady's threat as empty. She'd shown him disrespect already and he knew she would do worse if allowed. He guessed right. The lady stood right under the prisoner's roof and looked. The serpent stared back, standing guard, ready to strike. She dared not free the prisoner.

"I couldn't sleep,' she said, 'the whore need be with a man."

When she spoke, she sounded plausible, mostly because of the pains of her wound.

"Then you should come here. I am not dead yet."

She put the stick he was holding away.

"You should tell your boy to take a walk."

The old man clapped his hands and the serpent went the other way. It moved faster than the captive thought it would.

"And the thief?"

"We should hang him to the other side and make him face the hill."

"Yes I will, but do not do anything funny. You'd pay for it."

He untied the captive and pulled him away to where there was a pole.

"She said you should look at the hills."

The lady struck from behind, heavily with a stick.

"You were right when you said you were a fool."

She wound the rope around her arms; it smelled foul as it was made of an animal's hard tail and not well preserved (it was to be changed every day).

"Where do we go, to the river or the hills?" The prisoner panted. She looked at him with dispassion.

"Don't make me regret doing this. I hate them cowards and fools who think the world is so small there is only a river and one hill."

The old man lay on the floor, groaning. She looked at him and almost decided to help him up. Making decisions was an impossible task for her but this time, she stopped looking back. She packed some food, shouldered the deer meant for the next morning's feast and ran away with the prisoner. They both hid in the bush, and tried to decide which way to go. They could see the old man as he rolled on the floor. Shouts of pain woke dozens up and they besieged him.

"Dappanu's men attacked him!" one of those loyalists yelled, the one who arrived latest because of his clumsy gait. The old man replied it was not his adversaries.

"One of our own had turned against us. She absconded and now I am like a man without a roof."

The man who supposed Dappanu's men attacked, hissed.

"I wonder what is so special about that lunatic."

He was still harboring a grudge. He was the only one among the cycle of the old man's supporters who never got to see the lady at night.

"What manner of man are you?' another said as he helped the old man up. 'you punish thieves who sell our things to the monkeys while your adversaries harbor them and treat them as heroes. How do you think a good man can lead bad people?"

"I am not a good man,' the old man replied 'none of us is. Our wrong deeds are commensurate with those of the thieves and those who harbor them."

THERE WERE NO such lands in his world. He marveled and tried to remember a thing but every time the lady with whom he absconded asked why he was pensive, he'd lie it was nothing and keep going. They took the path never walked before, westward to the plains of ice sheet. He knew there would be an end to it. On the fourth day of their aimless journey, just about when they ran out of food, he found he was right. There was a mighty deep pit on their way. The end of the world! They had to turn back to face a bleak reality.

Lā kēnu was the first to rise in the morning that followed. Right at the mouth of the steep, she stood, her long hair floating in the cold wind. When Uncle Bode opened his eyes, he admonished her for endangering her life. She did not bulge. She had been groomed against fear. Her destiny, which she had freely altered, was to gather men for the purpose of a man's conquest, the old man from whom she fled. Her breaths were short and heavy as she stared. She opened her mouth to breathe. Her heart was freezing, yet she laid open her body to the air, like a bird wanting to fly. Probably she did so to honor the unknown God whose face she thought she saw as infant. Many people had died in the cold, especially those who didn't will themselves enough to live, those who failed to get an animal's skin to blanket their bodies. Now, Lā kēnu opened her arms like a possessed woman, nude as a newborn. Her companion rushed to sheet her when she began to gasp.

"You have come this far to get yourself killed?" He avoided looking. Be it fire or a deep dark hole, he didn't want to know what it was that laid beneath the land.

"There is a step there' Lā kēnu pointed forward. 'We could get to this beautiful place through the steps."

Uncle Bode felt a bright reflection fall through the cornea of his eyes. He raised his head. Before them was a white and immaculate land, extending to the horizon. Lā kēnu was in fact mesmerized by the magnificence of the view. Her father had told her about the lowland before. It was the only hope of the people of the earth, the only thing that would safe them from the imminent flood that the wise men of those times said, would end all forms of life. There had been times when the ice from the hills would melt, causing flood and killing families. Now that thick glaciers of many years had formed, the next coming of the sun would spell more doom. If only the flood could cut into the rivers and make its way into the white lowland, the world could be spared an apocalypse.

"Many believed the white land would drown anyone who steps on it," Lā kēnu said.

"So why climb down the steps?"

"To see if they were right. We'd touch the ground with a foot and if we do not drown, we'd go to see what lies beyond."

The sun was already receding when they got to the bottom of the steps. They were famished and too tired to rejoice but somewhere in their hearts was the pride of having desecrated an old fable.

Shortly they found the strength to proceed. As they walked, their feet made impressions on the chalky ground and the twilight threw their shadows besides them.

IN THE morning, he rose to make another fire. Lā kēnu tiptoed to his back, scaring him with a thing that looked like snake.

"There remain nine others who are like me. I feel the need to bring them with us."

"Of course, we'd return and surrender. There are no more foods and from the look of things, there are no plants ahead."

Lā kēnu kept silent for a moment. She was unsure about what she wanted to say.

"Is it true that the monkey men have surrounded us with shelters, holding us back from going beyond the valleys to take more places?"

Uncle Bode frowned contritely, he couldn't remember. He was starting to seem like a blockhead- a nightmare to the lady of terrific foresight. Lā kēnu smiled to end his uneasiness. His beautiful face and broad chest was helping her to stand his ignorance.

"I told Asiru, that old fool. He is more concerned about fighting his own brother and leading other men in a besieged valley than spreading out to conquer his true enemies."

"It could be wise, staying where your comfort lies and it could be foolish to stretch your luck."

Lā kēnu stood up and spoke. It was not in her training to sit while discussing real issues.

"No luck awaits the craven. Even in the comfort of their valley, the flood would come someday and drown them.' She looked away with a sigh, 'No one listens when I say this; even Asiru who thought me to be this way- his mind had been corrupted with another passion."

"You speak ill of the only people I'd known all my life."

"Evil people, you mean? The monkey men mate in the open and eat the flesh of another. They steal and kill."

"But our own people are not better."

Lā kēnu would not let him finish.

"In deeds, yes, but in their words and their songs, they fair better."

Uncle Bode yawned and looked as far as he could.

"In the land of the monkeys they treat me like one of them, and I am revered but the people of my own stock call me thief."

Lā kēnu took his hands, and looked ahead too.

"You wish to bring the two tribes of men together."

"How do you know?" the focus of his eyes shifted from the far to the very near.

"From your breadth,' she said. 'Men breathe hard when they conceive a new thing."

"That old man had trained you so much you think you know everything." His voice was meshed both in envy and contempt.

"Tell me, teacher, how do I bring the people of the world together?"

She assumed the posture of the teacher that she was called, never coy but firm and impervious to the sarcasm that she sensed.

"How many of them monkeys and men live in the valleys and the mountains?"

"I don't know."

"'You are not sure? Probably you don't really care' she raised her voice and the muscles of her neck showed.

"You should be versed in everything to accomplish that. You should know how to save this people from the coming flood, and the beasts that migrate from the east every time the snow seizes to fall."

Uncle Bode repositioned anxiously. He was having the most ambitious discussion of his life. Though he lived among creatures whose only concern was food and mating, there was something in him that testified that she was saying the right thing.

"How do I save them from danger?"

"You save yourself first from covetousness and all vices that make men common."

Uncle Bode stared her down, making her be the girl she was supposed to be.

"It is funny a man who clearly lack honor told you all these."

"Honor did not take away his instincts,' Lā kēnu remarked. 'Only men who defy the norm and do what they know to be right wouldbe reckoned as great."

"Sometimes I forget who you truly are."

"A whore?' she yawned unashamedly. 'Asiru's dream was to have myself and nine others give birth to the army. What we do is for a noble reason."

"So the murdered kid was your son?"

She threw the blanket to her back and started walking.

"No. He is one of our own."

"And you were trying to run away?"

"I wanted to see how the land looks like. We planned to take everything to ourselves but now I have found a man's only true passion is to outshine another."

Uncle Bode stood firm and hollered.

"I will stop the enmity and unite all the tribes. Everyone would journey outside the valleys, knowing the world is one and that no one would harm them."

Lā kēnu laughed.

"Asiru said nicer things yet he faltered when he tasted power. If you think you know something that Asiru or Dappanu don't know then you live in a fool's paradise. Sometimes power thrives on controversy and disunity."

That morning, he spent much time thinking, wondering if he would become like the two old wise men of the land. His sorrow labored his brow and he slept away the day. The cloudless sky and the desolate plains underlined the feeling in the air. There was no hope, not in any man.

SOME TIME in the middle of his sleep he saw a hunched back man walk by. The second time he did, he lifted Lā kēnu 's head from his chest gently and followed the stranger.

"Who are you and what do you want?"

The light of the full moon showed upon the man's face, and it was white and wrinkled. He looked right through the one who called.

"Don't move, you monster!" Uncle Bode's voice was shaky though he tried to pretend not to be afraid. There could be more of those sad creatures with white bodies and long beards.

"This is my home," the man said at last and attempted to move on. He must have come to see if the intruders were violent, never meaning to even disturb their sleep.

"Home?" A sudden sense of superiority set in, and he put his hands on his waist, wondering why a man would live without a shelter.

"We live two moons away, six families, happily. We take turns to keep watch over the gate to our land."

Uncle Bode laughed,

"Silly man. Your gate is so wide a legion cannot keep watch."

"You must follow me and take some food. If we hasten you could meet up with tomorrow's afternoon meals."

"And how do you know we are not dangerous? Why do you want to open up your gates to strange men in this world of hatred and suspicion?"

The bearded man was speechless for a moment

"No one comes here with no food except he is in real trouble. Our favorites are runaways."

He helped them with the spare blanket and they moved westward. He was delighted in their decision to follow him and he spoke as they dragged their feet upon the chalky earth.

"The lowly village, several kilometers from your own system of valleys and hills is situated in the center of a vast lowland area. Our fathers chose that place to keep away from the bullies, men who speak so arrogantly but leave their scrotums dangling below their pants." He laughed, waited and laughed more till his belly ached.

"Some men fled there during the streak of violence that saw monkey men conquering men who could speak and fashion weapons."

He paused and faced down. Memories of the war still pained his heart.

"Though many people left for the lowland, our numbers did not increase over time because of the climate. Some died, leaving their kids to the care of no one. Many kids died, as it was impossible for them to kill animals for hides, to save themselves from the freezing cold. Later, we figured every child without a father belonged to we fathers. We learnt how to care. Few of the kids who survived grew up into strong men and women, moving farther into the west as rumors of temperate woodland increased. The land is left with a desolate generation, fast dieing away, thirty-five people whose interest had turned away from greed and whose delight was only in finding truth. We live quietly, consciously turning our ears away from the noises of the valleys and the rumors from the western lowlands. We are comforted by what we know, that the time of fairness and calm will come."

He spoke so beautifully that they never complained about the distance. Suddenly, they realized a structure taller than every adjourning trees was ahead and that a little crowd was waiting to receive them.

"Welcome to the land of wisdom where rulers are made," the man said. He had been away for a couple of days himself. The people paved way for him to pass through, some genuflecting. He was accorded immense respect though he didn't seem like the oldest.

He toddled through the narrow path fashioned among the people. He greeted them and explained who the visitors were. He beckoned to the two as he walked into the jungle, the first woodland they would encounter in three days. They trekked to the stone house inside the thin wilderness, the gate of which seemed to lead to a dark cave.

"I am sure you are thinking it is time to eat."

Uncle Bode grinned almost like the old man.

"No, we are occupied with curiosity."

"And why not ask questions?"

There was no reply. The old man sat on the leafy floor and tried to be a little friendlier, he seemed to be proud of his shelter, hanging over them.

"I am not impressed that you didn't asked questions,' he said, 'see, many things have passed by."

Uncle Bode replied almost timidly.

"I should not ask about everything I see."

"Then you feed your mind with nonsense? Assumptions? Great ruler you say you want to become and you let a moment go slip by, not learning."

Uncle Bode jerked anxiously.

"Are there great rulers anywhere?"

"There should be. The world is large my friend."

"Large, but I wish to make it sane."

"Your chances are slim. Men have grown in wisdom more than you can ever imagine. They know a lot that you don't know. They know that they are supposed to strife to attain a nature far greater than the natures of the tribes of men who live on the face of the earth."

He paused for a moment then continued,

"Fate might have assigned to you a nobler task."

He walked into the stone house and they followed him.

"Such is alien even here- that which made you to hold hands in one accord and to trespass the unknown with courage, the same thing which qualifies you for this revelation."

HE HAD BEEN hospitalized again. It took him a couple of minutes to remember what happened. The last he remembered of himself was the night he saw a note at his door. Whoever brought him to the hospital must have broken the door to come in. There must have been one hell of commotion. When he saw Kemi approach, he tried to recall fast as not to upset anyone, for the smile with which she came, he could not afford to ruin. She was tall, she was huge, and she was the policewoman who helped him find the kidnapped baby that Sola Aderomoke brought from Ezukala during the last Christmas. Besides his bed was Doctor Akinola, he could not forget that man.

"I didn't take the drug this time."

Akinola bit his lips and scratched his brow. He must have been worried and from the way he nodded, it seemed like drugs was not the issue anymore. Uncle Bode had blacked out for too long and schizophrenia could be a possibility.

"The baby called my name this morning,' Kemi blew an awkward smile, 'unfortunately, I received a message from the Child Care Commission that Sola Aderomoke wants him."

"Sola, did she call?"

Kemi acted as though she didn't hear. She could still feel envy even though anxiety was the king of the moment.

"How long have I been here?"

"Two days."

Kemi held his hands more tightly and knelt beside him as he wondered.

"We have made contacts with Doctor Olanusi, everything will be fine."

He tried speaking of other things to repress his fears.

"I guess she's flying with the baby."

"Yes, she is."

"Did you tell her what actually happened?"

"Yes," she lied, and her conscience held back the tears.

17

JOHN Edison, the statesman cousin of late Baker Edison arrived in the hotel venue of a nieces' wedding ceremony with a battery of guards when the event was about kicking off. He had his own way of stealing people's attention, the same way by which he made them think he was humble. Born three decades earlier into one of America's noblest families, he never had to tie or untie his own shoes by himself till his College days. When he was four he had discovered that magnets could be made by stroking opposite ends of a bar magnet on a ferromagnetic substance but was disappointed when he learnt that he was only rediscovering what was figured thousands years before. At seven, he had started learning two extra languages, French and German. He had read about little Newton conquering a Physics Professor and he had promised himself to be another Newton, a promise that he almost kept. He was a renowned inventor and shortly after the evil of 1996 he'd published a blueprint where he advocated total takeover of all machineries of destruction, purporting that it was dangerous to leave certain technologies to the hands of barbarous individuals. Many thinkers had dispelled his ideas as rabblerousing and insensitive to the core human values of mutual respect and trust.

James Mendel, the newly appointed American negotiator to hostile nations arrived few minutes after John Edison. His ideologies had been identified with Edison's and his widely anticipated meeting with the man was celebrated in the pages of the newspapers. When he entered the hotel hall, many eyes watched. Everyone wanted to see how it looked like- the meeting of two giants who shared the same views on international diplomacy and war.

The bride rushed excitedly to meet James Mendel, brought him to where John Edison was and beckoned to Sola to come around.

"I arranged this meeting," she giggled.

"It's such a nice meeting isn't it?' James reached for John's hands.

"You always say my mind and sometimes I wonder if I need open my mouth."

John scowled as he made effort to recognize the face. Though he was a widely known achiever, he didn't know James Mendel, didn't know any man who trumpeted ideas and never got to the very place where raw decisions were made. He was a lowbrow technocrat who said only what he found to be technically correct and not necessarily what was scholarly.

"I must have been seeing your face on the TV too,' said John 'It is so familiar."

He began to think and he burst out.

"Mr. Mendel...Breatman High School, Philadelphia"

"You were my student."

"Yep,' he gasped, 'for six months or seven. Sorry I couldn't remember the face on time. Wasn't thinking about you then, I was busy thinking of how I could get out of Breatman and become a Rockefeller."

"I see where it comes from, your big demagogic blueprint."

"You used to spend forty-five in a sixty minutes lecture, making those theories."

"I can see you were truly my student."

"Yes sir. You were right when you talked about enforced disarmament. War technology is growing without bonds."

"Yes. You guys have been having destructive inspirations lately. Your new machines would end the world!" James Mendel looked around to be sure he hadn't spoken into a pressman's microphone.

"We intend it to ensure our military superiority so as to enforce this disarmament,"

"And what do you do with those arsenals after you must have freed the world of threat?"

John Edison smirked "I am not the Commander-in-chief."

"I see.' James gasped 'you should be smart enough to know the politics if you can be so brilliant as to formulate such weapons, buddy."

He paused to blow a we-aren't-ready-for-your-questions-yet smile at the pressmen who were just concluding an interview with Sola Aderomoke.

"I trained my kid in the way of the lord, I tried to make him not to hate but last year, my boy broke his African friends' head because he called him albino."

John smiled, erroneously inviting those pressmen.

"He called your son albino, yes it is not abusive but the context in which he said so, I believe is racist, so he deserves a smack on the head."

"I wasn't disturbed by his action but his comments,' James whispered because pressmen had arrived with their annoying smile. 'I was disturbed because he bragged about me and called the African boy's father a lazy man who has provided no lasting heritage."

"I see this is where we differ. You think even we could be potential agents of evil."

John's whispering was more obvious and James became uncomfortable with it. He waited impatiently for the discussion to end.

"If we do not hold back some powers to ourselves, we endanger everyone. We cannot distrust our kids and ourselves, there has to be some good guys somewhere."

With apologies, James and John turned around to face those men. Sola Aderomoke waited to exchange greetings with the two of them. James held her hand, almost removing the gauntlet.

"I am launching the New Generation Foundation tomorrow, would you like to be part of it?"

"Yes." She wasn't sure if she'd like to be part of it but the optimism on James' face could not be defied, more so because he mentioned the New Generation Foundation like he believed she should have heard about it.

He need not use a public facility for the event. He'd designed his home, his everything in line with his plans; a plan that would culminate into raising a generation of individuals who he said, would ensure that the standards of his country concerning the human dignity is preserved. James Mendel's million-dollar mansion affords the view of many types of scenery and from the top of the multistory building where he lived; one could see what his infant grandchildren used to call the whole of Manhattan. His weekdays were quite uneventful. He would rise by seven in the morning and disappear into his house office where he did nothing but append signatures. His duty as the proprietor of his business did not even include giving instructions. Although he once tried to lay off many workers, he discovered they were just indispensable. He'd built around himself a small group of loyalists who honestly or not, shared same view with him on what he had grown to believe so passionately that the latest defense technologies would fall into the hands of the faceless deviants one day.

On the NGF inauguration day, he stood in the gallery watching the road that led to his house. He was anxious though it was silly for him to think that no one would grace his invitation. The media representatives were already seated but he was not yet in the right mood to grant them interview. He took a time to watch the giant oil painting of himself that was presented by the hockey group he sponsored. In the picture, his bears looked much like Abraham Lincoln's. He never designed it to be so, but like many kids of his time, he'd grown up to look like the man he enjoyed reading about most. Maybe it was his constant preferences at the barbers' shop. There were many like him who shared his ideology but he differed because his' was not a conscious effort to be statesmanlike.

He stood wondering, His mind was absent and he did not know when the time he was waiting for passed, when a car finally passed the idle road.

John Edison stepped down from a dark Sovent and followed the usher stationed at the gate to James' private office. James Mendel went to welcome and shake hands with him. He forgot as many times he remembered that John was once his student.

"Is she here, the SBC girl?" John asked as casually as he could, but James was clever enough to know from the way John spoke that the name had been playing in his head since the last time they saw.

"She called this morning and promised that she would be here."

"She's married? She's got fine legs."

"'And face too."

"She's got long eyebrows, is she from the Caribbean?" John chuckled.

"No, she is from Africa' James said as she offered John a glass of wine. 'She will return to Nigeria next month to set up the Lagos SBC office. She doesn't wanna go home, she's been threatened by some old friends."

"She told you all these?"

"Yes, she is like a daughter."

"She could be lively."

"Really."

He took the German wine said to have been discovered from a World War time cellar and auctioned for sales in commercial stores across the nation. Strangely, he did not make a comment about it, unlike many other sophisticated people James had served. He was indeed consumed by his mission and it was unusual the way he carried his admiration for the teevee girl.

Sola entered the office and walked towards them. James whispered one more word as she drew nigh.

"They were right when they said I'd love doing this."

James stared, wondering what John meant by 'they'

"Good day Mister Mendel and Edison," Sola said bashfully. She was in a grey wooly jacket and a blue undershirt and jeans. James bowed her into his office and started a casual conversation with John who had grown seriously indifferent. When he got the chance, John wasted no minute to run to the private office where he found Sola fiddling with some journals. Uncertain John took a volume of the journals and opened the pages at random.

"I wonder what Mr. Mendel is doing with all these."

He knew that he sounded like a jerk. Even John Edisons sound stupid sometimes.

"Shall we go and ask him why he is keeping dusty journals in his office?"

Sola meant her response to be funny or friendly but there was something about jerks that really attract contempt. She moved to the door, unwilling to carry on with the dry conversation.

"You are returning to Nigeria next month, aren't you?"

"Si" she replied twirling. She almost fell for the smooth floor and the high-heeled shoe. She smiled as she inspected her cramped feet, making it all look graceful.

In the twinkle of an eye, James' luxurious office had become crowded with eminent diplomats and leaders of thought. Someone introduced the guests. The man working on the perpetual motion machine, owner of the world's largest insurance firm, legislators and dozens more. James mounted the little dais placed behind the office desk and smiled as he watched those faces.

"This is a great reunion," he said and was given a round of applause. He wasn't a great speaker. His speech was rather simplistic but with an admirable sincerity in the tone of his voice.

"Sometimes in recent history, the world began to realize the obvious necessity of individual's obligation to improve on themselves to bring about better societies. Many laws such as laws forbidding interracial marriages were made so as to give rise to pure races of people with superior qualities. But we have found in men to whom history bequeaths greater honor that the races of men shall not be defined by physical attributes but by the contents of the characters. It is they who understand freedom and equity and justice and they who work for the restoration of the world into becoming peaceful and livable that would be reckoned as supermen that Nietzsche passionately but erroneously described. It is they that our lord, Jesus Christ said, will recognize the kingdom of God."

18

WEAK and drunk, Uncle Bode gazed at the bottles of beer before him as though he was surprised that he took six. He remembered that someone was trying to tell him a thing.

"I beg your pardon," he managed to say at last. He'd tried vainly in the last fifteen minutes to make a sense of what that gentleman told him. His eyes opened to reality again- the reality that he was caught trying to perform sexual acts on a minor and that he was being blackmailed.

"There is a mafia here wanting you to divulge classified information to them sir. I advise you take less bottles because their plan is to make you drunk and leaky," said the man in a designer suite and shoe.

Uncle looked at him as yet another bottle and ordered him to leave. He knew why he got himself drunk, and he was certain that nobody lured him into it.

He stared at the long passageway connecting with the doomed reception. It was long, illuminated with a bluish white light, narrow yet wide. He absorbed himself in the stately ambience of the place. Opening his eyes, he saw the manner of people he had always wanted to be with. Cute and courtly. That he was their superior was difficult for him to believe.

He tried to guess the time before checking his wristwatch but the phone rang.

"Tunji and the ibo guy... ' Kemi's voice came high-pitched from the phone.

"Obi," Uncle Bode supplied.

"Yeah, they have been rearrested and the case has been taken to the law court."

"How did you know?"

"An officer told me on phone."

Uncle dropped the phone and dashed to his car.

He checked the time. How it had run to the twelfth hour he could not explain. He became anxious. Staying in the office, the guesthouse till the middle of the night was very unusual of him, even when he had to take some beer.

"I have been calling since nine o'clock but nobody picked the phone," Kemi raised her voice above the noise of the hair-dryer.

"I must have been drunk."

"Very unusual." Kemi said his mind.

She came from the back door, smiled as if she was only fooling around calling him. She was in a brief casual wear and her hair was shimmering.

"They said the Tunji and Obi case would be heard for just few weeks, it is a straight case, not complicated and there is a rumor they are going to plead guilty."

"I warned you," Uncle flared. The lady's calmness was annoying him.

"We don't have to shout in the public do we?' she said with an inscrutable smile, locking her eyes in his'. 'We needn't watch our dirty pants in the public."

There was a way she stressed the 'public' word that almost made him laugh. She had just called her cozy, little apartment 'public'.

She had a consistent way of hypnotizing him. Uncle clung her to his chest. Gradually she was becoming beautiful to him.

"But I was the one that was wronged, not the government. Those guys used to be my friends and I do not intend to send them back to jail."

"It doesn't matter who is wronged especially when a million Naira is involved."

"What for?" he tried not to jerk

"Do not tell anyone this. Today I received one anonymous call from a guy who seem to be interested in the case."

"Who?"

"I said anonymous, maybe some vindictive fellow who wants those guys in jail."

"And you took the money?"

"He paid into my account before calling."

Uncle Bode fiddled with her hands, trying not to be forceful but to persuade her.

"Please return the money.' The pace of his speech betrayed his emotions. 'Return the money and close the case, I sense everything is all about me. I think I am being followed. I would be implicated."

"If it is your friends you were trying to protect, trust me, I'd mess the burden of proof, I'd do it in a way nobody would feel betrayed and we would be a million naira richer for it."

"You do not understand."

Uncle Bode quitted playing with her hands and slapped his own head instead.

"Tell me the truth, Olabode, do you know about the kidnap?"

"No, I don't."

"So why fidget over anything?"

"Abdulkarim wants a favor I cannot grant and I guess he's doing all these to get me."

Not bothering to inquire about the details, she sighed.

"I will see what I can do about it." She spoke like someone died. The lost of a million naira could be agonizing.

"Thank you."

Uncle Bode was happy he hadn't overreacted.

She stretched her hands, releasing herself from his boring embrace.

"I hope the information have not been sent yet, it could be difficult quashing a criminal case when started."

She opened the door to the kitchen and a sweet aroma passed through the chimney. Uncle Bode pulled her back to himself, almost disengaging her bones. He did not speak but the word in his eyes was of pleading. Should it be true that Abdulkarim was behind everything, he'd surely go to jail.

HE GNASHED his teeth half-consciously and said to the gentleman browsing through the library at a corner of his office room.

"I think we've met." The coffee had burnt his tongue. He had been having little accidents since the morning of that day.

"Sir, I was the one who warned you against taking too many bottles last night," said the Principal Marketer.

"I see,' Uncle Bode yawned, 'I like your tie, how much did you get it?"

"Seven hundred naira," the man replied coyly.

"You're kidding, man, isn't this the seven thousand naira one?" He sat up and spoke more seriously.

"PM, you sounded like you know a lot about the mafia last night. Tell me who they are."

"I am sorry," Douglas stuttered. He could not trust the walls. He glanced at the windows. His actions were becoming funny but he explained why.

"Those guys have this unbelievable network."

"Never mind, I learnt this place is sound-proof."

"Yeah but nothing is impossible here."

"But who are those nasty guys?" Uncle Bode quaked and the PM replied in almost equal intensity.

"The Storekeeper, Accountant and your Secretary, they are the ringleaders and they carry half of the office along."

He looked at the doors again, implausibly this time.

"No need for probing, the second man to you would always be the Judas Iscariot"

Uncle sighed, not for fear but to let out the tension of the past few minutes. He'd uncovered in his mind, the plot and the joy of wisdom underplayed his predicament.

"Let me leave before they start wondering what I am doing here" Douglas hurried to the door. Uncle reminded him he had not taken any book and he replied he could not find the financial yearbook 1996 he was searching for. Uncle Bode ran his fingers through the middle shelves. The financial yearbook 1996 was conspicuously there. He gave it to Douglas who walked away, speechless. He tried to remember if he said anything about the financial security codes or the preliminary report of the secret probe panel set up by the central office before his deployment. He could feel the anxiety in the air. The fate of the big fives in AAF was in his hands. If he could bring the probing to a logical conclusion he would at least be able to close his eyes when he sleeps. The Principal storekeeper, he gathered had survived four instances of probing, likewise the Principal Accountant. It was only the Branch Managing Directors who refused to play that lost. The big three were on suspension again and there were no indication yet that they would come with a magic or trick. The road end was in sight for them after six years of corruption. Maybe Abdulkarim didn't have a hand in it; maybe Uncle Bode was only being paranoid.

Uncle decided to call Kemi to ask if she'd have only luck retrieving the Tunji and Obi file. She hadn't.

THE MAGISTRATE. Old and tired. He shouted the clerk down, playfully.

"Will you be quick, please? I am leaving this place exactly 1pm."

He looked over the faces of the six people seated and the two policemen as if he would pass a sentence on them.

"Kidnappers are not always lucky with me," he joked but his smile was more like a threat. It was being rumored among those who believed in everything that his little boy was once a victim and that he was known for finalizing cases of Kidnap in manner of days. It was taking forever for the clerk to gather her acts. The Magistrate leaned over his desk to screw the slack hinge of his goggle. His jacket was as stale as the furniture of the courtroom.

"Obi and Tunji," the clerk mumbled to buy more time. She finally announced there were no second witnesses. Proceedings would commence without one. It appeared the duration of the lawsuit would be really short because there were rumors of plea bargain. Moreover, the defendant had tactically admitted guilt in his statement.

"The fact that the suspects returned the baby willingly, under no pressure or mental subjugation or any extra-ordinary intervention should be understood. It is fit for the court to see the gentlemen as repented, therefore temper justice with mercy."

Everything looked so simple, yet so tricky because Uncle Bode was indicted in the same statement. His lawyer called him in the morning, saying that he had been served and that he should go for the plea bargain. Any other option, according to him, was no option at all. A huge joke was staring Uncle Bode in the face. He could feel the conspiracy in the air. It was thick, it was menacing. No one is to be trusted.

"Misters,' the prosecutor began strongly. He was full of himself. 'Do you realize that you have succeeded in frustrating a promising citizen out of her fatherland?"

He turned around to face the magistrate.

"My lord, I would like you to see the case in this perspective: the actions of these suspects are prejudicial to the country's image and treating such with a kid's glove would speak volume of our character as a nation."

Defending Attorney raised the same point he'd been hammering since the very beginning.

"I understand this case was resurrected after the maximum duration stipulated under the law. Also, the plaintiff has made it clear that she is unwilling to proceed with the lawsuit."

The prosecutor objected that the state was the litigant and the magistrate nodded. He raised his head for the first time in five minutes. His own concern was different.

"Can I see the abduction documents or any substitute?"

He received the papers and took a quick glance at it, then passed it on to the clerk.

"I understand MisterOlabode Oladejo once had a cause to visit the psychiatric hospital for treatment but this is never for antisocial behavior as the accusers may want to suggest. The plaintiff's plea is hereby struck out on this ground. However, I may feel compelled to demand for a comprehensive report to ascertain the position of his mental health."

The prosecutor on getting the magistrate's nod draped his arms over the dock.

"Do you know these young men?"

He pointed at Tunji and Obi across the room. Uncle Bode affirmed that he knew them.

"What is your relationship with them?"

"We are friends," he replied.

"Are you aware, Mister Olabode Oladejo, that your friends have finally confessed to this court?"

"About what?"

"Maybe we should ask you, sir."

"I don't know what I am supposed to say,"

Uncle Bode tried to be strong but every moment, his fears were made real. Tunji avoided eye contacts with him. Obi stared, but there was no look of friendship or solidarity on his face. It was the look impunity.

"Could you repeat what you told the court in everyone's presence?"

The prosecutor summoned the duo.

"With your permission, my lord?"

Tunji moved to the dock and Obi followed. They were both looking fatter, and much older.

"Mister Oladejo asked us to take the baby."

"To kidnap the baby right?' the attorney's face was lighted with a curious smile. Perhaps he wasn't so confident before then that the two men would confirm the police report.

"Why would he want you to kidnap the baby?"

"He feels it was a distraction to his relationship."

"Were you paid?"

"No we aren't paid. We are pals."

The prosecutor took a bow and the defendant took the stage.

"I maintain that the timing of the filing is suspicious, my lord.' He walked slowly to the dock. His gait was meant to intimidate the two suspects and make them loose confidence. 'Except of course the court is not interested in the mechanics I'd ask a few questions before proceeding with the..."

"You may ask your questions," the magistrate said.

The attorney stepped forward, visibly energized for the new moral right bestowed upon him.

"What is it that you did not know more than a year ago that you just came to know? What inspired you to turn yourselves out to the police?"

He saw that the two men wanted to talk but quickly raised his voice to stop them. He wouldn't have them quash his examination halfway.

"Perhaps guilt, a genuine change of heart, vengefulness, the desire to see the walls of the prison?"

"I don't know if you are aware that a court liaison had been feeding the legal department with details of your conducts ever since you stepped your feet out of the dock last year. Your attitude has been reported as unchanged, and your pattern of life as reckless and capable of degenerating. What then is the reason for your recent action if not to bully your one time friend into paying you to free himself from this mess."

There was no objection but the magistrate obviously did not like the question.

"Could you please reframe the question, mister?"

"What do you pray the court to do gentlemen?"

"Why jump the gun?" the prosecutor sighed with scornful countenance. He apologized when he realized everyone noticed him.

"The quest for truth, barrister, is the ultimate right of everyone." The magistrate explained thus rendering the questioning impotent.

Tunji answered the question anyway, having had enough time to think.

"We didn't file a suit, the police did and we were told the easiest way to walk out of this place as free men is to speak the truth."

After series of examination and counter-examinations from both parties, the defendant applied for leave on behalf of his client, Olubode Oladejo who was billed to travel in the middle of the week.

Uncle Bode had received an invitation from the prestigious Institute for Contemporary Studies in New York and would like to attend to it. Ever since his name appeared in a journal that featured Doctor Akinola's article, he'd been receiving mails from the ICS to come share his experience, his dreams. He agreed to go only when he learnt that all traveling expenses would be refunded, maybe in double folds as Akinola boasted. He was to be picked at the Kennedy International Airport Hotel by 6:30am Thursday morning and chauffeured to the ICS headquarters where he would meet with the world's craziest professionals.

"EVERYWHERE seems so busy even at seven o'clock."

Finally he got the driver laughing. He'd tried from the airport to no avail and at certain times, he would feel like he was being kidnapped or arrested. He didn't know beforehand that he was in a place where unserious things were to be delayed till afterlife.

"You may come down here," the driver instructed.

He alighted and was received by the director of the institute himself.

"Thank you for coming," the director said tersely and turned his back. The early morning breeze was making Uncle Bode's face dry and white. He shook and hid his hands in the pouch of his tailcoat. He wasn't sure about anything- the suitability of his dressing, if he should talk or if he should follow the director. He found he was not as important as he presumed when the director admonished him to check the menu he was given for directions and stop following him. He felt stupid. He should have taken a look at the paper the driver handed him in the car few minutes ago. He was scheduled to see the Chief Medical Officer by 7:15 who would in turn take him to psychiatry experts expected to exercise checks on him. He took the lift to the fifth floor, office of the CMO and met a gentle man at the lounge.

"You are a bit late, sir."

He was only five minutes late but lateness was as strange to them as the ethnic rituals of a Saharan village.

"Lets get down to business," the CMO waved his hands. He asked for Uncle Bode's medical card, the chip he was told to bring along with him, that he got from a Lagos hospital the previous day.

The CMO processed the chip in the computer and a page showing Uncle Bode's medical history was displayed. He clicked on the Mental Health menu and navigated to the Magnetic Response Imaging. Activities of the hippocampus were unbelievably high. The blood vessels were several times larger than normal. The right and left frontal lobes could be seen as red, indicating serious hyperactivity and the brain was having enlarged ventricles. There were also unusual levels of serotonin. The CMO penned some recommendations on a piece of paper and directed him to few other offices in the same floor.

By 12pm, he was ushered into a conference room. There were three men and two women at the table, all in various shades of dark suits. The one sitting at the right edge of the rectangular table was the first to catch his attention. He was an obese man, very bare headed with an imposing mien. With the way he fidgeted his hands over the table, he seemed ready for a confrontation and the way he looked at the faces of his colleagues, it appeared he wasn't alone.

Just about the moment Uncle Bode took his seat, at the far end of the 7 meters table, the fat man greeted.

"The cashier is to arrange for your allowance, sir. The board has decided to increase it by fifteen percent."

Before Uncle Bode could give his thanks, the man had gone straight to the point.

"We all know there is a young German, Federich Zurich by name, whose account we find to be plausible, especially where a mention is being made of a tribe of men with unusual abilities. What we do not know is you. We do not know if your own testament was inspired by his own"

"No sir," Uncle Bode was not sure about what to say. He could not damn them; he had been given a reason to want to assert himself already. Initially, he expected to be listened to and not to be quizzed like a schoolboy but now that he found he was no more than a suspect of fraud, he lost balance and he stuttered. Things would become more difficult for him if the board gets to know that his girlfriend, Kemi, is the German's ex.

"From the journal of last month, Doctor Akinola of the Nigerian University said that you, Mister Olabode Oladejo saw a place of white sand in your dream. He also described the mood of that place."

"Yes sir." Uncle Bode tried to salvage his reputation by appearing more convincing. He stopped fidgeting but the effort with which he did that brought fluid to his eyes. He winked uncontrollably as he spoke.

"The land was like three hundred meters lower than the outlying one and it was all chalky."

"Very well mister, we have an artist's impression of the details of your description."

He switched on the twenty-nine inch computer screen at the right corner of the room.

"Which of these sir, best suite the one you saw in your dream?"

Uncle Bode fevered as he pointed at the fifty-fifth option. The picture on fifty-fifth slide was a perfect fit. His breadth became faster as the operator zoomed the three dimensional picture to view more of the landscape. He felt like he was being teleported into his dream.

"It is okay sir, I have seen it." A droplet of tear blew upon his eyelashes as he looked away.

"Would you like to view more slides? We have four hundred and eighty-five of them."

The gentlemen gazed at one another in disbelief. Uncle Bode had chosen the same slide that the German picked two months ago in a highly secretive session.

"Various accounts received from different parts of the world points to a common direction,' the man seated next to the fat guy remarked. All voices subsided, leaving his'.

"By extrapolating the geological and ecological features of the white cliffs of Dover and subjecting them to the conditions theorized by great geologists, we arrive at a description best represented by the features that a few gentlemen and ladies saw in their dreams."

He stood at the fat guy's bidding and moved closer to the touch screen. Everyone looked with undivided attention as the man navigated the computer animation to a link with the caption: THE UNRECORDED HISTORY.

"Without apologies to the Harvard don who dismissed these analyses as the ultimate triumph of mysticism over science, I make bold to say that we have found a thing more convincing than the science we used to know."

Theoretical map of the ancient world appeared on the screen. The operator zoomed the diagram to the upper hemisphere, downward to where Europe was expected to be.

"At this prehistoric time, the Schelde and Muese rivers were farther inland and they were transected by tall hills."

A modern map of France showing the river sites appeared and the picture faded contiguously into another one.

"Through series of natural transformations; breaking and falling of rocks, chiseling, formation of moraines, drying up of streams and formation of new rivers, we arrive at this."

A new picture showing the same location around the Strait of Dover emerged.

"Here is the Strait of Dover as it used to be, about thirty thousand years ago. As we all know, it used to be dry land and prehistoric mammals freely traveled between France and Great Britain."

Uncle Bode, now calm, recalled the things he had been seeing in his dreams. The animation was a perfect representation. The institute had been working round the clock where necessary, ever since the German had described the old time world to them.

"Close to the white cliffs of Northern France was a prehistoric settlement where the German and apparently Mister Oladejo lived."

"In the dream," the fat guy cautioned.

"Yes, in the dream but I am beginning to suspect that they dreamed of what actually happened at a tiny prehistoric country."

The operator toured the animation of that ancient country to a place of chalky earth. Uncle Bode noticed the mighty hill of his dream that he used to see from every angle. The one in the animation was same but there was a sharp contrast at a point. He never saw an ocean in his dream, not anywhere near the hill.

"Yes!' The operator clenched his fist as the tour reached the part Uncle Bode remembered to be near the pit, the lowland. 'This is the part the German called the end of the world. He said families were compelled never to go there. In his words, it is a pit of white foam where people drown."

The animation showed as little geological changes occurred with time. Digits running at the bottom of the slide, Uncle Bode understood, were representations of the number of years it took for those changes to occur.

"But there is another account from a Nigerian, that the supposed white foam were not all foamy. Mister Oladejo posited that it was chalk and the journal recorded that he actually walked over it in his dream for three days to another human settlement."

Now the animation had run for ten minutes, representing ten thousand years.

"Mister Oladejo was able to walk from France to Great Britain because there used to be dry land in what has become the Strait of Dover today."

The animation showed as a great flood came upon the lowland, and as the ocean from the north cut through, forming a narrow sea. The part Uncle Bode saw in his dream, that he thought was the end of the world, faded out and then came the picture of the white cliff of Dover.

"It is crazy but I cannot help concluding that some of us are remembering how life used to be, many thousand years ago."

HIS EYES were shut. Like a man in deep introspection, he was. He saw the future as he closed his eyes, the future from which he had come. Firelight fell upon his face and he winked. His mind was more at home now than it had ever been in this old time world for he saw life and a tinge of muddled joy.

The man with white face and bears whom he met together with the lady, Lā kēnu , spoke to them. The man sat on a stone and held a lamp above his shoulders, shining it down to their faces.

"One day,' he said, 'this place shall become an island." He gazed far at nothing. His breadth was audible.

"Someday,' he said again, 'many independent peoples shall rise. And why not rise? Eons before this time, many colors emerged from white and many passions that used to exist as nothing came into being. The Father let it be, for His light shall remain white even when many colors are cast unto it."

Finally he smiled. It was an uncommon thing to smile in this silent world.

"So shall it be among our people, there shall be many truths but among those truths shall be the ones that would lift them from their pettiness into becoming like the lords of the ancient times."

"How can I be lord?" Uncle Bode asked.

"What is the truth?" Lā kēnu inquired, simultaneously.

The man chose to answer Uncle Bode first.

"You want to mix the tribes and rule the world?' he chuckled, 'you will have to develop a new feet, as thick as the horse's to accomplish that or you will have to ride on the back of a winged beast." He laughed and bent his tummy to put the muscles back in place.

"There are hundreds of villages like yours, scattered all over the world that sees the same moon that you see tonight."

Uncle Bode droned disappointedly.

"Then I suppose my plans are stupid."

"Indeed they are,' the old man replied. 'Only a god would stay two warring armies unhurt."

"Only we believe the white substance at the strip of land behind us is not dangerous. Only we are the ones who pass five nights without sex."

The white-faced man was speechless. He hung the fire lamp to the natural hanger besides his pebble house.

"Good luck to you if you want to mix the tribes,' he said at last. 'Believe me, one shall outdo the other. One shall drive the other to extinction."

"You suggest I do nothing?"

"Do what you wish, man. After all, the tribes are not all that different asides that one does not grace itself with enough privacy.' He laughed. 'One is dumb and the other can speak but the dumb one knows the songs of the ancient lords, a piercing irony."

Lā kēnu was particular about the last comment.

"Is it really true that such creatures exist? Men with wings?"

"Yes, I think they exist.' The man's sardonic smile was bigger than usual. 'I grew up learning about the fable just like you, but now I think I have found a reason to believe."

He stood up

"Follow me."

Uncle Bode and Lā kēnu followed. Now, they had developed the habit of holding hands.

"The tale was passed through the ages. Many seasons before this time, balls of light used to fly in the skies at night. One day, the balls fell upon the earth and they were men- beautiful men with wings. Today no one sees them again; no one knows where they vanished to."

"Except the monkey men, I think? In their folklore, their fathers learnt an ancient song which those winged men said, used to be their song in times when a new star is born."

"Yes it is true' the man replied. 'Monkey men taught a few of them real men, but those men were afraid to share it for fear that they would be seen as associating with the monkey, a forbidden act."

"Teach us." Lā kēnu leaped forward. She walked faster than the two men as they approached the rolling lands.

"I don't know the song," the old man said. He faced Uncle Bode, 'you said you grew up among the monkeys, you should know the song."

Uncle Bode looked away ashamedly.

"I don't remember things. I don't remember anything."

He lied when he said anything for he remembered the image that passed through his mind that day. He remembered the warm, noisy world of magic and clothed people that he saw. He remembered the walls of the house were smooth and multicolored.

"What about the song?" Lā kēnu asked.

"It brings courage and happiness. Monkey men desecrate the song yet it brings them courage and happiness. They do all manner of evil yet they enjoy because they know the song."

"How pathetic that creatures without the power of speech knows a song real men do not know," Lā kēnu said to herself.

"And what will I do with the song?" Uncle Bode asked.

"Maybe if you sing it and teach people, you would be able to build a new world; a world of harmony and peace. You would say to the mountain to shift and it will."

"I will go find the song," Uncle Bode asked Lā kēnu with a nod if she would like to join him. She nodded back. The man, impressed at their resolve, smiled widely, and hopped with excitement. His smile melted into awe as he spotted the wonder of the world, five hundred meters in every side, like an hexagon. The inscription on the rock showed many colors and each of the colors changed from time to time. It surely was not a design of monkeys neither was it of men.

"You should abide in your mind not only good songs but also good thoughts' he said, consciously desisting from passing a comment on the huge work of art that laid before them. 'And when your eyes are fixed only on a tiny light, you shall find peace."

THEY TOOK one abandoned road as advised. It was the only route through which they could get to the territory of the monkeys. It was also important for them to take the tiny footpath to avoid zealous villagers who would want to insist on hosting them to morning feasts (and it was a very rude thing to decline such invitations.)

They walked many days through desolate plains and mountain passes and sparse woodlands. There were many fruits in the place, but they found there was hardly a thing without an owner. Squirrel-like animals and rodents owned the grapes, cherries and oranges. Mastodons and horses came out at intervals to eat from the short trees. Erring goats were for the huge cats and other strange carnivores. Uncle Bode and Lā kēnu took everything and ate in the very eyes of the owners. They seemed to those shy beasts, the most ruthless of all creatures. All animals maintained safe distances, staring at them but a few daring and mischievous rodents came forward to have their own share of the harvest, the stock that the couple had piled on the ground. While Lā kēnu checked the greedy ones, Uncle Bode would climb rocks to watch the beautiful terrain. He loved to say that he was watching out for enemies just to remind the lady of his importance. Her bravery and astuteness, he felt, was undermining his place as a man.

One of those times he climbed to watch, he realized that the thin structure he used to see in the horizon was not a tree but a man-made structure. Even the white-faced man was wrong to have suggested there was no human settlement around. The couple set forth, missing their bearing several times. The structure was farther than they anticipated and a fairly tall hill blocked their view, making it difficult for them to know if they were on the right path. They slept in the open, burying themselves in bundles of blankets. The light of the dawn was not enough to wake them, but they rose as the sun came shining down. The structure was only a few meters away now and many people surrounded it. He'd seen a gathering of such magnificence only once in that ancient world, and then, some trespassers were being hung to death and left as a spectacle somewhere near his shelter. People did not gather to see a dying fellow like they used to do in his own land, not this time. They assembled to watch a group of musicians sing. When the people sang, they sang with all their hearts, not minding the raining snow. So enthralling was their song that they failed to notice that a couple of strangers were staring from a short distance. Barring the imps who ran around throwing stones into the assembly for their own amusement, the place seemed like Eden. Uncle Bode seized one of those erring kids.

"Where is the way to the land of the monkeys?"

"I don't know,' the kid said. His bones were so thin, he seemed like a mosquito in Uncle Bode's hands yet he felt no fear. 'Please leave me alone, I don't want to miss the best part of the party."

"So you do this all the time?" Lā kēnu asked.

"Yes, whenever the singers feel like, they play for us and most times, the village pours out to sing together. It is our sacred song, the song of heaven."

The boisterous place became silent as a man who seemed like the village leader approached.

"Greetings to you and your people' Uncle Bode stepped out and curtsied. He felt relieved when he saw the man bow in return. 'We are only traveling across the wilderness and we think we are lost."

"Where are you coming from?" the man walked him to the midst of the people who stared unashamedly at them.

"Where we came from, we cannot return to."

"You are being followed," the village leader disclosed, 'three men have been here today, searching for a man whose description matched your own."

Uncle Bode sighed and Lā kēnu looked away, avoiding his eyes, "I guess we'd better left for another place."

"No. You are safe here. We will protect you and if by any chance they prevail, we will include it in our pact that you remain untouched."

"Pact?" Lā kēnu muttered. She'd forgotten she was supposed to be quiet.

"Yes, we have a pact with the peoples of the valleys and all villages to the west of the river. Even Asiru and Dappanu's factions are talking now. The monkey men are threatening every human and it is only natural that we cooperate to safe our lives."

"Monkeys?' Uncle Bode's eyes met Lā kēnu 's at last. He was not sure if it would be wise to disclose he was their leader or used to be."

Lā kēnu took words from his mouth.

"I guess the monkeys are not as dangerous as you suppose,' she pointed at Uncle Bode, 'he once lived with them and they treat him as a leader."

The man was amused by her comment but he believed it.

"The monkey men have become more capable of destruction than ever before. I guess you have been away for so long that you do not know about the news of the moment."

"What is it?" Uncle Bode tapped his feet to shake off the snow, getting ready to pay attention.

"Asiru had given too much to the monkeys in his bid to become the leader of his people,' the man said. 'Now he has been murdered and monkey men have taken possession of the armory."

"We could make more knives and catapults."

Uncle Bode assumed a straight posture, ignoring the soberness of his companion. Lā kēnu wept at the news of Asiru's demise but only her companion understood how she felt. It was a funny thing to weep at the transition of a man into another life more so because people died of cold and fever every day. The village leader beheld them with suspicion for he had noticed many strange things about them in their short moment together, things like the feelings of affection. There were no such feelings or culture in the lands of men or monkeys. The only things that mattered were food, sex and power. It was even a shame for a man to be seen with only one woman as he would be considered lazy or called a miscreant who is unwilling to multiply himself.

The village leader said, "even if we work all day we may not be able to produce a tenth the knives in the custody of monkey men. Word has gone round the villages. Every man is to gather in this place to hide, maybe wait for the worst."

"You will do nothing while they take your land?"

"Perhaps the land belongs to them.' the village leader remarked, 'and there is a good news; we will negotiate and trade our holdings."

Uncle Bode shook his head in disbelief.

"What makes you so sure we cannot fight back?"

"History,' he spat on the floor, close to Lā kēnu 's foot to register his contempt for her emotion. 'Too many times we have tried to fight them and we have failed. Come to think of it, our villages are sited in the valleys and never on highlands or plains. Monkey men travel freely in the open, even sneaking to our midst at night. To serve them might be our destiny."

Uncle jerked as the village head spoke those ignoble words.

"Give me your word and I will gather the men."

"Do not trouble yourself,' the man made himself yawn. 'I have looked into the eyes of those men and I know for sure, to serve the monkey men is their secret wish."

"I do not understand why anyone would want to be slave to a witless master."

"The reason is simple. Our wit consumes us and the authors of our arts leave us in the middle of the wilderness like petty wanderers. Asiru thought us to be strong yet we found he was the weakest of all men."

"You dare not speak of him so," Lā kēnu interjected.

The man exhaled. 'Asiru thought us to be firm but we saw that he wavered more than any other man. Only the ways of the monkey men bring pleasure."

Uncle pondered on those words. He was motionless but his face brightened a little as he resumed talking.

"I see how pleasurable it was for your people when they sang, this afternoon."

"Oh, the song,' the village leader shrugged 'we enjoy it so much yet it is a painful irony. People believe a tribe of men came down from the skies to teach our fathers the song. There used to be a time when people make it to the top of the high mountains just to sing.' He looked to the mountains and there was unbelief in his face. It sounded like a fable even to him. No man can make it to the high mountains except he flies.

"Let men find pleasure only in singing and let them shut their senses to other forms of pleasure for the purpose of this war. Let them see that their home is being threatened."

He looked straight at the man

"Could I speak with your people?"

"Yes," the man replied softly

Villagers formed a circle around him as he called their attention. They'd been watching in the past moments.

"Our home is being threatened,' he said at the top of his voice. 'Your shelter, your barns and your animals are on the brink of destruction."

The people moved closer and listened. Their faces were wrinkled for the nasty climate, their eyes more than elliptical. Almost all of them had very bad dentition and their imprudence became more apparent as they scrambled to be in a considerable proximity to the stranger. There were no traces of anxiety on their faces and Uncle Bode seemed to be making a mountain from a molehill. His resolve was shaken for this reason but he looked at the mountains and he felt a shadow of evil coming upon the land, consuming everything on its path.

"It is true we have tried and failed many times. I was only a toddler the first time we did. Winning seems impossible.' He walked in the middle of the tight circle. 'I know you say to yourselves; there is no point in being free and who says we cannot eat and merry even as slaves? Believe me, the tribe will not stop at making you slaves. They will make you starve; sleep with your women in your very eyes. They will kill you the day you muster courage to protest. Why not stop them now that you have the chance?"

His eyeballs dropped as he finished speaking. Two men withdrew from the meeting and his eyes followed them, unconsciously at first. They returned with dozens of knives.

"This is all we have to fight," one of those hefty men said. Uncle Bode curled his arms around their shoulders and stood between them. Their bodies were sweaty even in the cold and they were the only nude ones in the village of forty-eight people. They had given up their blankets to orphans whose parents died in a recent pandemic and they were yet to get animal skin to make another for themselves. They were the first to make such gesture and no one understood why. All villagers believed they did so because they were having carnal knowledge of those orphans. The concept of love, to the people of this world was as difficult to understand as celibacy is, to the randy. The two men had pioneered one more thing- yielding to a stranger who was equally weird. Even in the minds of these tactless men, it was understood that likes attract and that an unseen force was in the process of transforming some of them, turning them into graceful mavericks.

Uncle Bode, dwarfed in the middle of those men, spoke to the people.

"To those of you who still ask; why need we fight, I say that you are responsible to the soil, your own selves and your children."

He turned his back and bended to take one of those knives lying on the ground.

"I heard you sing a song this afternoon and I saw your faces. Even the sun looked beautiful upon your land while you party."

"It is a very old song' one of the two hefty men interrupted. His gesticulations betrayed nervousness and subservience.

"Our fathers learnt it from monkey men and those monkeys told them that some pretty men, plenty, came from the sky to live among them long time ago. Those men thought them the song, said they used to sing it in heaven."

"It shall be our song in war," Uncle Bode grinned. He packed remaining knives, rolled it in a blanket and announced.

"Remember there will be no parity after this war. There is no standing. Every man shall either become slave to the monkey men or subordinate in the new world."

He never meant to threaten but people came out to join the two volunteers as he spoke. Words of threat had paid off. He would use similar tactics in getting more warriors from other human villages. He would also make them sing for he bore the witness that people almost seemed transfigured when they sang.

IT REMAINED dark, perhaps the sun was hesitant. There came whispers of a multitude from the tops of the mountains. Uncle heard it in the middle of the night and he did not stop hearing it, even when a lone morning bird sang. He thought he heard the sound of drums beating at long intervals. War loomed over the part of the world that was known to men, and the sky was silent, thick with sober clouds.

Beside Uncle Bode, Lā kēnu lay struggling to open her eyes. She was having a nightmare and Uncle bent over to wake her. The sound that she made in her sleep was like the beats of drum. When Uncle tapped her shoulders, she flung her arms and screamed. When she realized she'd been having dreams, she calmed down and breathed a word.

"I hear voices."

The cries of mammoths and mastodons had taken the place of the drumbeats now, and the morning bird had flown away.

"This land is cursed,' Lā kēnu mumbled. Her chest heaved and her eyes became red with horror. 'I saw nothing but I heard voices. *Too great lord, the power you have given unto them. They shall rise against you by what you freely give.*"

Lā kēnu looked upward. The ambiance of the world was as horrific as her nightmare's, if not more.

"What is happening?"

Uncle Bode shrugged off her question.

"Just go on with your story."

"Yes, I heard another voice beg that they be guided unto goodness." Her breath had become even now. "Someone replied that the people of the earth would choose for themselves which is more pleasurable to behold; the light of the Father or the lights pretending."

Lā kēnu choked and Uncle was so impatient that he encouraged her to continue.

"Someone exclaimed; *a great new thing beckons at our timeless history, that creatures like us is to live away from the light of the Father,*' she looked sideways into Uncle's eyes and her fears subsided, 'another replied, *even in many shades his light shall remain as immaculate and the gods of the earth shall find the truth.*"

She smiled as she remembered one of the voices she heard in her dream. *He loves to be loved in many ways, for Him*

to put excellent beings so far away and their love to test.
Uncle gave up trying to understand. He sighed and asked
if that was all she saw in her dream. Apparently, she grew
a little defensive and her willingness to be taken serious
made her to raise her voice.

"I heard one of the faceless men proclaim to another; even
before the people sees corruption, you shall."

Lā kēnu stood up and held the blanket against her chest.
Her gaze was on the mountains and her stare was like the
enemies were ready to envelope them.

"Then, the dissident swore that he would not behold
darkness but the people of the earth shall. A long silence
ensued because someone had spoken irreverently."

It seemed she understood her dream perfectly because she
clenched her palm against Uncle Bode's face and said,
"this war was begun in ages past and it will be fought
amongst us. Should the brutes win, we will never see what
is meant for our eyes and we will live for nothing."

When she mentioned 'war', Uncle noticed that a crowd
drifted behind her. He looked above her shoulders. Battle-
ready men and women were dragging their feet upon the
icy earth, approaching in silence.

"The army awaits your command, sir," one of the two
hefty men who first volunteered to fight announced.
Behind him was a host of men, some jittery, some
courageous, some fleeing their lands for the fear of dying
in isolation and some seeking only the pleasure of rubbing
shoulders with fellow men. There were huge ones whose
principal diets were fatty foods from the forests of inland
Europe; there were thin ones who took cereals all their
lives. There were dark ones, whose skin, having received a
greater share of sunlight, had learnt to produce more
melanin. There were blue-eyed ones and hairy ones,
different people from different villages. They had come
from the farthest parts of Asia, Europe and the regions of
the river of Nile. Few days before, word went round that
the Neanderthals were spoiling for war. Many brave men

and women formed shields and escorted hundreds through mountain passes and secret pathways into the village, venue of the first camp in prehistoric warfare. Pregnant women were made to stay in different camps, shielded by walls of woods and warriors. Some of the infants saw the soil for the first time in their lives, as the feet of so many people melted the ice, forming wide, dirt-like lines in the middle of the white moraines.

The sun was still not rising. Uncle would have loved to do a quick head count of volunteers but it was dark. He could feel only the breath of the soldiers and he could tell there were thousands.

"Should we wait for the first attack or should we make the first move?" One of the foremen asked him.

"You should take orders from the village heads, I leant there are over a hundred of them amongst us."

The man sighed, and rubbed his eyes. He had spent the whole night organizing. "There are too many of them here and if we should dig into their ranks and choose someone to lead, we'd be fighting ourselves rather than the monkeys."

"Okay, you should ask if they'd obey."

"They will, they asked me to tell you this," the man leased a smile to his ugly face and patted Uncle at the back.

"Where is the face of the sun?' Uncle said to himself as he moved to speak to the army. He was apprehensive but he reminded himself, the cost of doing nothing.

"Greetings," he roared and the people mumbled in reply, "greetings."

"I do not know why the sun has refused to rise when we need it most." He moved into the lines of the warriors and they made way for him. "I would have loved us to see the faces of one another but I think it is even better this way, for we shall not see the faces of them monkeys that make us fear. We shall stretch forth our sharp sticks and aim our stones only at those who make the sound of monkeys."

Suddenly, a loud noise came from the borders of the

camps. The enemies became restless and they prepared to bulge in. it was rumor until then and many hearts fainted for the rumors were true. Even the foremen wavered.

"It is rumored that monkey men fair better in the dark. Do not think that nature takes sides with them; the sun's failure to shine is to save us an illusion that would have made us retreat."

He walked into the lines. He never knew there were so many humans on the face of the earth. Historians said they'd been hiding in the valleys for many hundred years. He was also astonished what he had accomplished within a very short period. He'd made hundreds learn the old song which he hoped, they would sing in war. As he moved farther into the lines, he hummed the ancient song, his voice marrying the fretful silence that enveloped the world. His lips became heavy, his kneels weak. At first it seemed like no one would join in singing but the world came alive when he started the first stanza. The voices of humans soared. For the weak, it was horror, for the strong, it was joy.

The army lighted their sticks and mocked the sun. Front liners who saw the enemies from a far horizon leaned over and screamed, "The enemies flee!"

They waited for the next directive, anxious to pursue, almost breaking the lines. Uncle ran from the rear and thundered, "*Dapānu!*"

The armies of men chased the monkeys to a strange land, Uncle looked from one of the hilltops; the monkeys outnumbered the army of men greatly. He saw it was folly to try taking the earth. They were the tenants and the monkeys, the owners. Nature was blind because the brutes were meant for the top. Still looking, Uncle noticed the warriors had not stopped singing. His brow wrinkled as he tried to listen, the wind tricked his ears and blew him the song of redemption. He was enchanted and his hope was refreshed.

"Master!" one deserter who had come to hide in the hilltop

called, he regained his consciousness and quickly ran down the steep to join his people. It wasn't as beautiful down as it was from above and it wasn't true that the people sang. He tried to catch up with the front liners and when he finally did, he saw the giant work of art that the white-faced man showed Lā kēnu and him, few days before. The monkeys had run into the caves beneath the rock on which the wondrous design was inscribed. Not very many knew prior to that time that there were such places in the world. They stared as colorful films rolled upon the face of the rock. The army of men encircled the mountain, standing alert for fear of ambush. Learned men sent words that the enemies might have been suffocated. They waited for the drum of victory to play but something happened that paled their joy.

One of the ladies who occupied the back lines, the one who had come with the leader of the army, Lā kēnu advanced to bring the final words of the scholars. Uncle stood in awe for she reminded him of someone he knew in another life. He tried to place the face. A word came to his mind, *would you like to join my crew, see how we make the news?* Memories of Sola Aderomoke came to him, Lā kēnu was her! He became half awake into the modern world. His phone was ringing. He walked up to her in that dream.

"Muĥebti."

An anonymous bowman struck Lā kēnu from behind and she fell to the ground. He raised her head. He could remember the modern world now, the world in which he would wake up to. He had come to recognize the scar on Lā kēnu's neck, the semblance it shared with Sola's. The lady tried to be stoic as she pronounced the words of the wise men.

"The monkeys have run to doom, the world now belong to men."

She said one more word before her lungs shut down.

"Promise that you will find me."

19

"BOLLOCKS!' the fat guy of the Institute for Contemporary Studies yelled, 'I cannot publish these things in the journals, my job would be on the line."

"But the institute is independent of the government," his colleague said.

"So they say,' he looked away to avoid all forms of eye contacts. 'Even if it is independent of the government it sure is not above the law."

He breathed hard, inadvertently into the cup of coffee, steaming his face. He always sipped his coffee noisily, not minding who got irritated and this time, he did it more obviously. He had taken enough of the stories of dreams and vague world and now he was determined to put an end to it all.

"We have been too carried away to see that everything was a grand conspiracy of those who do not know of better ways to hypnotize their fellow men than to speak of spiritual things."

The second man spoke firmly.

"We work for the science community and not for our personal interest. Only the truth pleases science, not politics."

"Indeed, science itself was unfair. Charles Darwin wrote about a biological war; the fittest getting rid of the weak. Paul Galton spoke about dissimilarity in intellectual capacities from races to races. You and I know these things are true yet we conditioned ourselves to believe otherwise because of our love for the tenets of our country; freedom and equity.

"Maybe we have misunderstood the lessons of science for too long."

"You disappoint me to speak for racism and hatred, friend."

"I do not speak of hate, sir. Mister Olabode Oladejo's

hypothesis of men waging war against the Neanderthals could be of immense importance if we try to understand it in the right context."

"No context would justify genocide. To publish that human race is responsible for the sudden disappearance of the Neanderthals in prehistoric times is to glorify segregation and genocide."

"But the Neanderthals attacked. It was an act of defense and not genocide as you alleged. I guess someone who is wiser than all of us wants us to know something, that he made several people from all over the world to have these dreams."

"Someone?' the fat guy opened his mouth like he was surprised to hear his friend speak so. 'You mean God? Where was that someone when innocent people die in earthquakes, when my boy was killed in a temple in Bohpal? So now He cares?"

He dropped the mug from which he was sipping and it slipped from the table and fell, breaking into pieces.

"Everything makes perfect sense to me now. The war against the 2018 World Law Reforms has already commenced."

"No one knows about it yet, except in the Hague."

"Even in the Hague there are church apologists, people who would stop at nothing to see their religious heritage survive."

"No one feels threatened by the advance of science. No man is desperate to make a set of believes he is unconvinced of seem true."

"Lie' the fat guy hollered 'fathers care about their daughters, husbands about their wives, how do you mitigate adultery or fornication without making them nervous?"

"And you suppose unchecked liberty is to our advantage? We have found times and again that all these things serve to reduce us into guilt-stricken, purposeless and unhappy people."

"Guilt is the church's making,' the fat guy touched his friend by the shoulder, persuading him with tenderness. 'It is a false feeling that makes us weak and unhappy. The 2018 World Law Reform could bring an end to it all and people will live to be proud of their humanity."

The second man, shocked to know the rumors were true, said softly,

"Every man dies but it seems to me a greater promise that assuming a state of existence higher than man will make us end our lives in hope for greater happiness."

The fat guy looked away.

"What do you want from me?"

"I want you to write no dissenting report. You will write and we will publish what you and I know to be true; that the claims of those sixty-two ladies and thirty men around the world are consistent with scientific findings. You will write that men once formed walls, two hundred kilometers long to defend their home from the hands of raging brutes."

The fat guy sighed. "Sounds humanistic, I thought you were gonna mention that they fought for God."

"To heal the world is to fight for God."

"Don't make me change my mind,' the fat guy hollered, 'you know how you sounded yesterday? Like there was a bet between good and evil to see whose side the people of the world would take. How shallow. Even clergies would feel for you."

"And would it be more outrageous if I said that that the greatest mystery of the book of Genesis has been uncovered? The mystery of creation."

It is the second man's turn to stroll across the office now, and the fat guy's turn to listen with astonishment.

"Let us create man in our own image says the book of Genesis. Why is this sixth day creation the only one with a pre-creation name? Even the moon was named only after it was created. I suppose the Neanderthal is the man being referred to and he was to be created in the likeness of the heavenly hosts."

"You should say this to a creationist, not me,' the fat guy tried to walk away but the second held him back and grabbed his shoulder. The second guy had evolved more proves in his mind.

"Yes it sounds amusing to you that a God made things become with words but it seem to me a greater amusement that the tree of evolution is being broken at the most crucial point. No one has successfully linked *Homo sapiens* with the less developed Homos."

"You lie' the fat guy demurred, 'the modern human has been linked with *Homo erectus* and even earlier primates. Even if there are no links, we mustn't descend from a known hominid for us to be recognized as being part of the evolution tree."

"It remains a mystery, how the first modern humans with fully developed brains emerged at the tail end of all pre-modern human history. It has never been uncovered, what truly ended the existence of all Neanderthals. The advent of intelligent human being is independent of evolution."

He picked the booklet lying on his desk. His draft was almost done but the most difficult part of their work, apparently was harmonizing individual reports. They were to come up with an historical document that would become a backdrop to the conference of 2018. Whoever convened the board did so to ensure a fair conclusion is being reached as different people from irreconcilable backgrounds had been chosen. The fat guy was atheist- an aggressive atheist, a couple of them members of the board were agnostics, three were deists and even among the remaining folks who claimed to believe in creation story, only one belonged to a church. One thing that was common to them all was they never exhibited deep passion for any line of thought either in their career or in their publications. They were respected teachers, justices and statesmen. A great mandate rested upon their shoulders – to test the validity of the claims of a few young people which policy makers said, would shake the foundation of every belief system. Their mandate expires in two days and they were yet to reach a consensus. Now the fat guy is being confounded with the closest of the creationist theories to Darwinism. He found himself listening, even entwining his fingers.

"Remember when you asked me one of your nasty questions about the book of Genesis; what Cain meant when he told God that he would be killed if found in the open?"

"That the generation of biblical Cain lived at the same time as the Neanderthals?" the fat guy endeavored not to sneer.

"Yes, but we both know that the Neanderthals lived freely in this lost history while the real men, the children of Adam were confined to a safe place in Eurasia after a major exodus from Africa."

"Sounds plausible,' the fat guy remarked, 'of course if only it is true that the boorish race never mated with men as suggested in the July 11, 1997 issue of Journal Cell but as we all know through a May 2010 report that they borrowed cultures and even interbred..."

"Even if they interbred, it must have occurred in isolated cases. The 2010 report say *there is no evidence for gene flow in the direction from modern humans to Neanderthals*. I tell you, we were created from their fossils and bestowed a mind and a purpose to have dominion over the beasts of the earth."

The fat guy paused to think, his eyes heavy with contemplation. He remembered the Bible said that the first human was made of dusts, and how paleoanthropologists seemed to have arrived at a common notion that all human populations arose from a very little number, from Africa to migrate to Europe and overcome the earlier hominid colonist, the Neanderthals and the *Homo erectus* in certain cases. The manner with which the brains of the first human beings evolved, he realized, was drastic and couldn't have been accounted for by the usually slow processes of evolution.

"What do we gain by rewriting the origin of man? We will only start a new thing that will be ridiculed in no time."

"We stand to gain wisdom,' the second man replied, 'we will get to know our history; that we were made by God and of God. We will get to know why we are here."

"And if we don't?' the fat guy was losing his temper again. The death of his only son in Bohpal was making it difficult for him to acknowledge God.

"What happens if we decide to be oblivious of these things, and forge ahead with our curriculum anyway?"

"Then we might miss the greatest evolution. If we do not make conscious efforts to evolve then we would become endangered species whose history, however grand, shall be lost to the endless stretch of time. We are meant to evolve as did the early homos, just one individualistic and supernatural evolution that will make us become supermen."

The fat guy looked into the eyes of his colleague.

"You speak like Nietzsche. And it is so ironic because Nietzsche blasphemed against your God."

"Yes he did.' the second guy mumbled. He stuffed the booklet he was holding into a bag and headed for the door. 'It is a secret yet it lays bare for us to see. Hardly was there a scholar in history who does not know about this and it was a surprise to Jesus that Nicodemus never knew. Whoever does not evolve would make true the propositions of unbelieving fellows that we are just a biological piece whose existence ends with death."

20

JOHN EDISON APPEARED from the staircase and beckoned Sola Aderomoke to join him. He was in the traditional suit of the Edisons, a design made popular by his own father, Christian Edison. He looked terrific. He had come with Sola for a brief summer vacation in the family country home from where they both agreed to take a pleasure flight over the counties. To the countrified, the house was just another piece of badly designed edifice. The front yard was littered with leaves and animal dung. The landscaping seemed shoddy and all the same it sat a fabulous three story plus underground mansion that Entertainment Channel claimed is worth many million dollars. For a decade now, the family had kept the tradition of coming with cooked foods and video games to the building every first weekend in September. None of those holidays really ended serving its purpose but they kept doing it anyway as it was the only time of the year apart from Christmas that they communicated as family and not as business associates. Summer vacation of the year 2001 was a little special and a little unnerving for Christian- the foes of many ages would stay together under same roof for three days. It was his new wife Lauryn's first, and his sister Baker Edison's too. Baker never pretended to like the new lady, never pecked her like she did almost everyone. When she phoned Christian to intimate him about her willingness to join the family for the vacation, it seemed like she was really coming for Lauryn.

Lauryn was Christian's fourth wedded wife, nagged in lifestyle magazines for being uncultured and frivolous. She suffered hatred and ill will of almost everyone. People who disliked Lauryn might be doing it for a reason they aren't even aware of. They said it was because of the manner with which she kicked the latest wife out, some blamed the hatred they felt on her fashion sense. Only a few were discerning enough to know. She was too unsuitable for the Christian Edison they knew and admired. She was an insult to their psyches. Christian was the name that inspired their children and the force behind the courage they felt. To see a supercilious twenty something year old by his side every now and then was a bit harsh on their minds. They would learn in no time to separate the quality of people's private lives from the public life.

Christian had decided to keep faith only to prove the press wrong. It was his duty, like one of his many responsibilities to his community, to discourage hearsays. All the ladies who ever came his way were bad and the ones who weren't originally wicked learnt to be. A Psychologist friend told him that it was his own making, a fall out of paranoia and sexist altitude of his that was borne out of unfounded fear for dishonest women. He had divorced his first wife, mother of John because she dared pressurize him to include her as a direct beneficiary of his firm, the second, mother of his only daughter because she was too close to his business associates. He smiled at cameras anyway, like Lauryn always did. He wrote books on success, designed what he thought it looked like and illustrated to people at will, how to attain it. When he talked people listened and most of the times after talking business he'd mention relationships. He'd teach them how to be successful all round. Nothing really mattered, not his struggle with alcoholism and recklessness, nothing except that he was just he.

Sola Aderomoke had been to many stately places yet she felt a thing for the opulent designing of the stairs. Slowly she climbed, her eyes scanning through the rows of picture that lined the walls. The pictures were being arranged to chronicle the life and times of the Edisons. They'd come so far and seeing the wall album, Sola understood why people listened when the Edisons spoke. She'd listen too. Just as she was about climbing the last step upward, the much talked about Christian took her hands.

"You must have been hearing lots of news about me' he said with an adorable sense of self-awareness. Sola nodded and forced a smile to her face. She'd only heard about him from John but she knew the purpose of that smile on his face. He was the rich merchant who raised controversial issues in the dailies every time, risking his own reputation and setting himself to the pillory.

"And here is my sister, Baker."

Each of those nanoseconds, she tried to figure what Baker Edison could possibly love about her. She was a celebrity with the crowd no doubt but she was never sure about the professionals. Perhaps they hated her, their body language said so. No one ever congratulated her even when she bagged the prestigious Media award in London. They always came up with excuses to avoid her each time they were scheduled to meet at an event. Even with the glamour and pomp, she still felt like an amateur and she felt so far away from the traditional captains of the media industry. Now she was coming face to face with the most important personality of the television finally, to know the truth.

Baker was the least among the big sharks that she ever hoped would like her. From the very beginning, she'd pictured Baker as an old, unhappy nitpicker. It seemed like she was wrong. Baker smiled and trotted to her. Her sudden love for the news girl was either intended to spurn Lauryn whom she had purposely come to frustrate or borne out of genuine enthusiasm because of the rumor she was hearing about Sola.

"Congratulations," she said

Sola looked to the ceilings, wondering if she was being congratulated for the media award of the past year. She creased her face into a smile and thanked Baker, not bothering to ask questions. Baker literally stood, staring and grinning. Sola smiled back, not having a single idea what she was supposed to do. She was inches taller, and the heels did not help. Baker strained her neck and gave Sola that funny gaze till John finally came, saving her.

"Time for the poker"

Baker hurried to the table at the room center. The game was her favorite. At first John acted as though he was going to join in the game but he pulled Sola by the hand into one of the rooms.

"You should talk your way up, these people could make you a big deal in the teevee."

"Your aunt?' Sola chuckled and faced down. John was fumbling his hands over her chest.

"I am already made up," she said.

"Are you sure?" John whispered and tried to lay her back on the sofa. She offered only feeble resistance like she'd always done in her life. Her regretful countenance notwithstanding, she led his hands over her body. John would have none of that. The romp was not of love and he intended it to be far from mutual. He seemed like a predator and he panted like the men who constantly abused her in childhood days.

"You know why Baker gave you that long look?" his breath passed into her ears, making it itchy. She was uncomfortable but she did not wriggle. John's weight was pinning her down; at least that was what she wanted to believe.

"A big conglomerate in London is offering a media contract. You are to be paid an advance of £20 million," John said slowly because he presumed the great news needed time to sink into her head.

Still not moving, Sola asked how he came by the news.

"Baker told me this morning,' he said, 'but this is not charity. You are to promote their cause as vigorously as you can on the television. They'd give you money and more fame in return."

"What makes you so confident I'd be enticed by money?"

He took his time to answer, looked sideways and sighed. He saw her eyes on the adjacent mirror. Indeed he was holding her down like a predator and she was like a vulnerable prey. Her eyes were drawn and her temper, wistful. The fellows of the Human Renaissance were right about her. How they arrived at that conclusion about the girl's physiology he wouldn't know but the brains of the HR had proven to be all knowing. He'd seen they could be more than just perverts. They were psychics who knew how to get to anyone. They told him she'd ask that very question but the response they suggested he gave was spiteful. It was difficult envisioning that the lady of graceful mien would take such insult from anyone.

"What makes you think so?" she asked again, releasing herself a little.

"Because you live only for fame and money, without it you are nothing but a wretch."

She smiled and dropped her face.

"Tell me about the contract."

He tried to breath. He couldn't believe his ears. The lady was a masochist.

"You'd host three hundred sessions of the largest talk show ever.' He stretched his arms to pick the piece of paper he'd earlier slipped under the sofa.

"Is my agent aware of this?" her typical demeanor reminded John of her personality, almost daunting him.

"This is squarely between you and the sponsors. You have a lot of work to do. A lot of people to work with."

"Sounds like a propaganda."

She finally rose.

"Propaganda is an unfairly demonized expression. All that matters is that a group of people want you to help them promote what they know all their lives to be true."

She wiggled her hair, wordlessly beseeching him to speak on.

"It all started in 1985 when a few guys suggested the science community deciphers the composition of the human genome,' he said. He picked his words slowly as it was important for him to be understood. 'The United States Department of Energy sponsored many laboratories across the states and collaborated with many foreign countries who conducted similar projects. By 2003, the total sequence of the human genetic makeup had been determined. We had never come closer to one of the most puzzling questions of all times- why we look the way we do, and why we behave the way we do."

Sola acted as though she was unaware. She enjoyed being patronized. She was more ahead than most people she'd met anticipated. She'd being to the DOE, and she'd talked with a lot of professionals there. She knew about the science; knew that the genome was the thing that differentiates all living things, from humans to the dogs and the birds. She knew that the genes contained information necessary for the formation of proteins, which could determine even individual behaviors. Through mapping of genetic sequences, she knew, the world could learn how to multiply desirable traits. She was aware that the DOE spends 5 percent of its budget ensuring that restraints were exercised. There was no need to let John know that she was aware.

"Think of the possibilities,' John extended his arms, 'knowledge will not only improve our chances of living longer, we could also clone supermen!"

Her dimples betrayed the thoughts in her mind. The whole game was all too familiar. The guy he spoke with at DOE had told her about the crazy Human Renaissance group who insisted on cloning super beings. John was probably a member of the group.

"Unfortunately, we cannot make progress because of the world's emotional baggage and because of many inhibitive international laws. We need you to enter people's heads."

Sola giggled, her face reminding John that she was only twenty-three.

"Now you are really making me to feel important,' she covered her mouth bashfully. Fairy tales couldn't have been more ridiculous, she thought.

"The Human Renaissance needs you' John said, 'it took a couple of renowned sociologists to arrive at this."

Again, he remembered he was not supposed to speak nicely.

"This is your only chance to remain in the spotlight. This is the future."

IN THE NEIGBORHOOD where John Edison grew up in, people say that every available girl was his'. They couldn't be more right. His rich peers had been unsuccessful in living above stereotypes- carousing in the streets, finding trouble and some girls to impress, John was never left out in all these but also included in his routines were the things only expected of 'losers'. Somehow, he managed to enjoy the loyalty and love of both sides and no one thought his action as phony even when he fought his friend for mishandling a lady in one late night party.

Since his fifth grade years, John loathed seeing his mates treat a loner with disrespect. He obeyed traffic rules when he started driving, tried to drink responsibly and stayed out of unnecessary troubles. He acted like he was keeping only one girlfriend too. Unlike most of his friends, he was his own dad's best pal, traveled the world with him for ambassadorial meetings. He enjoyed not only lodging into five star hotels on those tours but also series of fierce debates with his father about climatic change and politics of different countries of the world.

One of the things he seemed to share with his father was hatred for perceived Vatican's influence over Europe. His father, Christian Edison could not but nag and wonder why many people chose to align themselves with unattested ideologies. Each time he was driven through the narrow streets of big cities he would stare at outlining cathedrals, shake his head and complain about the location of those opulent structures. "The world is crazy," he would say, and sink himself back into the piles of diplomatic papers necessary for subsequent meetings. Nevertheless, Christian encouraged John to attend Sunday Masses with his mum. He made John read widely that the boy might find a thing to believe and not become a disillusioned adult that he was gradually becoming. There seem to be unbelief in the blood of the Edisons. Maybe John would have grown up to be moderate if he hadn't encountered orthodoxy at all. Every effort of his dad to make him toe a different path led him to greater deviance, making him to become one of the greatest critics of famous tenets.

The first time John learnt about the proposed World Law Reforms, he leaped and copied the advertiser's address on to his palm. His original intention was to fund the promoters, the Human Renaissance group but he found he was the one who needed money. He joined the HR as a full time propagandist but not until he had helped in establishing the group in a few cities. He was named the new Chief International propagandist on his fourth anniversary as a member. He was paid twice better than he used to, as manager of a national conglomerate. He adored the leaders of HR for their understanding of the human condition; the grandees recognized the place of gratification especially where fast results were needed but he found one thing was mysterious about them- they were rather too specific in their choice of workers. The leaders of HR trail a few successful professionals while they ignore the scores of people who applied for jobs and contracts through the Internet on daily basis. On top of the list of those wanted professionals were Sola Aderomoke, the cute teevee girl from Nigeria. John's meeting with Sola was not by chance. It was his job and it was a plot. He was to talk her into coming to the HR, the place where they said she truly belonged. When the old billionaire from London commissioned John through the videophone, he said the young lady had abandoned her destiny for too long, that it was time for her to come back and join the true lovers of the world.

Like he promised, John flew Sola around, but the sightseeing was not as lengthy as she anticipated. He landed the little airplane in an isolated place and took a parked motor vehicle. Sola knew very little about the city, couldn't recognize a place especially from a high attitude. She knew by instinct that she'd been there before and she started having unpleasant feelings. The sight of the place was bringing an obscure but painful memory to her brain. Suddenly, she saw that she was right. The streets were familiar though most of the buildings had been reconstructed. The perverted orphanage and 'castle' must be somewhere near. The last time SBC did a documentary about the place it was reported that the castle had been auctioned to a wealthy hotelier. Sola always avoided going back to the place even when her job required her to. The castle had become a big tourist attraction and the pains that used to be attached to it had given way to elegance. History, whichever kind of history, sells in tourism and that was why the castle was being refurbished into a first class hotel.

Eleven years after Mister Gbajumo conveyed her to the countryside, she'd come back not to the same building but somewhere very close. She didn't utter a word even when John Edison drove past the familiar graffito, *I hate the police.* John didn't speak either and it was quite unusual for a New Yorker as the evil of 1996 was the slogan of the moment especially because of the recent news of the castle's auction.

Finally, they arrived at their destination- a moderate duplex, painted in white, flanked on one side with a tennis court and the other with a swimming pool. The compound was surrounded with a short fence, lined with artfully arranged Light Emitting Diodes. The place must look very beautiful at night. Sola noticed that a man was standing impatiently before the house, probably waiting for a cab or them. She thought she recognized the face. Surely, it was one of the constant faces in the newspapers or she must have seen it too many times in the SBC library. She'd met no ordinary man for so many days now and it was like life was interested in bringing only great or loud people to her path.

"And here she is at last, the wonderful girl of the television," the man enthused from a fair distance. Sola walked into his opened arms and curtsied. She never bended her kneels in greeting for anyone who did not see it as culture but there was a way the man called her name that made her do so. Apparently, John Edison was meeting the old man in person, for the first time too. They'd only communicated through the Internet and phones. John moved forward to shake hands with him. John was tall but the old man was taller. He was slim too and his shoulders hung his blue fitted shirt well. He was clearly an old man but he looked younger from afar. Even John was a little nervous in his presence. When John was done groveling, he faced Sola and said with an awkward smile

"Just call him Lord, he is the proprietor of fourteen multinationals, and emeritus professor in genetics. At the moment, we are preparing to celebrate a recent achievement of his laboratory.' He managed to quip, 'this man may be the next recipient of the Nobel Prize in physiology."

"If those thralls will ever let it happen," The lord responded. John was extremely glad for striking a chord. He grinned like a fool, forgetting to continue with the introduction.

"My pleasure," Sola nodded. The man palmed her hands and pecked her. His hands were limp in hers'. He seemed very sick.

"I am sorry this meeting would not be as long as I'd love it to be. I ought to be at the airport by now."

He led the couple into a disarranged private office room. The building, Sola understood, was to be vacated within twenty-four hours.

"As you must have been told, one of my companies wishes to introduce a daily television program which we'd love you to host." He fetched himself a sofa from a pile of rubbish at the room's corner.

"I told John the company would have to make their intention known through my manager."

The old man pursed his lips briefly and he continued talking like Sola hadn't said anything. It seemed like he had never been faced up to before in his entire life and he seemed oblivious of any appropriate reaction to petty confrontations.

"I have the contract papers with me here and I'd like you to append your signature."

He signaled that he needed the papers and John provided it.

"We will renew the contract next year September."

He took a quick glance at the papers like it wasn't worth many million Pounds. He'd contracted several professionals in a single day and he endeavored to establish good relationships with each of them. Consciously and carefully, he'd learnt the art of leadership and of persuasion. He was a genius, always inches ahead of Government Intelligence units. He'd incorporated the Human Renaissance in several nations across the Atlantic and his influence grew by the day, though he remained largely irrelevant in the politics of his own country. Among a little set of people scattered all over the world, he was a messianic figure. He was not satisfied, even with the groveling and the near-deity worship accorded him during his visits to the Caribbean. He'd designed, together with dozens, a scheme that will see the world embracing his religion of individualism.

He was under watch- the state intelligence was not slack in their duties but he gave them a tough fight, countered their counter-actions. He conquered their intellects for no one, not even the best psychologists envisaged that a man who seemed to believe in nothing could have so much motivation. When a member of the State Intelligence announced that the man's scheme extends to the year 2100, the poor staff was laughed out of court. No nihilist and individualist cares much about the world they leave behind, they said. Of all the things that drove men, there was none that could be accounted as motivation for him, not love or power. A great scheme stared the State Intelligence in the face yet they did not believe.

The Lord, like he preferred to be called, nursed many grudges for his nation and his reasons were simple. He dealt in arms business at a time the world pursued peace. He trafficked young people for sex and cheap labor in the century when the world was increasingly becoming contemptuous of the act. The very last thing that broke his camel's back- his human cloning business was being jeopardized by religious men.

In the beginning, when he was yet shy about his 'perversion', he came across Nietzsche's articles, *Overman*, the same piece which inspired good men unto goodness. The nineteenth century thinker, Nietzsche had blamed human misery on religion and traditions, proclaiming that the overman or the superman would bring the world back to her senses. Lord did not appreciate in full measure, this assertion, until many scientists started decoding the language of life- the DNA. "Inasmuch as we have known the secrets of the DNA,' he always said, 'we could clone men for our own pleasure."

Statesmen thought otherwise, and lord thought he knew why. The so-called men of power grew up in Sunday schools and they were too afraid to usher humanity into a new age. "If we could envision it,' lord always said, 'we could achieve it; take the world to the glorious age where science leads the way."

Lord thought his adherents that knowledgeable people whose mind had become freed from all forms of fear were the ones destined for greatness and they would overcome, as Darwin postulated, the weak. He became more resolved by the day- he found his own truth and nurtured it till it became a religion in his heart. He'd made tremendous progress about his New Age movement too. He'd succeeded in convincing the world that there were serious loopholes in the basis of every law. He wasn't a lawyer, but he showed deep understanding in almost everything. He'd achieved unbeatable success in his endeavors- main reason why the newly constituted International Law Convention invited him to present a paper in the March conference of 2007. He was the first to advocate for a Law reform, a campaign that resulted into the constitution of the Law Reform conference of 2018. He'd drawn extensive plans like his life depended on it and he'd seduced great people to his side.

The only man who really knew him, Doctor Olanusi once said to his face that his efforts at turning the world around was an indication of a major flaw in his life. He knew Olanusi was right. His original ambition was to build orphanages in every major city in Europe, then South America and Africa. He acquired properties and started an orphanage soon enough but a familiar demon kept luring his heart to the ladies'. He gave in, one day, and followed a pretty one to her room. The next day, he did the same thing, and the day that followed. He suffered the chastisement of his own conscience and the day Olanusi caught him with one of the orphans, he swore to change. He undermined his demons.

He continued abusing the orphans till he found a justification for his actions. His journey to the dark commenced when his personal psychiatrist, Olanusi told him that his madness could be cured by his sins. Since then, he had gladly preached the gospel of humanism and hedonism. He did not stop at that, he'd made many great people sign up to the incipient religion. He'd trailed Sola Aderomomke, whose destiny, he proclaimed, was to take the gospel to every home through the television. He had made John Edison to bring her.

Lord draped his arms over the window and stared at members of staff who were busy loading the trucks. Sola Aderomoke stood behind him and John, some meters away.

"They call it the land of the free yet they are slaves unto fear,' he puffed and turned around, 'they are slaves unto delusion."

"Maybe it is good to exercise restraints. The world would be in great danger if they should just jump at the promises of every new science."

"Crap!' Lord raised his voice but cautioned himself immediately, 'Crap,' he repeated, mildly. 'My company spent time, money, sweat and blood, trying to figure out a freaky content of the human genome, and now they wish to sacrifice my efforts in the altar of morality."

"SBC-TV reported it would result in a holocaust.' Sola chuckled, 'with powerful cloned men in our Armed Forces, all international scores would be settled in one minute."

"There could be danger only if the new trick gets to the know of idiots."

"It will, eventually. We have seen nations steal another's technology."

"I need you to tell them it will not,' lord fondled her. 'Men have worshipped an imaginary God long enough. It is time we invented for the world not a God, but a legion of gods who will fight our wars and construct our bridges."

"And they will be used for unjust purposes. Wicked men will take over."

"So said the lawmakers.' Lord sighed. He must have repeated what he was about to say, too many times.

"Is it not the design of nature for supermen to overcome the middling and strong nations to make the weak nations tremble? To pretend that all men are equal is to insult the most sacred tenet of nature."

"I guess you have a very bumpy road ahead of you, sir. Convincing a pacific generation about chauvinism is an impossible venture."

"Don't lecture me, young lady,' Lord interjected. The father of this generation knows nothing.' He paused and looked around the room for his laptop. "Thanks to this amazing nuclear base that we found from the scrapes of a rock surface, a few years ago, we have found that men could indeed do a lot more than fire guns."

He wanted to turn on the laptop to show a genomic map, but he changed his mind. Showing her a complicated pictorial representation of the human genome would make no difference, especially for a non-geneticist.

"Only a few researchers know, and we have resolved to make it a secret.' He grins. 'What you know gives you power!"

"What do you know?" Sola asked, her gentle mien toughened with inquisitiveness.

"That a group of extraterrestrials once visited southern England, many million years ago and he or they left an inscription on a rock surface for us to see."

Sola gave a knowing smile. Even in the awe-inspiring presence of the lord, she felt considerably calm. "I guess you got the DNA you spoke about from that inscription."

"From the scraps.' Lord replied. The DNAs are essentially the same with those of the modern human except for the genes that my laboratory recently discovered, could have allowed this mysterious, prebiological human race to fly. The ease with which we got the DNA is a testimony to my assumption that these people intended us to discover this ageless secret."

"Where in southern England is this rock?"

"We aint making it public yet, but geologists said the mountain used to be one-thousand feet high in geological times. I guess the artists must have been able to get to the top because they could fly."

Sola sighed, and she tried to relax. She'd shown huge interest in the topic to the lord's delight. "What if it is just a joke? Someone could be fooling around."

"No man or group of men is capable of designing the inscription we found on the rock in Mars. It changes color from time to time, like there was some machine inside and again, the inscription is more than three billion years old."

"Meaning there used to be a world more civilized than ours even in a period we used to think there was no life?"

"Obviously, that is what our discovery is making us to believe."

"It could be angels," Sola giggled to soft land herself in case her contribution would be tagged silly. She wasn't all that silly. Leaders of thought and clergies were theorizing angels already.

Lord gave a stony look, "Religious folks are celebrating, but I wonder why they have all become materialists all of a sudden. I thought they said the things of God cannot be explained by material things."

"Grabbing the easiest choice isn't a crime, is it?" Sola smiled, more because she just discovered that she was evidently not out of touch with reality.

Lord rushed into one of the rooms like he was going to take something but he returned empty handed. He seemed freaked out.

"We must not leave our destiny into the hands of them cowards who think there is someone up there, especially when an ancient wisdom gives us a promise of immortality."

Sola examined him; "You need to take it easy, sir. You should, maybe, see a therapist."

"How dare you?' came a thunderous shout that drove the room into a moment of quietness. Even John was afraid. Sola quivered and she slipped a word of apology from her trembling lips.

"Don't be sorry, dear.' The old man had suddenly calmed down. 'You are right. I need a therapist. I used to have one, a Nigerian. Doctor Olanusi weathered my mind with the thoughts of common men but the thing that made me great and successful also deprived my mind of the peace of common men."

Sola wondered why lord talked like some old-time knight. Her shoulders dropped, hanging like it used to, in her moment of apathy. She gazed at the man like she was seeing more than a mass of flesh.

"I learnt you own an orphanage in England.' She attempted to close up the gap between lord and her, but had a rethink. The old man's temper was volatile.

"What makes you care for orphans if you are as heartless as Doctor Olanusi suggests?" she smiled faintly, either because she loved what she just said, or because she wanted to extenuate her sensitive comment. Lord closed up the gap, bringing to life, her little fear. He placed his hands over her neckline and examined the little scar on the neck. His actions were senseless. He was a mad man. People said he ran mad at work, one day when he thought his computer systems in which he documented series of genome sequences had crashed.

"I care for children.' He said like he was not offended, 'I care for all the downtrodden."

"You do?' Sola tried to be calm though it seemed like lord would strangle her.

"Someone have been talking too much and I know it is the doctor."

"Doctor Olanusi only mentioned you in a private discussion, and it is not like he has been talking to the press."

"I learnt he is writing memoirs and my eyes are on him."

"I swear he is lying low,' Sola insisted but the old man kept fuming.

"Olanusi is a traitor. He encourages you in your presence and turns his back to criticize you."

Sola gave up explaining and she turned her face down. She swallowed the saliva. The thought on her mind was of safety. She tried to believe that she was safe, hinging her doubtful assumptions on the manner with which the old man spoke. Lord spoke like a child when he complained about his old friend and personal psychiatrist, making her to wonder how he carried on in more difficult situations.

Lord's attention remained essentially on the scar at Sola's neck. He rubbed his hands over the lump.

"I did this. I am sorry that I hit you."

"You didn't hit me," Sola replied, her composure dwindling.

"Yes I did, a long time ago."

"But we are meeting for the first time."

Sola jerked her body away from his grip and ran to get her handbag. Fear built up in her till she lost her manners.

"John, we must leave now. Please take me away from this place!"

John walked up to her, throwing his hands into the air.

"I am sorry, sweetie, but we cannot leave now. You gotta listen to the man."

"Am I being kidnapped?" Sola gasped. Her whole face was filled with horror.

"No, you are not.' John replied but did not add the kind of smile that she desperately needed. 'Just listen to him and do whatever he asks of you. You will walk out of this place a millionaire."

"I am no longer interested."

"No, you are." John advanced to lock the door. His countenance had suddenly changed. He avoided Sola's eyes when he spoke.

"I think it is in your best interest to listen."

The old man, miffed by her behavior, clasped his hands to his back and spoke fiercely.

"Perhaps, we should clone ladies who know how to turn down a man's advances."

Sola stood completely awed by the new face of cruelty she was beholding. Her eyes seemed swollen and tears watered her face.

"I guess it is time to take you back the memory lane,' lord said as he strolled around the room, 'the Human Renaissance brought you from...Lagos, I think?'

"Right, sir." John answered on her behalf.

'We brought you from nothing and made you into something within a short duration,' he chuckled. 'Probably, you thought everything ends with the so-called Evil Day of 1996. I expect a lady renowned for ingenuity to know better."

Sola tried to speak but he did not allow her.

"We own you, we know what you want and what you need. We own the future."

A staff member interrupted him.

"The contingent has edged through the airport. They should arrive in Nigeria in two hours."

"Brilliant! I told you the security unit is overrated."

"The driver waits."

Lord rubbed his hands together with an air of finality.

"Even though the enemies love to portray us as bullies, the truth is, we are not. We will leave you to either take this offer or fall to the wayside of destruction."

He threw the papers to her face as he made for the door.

"You should fill these, scan and mail them."

He moved over as the driver packed his things to the car and he apologized to the man for taking so long to prepare. The third Sorento in the convoy was to drop Sola in her place and John was billed to follow the last contingent to the airport.

"Remember, this is the ultimate showdown.' Lord stooped to look at Sola in the eye. 'The world is about to witness a great war and the minds of our people is the prize."

John took the front seat of the waiting motor vehicle. "Over there,' he pointed at the car at the rear. 'It will take you to your place," he said, still not looking at her face. Lord joined him and the car drove off.

THE FAX read:

"Area under watch evacuated, monetary exchange between the HR and terrorist organizations confirmed; Washington under threat. Mister Bay turned lazily in his bed and droned.

"Constant attention seekers....so paranoid. The State intelligence guys need a therapist."

His wife was awakened by the humming sound he made. It was irritating but then, being peevish seemed like a necessary distraction from the constant pressures of their job. Too many times, the couple had started their day on similar note. They'd made so much money they didn't even have the time to spend. Their five year old kid now call them mister and missis. They couldn't make more babies like they originally intended. The contract investigative job was taking over their lives.

Mr. and Mrs. Bay lived in the same estate with the most watched individual, lord of the Human Renaissance movement and they kept track of his activities. Mr. Bay was convinced beyond doubts that the old man and his cohorts were complacent in the evil of 1996 but the nasty clique always had an alibi. Mister Bay's faith in his own conviction was shaken when lord acquired a property in the same estate that he supposedly knew was under watch. No one who narrowly escape justice comes back to the face of justice, the State Intelligence chief used to say. No one seem to have a satisfactory insight into the motives of the old man who the prestigious British Life magazine reported as fast assuming a messianic figure in different nations of the world.

At first, Mister Bay chose not to believe the news of the sudden evacuation but he found himself getting worried. Not even the cameras or electronic trailers of the estate could be trusted. The HR guys were apt in beating all those features, as though they belonged to a greater civilization. Should it be true that the guys have eloped, Mister Bay's well-intentioned actions of the past fortnight would amount to negligence. He'd been warned. He should have arrested the leaders of HR when the hint first came that they were transacting with the rebels. Several thoughts flooded his mind. He reached for the phone box and dialed the Special Intelligence Headquarters.

"This is Mister Bay, code number X156, I wish to confirm the message."

"Confirmed," came a feminine voice, almost immediately.

"What do we do now?" Mister Bay endeavored to be stoic and professional.

"Another message has been sent. Top security officers are meeting presently. You should hang on for instructions."

Mister Bay leaned against the bedstead, panting, and a mischievous smile sneaked to his face when he discovered his wife was watching.

"You're gonna father a bastard?" Mrs. Bay joked. She'd been observing for the past one minute. Mister Bay laughed, even though the lines of anxiety remained on his face.

"What makes you think someone is pregnant?"

"Because I heard a female voice over the phone and I saw you beating up yourself."

"Too bad I am too busy to cheat."

He knew what his wife wanted- some reassurance, but he was tired of giving one. He'd spent the previous nights explaining how she was more attractive than all her friends. He dragged his feet on the smooth floor as he walked to the bathroom. Mrs. Bay intercepted. She was going to pick quarrel should he struggle with the bathroom door like they always did every morning. Mister Bay allowed her to go first, not holding her wrist like he would have. The phone beeped as he moved away, making his action seem incidental.

You are being connected for video conference call. Online meeting is to commence in five minutes, the message read.

Mister Bay went to put on some clothes and he waited for the signal to come up. The computer had been on, all night. He tried finding a good excuse in his mind but there were none. He would settle for a ridiculous one, at least that would be better than making apologies. Apology was indictment in the security world, and it was better to insist on having done whatever is being done for a reason. Through the moment, Mrs. Bay's shameful vexation disappeared.

"What more evidence do we need to nail those guys,' she asked from the bathroom, 'hesitation could turn out to be costly, you know?"

Mister Bay clenched his fist with regret and gnashed his teeth. Unknown to his wife, they were paying the prize of hesitation already. They had lost the chance of killing off a most dangerous religion when it was still beatable. Bay groaned as he waited to see a green light on the camera. The waiting was tiresome but it was useful, as he needed to defend the decisions he had been making for the past few days.

"Mister Bay, we hope information have reached you that the guys under surveillance have left the country for an uncertain destination."

"How uncertain could their destination be, state security has the database of all flights, both private and public."

Mr. Bay knew the security chiefs would blow things out of proportion. He raised his head.

"I could come around, sir."

"To Washington? Nope. We need you in New York more than we do, here. You should stay and provide necessary information to a team of experts we will be referring to you."

Mister Bay nodded and just when he was about breathing easy, another person said, "we have a feeling that our national security has been jeopardized."

He looked up to see who was talking, hoping it wasn't the person he thought. A very senior security officer was in the meeting, a serious indication that the situation at hand was grave or potentially so. Top officers were dressed in full regalia, looking battle ready from the computer monitor.

"Mister Bay, we would like to run by a few things with you."

Mr. Bay wiped his face with a handkerchief, swallowing the saliva he'd prefer to spit out. He beckoned his wife to stay away from the camera. She had just taken her bath and she was nude.

"I am listening, sir." He said to the Special security chief.

"Over the years, we have been talking to the special commission established by the former chief of the state Special Intelligence Service in 1996. What the commission does is to read every book the so-called lord has ever read, simulate the developmental stages of his life, you know, they do all those crazy stuffs just to get to his mind."

Mr. Bay cleared his throat, and his eyes became less fuzzy, a thing the handkerchief had consistently failed to achieve.

"That is brilliant, sir," he said

The security chief continued talking in a restrained pace, as though he was reluctant to share the information.

"Early this year, we discovered an essay that lord wrote for a college editorial board thirty-six years ago. The essay was never published but we found it among the slush pile of the defunct student group. Lord wrote in the third paragraph of that article that fear is one of the most employable forces in driving people to do a thing."

"Yes, my wife said that he spoke about fear all the time," Mr. Bay interjected to show he was still getting the signal.

"Lord went further to explain how the fear of thunder and earthquakes led human ancestors to assume the worship of the sun and other items. He expounded on many theories of fear so vividly that we cannot but suspect he is resolved to blackmail the nations of the world into adopting his fascist religion."

"And what do you think he is up to?"

"To create fear and make us abandon the doctrine of compassion and democracy and equality. It is only then that we could agree to his supermen project."

A senior police chief spoke from the second row, "lord happens to bear no similarity in ideology or in any way with the enemies but he made pact with them because he wanted to teach us a lesson."

"And I guess our own lesson will be the first to be learnt," an officer representing Inland Defense posited.

The old commanders chorused "yes", not minding that a junior had spoken and one assertive voice rose from the hubbub.

"The special commission reported that the Human Renaissance apparently does not know the details of the partnership. If by any chance the HR holds sway in the relationship, I bet they would want to strike on a day of significance. The president speaks at children conference in Washington today. I am afraid lord may choose today because of his affinity for children."

"Too remote!' the thin, goggled lady in unknown uniform protested. 'You are cramming too many assumptions into a single hypothesis."

"You accused me of the same thing five years ago; proposing a theory that is remotely connected to issues at hand but now, we all know the truth, that the Human Renaissance is complicit in the evil of 1996."

"It is not our job to debate on the next line of action, another force man remarked. 'We should stay alert and wait for executive instructions. Remember, a group of men and women are behind doors, trying to reason like lord would, and picking his brains. We should wait for their report."

The lady in brown uniform shook her head, "wait for people who couldn't tell the only man they were employed to watch is absconding?"

Mr. Bay felt his heart move. He knew it was time to speak up less he bears the brunt.

"They told us he is absconding but we didn't have orders to arrest him," Mr. Bay remarked. He couldn't believe his ears; the silence that ensued.

"You didn't have the orders?"

"Not only that. There are no evidences. We intend catching lord by the fist this time, because the last time we took him to court, he made us pay millions for defamation. The man is a genius; I couldn't have believed he would survive the case of 1996. The way he operates, you must believe me, is somewhat mystical. He doesn't have to be arrested and bailed again. He doesn't have to know that he is been watched this time."

"Whatever you say, man, you were contracted outside the constitution and you are expected to use discretions where necessary,' he sank into the chair. 'This is what you get when you employ the overqualified."

Just before he finished talking, the police chief bawled "He would escape justice once more if we should arrest him, he is not human, he has some powers. We intend killing the man on action, we planned to gun him down as he flees."

He sucked his lips and looked away as he quivered. He shouldn't have disclosed such information, not in the presence of junior force men.

Even his reasons would not absolve him of the blame, that he suggested that lord was supernatural is unprofessional and would land him in greater trouble. A troubling bombshell had been dropped, even in the middle of a crisis.

"We have only few hours to decide necessary security measures that should be put in place. There isn't much time for blame game," Chairman of the joint meeting remarked.

MR. BAY clung to his podcast in anticipation of an event, any event. He dragged his feet as he strolled down the walkway that connected his house to the estate's central garden. He'd lived in the hilly street with his wife for three years. It was a working day but he had been instructed to stay at home. He wasn't told exactly why, but he knew an anti-terror unit was to be dispatched to the estate and he was to show them around. Their mission, he hoped, was investigative but he might just be overrating his superiors, the generals might just be having a wild dream of finding someone to arrest.

About three hundred meters behind, his wife waved and asked to join him. The couples were the only ones in the fenced estate of one hectare. He beckoned her to wait for five more minutes and tried to hide the mischievous smile that was forming on his face. The sight of his plumb wife longing to see what lay ahead amused him. He was the senior de facto, although the agency with which they worked thought otherwise. He knew how long five minutes was, for his wife. She would come join him in few seconds anyway.

Mrs Bay jumped over the railings and dusted the back of her jean trousers, ready to leap over the swamps to join her husband. The first blast that sounded from the metropolis, 2 kilometers away South East, threw her off balance. Mr Bay came for her and he laughed for no apparent reason. He must be undermining the threat the huge fire was posing to them.

"I told you they'd pick today," Mr. Bay panted.

"What do you mean 'they'? Do you think honestly think a mafia is capable of holding a nation to ransom?"

Another blast came before Mr. Bay could respond and the noise that followed showed the streets were panicking.

"So what would be their targets if they were to attack?"

"I don't know but I have a theory."

He scratched an insect off his temple, staining his face with mud.

"You spied on these guys for more than a year, testified to the fact that they have far reaching plans yet you doubt their existence?"

"I do not doubt their existence' Mrs. Bay hollered, her voice accompanied by an uproar of alarms and police sirens, 'only their capacity to constitute a major threat to the security of a nation I doubt."

The frequency of the blasts got him worried. He became pensive and for a moment, unsure of what to do. His doubts melted away as he shook off the Mistle toe that clung to his boot.

"I agree it is impossible to fight a nation and win, especially from the hood."

A flame of fire rose above the gardens as if to warn him but he wasn't deterred.

"Come on," he waved his wife to follow him as he ran to the only structure within that axis of that estate, his house. They were followed by gunfire but they managed to shut the proof metal door behind them and Mr. Bay crawled up to the bedroom.

"Why?' Mrs. Bay panted, 'why are they after us?"

"Because we have the key to this mystery," Mr. Bay took his palmtop with dire urgency.

"Never once have I taken them as a major threat."

He needed to do many things within seconds and he better be quick about it.

"Please call for help."

He tried to take a deep breath. He waited to clear his head of all strains. He needed to remember nine successive passwords to gain access to the network of Defense Bureau.

Mrs. Bay returned in a minute.

"Help is coming."

She saw that her husband was totally engrossed by the thing he was viewing on the palmtop.

"What is that," she whispered as she pressed her cold, shivering body against him. They knew the silence and calm of the moment was intermittent. Mrs. Bay lay on the floor, and stared at her husband's face that was lighted with the purple light of the palmtop screen, expecting the next blast, a big one that would, most certainly end their lives.

"What you wanna know will be useless for everyone if you do not find us a way out of this place."

Mr. Bay jerked forward, and smiled to himself like he just remembered something.

"I am not the only one who knows,' he said, 'this is what our leaders had been keeping away from us from the past twenty months." He dropped the computer joltingly as bullets flew through the window. "Leaders kept this secret close to their chests as not to create public hysteria. The German who suffered schizophrenia said many things, far more than was published." He bended over and narrowly escaped being shot "Remember the rock having an ancient inscription that the German spoke about? It is untrue that people who were lettered in semantics failed to unravel the meaning of those ancient inscriptions. They did in fact explain every bit of it, working in conjunction with award winning geneticists. The design was a message from an unrecorded past and it was meant for us."

"What is the design about? Where did you get your information from?" Mrs. Bay asked but she seemed barely interested because of the look on her face. Fear had taken hold of her heart and nothing mattered to her except to live.

"I stumbled upon it last week when the classified weblink developed a fault. The fault never lasted for more than a few minutes but I retrieved many hidden passwords and learned them by heart. I didn't go back to that link for fear it would be traced back to me but I guess there is no reason to fear anymore."

"So what are the contents?" Mrs. Bay asked in a teensy voice that betrayed hopelessness.

"Several thousand years ago, during the Ice age, an unidentified, highly sophisticated race inscribed series of genomic codes onto a rock as if it were meant to be discovered. Through the German's guidance, the rock was discovered and it was carefully protected by powerful authorities. Semantics discovered its purpose after a year of marathon research and consultations. They said the codes were guidelines to the making of genomic construction that will make the human race capable of flying, making fire, and even to attain immortality."

"Sounds good," Mrs. Bay muttered, her face became pale, and her spirit dulled.

"But the German warned against it' Mr. Bay quickly added, 'he said an invincible wickedness will emerge if we dare to synthesize those DNAs or clone human beings using the knowledge of that ancient inscription."

"Unusual abilities, immortality...sounds like gift from God. Our geneticists should go back to the laboratories," Mrs. Bay said. It was a little surreal, how her senses had managed to outwit her spirit.

"So said a faction of those contending groups. Many leaders believe it is divine; the revelation, but the German cautioned it is evil. He discussed a popular myth in bringing home his assertion; the origin of evil as recorded in the Bible."

"Oh, Bible' Mrs. Bay sighed and the deep breadth she took helped bring back some life to her face. There hadn't been a bang now for the past twenty minutes.

"The German had proven himself to be authentic and almost every world leader who knows about everything takes him serious."

"And does he really have to quote the Bible to foster his authenticity?"

Mr. Bay faced the palmtop, ignoring the query.

"I cannot believe so many leaders know about this."

He was annoyed because of the side his wife was taking and he melted out his usual punishment for her- his silence. He read a long text from the computer, not saying a word but he spoke after ten minutes.

"The religious-minded among them said the genomic maps and the letters on the rock were authored by fallen angels. There is also an antithesis that those human-like beings meant to make good their promise to the people who lived in the valleys in that time, by leaving those codes on the rock, hoping they would learn science quickly, and make use of the knowledge. These set of infidels proposed that the dwellers of the valley were sacked from the place so as not to discover the secret."

"And who is to be trusted?"

Mr. Bay shook his head in surprise.

"No wonder the world leaders bargained to make this secret. People are so unfaithful they will disown God because of this vague promise of immortality."

"It has always been the wish of men to live pleasurably and to live forever." Mrs. Bay said.

"Forever we will live, but not like this,' Mr. Bay raised his voice. Whoever it was that was trailing them must have an idea where they were hiding now.

"This is an ageless conspiracy and not everyone is noticing. We are either being ensnared by a civilization far older than ours or by a timeless enemy."

Mr. Bay laid his back on the floor.

"Considering the manner of people who wants this Greek gift, I am convinced that an aged conspiracy is to be perfected in our own time. Even their proposition lacks merit because the secret was not at any time shielded from the ancient population. There was no life on earth at the time the design was crafted on Mars, no human to which a promise was made when a replica was inscribed on a rock in England. The people who made the inscription were extraterrestrial, the German said they were evil, and their purpose was to ensnare humankind, the creation which the creator proposed at that time into blaspheming."

"Then I suppose the lord of the castle is aware. He loved life and hated that he was getting old," Mrs. Bay remarked with a croaky voice.

"Yes he does. He formed a network of skeptics across nations. He is determined to give the conservatives a run for their money."

"All these while, politicians knew who their enemies were and they risk our lives finding out who they were?"

"Everything is game to them. Even the believers, a great number of them aligned with the spiritual not because they loved it but because they needed power and religion gives power. There are no good guys in this conflict."

A noise came from the city center. Fire-fighter motors sped across the streets and armored vehicles rolled. The nation was under attack and so were the couple.

Mr. Bay tried to move his stiff neck. He was anxious for his little daughter who stayed with a Nanny five kilometers away. He tried to undermine the mood in the air and he continued talking.

"Why do you think lord escaped the jail in the case of 1996? The rebels, I say, have a symbiotic relationship with our leaders and none of the two interests wanted open confrontation."

Mrs. Bay asked with genuine interest for the first time, "how?"

"The Human Renaissance owns the key to a code which could see people living a very long and healthy life, governments of industrialized nations felt they needed to exercise caution, but they still need HR anyway just as the HR needs the government to legislate and make their business legal."

"And they both agreed to keep it under wraps?"

"Yes,' Mr. Bay replied, 'everything would turn to one big war if people come to know about it."

"And we are people. I guess that is why someone is after us."

"They must have discovered that their networks had once been compromised and they must have traced the porous links to us."

Mr. Bay, still lying on the floor, rested his head on his wife's limbs.

"This is it, girl. Help is not coming. Everything we said here, I have recorded and I will send it to Sola Aderomoke. It is not all for nothing."

21

UNCLE STOPPED talking and he rubbed his chin. Befriending staff members, for him, was almost impossible, partly because of PM's allegations. The only person he could possibly trust was the PM. His face, his voice, his tie and general style easily gave him away as trustworthy. Uncle judged by those things. He had his own parameters, which he adhered to, not minding how many times he'd discovered the contrary. Uncle told him stories until he had to start recycling old ones and PM carefully ensured he didn't regret anything he did. PM reminded him with every opportunity that he, Uncle Bode was the boss but Uncle forgot as many times as he remembered. He did not feel like he was in charge. And he was right.

The harmattan had its way in him for the first time in that season. His lips cracked up, and his hands felt dry. He grew more restless and unable to keep his latest findings to himself. The probe panel that he commissioned a fortnight before had come up with incredible revelations and he needed to tell someone how skilled an administrator he was.

He took a bunch of keys from his pocket and unlocked his filing cabinet. He was not sure of what he was doing but an eager inner voice kept telling him he couldn't afford not to trust anyone. He took the rough and thoroughly sealed parcel in the lowest cabinet and slammed it on his desk to shake off the dust.

"This is a revisit of the case of 1996, a complete report that will lead the way in sanitizing this division. The wolves cannot escape this time. We have caught them by the arm."

Like he wasn't impressed, the PM stared on. It was apparent from his face, a struggle to remain undaunted.

"If that report is anything to go by, then more than half of our work force would have to go for it."

"Yes,' Uncle shrugged, 'there are many promising professionals out there looking for opportunity." He could not believe the rather prejudiced comment was coming from him. He sounded phony in his own ears. He did not know what he really wanted or what it was that really sickened him about the company's old financial inappropriateness report but there was something about the dating of the crime that made him suspect there was more to it than the ordinary. The company's executive had acted as though they were compelled to. None of those indicted staff members benefited from the fraud but two expedited money transfers had occurred on a single day in favor of same foreign organization. He became more confused when he found the Human Renaissance group; the famed worldwide organization was the recipient on both occasions.

"Do you really want to know why the report of 1996 was passed up?' The PM tried to hide his anger. 'It was abandoned because the management realized the consequence. The board would start a holistic appraisal of each staff like it was done before we were employed. Issues bothering on private morality would be raised."

The way PM looked at Uncle when he talked about 'private morality', Uncle could not help suspecting that he was being gagged for something he'd done. He knew it from the way a staff was reproached for advocating tougher penalties for pedophiles in his presence. The cautioning and the apology easily pointed to one thing- the news of his sexual impropriety was known to them staff members.

 He stared down for a moment, and his eyes became unusually moist.

"PM, if you fear indictment you should tell me."

"Who...me?" PM stuttered but quickly regained his poise.

"All I wanted to do was to restrain you from creating a great upset in the company."

"And I should do nothing when millions are missing, when we are being pushed to the brink of a financial crisis?"

"You should maintain the status quo, sir, because we consider personal morality of staffs as equally important as their financial appropriateness."

Uncle sweated and it felt like a bubble of air passed down his auditory canal. *I know you are up to something,* he wanted to say out loud but the word left his lips as a whisper.

 PM left the office room and Uncle followed him to shut the door. He saw Musa Abdulkarim through the window that was next to the door, waited to read the man's countenance. Musa's visit to the guest house must be routine because he held a file and smiled at the doorman. Uncle became disturbed when he noticed that Musa walked faster than necessary. Abdulkarim must have made good his promise to tell his son about what happened at the clubhouse. He followed the elevator's timer in his mind and he proceeded to the door in the fortieth second. He couldn't be more accurate.

"Good morning," Musa offered his hands.

"Good," Uncle grabbed the arms too tightly. Musa declined his invitation to enter the office room.

"Someone died," Musa handed him the certificate of demise that was posted to Uncle's former office, that morning. The name read Nkechi Oladejo. It was funny that a person had a first name and a surname from two different cultures. He quitted smiling when he realized the mail was truly meant for his office. Sola Aderomoke must have dropped his address when she made the application in the National Planning bureau.

"Someone I never met," he quickly told Musa who had become replete with guilt for the casualness with which he delivered the mail. He remembered something that made his eye fly to the part of that certificate where parental information was written. He knew his sister used to answer that name.

"This is..' he wanted to talk, but he was too sensitive about anything that had to do with his family. He could not believe it, but he knew when things are lost, they could be found anywhere, even in the most ridiculous places. He'd finally discovered the identity of his sister and mother with whom he was separated in the late 1970s. They were both late. He closed his eyes to let the sharp feeling of pain that passed through his body subside. He'd always hoped for a happy ending but the past seemed to have passed. He could only hope for happiness for the future.

"The lady your ex helped to keep her baby, right?" Musa tapped his shoulders.

"Yes," he smiled and rubbed his face, 'I should have shown more interest in the poor lady."

He still remembered childhood stories of why it is good to be good but he was astonished how life had thought him another lesson on being kind in its most literal sense.

Musa sighed, "It's over now, and you have learnt your lesson."

Uncle looked at him. The man doesn't have any idea how difficult the lesson is and will be. Uncle realized how much he'd missed Musa; one man who reminded him of how religion had made the lives of some people fine. Musa recognized that gaze, and he was flattered.

"Pearl is acting weird and I hope you'd come to talk to her."

"Weird?"

"She...' Musa scratched his head, 'how difficult was it for you, the challenges you faced?"

Uncle sighed. He'd forgotten that he'd told Musa about his disorders before. He'd forgotten how close they used to be.

"I'd come talk to her."

He examined Musa's expression when he said he'd come to her. He needed to be sure Musa wasn't in the know of his misdemeanor.

"Thanks," Musa winked at him and left.

Uncle shut the door and feelings of pain rushed at him. He'd held them back for too long.

THE CAR steering in his hands seemed to have become more flexible. He whistled a long forgotten folk song as he drove into the street Olanusi lived.

He was the one nursing unpleasant feelings; the Abdulkarims had moved on, even Musa who had gotten to know about his sin. Uncle hoped he wasn't presuming too much but it soothed his psyche, the thought that everything had fallen into place, the thought that he had atoned for his misdoings with the tragedy of his life.

Abdulkarim had secured another accommodation for his fugitive friends who wanted 'asylum'. The man was the most disadvantaged now, having revealed that he dealt with an anti government cabal. When he saw Uncle that afternoon, he spent a great deal of time trying to circumvent the truth. The pressure and the fears were all written on his face, he prayed everything ended soon. He would, given another chance, flee from such relationships. He was regretful and it reflected on his words, the manner with which he served Uncle Bode and his son the wine, that afternoon. He was a good man but his phobia for failure in business had led him into allying with a group of influential people he never really understood.

Finally, Uncle arrived at the country mansion of Dr. Olanusi, a two-hour drive from the Abdulkarims'. His excuse for visiting was to book an appointment for Pearl who the family said, was being or trying to be antisocial.

Uncle had gotten to learn the truth when he spoke to her. She'd only being finding it hard to draw the line between what she always saw in the Music TV and what obtained in reality. The family was worried for her recent behaviors, the smashing of a mate's wheel screen in a fight, unnecessary theft at a nearby grocery store...while Uncle negotiated for a parking space at the artful community hospital besides Dr. Olanusi's Iluimo home, he didn't think about those things. He had come for an indulgent discourse which he feared the doctor might not like. He wondered if the great psychiatrist would lend his ear when he speaks of superstitious things. He'd try, even though he stood the risk of seeming like a fool.

From the very beginning, the look on Olanusi's face suggested he knew Uncle was being insincere about his mission to the place.

"One more thing, doctor," he tried to be casual but it was obvious he was about to say the main thing. Insincerity had made him forget that a counselor or psychologist was what Pearl needed and not Dr. Olanusi.

"I had the dream again."

Dr. Olanusi was silent for a moment.

"And how was it?"

He repented from feigning ignorance.

"Yes, I learnt about it from the journals. Reputable researchers are saying that it really happened in southern England about thirty thousand years ago, what you dreamt about."

"May I share with you one more thing I didn't tell the institute?"

Olanusi strolled to his private study to fetch his manuscript.

"Go ahead."

"The lady I saw in the dream, Lā kēnu...' Uncle was undecided but he continued, 'the institute confirmed Lā kēnu was the translation for 'infidel'."

Obviously, he had digressed to give credibility to whatever he was going to say.

"While I raised her head, I looked at the face closely and I remembered this life, the lady was Sola Aderomke, my ex."

Dr. Olanusi laughed. He'd listened to more ridiculous things in his fifty-two year career though.

"You must forgive me, Bode, but I cannot but laugh, seeing that a solemn matter is to be turned into an epic of romance."

Uncle joined the old man, the best he could do was to laugh at himself.

Olanusi touched Uncle compulsively.

"On the other hand, I must admit that the reality of conjugal passion is as mysterious as the concepts of existence itself."

He sighed, "You made a wise decision not telling the institute about your private business. Tell me, where is this Sola Aderomoke?"

"She works in New York."

"Are you going to tell her about it?"

"Yes, and I don't know if she would think I am being superstitious."

He remembered he had not been communicating with her but again, he need not tell Olanusi, things are usually more complex than it always seem at the surface.

"Go make yourself happy." Olanusi removed his hands from Uncle's shoulder. Uncle Bode felt a love for him, that moment.

"And one more thing that was not published in the journal,' he said, 'the man with white bears that I saw while journeying through the plains in the dream told me this."

"What is it?"

"He told me that it is equally important for everyone to feed their minds with kind thoughts, store up the right things in it, as it is important for them to treat another fairly. It is the mind and it alone that will persist when most other things cease to matter."

He left and shut the door behind him, leaving the old man in a mood of rumination.

WHEN HE SAW Uncle Bode at the door again, he gave a knowing sigh. He was between the devil and the deep blue sea. His mind was that sea, which he learnt would persist when other things fade away. He chose to go with his mind as he nodded Uncle Bode in.

"I know you will come back."

"Yes doctor, I knew there is something you know that no one else know."

"No one?' Olanusi chuckled, 'you speak the extreme to say no one." He walked slowly to his table and ran his fingers through the long essay of his'.

"Many hundred people know. Obviously you dream of a time never on record, but the wise people of the world make others believe only what they want them to believe."

Uncle Bode took his seat and raised his head to the old man who stood close to a desk.

"Wise men?' A smile followed a frown on his face, a meaningless expression. 'I think no one should feel threatened if I dream of the past. None of them wise men existed at that time."

"Yes, boy,' Dr. Olanusi scowled as he spotted yet another typo in his essay. He had spent eternity editing it.

"And when I say wise men, do not think of villains or the one-eyed bad men you used to see in James Bond's movies. I would not call such men wise. The wise men I tell you about are noble fathers and mothers who hold true love for the world. They have seen that men lack the will to love many things all at once. They have seen that religion divides and they wish to build the world where the man next to you is your god. You threaten their vision by bringing another prove that there exist a celestial intelligence."

Uncle Bode scouted for words as Olanusi wrote a thing in the middle of the lines of his manuscript.

"Is it religion that divides or men who mold falsehood from truth? Even in the absence of all these things, I know people shall devise a means to perpetuate wickedness, a reason to hate."

"Yes it is true,' Olanusi's face was lightened with admiration. 'My lord taught us that goodness preexists and that evil comes to the mind when we become corrupted by the world's fallacies. We begin to love money when we realize that costly things are better than cheap ones. We begin to cheat when we realize how important it is to succeed."

"Then I suppose the answer is in de-emphasizing material things?"

"Yes' Olanusi hollered, 'he told us to take succor in nature and all that it has to give. He said that sex was the fee gift of nature, meant to mitigate the illusions which material things cast upon our minds."

Uncle Bode turned his head down and fidgeted.

"Doctor, you must stop talking now..."

"Why should I?" Olanusi smiled back. 'I cannot wait to tell the world about this madness, this unfolding drama."

He rubbed his face to cure himself of his dizziness. He never enjoyed conversing with a common man and doing so made his mouth feel dry and his eyes blurred. He felt like he was droning or soliloquizing. He'd speak all the same.

"Those great men, their fathers carved their own gods from their own human minds and now that they have repented, they wish to heal the world and turn history around."

"Too bad we are merely dolls in the hands of these aristocrats of yours," Uncle Bode sighed noisily but Olanusi ignored his comment. He sensed disrespect but he knew where it came from- a frustrated heart trying to fathom the complex theories of an emeritus. He expected anyone to know it was an obvious generalization, purporting that all great men had repented.

"Many great men find it difficult to relay what comes to them in its original tongue. They abandon truth and chase after their own passions."

Uncle Bode scratched the back of his ears. "It is true."

"How many times have you told your dream in your own words?" Olanusi gave him a close look.

"Almost always," Uncle Bode said after a bit of hesitation and he sat back, feeling more relaxed.

"You see friend, when CNN interviews you and ask how it is like for you, struggling with this nameless disorder, you'd say something sexy to look a little more hip."

"Of course, doctor, I hate to say that I read comic books about saber toothed cats before going to bed and I hate to say that I abuse drugs."

"But the truth?" Olanusi hollered. His temper had shortened with the little remaining for him to finish his book.

"The truth will make a nihilist of me,' said Uncle Bode, coldly. 'Nothing makes sense except we make it fall into shape."

"I see,' Olanusi sat close, 'the big irony remains. We are encouraged to seek knowledge yet we find that it is all vanity. Great men end up as though they are nothing. We are being mocked."

He stood up again and strolled away like he was remembering his lines.

"Nature abides in some, the soundness of mind to understand how things work. I happen to be among those lucky ones, having obtained the highest college degree at twenty-nine but I find I was being ensnared into not acknowledging this celestial intelligence on whose scrape I feed."

EVERYONE WANTED to hear from him- Doctor Olanusi. The widely exaggerated news of his exploits as a psychiatrist was legendary. Now that he had accepted to speak at a University function, everyone was caught up with a common feeling that they were going to hear from an icon who clearly belonged to a faded generation. No one knew why he had chosen to speak at a student forum after turning down invitations from big companies- an act, which further established his assumed reputation as an eccentric intellectual. Rather than wonder, his kindreds arranged themselves and traveled down in buses to the university hall, venue of the annual event of an insubstantial student body.

Doctor Olanusi arrived early with his wife, and he mounted the podium, several minutes before schedule. Five minutes into the discourse, a multitude of boisterous young men and women besieged the hall, negotiating for better views.

The old man had aged gracefully and his skin glowed under the bright halogen light. His silver hair was good to behold, and the smooth piece of suite, which perfectly fitted his little frame. He was a little distracted as more people surged in from backdoors. Perhaps he was annoyed at their impatience and uncouthness. He tried to delay his speech till the crowd settled. He smiled in the face of the chaos. His wit had gone nowhere.

"One of the things I have come here to do today is to dispel many old time rumors surrounding me,' he said, 'It is untrue that I cure mad people by simply talking to them. I am not a miracle worker."

He chuckled and watched the crowd calm down.

"It is also untrue that I conduct regular mental checks for British officials. I'd be a billionaire by now if it is true and there are better psychiatrists in London anyway."

The crowd grew more tumultuous, laughing, shouting and jeering for his unacceptably modest comment. He had shot himself by the foot, and he would have to work even harder to keep them silent.

"What I am about to do today is not the easiest anyone could do, especially in the presence of his family,' he bowed to his wife who sat in the second upper row and she waved back. 'As difficult as it seems, I feel it will amount to giving myself the best birthday gift ever, and you young men, an invaluable thing."

A session of the audience jeered. He was known to be miserly and it annoyed them that he wanted to give something not money.

"Tomorrow marks the sixty-seventh month since the most inhuman act of modern history was committed,' he started. 'Three hundred boys and girls who served under an illegal organization as sex slaves were killed. But make no mistakes, while they served, they did not just do what they were told to do for the sake of money or because they enjoyed it but they served with set goals on their minds. These three hundred people were promised affluence, satisfaction and most importantly, a life where there is no guilt or judgments or obligations, the same factors which relegated them to the bottom of the social ladder. They died, more than half of them in a strange country. Only a few among them had traceable family records."

Doctor Olanusi looked at his wife to catch that look on her face, the look that always came whenever she felt proud of him. She was an incredibly brave woman and she looked a little too young for her husband.

"Many of you watched it on the television but you did not see more than the interior of what has become the most mysterious building in the world. You never saw the beautiful faces of the victims, never heard them speak so intelligently about their grievances. I saw everything because I was there."

A dreadful silence came over the two-thousand-capacity auditorium.

"I was at the castle on the evil day of 1996."

He tapped the microphone nervously. It had gone off.

"Haven seen all these, I do not have to wonder anymore, why people unleash mystery on their fellow human beings."

The microphone came on again just as he finished the remark."

"Since my return to Nigeria in 1996, I had promised myself and my wife, who happened to understand faster than I, to share this story with you."

The microphone made a sharp, discomforting noise. Olanusi's two phones were ringing and the waves were interfering with the sound system. He beckoned his aide to switch the phone off and he continued.

"As a student psychiatrist, I realized how wanting our textbooks are, concerning the nature of the intelligent man. Fate put me amidst the world's soundest and I observed a disturbing reality that people who commit the most unspeakable atrocities are not some crazy folks but very sensible individuals like you and I."

His hands trembled on the podium as he looked at the crowd. There were no empty seats and more than half of the people inside were standing on their feet.

"The Human Renaissance group which you all know today as notorious started with good intentions as did almost everything that exist. Even though they loathed organized religion, they also hated every establishment that hypocrites used to further their private quests. They mulled over the concept of human alliance. Humanity was to ally against any phenomenon that tries to undermine the yearnings of their flesh, be it religion, or political groups or social hierarchies. These people were hardworking individuals whose first major mistake was to deny the stark reality of every community that every private interest which conflict with the public one is best done away with. And this is where they falter, as they failed to provide tangible alternatives. They wanted to devote their lives to seeking pleasure, therefore concentrating on less grievous atrocities. They despised inhumanity but their love for little sins drove them into committing greater sins that made original sinners seem like saints."

He noticed many people were looking at the door behind him and he looked back. Three men in gray suites were arguing with the usher who manned the VIP exit. He beckoned to the nearest of the men.

"State Security Service, I suppose?"

"Yes sir,' the guy in dark goggle replied, 'we strongly advice you suspend further revelations till we get to our office."

"You came a little too early. I plan to finish with my speech."

"But you put the security of this place in jeopardy, sir. The Human Renaissance will stop at nothing to remain anonymous to the common."

"I am not leaving yet," Doctor Olanusi protested, starting a drama and making the hall unquiet. He clasped the microphone to his chest and he spoke hurriedly. He was anticipating violence.

"I was in New York and I was talking to the famous Bishop Collins in a room overlooking Sola Aderomoke's when we started hearing police gunshots."

The three men tried to seize the microphone from him but he clung to it and shouted at the top of his voice.

"Yes she was there, the famous presenter, ask her. They trained young people who showed great promise and teach them for the purpose of their so called ultimate takeover."

The crowd had become really unsettled now, and rumors went round that all exits had been shut.

"You endanger the lives of these students if you keep mentioning names."

Olanusi could not understand why the media gadgets of the hall were being destroyed and why people cramped one another at the doors.

"Felix Hudgher, Davidson Stunt, we belonged to the London branch of the HR. I warned them against releasing the gas into the air that night, they did, and we escaped through the upper cubicle to Hammer Craine's private helicopter."

"Doctor, we might be forced to repeat the same if you continue like this."

"I knew you aren't SSS," Olanusi whined. He looked at his wife to be sure that she was safe, but not directly as not to remind his assailants about her. "Let these kids out of here and I will follow you."

"Too late!' the man in gray suite wept. It was a grisly sight, seeing a six foot two inch guy with smooth hairless scalp and fierce face, weep. 'My lord was fair to you. He gave you everything and he retired you with fat gratuity and how do you repay him, speak of his mistake among kids?"

"They are just students' Olanusi panted. The microphone had slipped off his arms now. 'They do not know my lord."

"Sure they don't, but what about the church and our friends in America? You spell doom to the world you live behind because no one would trust again."

"But we do not cover our sins with greater sins."

The man drew a gun from his jacket, causing the crowd to be more terrified. Many lay flat on the floor while others struggled with the doors.

"You should think about this on your way to hell; if it is really worthy to jeopardize the lives of thousands because of your personal quest for truth."

Gunfire ended the rage and the groans. Police commandos descended from the ceilings, shooting to warn.

"Drop your guns now or face our superior fire."

"We are State Security Service." The men flashed their IDs from the stage.

"You lie. The SSS has no such mandate. Drop your guns before we proceed on proper identification."

More people ran to the door, as news came that it was to be opened. Another version of news had it that a killing gas had already been released to the air.   Suddenly, the door gave way and people surged to realize they were to move slowly through an artificial, makeshift tunnel of censor gadgets and security officers. People were anxious because of the rumor of poisonous gas but the security men would not compromise. They had to move slowly. Some lay on the lawn in front of the auditorium on passing through the checkpoint while others toddled to the waiting campus ambulance.

22

THE GLASS, though meant to provide a view of the Manhattans, afforded the sight of a burning sky-crapper.

Sola Aderomoke seemed to be the only one who noticed it from the penthouse book café that she was. She had come to wait for Mrs. Bay with whom she was scheduled to take launch in a continental chef, sixteen floors below. She needed to seek her counsel on Uncle who had called her on phone, the previous night. She had problem reconciling what she saw through the glass with the ambiance of that room because of the sublime classical instrumentation which played, accompanied by the buzzes of young adults who had come to read or to exchange ideas.

The cup of coffee that she prayed a waiter to prepare arrived at her table. She asked the Persian if he could see what she saw from the glass.

"Gosh."

Visitors and workers rallied to see what it was. One of the twin buildings of the World Trade Center was on fire and in their very eyes, a plane crashed into the one adjourning.

Sola Adermoke took her phone to take a snapshot but she found that she had received a new video from Mr. Bay. American adversaries had finally attacked through the aid of the Human Renaissance leader, lord of the castle. Mr. Bay mentioned in that video, "Lord hopes to sway the mood of our leaders and make them change their conventions ahead of the proposed 2018 World Law Reform. This radical turnaround will see the nation adopting the so-called 'wisdom of old', which was inscribed on a simple rock in England."

Sola hid her phone as she felt the breath of a man behind her shoulders. People crammed on one another to see the burning tower but one of them seemed to be more interested in the video that played on a phone.

"The bad news is that our security has been greatly compromised.' Mr. Bay said to his wife in that video, 'If lord could go as far as aligning with people who stood for the things he hate most then he could do anything. He could disregard all conventions, make friends across the globe and start cloning super human beings and if the claims of the semantics are true, then an end might come for this egalitarian era because he would raise an invincible and immortal population."

Sola looked sideways, the man at her back had gone to speak with another man, and they both stared at her. Almost all of the one hundred and sixty people in that room made calls on the phone, asking about their families and friends', trying to know which road was safe to take.

"And the good news,' Mr. Bay said in the phone video, absorbing Sola's attention once more. 'The good news is that this deadly relationship will not last as their differences are irreconcilable."

She wasn't sure if the video had ended but a call that came in seemed to have obstructed the pictures.

"Hey there."

People grew restive; afraid of what might become of the street they were, should the buildings fall down.

"Olabode, I don't know what's happening here.' Her voice was quavery. 'I am at the centre of a martial attack."

"Hello..."

The phone line seemed to be breaking.

"Our own building is being evacuated...we don't know what's going to happen."

She'd started weeping uncontrollably.

"I can hear you now," Uncle shouted from the other end. The noise was making it difficult for him to hear. He'd planned to tell her about the dream, not sure about the part where Lā kēnu died, but willing to gamble and mention that he promised in that dream to find her. He felt like a rock thumped his heart when he realized that events might be playing out his dream.

"O my, you should go out."

"I am not sure if I would be able to, a couple of guys are coming towards me now, I am afraid they are harmful."

"Call for help!"

"The place is in chaos, no one is listening." She screamed out loud, "Help!"

Uncle knew she must have run.

"Oh my God, I am in..' she wept, 'I am in an empty room now, no one is noticing...they are after me."

"Please call someone." Uncle must have talked to her or to someone beside him that he hoped could be of help.

Someone fired the gun, bringing their conversation to an end.

Sola Aderomoke rang his phone after twenty seconds.

"The door is to be opened. Everyone is out of the building already."

She must be looking at the streets from the window. Now, she wept agonizingly for her death was nigh.

"You know, I have become too dangerous for these guys, knowing their plans and not willing to work for them."

"We have made some calls. Hold on, and please try to be safe for another five minutes."

It was amazing how a man in Lagos tried to save a lady in New York, several hundred miles away.

"I can hear you clearly now,' Sola said more calmly, 'we aren't so far away after all."

"No, we aren't. Please be safe, I will come...come find you, I promise."

WHILE SHE was covered with the police sheet, she remembered how she escaped the evil of 1996, and how she felt like a princess in the police car.

Hundreds had been reported dead in the attack but the multitude that descended on the ground zero, SBC's new epithet for the site of the collapsed buildings, chanted.

"Nigeeriaa!"

She wondered why, bended over to ask one of the men who were taping off the site.

"Did I pass out?"

"You were unconscious for three hours,' the man replied. 'Your assailants have been arrested."

She watched the crowd applaud, wonder in her eyes, freckles on her face.

"They greet you because your fiancé, if I may call him so, helped avert what would have been a great holocaust today."

She bowed to the cheering rescue workers and turned to the man beside her.

"Who...how?"

"Through the help of Bode and one Abdulkarim, the leaders of the conspiracy have been arrested. Their plan was to attack three major cities all at once, and Paris, and London."

"Yet this happened."

She gazed at the rubbles and the lifesavers who had now gone back to work. Tears blurred her sight and the sound of sirens filled her ears. She turned around and allowed the tears in her eyes to drop when she heard a familiar accent from the television that was just three feet away. A couple of officers were following the news from the TV, in the open air. When the water in her eyes permitted, she saw Uncle Bode's face in the television. She dipped her hands in the pocket; her phone had been ringing for quite some time.

"You need to see your face on SBC, girl. Weeping, weeping."

"I thought you are in the middle of a press interview?"

"That was an hour ago,' Uncle Bode laughed. 'And I need asylum from the press agencies here."

BOOK THREE

23

May 16, 2287 6:00am

MY EYES had become heavy, having stayed
awake for most part of the night, writing. The
dawn had arrived at the curtains. The day is here.
I remember Uncle Bode's cousin, my second
cousin and I will inquire just as I have inquired
about others through the Universal Bio Pool, the
web having the data and tracking devices for most
of the ten billion people of the world who lived
within the last three centuries.
Uncle reunited with his sweetheart, keeping his
rather predestined promise but never telling her
about the intimate chapters of his dream until
their tenth anniversary as couple. Kemi flew to
Germany, and relived old times with her love
before his eventual demise. Mr. and Mrs. Bay
were rescued just like many other people on the
danger list of the Human Renaissance, that day.
Inspired by the way global intelligence had saved
their lives, they took up voluntary humanitarian
jobs that saw them traveling to the former third
world countries. Chekhov languished in illegal
detention for months before he was finally
released, continuing with his research in a quiet
community university. He visited Lagos one more
time with his daughter to advance his book, *The
Probable History of Life*.
Now that everything has passed, I rose up to
unwind and danced to the music in the compact
disc I had bought in the street. The song was
rather too fast, but I would learn, if time permits,
to be entertained by it. I had ordered old time

songs and it will arrive at my door before noon, just in time before my family come visiting. They had promised to come with a descendant nephew and I cannot wait. I would receive Shedrach later in the day, the only one among the new arrivals who wishes to share our story with the world. I must keep my excitement in check, knowing that today might be the last for us as free people.

I hope to post this piece to the press before 8am this morning. I am yet to finish with it, but I'd craft a conclusion, lest I be denied the luxury.

IN THE TIME of the great Alexander of Macedonia there lived a Greek who once walked through the streets of Athens with a lamp in the day, saying that he was looking for an honest man. Needless to say, there was no single man whose ways and thoughts matched entirely his gestures and speeches. No man truthful to his own self or faithful to his own faith.

 Sometimes he lives in the mirage of what he will never become, denying himself the fullness of his being, yet cheating on the creed he professes, dishonoring his own person. He tries, and for every trifling effort there is no applause for the challenge bestowed upon him is enormous. From the dusty plains of Sahara to the basins of Amazon, there is no man faced with lesser test. To hold his head high in the midst of a mad crowd, find cheer as sweat drips by his spine, to keep his shoulders down in the face of flattering accomplishments and the toughest of all to his heart; to forgive those who merit the gallows. Lying passively in his marrow is that silent quest. Can he do more than he used to, live life as he would love to, with an aura of peace and contentment? In moments when he comes back to himself he feels an ethereal feeling in his heart, so close to happiness, he could dare call. He will find the best homilies are too difficult to practice. He will see that the best preachers are human after all. He may come to the conclusion that good does not evidently pay off, but the veiled feelings of his heart could be trusted. Amidst the rumblings of the world and the murmurings of his mind he shall find there is some good in what is good.

24

IT ELUDED us for sometime; strength to harness the mines running deeper in our hearts than gold is at the crust of the earth. One morning we realized what we needed to fly was right there with us, that there was hope.

That morning I woke up from a dream of home that left my heart pained with a strong and sore feeling of nostalgia. We had been there for so long. Though it was an endless wilderness, we had made a portion into long stretches of farmland and pools, for there were clear, healing waters under the surface. We had made lights from the cells of the ship, making use of the powers of the tiny quantum of the sun that reached us. There was a sensitive part of the cells we adapted that stored the little waves that entered Mars' atmosphere, using the powers to suction waters from beneath the surface, also sprinkling waters to our farmland, tenth the size of the island of Príncipe. The guy from Angola multiplied a bacterium species he got twenty feet beneath the surface, improving it to be able to collect enough energy from the sun for the plants to produce food.

Most worthy of all mentions were the little ones who grew up to know not another home, the true Martians. There were over a hundred of them, half of them females. The one whom we loved to call the prince of Mars often narrated his dreams to us. What came to us feebly in the middle of the night had stared him in the face many times in broad daylight. He told us and we fathomed it was a people long lost in the history of histories that he saw. Also we were mindful of the possibility that we might have been brought there to learn about the past but for a reason we would not know right away. Even in the times which precede the formation of the earth, evil had become defeated, and betrayal and wickedness and everything the conscience of men deem as improper. The 'little boy' said there would come a time when the world would come to another hill of Megiddo and that they would need a reassurance, a heart to defend their home.

Thus we lived in the peaceful and surprisingly cheerful settlement for many years, aging about four times less than normal. Shedrach said it was a consequence of the lilies we grew to include in our diet, also of the healing waters beneath the surface that we took. He had become a professor now, a special committee of nine people pronounced him one after reaching the targets and making new discoveries that endeared us more and more to the harsh atmosphere of Mars.

We'd lived here so long that memory of home seemed far and hazy but that night I remembered vividly how it used to be at home and in the morning I was woken by a soft, morose whisper.

Nana, the lady astronaut from Ghana was calling her son, the first of the children to be born here who had become a great-grand father himself. She lowered her voice apparently to know what it was she was seeing in the sky before she raises alarm. I came from my tent, just like a hundred and fifty others but did not raise my head to see. I moved close, staring at her eyes as she stared at the sky. There was a flying jet in her teary eyes. It had been long since we last saw a thing that flew. Weakened by unrestrained eagerness, I remained, not turning around to look. It seemed much better to stare at the sight that came to us in the eyeball of who dared to look. A familiar feeling set in, a sharp feeling of great anticipation that would have kept me moody had it been with me all the years. Nana smiled brightly as she looked on, the wrinkles on her face moving in waves, tears rolling over.

"Home of the free," she muttered.

I turned around to look. An ark the size of Titanic with flapping wings was flying by! At the left side were flags I could not remember and a caption in large fonts, dotted with smaller ones in the languages of the world.

Home of the free.

Shederach ran into our midst as we marveled.

"I said it. They will come for us this year."

Nana shushed him and said quietly, "It is long known that the Earth and Mars will only be 35 million miles apart in 2287, about five times closer than it used to be."

"I guess they will come in large numbers,' the captain joined. He had become old and limp. 'The world must have become unstoppable now." He went for the red giant flag inside our good old laboratory and tried to flap it as though our farms and houses were not visible enough from above. We stood and watched as the space shuttle that was in the form of an ark passed by. The captain kept flapping with the last iota of energy he had. He had been sick for a while and the healing waters appeared to have lost its effect on him.

"They can't just touchdown anywhere," Shederach supplied. "They must have an agenda, you know."

Nana gave him the same kind of look she did the first day they saw.

"Seeing humans on Mars, is it not enough agenda?"

"They must be thinking that we have perished when we lost contact," another person said.

"Who can ever believe it that we remain," the captain panted. He was still resting his back on the rock upon which he stood to call attention a moment ago.

"How big the news will be,' said another, 'I wonder if CNN still exists."

We kept looking at the flying ark as it got smaller and smaller and as it disappeared to the sky of many shades. Our eyes were swollen with great anticipation and those of us who came several decades ago were hit by a killing fever. Just as we stood, some of us holding our breasts, the 'prince of Mars' came talking even when he had nobody's attention. He was the only person not awake to see the giant ark. He was a lazy man but from his laziness he had made a useful career; learning about everything that was, and everything that is, teaching us about the things of the world that made us believe there was a sense to it all.

"One point nine, three five four point eight north..." he seemed unsure of what he was saying.

Nana laughed nervously, trying to hide her son's perceived stupidity.

"My boy reads too much from the library and ends up sleeping, missing the best parts of the day."

"North-south or South-north I am not sure," he tried to ignore his mother who now grew furious with him.

"Meridianai Planum, near latitude one point nine degrees south and three five four point five degrees east. The site Opportunity landed in two thousand and four."

She threw her scarf down, angry at herself and at him.

"And you don't even talk like a scientist."

Captain whined from the place he was laying, "Let him, Nana, he is the prince of Mars."

"Prince of Mars my foot,' she proceeded to help the captain up, 'you indulge him and make him lazy away, dreaming about things we hardly understand, things not his business while others are working to make this place look a little more like home."

The captain chuckled, not minding who gets irritated.

"We have been able to achieve this much and sustain ourselves in this unlivable place only because someone we don't know holds our hands, makes our little efforts to flourish."

Nana shook her head dismissively but careful not to upset the captain.

"Hard work sustained us and I feel so ashamed that when other people work, our own son sleeps only to sneak into the library in the night to read things he would throw back at us to win cheap points."

The captain sighed.

"If I will ever set my eyes on Lagos again then this man might just be the answer."

It was obvious he was trying to undermine his illness.

Nana smiled. She had adored him all the long decades.

"But if even the ark is going to land at *Meridiani Planum* like prince said, how do we get there, how do we know?"

The 'prince' cut in, spoke like he was in trance.

"I have always known what part of this globe we are."

The guy from Angola turned his palmtop on, ready to take instructions. The full map of Mars as deciphered more than two centuries ago showed on the screen.

"We are we are...." He fumbled his hands over the screen, 'we are here." He pointed at Gusev, his chest heaving.

"Young man,' Shederach burst out 'we are not some bunch of idiots here, okay? We can't just embark on a journey without having a concrete basis for our actions or what to expect."

"We are in Mars!' another joined, 'a cursed wilderness for all I care. There are volcanoes and quakes everywhere, so many funny things; we are only safe in this valley."

"And we can breadth only here," one more person supplied, one step out of this place we'd get fried by the oxides."

A revolt commenced but only succeeded in making everything easy for the captain.

"Everybody has the right to stay behind,' he shouted at the top of his voice, ending the impasse. No one knew where the strength came from, not even him.

"We are going to the ark!"

A dozen of young men born in the planet crowded around him, one of them holding the radar machines they had been making for twelve years. Their faces were alive with youthful vigor and curiosity. They knew no other home.

Two days later, we set on a journey to *Planum* on five trucks and two new ones the engineers among us had just made. Climbing the steep of our abode took forever. The walls of rock and sands six hundred feet high, surrounding our place half the size of Lagos Island had provided an atmosphere like the Earth's in a chemical reaction Shederach never deciphered, a major failure of his'.

As we passed through the quiet plains, I remembered what we had learnt. A tribe of men once lived here, happy and merry till they committed great blasphemies, getting the planet cursed. I remembered the book of Jude, the part where it was mentioned that the lords of those times left their own habitation to take another place, away from their first home. I remembered Chekhov and all that he had said about the dark matter.

Planum was not as far as we imagined but when we got there I had already fallen asleep. I woke up to see a huge shadow at the horizon but the further we went, the farther it seemed. Our eyes were fixed on the large object that eclipsed the surface ahead of us. Our senses of perception were being tricked and it was hard to tell what it was, how big and how far. Sure it was immense. There were tears in the eyes of almost everyone in the truck I was, and there were no communications as the speakers stuck to our ears only made scratching noises. Afraid to move nigh, we stood a kilometer away and watched as the ark came apart, spreading out and out, almost noiseless till it covered over twenty-five acres. Our eyes were fixed on its farthest ends, horned with a giant tube that rose about a hundred feet into the sky, all of us perhaps. We did not notice at once that the ark has been shelled and that it was closing back, preparing to ascend. Though it was a technology alien to our own age, my fellows seemed to understand what was happening fast. Captain said the allied nations of the world had come to land an estate in Mars. Nana said a great exodus was imminent. The guy from Angola suggested the tube that rose into the skies was the chimney and also the entry point for would-be new entrants from space. He said the estate is being provided with a central system of conditioning that would create an environment like the Earth's.

All the while, the little gurus of ours were checking the radars for clues. The estate seemed to have been fortified with a dangerous arsenal that could get us killed if we move near. Also, radio signals coming from it seemed completely complicated as our gadgets and systems had been outmoded.

"And one chance stirs us in the face," the captain's voice came through the little speakers stuck into our ears. I had known him for so many decades now and I was certain he was about proposing something grand, something that might get us justifiably anxious about our lives. I looked to his face and Nana's; both faces glowed with a new determination to go home no matter what.

"The ship lives in thirty minutes," one of the boys with the radar announced, their faceplates were lit with the blue light of the hardware.

We gazed at the saucer that stood half a kilometer away, dwarfed on the horizon by the outstretched object that just dropped. The saucer was the remnant of the ark that just dismantled to form the estate. It flashed green light.

"Boys! Time is running," captain whined. He had never sounded desperate in those long years, never acknowledged another man's importance so. His face grew paler inside the transparent covering, and the readings of his heart showed that it would fail in minutes. There was a screen attached to our jacket that summarized our health statistics. It had been attached to everybody's back because of the principles of the old masters of the space institute who tossed us to space a long time ago; to watch our neighbor's back and let others watch ours. I saw the captain's back but I couldn't do much in the spur of the moment, our moment of truth.

"The saucer will take off in thirty minutes minus two," one of the boys said. They had been able to hack into an external system for the first time in twelve years of many failed attempts. Now that we seemed to need it most, the radar had suddenly started functioning, a miracle no more amazing than the miracles we see every day and everywhere. Everything happened fast and for me I was overwhelmed with the same feeling I had when we first set forth at the base in Oron, Nigeria, a strange feeling of rushing anticipation, quaint and intense. It was a solemn reminder of life back home, making many little things I used to take for granted seem great and meaningful. Now my heart raced, knowing that it was time to go back to a normal life that is bothered only with simple things.

WHICH is more worthwhile, the taste of a wine, sound of a good song and view of an excellent dancer, or the view of the skies? What does he gain, a man who keep piles of papers on his desk, trying to fathom the ways of the world while the dance hall beg his presence? Between the shrewd and the light minded, none seem to be more fortunate. There is no luckier person than who is convinced that everything is not a meaningless random cycle, that though the universe is full of dark void and endless complexities, a large chunk of what we do not know is happy for those who believe there is some good in what is good, that a reward awaits those who, with every little effort, heal the world.

I was thinking about those things, lost in thought till a jubilant voice came.

"It is headed to the Earth."

The large saucer before the sealed white estate freshly descended was heading to the Earth. We surged forward, mounting the slider that was moving rocks and heaps of sand into a large compartment of the space vehicle. Apparently it was an unmanned vehicle sent to plant the first human estate outside the Earth. At the door, we waited to be scanned, arousing a fresh fear in us that the time for takeoff might not be enough considering the long queue. Twenty people were yet to be scanned and only two minutes was left. They moved forcefully across the lines of lethal radiation, acquiring deadly ailments that would keep them hospitalized for months. We fell upon one another, some upon the cold rocks, securing bruises in their heads and chests. When the saucer shuttle took off we scrambled to look through the windows. The new white city was in the shape of America's Pentagon and as we ascended it became like a bright spotlight. We looked with awe till the dusts and moisture of the Martian sky blurred our view. There were few more white dots outlying the spotlight. Apparently the people of the world had been sending tens of such objects to the surface of Mars in preparation for a major occupation. Next to the chains of estates were rocks carved in human faces, the ancient art that Chekhov tried to talk about.

THE SHUTTLE quivered, waking some of us from our long sleep. We had slept for so many days, barely surviving, licking the next man's scanty sweats, laying our heads on the cold rocks in turns to keep ourselves from fainting. We expected to move close enough to the Earth to crash on it, careful not to end our long years feeling disappointed. Though we whispered to one another's ears that the end had come, the twenty-four of us who landed in the red planet several decades ago, there was still a pint of hope in our hearts but we were afraid to hope. We were resolved to consider ourselves lucky men who lived happily no matter what.

We looked through the windows and there was a blue reflection on our happy faces. There were no such smile more beautiful than Nana's and the captain's. No such embrace more tight and heartfelt. Our shuttle floated over Atlantic, getting positioned for a free fall. I looked into the other's eyes, as there were no mirrors for me to see mine. They were at the same time angry and thankful and humbled, they were feeling too many things all at once, thinking about a lot of things but the least of all their thoughts I could tell, was to go halfway around the world getting themselves celebrated. They'd borne the burden of knowledge and they'd become more desirous of simple lives, in the words of a great man; not keen on doing just a single great thing but desirous of doing many small things with great love.

IT WAS a sunny day in May 2287. The breeze of the ocean carried our shuttle back and forth. A lone boat appeared from the west and a sailor with a tall red hat matched to us, stood alert and cried 'welcome' in Portuguese. He chanted a command to a dozen of sailors who emerged with their boats from different corners, standing guard with their guns pointed upward.

"Mister, do you speak English?" He shouted from a distance, his voice almost totally subsumed by the sound of the waters.

"What a pity, they missed by a great range,' he said to a fellow seaman. 'We'd take them to Nigeria anyway."

"We speak English," our captain replied shuddering, when I relayed to him, the cries from the sea fellow. The speed with which our shuttle descended before balancing up and getting parachuted had damaged his nerves. He was the first to be taken into the first helicopter that arrived within just a few minutes to lift us. Marine physicians attended to him.

"Where are we?"

"Five, six degrees longitude, close to the equator,' the doctor answered. 'São Tomé is not too far away."

"How lovely."

The captain shifted to lessen his pains.

"The shuttle is NASA's but they planned to land it in Lagos in honor of the world leaders who are presently meeting there. They missed their target by a few degrees and got it landed here."

After being administered with the drugs, the captain fell on the floor and rested his weight on his hands as if he was genuflecting. His face was down and his breath was labored.

"What year are we?"

The soldier looked around nervously and whispered not with a Portuguese accent nor English but a kind of tongue I would understand the world had acquired.

"I nae havee orders wu speak with you but it is two thousand two hundred and eighty-seven."

We all nodded, seeing that our calculations were right (for earthly timing was different from Mars').

A strip of land was in sight now.

"But me havee orders to take you and ya fip'l to the Institute for Special Studies in Nigeria, sir. Some fip'l like to talk to you."

The captain smiled insolently.

"And do we have any choice in all of these?"

"Absolument, sir,' the young Marine replied, 'you may like to go to the guesthouse first, you and ya fip'l, you'd been paid for but I bet you don't want to do that. Y'attention seriously needed at the institute, sir."

The captain signaled the decision was ours to make and we nodded our approval. We flew slowly, quite slowly it seemed, to the institute. Several peninsulas had extended from Lagos Island. Magnificent flyovers, towers, cable rail road, interconnectors, road bridges and air garages unfolded before us. We watched the television and saw the news that was going round. *156 unidentified men recovered from Mars, space terrorism suspected.*

I looked down, my eyes never getting dried in an emotion I do not understand. Surely it was overwhelming to see the world you reckon as seven generations after yours. Not so many generations had passed in truth, as people spent more time in bachelorhood and spinsterhood. Also, life expectancy of the people of the world now average a hundred and forty for the 'old masters' and about a hundred for the 'new masters'.

Everything seemed surreal more because of the funny pressure I felt in my body systems and my sight, which had now become dichromatic. I looked down from the height of ten thousand feet to see a sea of tiny heads walking along a long strip to the garden island, which the soldier told us was the city the African Union freshly built over the ocean to contain the homeless, if there were any by any chance. The world's leaders are meeting there in the 'Laboratory of life' and ordinary citizens are getting unsettled and anxious about their survival.

A long time had gone by and the world had turned around, witnessing a gentle revolution. A crop of new men had emerged leading the world to relinquish the nuclear, and all tools of heavy destruction. Through them, nations of the world had become more peaceful than it had ever been. They'd taught men the principles of freedom and fairness and equity. Trees flourished and rid the air of poisons; waters flowed and harbored less pathogen. Crime rates declined because there were more resources hence less competition, because it paid more to enforce the law than to break it, also because people worked, played and got tired, having little time for unpleasant cohesion. With new technologies the world seemingly became smaller and faster and more worthy to live in but in the middle of all these, trouble grew. Evil came with a new face, more deadly and threatening to subvert every good thing the world had inherited. When it came it did with abounding resilience.

The soldier seemed to have grown wary of our intent and true identity but was gracious enough not to let it show excessively. Though he was under high orders, he seemed excited at the possibility that we were saying the truth. He felt uneasy with himself as he conversed with us but there was also an attraction he felt towards us that he could not resist. While we told our story, his eyes would brighten with excitement to become narrow with disbelief. On our own side, we marveled at his naiveté for ever believing in a single thing we said. Our story was weird, sounding dumb even in our own ears but to see a man consider it was more surprising than the story itself. We were oblivious of the truth that the people of the world had witnessed far more incredible things.

We asked questions and the soldier answered reluctantly. We got to know that the science of human genome sequencing actually came to see the light of the day but the science of the English rock was never put to use on the large scale, even with its promise of immortality. People now age gracefully to an average of a hundred and twenty. Ultimately, science came to her golden age, and technology and freedom. Once in the middle of those years the world came to a roundtable where all swords were sheathed and every man's agreeable interest was brought to balance but there existed a discontented cabal. Evil grew in disguise for the rain of knowledge that came upon the earth reached both the good and the bad. Now that it was fully-grown, a group of men whose fathers formed a renaissance against the world's newfound virtues took over the machineries of power slowly and methodically.

There was a time in the times of the supermen when people fed themselves with a lie that only virtue brings about perseverance and patience and determination and hard work. There was a time in the middle of those years when they assumed the kingdom of heaven had come upon the Earth. Yes it came and like it happened in ages past, darkness crept into the minds of men, growing till they found the courage to fight. Everything that they had learnt about racism, sexism, imperialism, slavery, intolerance and a dozen more were put to question. The nihilists and the relics gained control over the markets and the armies of the world, winning the souls of many great nations. Now they had set out to finalize their mission of many years- to change the laws of many great nations at once, and to include in many sovereign constitutions, their principles and make their leadership legitimate. The soldier who welcomed us said the guys had recently blackmailed an island nation into signing the papers, changing their laws.

Our bus descended gently to the park and the soldier told us the remaining part of the story hurriedly.

"They are everywhere,' he snorted, 'in the parliaments of many nations, in the industries, in the Banks, among the Force." He paused to answer his phone.

"Yes sir, we would be ready in five minutes."

He looked at the captain and Nana whose head was rested on the shoulders of her dying old husband.

"Leaders of the world are meeting in that dome,' he pointed at the giant building uphill, about five kilometers away. The builders had sited it upon a land two hundred feet above sea level for it to be seen from afar.

"We will take you to the laboratory of cerebral imagery where you wiould be quizzed,' he said proudly, 'this is the twenty-third century, and nobody is interested in lies anymore."

An insolent smile came to his face, damping our hope of having his sympathy. His countenance changed sharply as we got to the bus stop and as we alighted.

"Never mind, brothers and sisters, you are in safe hands... as long as we are sure you aren't enemies."

He finally delivered us into the hands of a new set of security officers.

We were divided into groups and led into dark rooms. It felt like a small room but hundreds of young men and women were seated, making notes. We had been taken to the usual morning practical class of mind baring technology, in the college. It was a ten-year-old technology in which people were hypnotized through electro-cerebral interference. There were no cables or connectors but a platform for the guinea pig to stand upon.

On the platform, I felt weightless and euphoric, my mind clear and freed from worries. I looked at the monitor that showed a chart of dates. The operator would enter specific dates to which my memory would flash. Whatever I remember, whatever my brain captured in that moment would be shown on the screen. The operator explained to me that a protein is being formed in a tiny compartment of the brain with every new thought, every new sight and every new thing we learn. It forms as tiny and massless matter. Through a somewhat radiographic process, these proteins could stream to provide considerable pixels that would be eventually transmitted to the screen. A few big names had discredited the technology owing to the fact that the final pictures would have passed through over sixty percent maneuvering before showing on the screen.

Having my head scanned was an enjoyable experience occasioned by sudden and intense headaches. I was not sure how authentic the strange technology was because I saw on the screen, pictures that I considered too extreme for my mind to endure. Shederach said there was an initially voluntary censor in the brain that fences off such images from manifesting in the conscious phase of our thoughts. I saw on the screen what I had seen that I forgot and what I had learnt in the wilderness of space.

One day in our twentieth year on Mars I became acquainted with brief flashes from the past in the time when there was no us and when the earth was filled with giant beasts. Suddenly an asteroid broke apart, striking the planets, destroying and tilting their axis. A thick fume rose above the earth too and all lives were lost; the beasts of the land and of the oceans. Errant beings fled around the Milky Way in search of a home, moving deeper into darkness, getting themselves more corrupted by the tiny whisper of free will that lay in the timeless space of gloom. They found a home where there was no star and they made fires that they might see. A long time after, when the Father had rescued the desolate earth, they set forth, traveling a great distance to the earth. They arrived in the era of the early men, the Neanderthals.

We have come to understand that somewhere around this time our first fathers and mothers were formed with a purpose to heal the land and have dominion for the witless men who existed before them had given in to wickedness. Soon, they became corrupted too, learning the ways of the Neanderthals; the race of men that existed before them who practiced every unwholesome act. Now we have come to understand why we were taken to the wilderness of knowledge to be acquainted with great events of the past. History was about to be repeated for there would be a battle for the soul of our home like it happened in the ice age when our fathers were surrounded by the crude men of old and challenged to a fight. There will be lesser war this time but a fierce debate between every good proposition and every flawed one.

"GOOD DAY, Ladies and gentlemen," came a placid and apologetic voice. We had been kept waiting for six hours in a guesthouse after long sessions at the laboratory. The institute's principal told us some psychologists would like to attend to us, that we must pass through series of medical tests before we could be allowed to pick the legal counsel of our choice for security and welfare reasons. This would be followed by a visit to the presidential palace to meet with two heads of state and the leader of the 'new world' who had come for the Centenary conference of the commonwealth of pacific countries.

"Morning,' said the man again, his face studded with an expression of pity. We had been lying on lightly cushioned upholsteries without food for the better part of the day. Some of us rose, yawned and listened carefully to his instructions.

"I apologize on behalf of the state police,' he said, 'you have been acquitted of all charges, but the world is puzzled and the government had developed keen interest in you and your story."

We looked stunned, not understanding why we had been swiftly vindicated.

The young man in plain dark suit chuckled respectfully.

"I know you are wondering how you could have been acquitted without facing the court of law.

These days, no one has the time anymore. We go to the courts in the computers, in full dimensional virtual world."

"We've got no witnesses, how did you...?"

Shederach wasn't sure if it was proper to ask and when he spoke, he sounded stupid. He searched our faces awkwardly for quick approval. He must have learnt about the technology, even from the days of the space institute and he would simply burst if he doesn't flaunt his prescience fast. He remains Shederach.

"You don't need witnesses,' said the good looking young man, 'we have bared your minds in the laboratory and we have discovered you are not space terrorists."

He signaled to the men and ladies who came serving coffee and continued, "The new legal system of the old masters, I mean the long developed nations of the world, has been revolutionalized so much that when you need a legal redress all you do is to go on the Internet, get a lawyer and connect to any virtual court who has jurisdiction for your case."

He paused for a moment, allowing the waiters to go round.

"We make use of the mind baring technology to know what has happened, no lies, no heartbreaks."

The captain cleared his throat, unimpressed by the new technology.

"And you go about baring all minds, budging into people's privacy, taking away their God-given privilege?"

"The world spent nine years debating,' he heaved a sigh, apparently bored by the conversation. 'Old man, we live in a free world and you can be rest assured no one is denied justice, no one gets his or her right trampled upon, except of course, that a mafia is presently trying to end all that."

"But our own rights have been trampled upon because you just took us to that cold lab without our approval."

Our captain was apparently irritated by the boy's condescension.

"You...' the soldier paused a few seconds to think. He checked on his wristwatch frequently because he was to spend only thirty minutes with us. 'Your own case is peculiar. You were suspected of space terrorism, the new and most dangerous arsenal a group or many groups of faceless individuals are using against sovereign nations of the world. Those guys have already launched an indestructible satellite into space. They hack into military systems and intelligence. Now they have the security details of all nations of the world."

"Ordinary citizens hacked into security details?"

The captain coughed profusely and Nana warned him to stop talking.

"I never said they were ordinary. They are people in high places, even people in the Wall street and in the holiest cathedrals and shrines."

"And what do they want?" came Nana's vibrant voice. Apparently she was helping her husband to ask his questions.

"No one knows exactly but most intelligence units of the world have come up with a common theory. We think they want to subvert international laws so they can practice their science, the so-called wisdom of old."

"I know about the wisdom of old,' Shederach took words from my mouth. 'so how did it go? Did the world ever learn about the inscriptions on the English rock?"

"A few rumors here and there,' the soldier replied. 'but there are no evidences of immortality, only weird abilities. Some people believe a tribe had risen from among the people who used Cheknosin."

My eyes brightened as I heard that old name. "Chekh..."

"Uncommon intelligence, malicious demeanor, such were the qualities of those people and their children."

The man looked at his watch again.

"I think my time is up. Now we will like you to have your launch and take a rest in the guesthouse. We have booked a room for each of you."

He smiled chivalrously, and looked at the most loving couple among us.

"Or maybe the ladies would want to pair up wu de spouses."

WE TOOK the metro connecting to the guesthouse, fifty meters away from the institute. We were taken through a solitary route purposely to keep us away from the sight of hundreds of curious students who wanted to have a look. A lot of them had besieged the Principal's office for ten straight hours asking to see us and even threatening to start a riot.

I would have loved to walk through the open, on the green lawn where young men and women lay reading and socializing. Short trees with outstretched branches dotted the beautiful yard of undulating contour. I had seen the young scholars through the glass at the Principal's office, holding tutorials, taking pictures, exchanging gifts; some taking their visiting parents round to meet their friends and teachers. I sense our presence had interrupted their complacent lives.

A tall silver haired man approached as I tried to pick one of the keys spread on the marble counter at the reception.

"Good day sir. I am uh, Nigeria's ambassador to this conference... a Senior Advocate."

"Are you...?" I stammered excitedly, I have got a lot of keeping up to do.

"I am a diplomat, representing Nigeria at the conference."

We walked to the restaurant adjacent to the large, domed reception area. Others were eating at the table already.

"I am excited to hear your story,' he chuckled, 'and I feel honored to meet you. The president sends his greetings, he will join us here on Friday, I mean on the grand finale."

We went round picking our food and a wine labeled 'Ondo'. I learnt it is the best wine around and it is made in Nigeria.

I took a bite from the meat and poured the wine.

"That Centenary conference of yours seems to be very important."

"The world is going to make far reaching decisions,' he said, seating up and dropping the table knife in his hands. 'A few things have changed and we need to update international laws. We need to know if we should tolerate religion, having seen that there is no God..."

"What?"

He continued, ignoring my objection, "we need to define murder and rape and everything again."

"Why?" I asked leaning over the table.

"Because the world has changed and we cannot be sure of what is right anymore,' he lowered his voice and continued, 'I learnt in school that about forty years ago a group of scholars around the world denounced the basis for our conventions, our laws."

I looked stringently at him, my eyes closing for the lights reflecting through my dichromic eyes.

"Who are those scholars?"

"People who...?"

"People who injected their systems with Cheknosin?' I chuckled and sat back into the chair. It felt so good speaking to a man who evidently feared me or needed my favor. 'Tell me, are they immortal now?"

"No, they are not, but they..."

"Why would they denounce the basis for existing laws?"

He leaned towards me and said, "Truth be told, sir, leaders of the world are being blackmailed into holding the conference but it is the only way out of a dangerous impasse. Tho' fípl have threatened to make flat every land that remains obstinate."

"What for?" I fumed and in that moment my heart skipped a beat as I saw a huge man at the back of my new friend, the ambassador.

"You talk too much, Barrister,' he said in a baritone voice, 'can I have a word wu'yu in private?"

"No," he declined sharply. He was visibly anxious about his safety.

"Barrister, I am sure you wouldn't want to be undressed right in front of every one here."

The strange huge guy looked at the gallery and eyed the security men on guard, ostensibly telling us that he was in control.

"What has he done?" I said, hitting the table. The ambassador pleaded with me to stop. "Am so fed up of you Nigerian, wonder how you made it to the league," the strange man said as he whisked the barrister way. Before I could breath, the captain had joined the table.

"He will be fine,' he said, 'trust me he will be fine and he will join you later."

"When?"

I stood up as though a snake was on top of the table. I was determined not to cooperate. I could sense an air of conspiracy and malevolence. Even the Mars returnees might have been bought over.

"All one, freeze!"

International police officers raced into the guesthouse and combed through the restaurant. They'd been deployed all over the conference venue. They were able to produce the ambassador and the man who tried to abduct him. The ambassador's jacket had been shredded already and his dazzling white barrister shirt stained with blood. Both the captor and the victim were walked through the passage door. I made a dart for the door, and flung my hands at the huge one. I was so foul. Everyone stood still, fearful for what might befall me. I had just tried to hit a 'higher human', a man who belonged to an emerging tribe fated to crush the world!

I was lucky for he chose to pardon my ignorance but I didn't realize soon enough.

The policeman held my fist.

"He tried to kidnap," I panted, 'I was just speaking to my friend about the conference and suddenly he came and warned..."

"Shh..' the sergeant shushed me, 'Nigerians talk too much."

He released the jacket to the ambassador and apologized casually on behalf of the tall stern looking man who betrayed no emotion. I observed he was unwilling to join issues with me but I glared my contempt when I had the chance. Even the ambassador smiled, his face showing a condescending admiration for my naiveness. "Welcome to 2287."

SHORTLY after launch, I retired to my hotel room and scrambled news materials. I needed a clue. I was lost. After sorting and searching for half an hour, I discovered a *Time* magazine late edition. The headline read:
World leaders consider giving in.
I read through hurriedly. I felt I was under scrutiny by some elements and I guess it was a grave mistake on their part for me to have found something to read. We were absolutely unacquainted in this world and a group of people who knew more than we did seemed like they wanted to keep us so. If that was not the case, I wonder why anyone would care what the ambassador told me.
I read a line from the speech delivered by one of the leaders, the day before, titled *We are alone*. He had mentioned, "It is time we took our destiny as men into our own hands for we have found no voice in the wilderness of space."
I remembered the soldier who first received us on our return from Mars talked about space terrorism and I figured the man must have given his speech in frustration. A great damage must have been done to the world, shaking the mind of the most resolute. I opened the fifth page to see the picture of Abuja under a fiery sky. It looked like Armageddon, like the world would end. I remembered what Ambassador said about faceless groups of people bullying nations of the world into the conference. I remembered what we

had leant in Mars and it all made sense to me the more.

"There will come a time when the world will be brought to her kneels and the people would need the heart to prevail."

I inspected the room and undressed. I was anxious for a lot of things but I needed to sleep. I had been offered the chance of a siesta which I understood was to last for only an hour. We must join the leaders of the host federation, Nigeria in a sub-meeting they had convened that morning to decide on which way to go. All attempts at legislating or making referendums had failed.

A YOUNG MAN entered my hotel room without knocking at the door.

"I need to talk to you, sir," he said almost timidly.

I stared searchingly at him. He looked sixteen.

"I learnt about you and others. It's really inspiring."

I crashed on the smooth bed and said, "Nothing is inspiring about us. It's a really weird situation we have found ourselves."

"I can see you were checking on these,' he picked the piece of magazine I had dropped impulsively when the door was opened, 'you must know a lot of things by now."

He moved to the study chair at a corner in the room

"May I?"

I nodded and he sat.

"Barely a month ago something happened that instilled a great fear in the minds of almost everyone. A good of faceless cabal made good their promise to destroy every artificial object in the orbit. No one knew they were capable of such violence but sadly, they did."

"Why did they do that?"

"Vengeance,' he said, 'pacific nations of the world launched an offensive and destroyed what they classified as Unidentified Flying Object in space. It was in fact the new satellite of these unknown elites. It is capable of imaging and running down virtually every military installation in the world."

"Vengeance?' I chuckled 'so I suppose both interests are even now."

"Not yet,' he supplied 'what happened in the two European cities last week also serve as a warning to those who wants to manipulate the conference."

"Manipulate?' I reiterated, 'whose side are you?"

"Peace,' he replied, 'I want peace; want the leaders of the world to embrace peace and welcome new ideas."

"New ideas from faceless group of people who promotes anonymous interest?"

"Faceless group of people who knows military secrets and have the capacity to destroy the world's ten biggest cities put together."

The boy's voice had become loud and bold. Suddenly he had become assertive.

"We do not want our families in New York or London or anywhere to perish simply because our leaders wouldn't shed illiteracy and allow science to take its course."

I looked away, briefly weighing his opinion in my mind. Globules of sweat formed on my face.

"Come to think of it sir,' he started in a more cordial tone, 'what they want isn't so bad, just a chance to overcome morbidity and become the supermen Nietzsche dreamed about. What they want is the realization of the ultimate evolution."

I looked intently at him.

"But men do not want..."

"Brotherhood.' he helped me finish.

I sighed, and chewed the tiny piece of meat that had hung within my teeth for the past minutes.

"Only a fool would merrily give up the chance to live forever, but I sense conspiracy, and I feel that the lies that was whispered to the mother eve, still echo to us."

"And you'd pass an eternal chance for the sake of an ideaology?"

"No, I wont' I replied, 'only that I'd experiment with a guinea pig...see what happens to the man who eats that forbidden fruit before I take a bite. I ask, mister, how many of them who injected their body system with Cheknosin survived the anthrax test?"

"None, but we have recorded cases where unbeatable geniuses were made even from idiots."

"Let the world hold on to the promises of eschatological transformation, while they live purposeful lives because theirs is no lesser than yours which had failed but which you held on to even with a seeming religious fervor."

Sobered by my deviance, the boy dropped his face and sighed. He faced the door and signaled to another young man who walked in and bowed.

"Look at this gentleman. His name is Jean. Jean used to be a devout man until he found his equally religious fiancée cheating on him with the man assigned with administering their planned marriage. You know what bothers me most? Jean caught them in a supposed sacred place....well, he live as a fugitive now because he killed them both."

He tapped his fingers and a young lady entered.

"Look at this fair one. She works in the brothel but local authorities keep hindering her, trying to make her go to school against her own wish, seeking to demonize the world's oldest profession."

He tapped his fingers again and a couple enters.

"This lovely couple had their business seized and accounts frozen because they run child porn sites on the Internet, because they made willing precocious children to do what nature gratifies."

He waved the next person inside, an old man.

"This man is eighty years old. He is a bitter man because his only daughter was brutally murdered in his own presence, forty-six years ago. He saw the man who killed his daughter at a train station last week and shot him dead for not having the patience for legal things. Now he is on the run because he would be charged for murder."

He looked at me, his face had become reddened and his eyes, swollen.

"Tell me what the people of this world think of justice."

"So what do they want.... the masked ones?" I asked with a tired voice.

"Freedom,' he yelled, 'freedom from the strings of hypocrisy and prejudice, from gratuitous philosophies and silly assumptions."

"What do you want from me?"

My voice, laden with boredom and a strong longing for unscholarly things, left my lips softly.

"What do you want from me? I am just a humble man who finds himself in this....this unusual situation."

"No, you are not just a man,' he said, 'no one sees what you have seen and remain common. We want you to seal your mouth and not frustrate the conference."

"We have not been invited to the conference," I supplied.

"But they will soon invite you. You must go there and speak of nothing that will frustrate freedom."

"You mean freedom from reality?" My voice was deep.

"No,' he said, 'freedom from what is perceived as good by a few selfish ones."

He asked the strange people who crowded my small hotel room to go out, making a single exception.

"Sir, I observed the look in your eyes when you spotted this one and I must say, I admire your taste."

He was good at making suggestive comments without sounding scandalous.

"She's got it all...and she's ours, body and mind."

I moved sharply to distract and make him stop. It was too improper to speak of a gentle lady so. Also, the lady looked too reserved to be unembarrassed.

He laughed at my discomfort.

"You are so in bondage."

"The young lady is hypnotized. You use her as your slave."

He could not stop laughing. He'd seen ahead of me, what would follow.

"You are so fake."

He took her hands and walked away.

"Sorry dear, for the wasted time. I havee better people for you."

I followed behind and told myself I wanted to see how people are being abused, if I should dial the social complaint number.

"You know what makes us thick, mister?' he looked back, 'we are so great that we do not force anyone against their will, like those arrogant fools."

"No one forces you too, only that you will end up in jail." I was becoming combative.

"And why do you follow us mister?' he asked, 'well, you may want to see this."

He pushed the large door before him. Every one of them who had come from Mars was inside the auditorium in an erotic revelry. I walked in, bemused to see Captain and Nana reveling with strangers, unclothed. Captain was seated on the edge of the tub, getting the scales of his skin removed (for we had developed a hard, russet skin). He was pale and he was dying.

"I know what you think of me now; a dirty old man."

He lowered his face in shame.

"I met a man here, a surgeon here...he promised to treat me. He gave me this,' he showed the money card in his hands and I saw how his hands shook. He had been given money worth buying three luxury estates. Apparently he felt lesser shame for having being seduced by money than by carnality.

I yawned and asked how I may join them.

AFTER THAT, we were taken to the countryside, somewhere in the emergent part of the ocean city. The young man who came visiting in my hotel room the previous night boasted it would make an experience more worthy than any other experience we might have had in our lives. We had been sneaked out of our hotel rooms to partake in the rendezvous but we were to return before noon when we were scheduled to meet with the leaders of the Nigerian delegation to the conference through the hologram.

When we arrived at the remote and sandy suburb, dozens of serious looking old men and ladies surged forward to receive us.

"Welcome to the camp of the believers," they babbled courteously as our bus descended in front of the wooden gate.

"Believers," I reiterated. I remembered Uncle Bode once told me about the people who greet that way. His wife had encountered them in New York when she was still very young.

"Welcome sirs and madams,' said the host, 'as you all know we have only an hour to get to know one another and to take you around. We will return you to your hotel rooms right before noon because we do not offend authorities. In view of that I pledge to take you back before twelve so you don't miss the meeting with Jim."

Our host had just called the leader of the delegation by the first name and he didn't appear to be namedropping. I was heedful of an impending danger but my fears were made impotent by the grandiose feeling of mingling with the world's greatest.

"This is the fofosed headquarters of the Human Renaissance in Nigeria,' said our host 'the mother city is in New York City and our tentacles spread worldwide. The last time I checked the Internet, our membership had risen to a billion, meaning if we were to be a nation we would be as populous as the United States and Canada put together."

I looked around in the site full of white sand and heavily fortified concretes. Many earth-turning and object-lifting machines were spread all over the vast area. We learnt a hundred acres of land in the ocean city had been acquired through a 'believer' on behalf of the group, the same way many properties worth twenty-five percent of the world's stock and assets had been acquired.

Hundreds of enthusiasts had come from the main land to witness the progress of the project; the estate that our host swore would be the costliest in the world on completion. There was a thing that happened at that moment that made me conclude I was stuck with wicked men and made me realize the world was just an hairs breadth away from falling into the hands of them who believed in nothing.

For the fate that befell a woman from the main land who tried to stop her errant teenage son from getting 'purified', I came to understand the end was near for the era of fairness.

The boy had been lost for days but the mother later fathomed where he had been, using the map of the Google live search technology. When she arrived at the site, scolding her found son, she was taken away by some men to a room not far from ours, beaten and humiliated. Her cries were agonizing but no one cared. I later realized I'd stopped hearing the noise. I inquired about the woman from our host who was tutoring us on the needs for the worldwide counterrevolution. He tried to downplay my enquiries, also tried to dissuade my attention as the woman's lifeless body was carried from the guardroom into a waiting truck.

"Tomorrow we will all wake up to the beginning of a new world where no man or woman will lord his or her convictions over another. Tomorrow the dreams of the great fathers of freedom would be finally accomplished."

"You talk of freedom and yet I have just seen a sinless mother murdered in cold blood right under your nose.' My voice was shaky and my eyes were teary.

"Sit down gentleman,' said he, 'I must warn, you should mind your own business ..." He seemed unsure of what to say.

"Murder,' I thundered, 'that is what I have just witnessed here."

"No, she wasn't murdered... only committed suicide. Coming alone to the enemy's camp is suicide. She is responsible for her own fate."

He looked at his wrist watch again. We were having just five minutes left.

"However, I will see to it that those guys are apprehended. I think they overreacted," he said, searching my eyes for a look of satisfaction. I glared my unmodified disdain instead. He gave a pregnant smile and growled.

"You don't understand, mister. We are children of those who had been wrongly condemned to face the hanger man, children of those whose heritage was turn apart by the so-called anti-corruption agents. We are those who were chased from school because we could not afford the school fees, because we aint so endowed to qualify for scholarships."

An airbus came beckoning as I tried to reply. Our time was up but I managed to talk anyway.

"Your final defeat comes when you give in to evil," I said and he nodded raptly.

"You shu'avee told us that two hundred years ago."

I turned away to follow friends from Mars who was filing into the bus.

"I bet you wouldn't say anything to Jim or anybody except what we demand you to say.' His voice was down as though he had been thinking, 'I bet you don't wanna miss the golden opportunity...you don't wanna throw away the chance to manage one of the biggest corporations in Africa."

I nodded and entered the bus. We were two minutes late for the meeting with 'Jim'.

ON OUR way back I'd seen how clueless I was about the true magnitude of the cold war between sovereign nations and the great masked ones who sought to change the world forever. I had been told how those great men bend the stocks to their side to press home their demands, how they had used blackmail and threat to tear down many great humanist and religious institutions. But their real intent no one ever knew as they brought tears to the eyes of men whose emancipation they claim to assert.

When our bus flew past the rural communities I saw the eyes of children and mothers and fathers dampened with fear. They had come out of their houses to see the huge arsenals facing the heavens and the big tank guns. Some faceless individuals had boasted to unleash terror in the magnitude never witnessed before in history. Intelligence reports had said, should the governments of the world fail to ratify the new proposals of these ones there might come a holocaust halving the population of the world. Though a few of those weapons had been reportedly destroyed in the Americas, the radio said thousands of many other unmanned and indestructible weapons had suddenly appeared at dangerous positions in different powerhouses of the nations of the world. With the frightening comments of the radio and the soft music Nana kept playing to mourn her dying husband, and the huge shadow that eclipsed the country area, I felt a fear that had come to my heart only when we approached the face of Mars many decades ago. There was a thick ominous cloud in the skies making children to cry and dogs to bark amidst the grave silence that enveloped Eko Atlantic city. Suddenly the day became darker as two huge structures appeared, forming dark spots across the light of the sun, casting their shadows to the ground. It was reported in the radio that a space ship jointly owned by the pacific nations was under attack one hundred miles above the surface of the earth.

When we arrived at the United Nations reserved area, only a handful of diplomats were around to receive us. Many people were just too busy making phone calls to their loved ones and picking their children from schools. We were ushered into the tall building at the middle of a busy business district. A tall building experts feared may be at risk for the lethal radiations said to be coming from the third unidentified object seen in space in the last two days.

"Good day, every one,' said a well dressed lady with a big smile. I was a little surprised to see someone smile in the middle of that chaos.

"I honder if it is a good day but am gonna say good day still," she quipped.

She made a few phone calls and took some coffee to douse her tension. Her kids were turning the next office room upside down, celebrating the chaos and the fact that they were having another school free day. Apparently her staffs had abandoned her for the day. She had lost control of them all, her kids and her staff but she was left with no choice but to prepare the hologram before she takes the kids and join her husband in Iluimo, a small town they perceived as relatively safe.

"Come on,' she said and then hesitated a bit, 'you are going to talk to a president of Nigeria. He is not here but you will see him as though he were around. You must treat him with outmost respect as if he were in this hall. Never try to touch him although I understand it's just a hologram."

She moved away.

"They are ready, Excellency."

A man seven feet or so appeared. Shederach said it was an illusion that he wasn't as tall.

"Am so sorry not to be here in flesh as we earlier planned,' he said, 'I am busy monitoring logistics of the conference."

"You can't be more here," Nana laughed (she stepped forward to stand in for her weak husband because things like that mattered to her).

The hologram was quite impressive and the images and sound were perfect. It seemed like he was right there with us, that we were only been lied to that he was not.

"I want to say on behalf of NASA and all space agencies to which your countries were allied that we are very sorry for how things went when you were lost in the planet of Mars many years ago."

He strolled round the dark auditorium, resting his hands on space. Probably he was resting his hands on a table in his office.

"The single fact that you survived those long years in a place we all believe can hardly support life is a testimony to the fact that we know too little about everything to jump into conclusions."

His voice was low and filled with guilt. He looked clearly tired of his tenure as chairman of the conference.

"At my study this morning I realized we shouldn't have given up to those charlatans who believe in nothing, for peanuts. We should have fought harder."

"No your Excellency,' Nana interrupted. Her voice was tender with empathy and she spoke eloquently, 'you only did what had to be done; sacrificed believes and creeds and laws for peace and life without which those laws would not have been useful anyway."

We respected her opinions as much as we did the captain's. Even the most shameful things she did with dignity. I was tempted to find my peace with inaction and with concealing a truth that might end an era of civilization.

The President moved closer to Nana more than was ethically permissible if it wasn't a hologram. He clearly needed a shoulder to lean on. It looked like the two were close and the puzzling images made me feel dizzy.

"If there is a God why does he seem so uninterested in the affairs of the world,' the leader said, 'why does it seem foolish trying to do what is right?"

"Whatever gives you joy is right." Nana looked right into his eyes, seeming with him like the mother she'd been to us all those years.

The president looked at her. Probably he had spent too many hours debating just that proposition.

"I can hardly tell..."

His voice was croaky and his hairs were silvered. He looked like a wise man.

"Forty years ago I was a reclusive countryside boy who loved to play the guitar and watch the sun set from our family barn. I promised myself then, if I could make it to this town and become a lawyer I would do my best each day to be a good man.' He snorted, looked away and continued. 'Forty years on, I am about giving up everything good men who ever lived fought for."

"History will forgive, Excellency, if at all you were wrong to appease those cabals. Good men seek to preserve the lives of innocent people even above ethical considerations."

Shederach coughed like a long comatose patient. He opened his mouth for the first time in so many hours.

"Home of the free...we saw a space ship carry the name...the ship we entered to get here."

"Yes...what about it?"

"What is it for, why are there so many estates in Mars like the world is gonna move there?"

The leader chuckled.

"We have only fourteen. Can hardly take the population of Abuja even if people were to be piled like sardines. The world is just experimenting, just trying to keep up with these mystery men."

Suddenly, his face became brighter and he smiled incomprehensibly.

"I think there has been too many good men elsewhere and very few of them in the laboratories and hardware workshops. I think those who truly love peace and brotherhood stay away from money and power too much that they have become victims of misrule themselves."

"But you...' Shederach stuttered, 'we have you. You are the chairman of the conference."

"Yes I am in a manner of speaking but over the years, true power seems to have returned to the race of men we foolishly thought had become extinct, the children of people alleged to have injected their body systems with Cheknosin."

"Race?" Shederach echoed.

"It is a hilarious concept from a school of thought. We do refer those who do all antisocial things as belonging to another race, meaning there are only two races in the world- the good natured and those who are driven by impulse alone."

"Great philosophy," Shederach remarked. He looked at our faces and burst out.

"Your Excellency, I think you should not surrender."

I nodded and my heart raced.

"We have been to the wilderness in space. The eyes of our mind have seen it all. You must stand against wickedness...'

"Your honor..." Nana and others tried to interrupt, their voices climbing desperately, but Shedrach did not allow them.

"Tomorrow is a day of war; a war that has been fought and won many eons ago. You must be strong to make what has already been settled come to past."

"I do not understand," the world leader replied, 'you scare me with your figures of speech."

The hall was getting heated and more desperate.

"If they were so sure of their capacity to destroy the world why would they try to stop us from telling you this?"

"Excellency, he is lying," Nana screamed. The nerves on her face had become swollen and she had become a little unlike the sweet lady she used to be.

Shederach whined as he tried to free himself from the gathering mob.

"Tomorrow is a day of war. Tomorrow is a day of victory."

25

THE YORUBAS say lazy men always hiss at the break of the dawn. There is a dawn no man love to wake up to, not even the men of war.

I had been woken from my slumber by the deafening sound of a blast. Early morning report had confirmed that military installations in forty locations from four continents had been destroyed. Somehow, the military capacity of negotiating countries had been reduced by more than a half. It was six thirty in the morning of sixteenth May, in the year 2287 but I hadn't woken early enough to hear the biggest news of the day. Pacific nations of the world had decided over the night not to ratify the proposals of the nameless powerful ones. By the time I woke, Shederach was already by my side, dusting his laurel; the one made from him in Mars when he was named a professor. He looked contented and proud of himself.

"Where are the others and where are we?" I asked.

"Your family apologizes, they cannot make it because all flights had been grounded and all roads, blocked. There are several minor crises, people are walking from Akure and Minna to stage a protest, everyone worried for their lives."

"The fear for what might happen if the world leaders refuse to give in?"

Shedrach nodded. "It is the D-day," we both said.

That morning, we were served a sumptuous meal and a police band played beside our table, an old song I tried so hard to place in my memory.

The Nigerian diplomat whom I met at the hotel four days earlier, waved from the adjacent table gesturing that he would join Shederach and I in a minute.

The music paused for a moment and we listened to the latest news.

"The Ocean city has been rid of all suspected elements, declared ninety percent safe by state intelligence units."

We clapped our hands merrily as though the war was over. In the next minute we had started a long exodus into the the heart of Eko Atlantic through the submarine tunnel. Tens of thousands of people were passing through but we learnt a greater exodus was taking place in the open, on the road bridge that connected Victoria Island with the ocean city. We marveled at their bravery for they walked pass gory sights, defiling the loud sound of bomb explosions all to make it to the conference. The radio presenter seemed mystified as he reported the great exodus in other nations to places where they would view the conference. All sources of electric power had been caught off and there remained only one functioning television service- the one that is owned by those unknown men. They had provided huge screens for chosen communities ostentatiously, hoping to air it to the world as their leaders grovel. Again it was a mystery how the screens had been mounted within the space of only one night.

 When we emerged from the tunnel, a loud noise greeted us, almost shaking our newfound confidence. The crowd that had made it to the ocean city through the bridge cheered as we moved into the fabled auditorium when men shall decide whom to follow.

Hundreds of people defiled the barricades to take a space in the mammoth square and inside the auditorium itself. News went round that ex-service men in a tiny pacific nation had taken up arms against suspects. Though it was too small a scale, an allied army of the pacific nations was encouraged by that little act of uncommon courage that finally demystified enemy's strength. Pacific nations overturned the ceasefire and struggled to dismantle all suspected enemy installations. Many things were lost, many that some people called the victory a pyrrhic victory.

THE END.

AUTHOR'S NOTE

WHILE studying materials for creation theories and various explanations for human origin, I was fascinated by the originality of my own conclusion (which might have shut my eyes to the veracity of opposing views), paradoxically also by the need to come across a closely related hypothesis, the absence of which would be the ultimate disproof of my rustic discernment. It is megalomaniac for anyone who is not a paleoanthropologist to discuss with full conviction, the events that must have taken place in prehistoric times but then again, the framework for the hypothesis is embedded in the plot of this novel and even the science and pseudoscience seem plausible, at least entertaining.

The last is yet to be heard about the great event that must have led to the emergence of the first modern human but there is almost a consensus among scientists that world population arose from a relatively small number of people in Africa, and not as it is once believed, from the scattered *Homo erectus* who lived in different continents in the ice age or the Neanderthals who lived in Europe (after evolving, perhaps from *Homo erectus*). It is unknown to science, what actually happened that culminated into the dramatic change in the cognitive abilities, hence the brain structure of the people who lived in Eastern Africa at certain time in history. Some have explained it away as 'mutation', a sudden change in genetic material but sharp changes in the morphology of hominids are rare in evolution. The wonders of the origin of the modern human being continue to pitch one theory against another. The road out of this impasse might be in the traditional creationist story.

Let us create 'man' in our own image, the bible says, not *let us create something* or *let us create a being in our own image*.

God was said to have formed the first man from dust (or the fossil of a *Homo erectus* who died in Africa), breathing into him the breath of life and commanding him to replenish the earth and have dominion, an order which he clearly demonstrated by migrating to Asia and to Europe to replace older populations. This hypothesis is fortified by the story of biblical Cain who feared for his life when he was banished from the habitation of his family. He wouldn't have been so jittery, I presume, if the people who lived beyond were of the same stock as him and it is now a scientific certainty that the Neanderthals existed as contemporaries with the first modern humans at a time in history, before their apparent tragic disappearance, another evidence of the new men's quest to take dominion of the earth. It is on this proposition that this novel is built.

The story is not centered on this material concept alone but it also purports that the creator, having created the first hominids many million years ago and leaving it to evolve over time to become erect beings (*Homo erectus*), still requires man to evolve to the superman.

Charles Darwin's story of natural selection and preeminence of stronger species seem very similar or analogical to Christ's teaching that [*it*] *suffers violence and only the [strong] takes it by force*.

A man said in the chapter 19 of this book that only one more evolution will make him become immortal. Here comes the major phase of the story, as there is a conspiracy, a false evolution, programmed by the 'people who once lived in Mars'.

Like the first proposition, it is the lack of resolution among researchers that provided me the opportunity of writing that a super-civilized tribe once visited the planet of Mars. There are evidences that there used to be waters on the planet. Many serious minded people had believed in the past that the planet of Mars used to be the habitat of a lost race. Some people still believe, even before the event of the 1976 Viking 1 image which showed what looked like an artificially crafted design in a large rock surface in the red planet. NASA had since disproved the assumption that the formation was artificial but some conspiracy theorists believe the American agency is only trying not to be freaky.

This part of the novel is heavily built on the biblical account of the fall of the rebels of heaven who left their first estate, as said in Jude 1:6, to another habitation. Traditionally, the serpent preceded the first man in colonizing the earth but the book of Revelations said; *woe to the inhabitants of the earth for the [rebel] is come unto them.* I could not help writing that a generation of the Neanderthals experienced physically, the fall of those beings who momentarily (over several thousand years) camped in the planet of Mars.

The original sin remains on the cards as the contemporary world comes in contact with the ancient device of the rebellious extraterrestrials (who once visited Europe) to corrupt human beings with the bad science of counter evolution.

ACKNOWLEDGEMENT

Thanks to my parents, Mr. and Mrs. M.I Apoola. No one keeps writing for so long without their kind of support. To Dr. Supreme, whose dutifulness made up for my negligence of household things in the period of writing this novel, Olubunmi, whose interest in the initial draft buoyed my hope for its wide acceptability and to Aanu.

No word is enough to appreciate Goke Adedamola. Thanks to Mr. Seun Banjo. I should appreciate Anwuli Ojogwu for reading the first draft and challenging me to rewrite. I must also extend my gratitude to the web community of literary minds whose kind words helped the work carry through. To the over two thousand members of the book's facebook group, and many others who I hope will understand, I say thank you. You were the ones who made me consider it a bad thing not to finish the book.

God bless you all.

You may like to join the facebook group; **Times of the supermen- a novel** or visit the publisher's website, **www.bateleuresources.com.**

EXCERPT FROM THE UPCOMING NOVEL BY *TOPE APOOLA*, "THE PILGRIMAGE".

"We can change the color of the grass within two days..."

The landscaper paused to see what it was that inspired more awe than his Botany; what his new client was staring at.

"...from green to blue, and to red..." he grinned and his enthusiasm vanished before the man could apologize for not paying attention.

"O...great," the old man sighed like he was done looking, but did not keep his eyes off the horizon. The sky was getting cloudier and frequent lightening, unaccompanied by noise, sounded a new warning. Since the last three days CNN had constantly reported that the heavens were preparing to cause the earth a flood that would rival Noah's. The surveyor had made him come to negotiate before the expected flood. The client showed up even though he knew the reason for the urgency. There was going to be a great flood that may cause water level to rise fifty meters above sea levels at coastlines. Even cities must be totally evacuated.

The client was a polite gentleman and the little contempt he showed was because he sensed he was to be defrauded. He could see it in the surveyor's eyes. Nothing will remain the same after the inevitable flood, not any recent transaction. Lagos will be half-submersed; even the inland federal region would be deluged for months. The man, trying to feign comfort in his deviance, fixed his eyes at the tower which stood alone in the savanna.

The surveyor followed the man's gaze and chuckled.

"That is the congress building, it occupies a hectare and it rises 100 meters above Zuma."

"Okay."

Though he meant to spite the sweet-tongued professional with his divided attention, he grew to be genuinely interested in the building. He tried to continue with the conversation of the rolling land that he was supposed to acquire but just could not ignore the splendor which stood afar off.

"It is true we still have the traditional National Assembly but the congress is where the bulk lies, even though it is supposed to be an informal institution."

If the surveyor had said that to satisfy the old man's inquisitiveness, he must have been disappointed because the man fixed his eyes on the white tower adorning the Zuma rock of Abuja and said, gently

"Congress...what do they do?"

"Basically the same as the National Assembly...some guys have taken them to the law court, claiming their meetings are illegal."

"I see," he scowled, and turned around.

The young professional had finally succeeded in making his client listen to the 'grass' talk.

"Okay, now...I'd suggest a color that is most suited for your eyes because I am aware you complain of mild vision impediment."

The man gave a stare that showed he was embarrassed that his health was public knowledge. He would resume his insolence.

He turned around to look at the windy countryside, her machines and vehicles seemed to be mute. Residing serenity next to great bustle was yet another trick of the mastermind, one of the thousands of people who lived at that time- the era to which the old man had returned. He had lived several million miles away from his home for a very long time, together with a group of astronauts who were lost in the planet of Mars, where their bodies saw no decline.

He quickly corrected the misconception about his vision with defensive aloofness.

"Partial achromatopsia."

The surveyor smiled. Apparently the word 'achromatopsia' had become dated.

"So how much are you willing to pay?"

"I told you,' he moved away and it was like he said with a yawn, 'a killer storm is coming anyway, and none of these would matter by then."

"And what if it does not?' the surveyor tried to keep his emotions in check. 'Sir, you may lose this one chance of getting the estate for this price. Costs are down because very few are showing interest, and whatever is making them skeptical would surely end this week."

The man moved nearer to the surveyor and realized he was only a boy. Even fourteen year olds now seem like men.

"And you...why do you think you'd be needing money?"

"Because I know the use of the news going round.' He stopped talking and on a second thought, muttered, 'the rumors were meant to appropriate money flow, make people jittery and hands off their properties which the government will then acquire."

"Hilarious."

The client noticed several air buses were dropping off people at the tower, the congress building. The place had suddenly become lively.

"The president has incurred huge debts in the research project he is sponsoring in Egypt, and he desperately needs money. I wonder how he had managed to co-opt our finest into supporting his hopeless mission."

"What mission?"

The client's heavy breath passed forcefully into the current of air as he looked away to the congress building. He knew the young man's type very well; he must be one of the unsuccessful folks who always took solace in promoting conspiracy theories, demonizing success. The boy eased into the client's stereotype completely, especially with his idiosyncrasy, the way he moved his head when he talked.

"His fascist mission. The president is taking lessons from evil advisers, in particular the Culture minister who believed we could teach the world our ways like the English once did."

"How unnecessary,' the old man sighed, still not enthralled by the conversation. 'I hope he would not seek to take the credit of our new found power to himself."

"He has already.' The client threw the measuring device in his hands to the green grass, and joined the man in looking, his eye muscle strained to admit the rays of the twilight. 'he thinks himself the most important now...and every high flier his servant."

He stopped and beheld the far sight, as multitudes swarmed around the building and as Air-buses roved in dozens. Even he could not sustain a grimace.

"The country's finest gather without requiring allowances to discuss real issues in that place from time to time.' He faced his client to spot the question he was anticipating from his face. 'Yes, the president makes geniuses work for him without offering monetary benefits. He promised them his own version of heaven- alluring to them and far cheaper for him to handle."

The man laughed to his own assertion,

"Crooked man he is, our president."

"And he'd managed to win every one to his side?" The man's question was clearly rhetorical. Now that the boy had joined him in discussing politics, he'd turned his attention back to the gardens. His restless eyeballs oscillated between the boy and the building.

"The president's messianic stature would change the face of this nation forever. It is good what he has brought to us, but I fear for the next few years when mere men would seek to enter his shoes."

"His peers would bring him down when he moves too close to becoming our god king. Good men are never meant to be absolute."

"Yes...' an enigmatic smile danced upon the boy's face as he stared dreamily into the field. 'He and his lieutenants think otherwise." He raised his fist into the air and said dramatically

"We live in the times of the supermen!"

The old man was lost, but he supposed the boy was only trying to mimic the president. One minute, the boy had called him evil, the next moment, good. He thought he understood where the little confusion originated from. Only few great men are truly good anyway, he thought, as there is almost no chance for the truly temperate to be noticed or achieve greatness. He smiled when he remembered his own assertions that he used to make when he was a boy, 'there aint no good people or bad people but the foolish and the wise. The number of his years had made him come to see the connection of wickedness and folly, of goodness and smartness. A deep smile accompanied the thoughts of his head, making the boy to consider him amused by his drama, his mimicry.

"Yes, the president raises his fist like Caesar. Like Caesar in the twenty-third century."

His effort at amusing the client inspired in the ill-humored client, an obligation to laugh.

"So what project is the president following in Egypt and why is it so costly he could not pay?"

He needed to say something fast to stop his faked laughter. The muscles of his face had lost the skill.

"An indulgent pursuit meant to buoy the stature of our people...to think big. He really thought big when he bought over a world class oil corporation just to take hold of their fields for the purpose of his research."

"He did? And what did he say he is looking for?"

The old man's word was enough to make a noisy headline, because of who he was and because he'd never meddled in the politics of his country ever since he returned from the long journey. His indifference, some have said, is hypocritical. With time, the world had learnt to let him be, forgetting him almost completely and allowing him to enjoy the fortune he had incurred from his very weird situation which dazzled financial institutions and changed the history of insurance.

What he is looking for? The boy couldn't believe that was coming from the sage, the best journalists had tried in vain to know his bias and now he'd opened up to whom he obviously disliked. The boy would give away everything before the man changes his mind.

"The president's private firm outbidded many large international corporations in getting the North-eastern Egyptian oil wells not only because he was interested in making money but to get access to the site talked about in *The Pilgrimage*, an eccentric history book that the media now report to have its roots in Nigeria."

The old man snorted, "The pilgrimage, everybody is talking about the pilgrimage."

"Yes, and no one is talking about the author, a totally unknown woman from the Western region of Nigeria, a total enigma who dabbled into almost everything, from singing to painting and cloth making."

"The media called her the resurrected *Marta Hari*," the man supplied, jolting the boy about his awareness. His otherworldliness was faked perhaps; he needed to do it to stop being reminded of how strange his life had been.

"Her private life is mostly unaccounted for, except that she willed gross properties to the old Christian sect that she devoted the latter part of her life to. It is said that she has a granddaughter who lives in Lagos."

ABOUT THE AUTHOR

Inspired by the growing optimism of the Nigerian youth, the author writes this as a major sequel to a series of articles he earlier wrote, and to commemorate Nigeria's 50th independence anniversary.

Born June 1984 in Akure, Tope Apoola studied Microbiology in OAU Ife. This is his first novel.

www.ingramcontent.com/pod-product-compliance
Lightning Source LLC
Chambersburg PA
CBHW060807030726
47503CB00002B/369